Praise for Lexi Blak Mercenaries...

"I can always trust Lexi Blake's Dominants to leave me breathless...and in love. If you want sensual, exciting BDSM wrapped in an awesome love story, then look for a Lexi Blake book."
~Cherise Sinclair USA Today Bestselling author

"Lexi Blake's MASTERS AND MERCENARIES series is beautifully written and deliciously hot. She's got a real way with both action and sex. I also love the way Blake writes her gorgeous Dom heroes--they make me want to do bad, bad things. Her heroines are intelligent and gutsy ladies whose taste for submission definitely does not make them dish rags. Can't wait for the next book!"
~Angela Knight, New York Times Bestselling author

"A Dom is Forever is action packed, both in the bedroom and out. Expect agents, spies, guns, killing and lots of kink as Liam goes after the mysterious Mr. Black and finds his past and his future... The action and espionage keep this story moving along quickly while the sex and kink provides a totally different type of interest. Everything is very well balanced and flows together wonderfully."
~A Night Owl "Top Pick", Terri, Night Owl Erotica

"A Dom Is Forever is everything that is good in erotic romance. The story was fast-paced and suspenseful, the characters were flawed but made me root for them every step of the way, and the hotness factor was off the charts mostly due to a bad boy Dom with a penchant for dirty talk."
~Rho, The Romance Reviews

"A good read that kept me on my toes, guessing until the big reveal, and thinking survival skills should be a must for all men."
~Chris, Night Owl Reviews

Submission Impossible

Other Books by Lexi Blake

URBAN FANTASY

Thieves
Steal the Light
Steal the Day
Steal the Moon
Steal the Sun
Steal the Night
Ripper
Addict
Sleeper
Outcast
Stealing Summer
The Rebel Queen

LEXI BLAKE WRITING AS SOPHIE OAK

Texas Sirens
Small Town Siren
Siren in the City
Siren Enslaved
Siren Beloved
Siren in Waiting
Siren in Bloom
Siren Unleashed
Siren Reborn

Nights in Bliss, Colorado
Three to Ride
Two to Love
One to Keep
Lost in Bliss
Found in Bliss
Pure Bliss
Chasing Bliss
Once Upon a Time in Bliss
Back in Bliss
Sirens in Bliss
Happily Ever After in Bliss
Far From Bliss, Coming 2021

Submission Impossible

Masters and Mercenaries: Reloaded, Book 1

Lexi Blake

Submission Impossible
Masters and Mercenaries: Reloaded, Book 1
Lexi Blake

Published by DLZ Entertainment LLC
Copyright 2021 DLZ Entertainment LLC
Edited by Chloe Vale
ISBN: 978-1-942297-43-7

McKay-Taggart logo design by Charity Hendry

Sign up for Lexi Blake's newsletter
and be entered to win a $25 gift certificate
to the bookseller of your choice.

Join us for news, fun, and exclusive content
including free Thieves short stories.

There's a new contest every month!

Go to www.LexiBlake.net to subscribe.

Acknowledgments

This is a brand new chapter in the series that has been the center of my career for over a decade now. I'm having a blast looking at these characters in different ways.

The younger men and women are taking over, but don't think that means the old guard will be left out. In so many ways, this is a new chapter in my life, too. I recently turned fifty and the world flipped and we're all figuring out how to navigate it. The one thing that didn't change is the comfort I find in writing these books, in inviting you to join me for an adventure, for some romance, for a few hours of respite. This Masters and Mercenaries series is set slightly in the future, and while there are definitely still threats, I hope you find it as bright a future as I have imagined it—a place where we can find love, find family, find a path to all of our dreams.

Except for the bad guys, of course. Screw them.

I want to thank everyone who helped turn this story into a book. As always I thank Kim Guidroz who is my family, my sounding board, the better half of Lexi Blake. My husband who holds the better half of my soul in his heart. Thanks to Maria Monroy, Liz Berry, Jillian Stein, Jenn Watson and Social Butterfly. To my agent, Kevan Lyon. To the best beta readers in the business – Kori Williamson, Stormy Pate and Riane Holt. Thanks to the lovely and amazing Lila Dubois for the cover.

To anyone who listens to audio, you know that Ryan West has become the voice of my McKay-Taggart team. I want to thank him for 29—wow—amazing narrations. I'm so happy to move forward with many more stories!

And thanks to you, dear reader, for following me once again. Let's see what happens next…

Prologue

Papillon, LA

Noelle LaVigne stood at the edge of the big deck in her father's backyard and sighed because she really did miss this place and her family. It was late afternoon and the heat of the day was only broken by the nice wind coming off the water and the shade from the big cypress trees. She'd spent many an afternoon sitting under those trees and dreaming of her future.

Most of her young life she'd lived in New Orleans, but she'd always thought of Papillon as home.

She missed the bayou and her family, but she was kind of ready to be back in her apartment. Sure there were problems waiting for her in Dallas, but she was optimistic that she could solve them.

Even Madison's murder, because she was almost certain her rival scientist's death hadn't been an accident.

Would Madison have tried to solve Noelle's murder? Probably not. She'd been a genuinely terrible human being who'd tried to make Noelle's life hell. Unfortunately, Noelle had been raised to rise above and all that, so she couldn't look the other way.

And she was curious.

"Hey, sweetie. Do you want something to drink?" Her stepmother walked out from the house where the sound of the game playing rocked the living room. The LSU game was on the big screen, and if her father and his friends' shouts were any indication, it was going well.

"I know I want something to drink." Lila's sister, Lisa, stepped out from behind her, putting a hand to her lower back.

An evil grin lit her stepmom's face. "You get water. And stay away from the lemonade because I'm pretty sure Zep spiked it with vodka. You've got at least another six weeks before you can even think about taking a drink."

Lisa was heavily pregnant with her first child. She and her husband, Remy, had taken their time. They'd been married for almost eight years when Lisa had announced she was having a baby. It had been fun to watch the big guy go pale at the thought. Lila was having a blast watching her youngest sister go through what she'd already been through twice.

Lisa put a hand on her belly. "I hope my husband is happy with one because this pregnancy stuff sucks."

Lila chuckled. "Noelle, I want you to listen to your aunt for the next four or five years. Pregnancy is not for you. Until you're a bit older, and then your dad is totally going to want grandkids."

Now she was pretty sure she was the one going pale. "No."

Lila pointed her way. "That is exactly what you should say. For now." She glanced out over the backyard. "Boys, that Frisbee is meant to be thrown, not eaten." Lila sighed. "I hope I'm right and that is a girl in your belly because boys...I'm lucky I still have hair. I was totally taken in with stories of how easy Noelle was. Then bammo, I spit out two boys and my life is one long test to see if I can keep two human beings alive. I'm a medical professional. It's what I do every day, but those boys...Jason, do not try to ride the dog."

Lila strode off as the boys started to chase each other, and inside the house she could hear the guys shouting their joy over someone catching a ball or something.

She'd never been into sports, but that hadn't stopped her dad from finding ways to bond with her. Her small-town sheriff father had gone to way too many science fairs to mention. He'd become a STEM dad and put up with chemistry experiments in his bathroom through her teen years.

After the accident that had left her in a wheelchair, he'd supported her when she'd learned to walk again. He and her stepmom had given her the encouragement she'd needed to make her dreams come true, and that was why she came over on football days whenever she was in town.

"You doing okay, kiddo?" Lisa asked.

"I'm good. I'm enjoying watching the kids play." Her much younger brothers were running around the backyard, swinging on the trees like the crazy little boys they were. She spent so much time in a lab it was good to get out and remember there was a whole world out here.

There was a world she could discover and explore and find out if she had a place in.

"Are you still feeling good about what we talked about?" Lisa kept her voice down. "Never mind. I can see you are."

Because she was smiling. She could feel it on her face. "I'm excited."

Lisa leaned over and patted her hand. "I'm excited for you, sweetie. You're going to have fun and make some great new friends."

Noelle went silent as her stepmom came back to the porch and checked the smoker that was currently cooking the meaty portion of the evening's supper. "Those boys are going to give me a heart attack one of these days. Are you sure you can't stay longer? It's been nice to have you here."

"We love you, Noelle!" her youngest brother screamed from the top of the slide.

"I love you, too," she screamed right back. She did. They were awesome. In small doses. She would be on a plane first thing in the morning and back to her super-quiet apartment where she would watch TV that wasn't a cartoon and sip adult "juice" boxes. She looked to her stepmom. "I have to get back to work. I normally wouldn't have taken this time off, but they shut down the lab after the accident. I got the word today that we've been given the all clear to work again."

They'd spent a week ensuring the lab was safe after the accident that probably wasn't an accident, but she wasn't about to tell her stepmom she intended to play Nancy Drew. After all, she'd mentioned to her dad that she was a little suspicious about a couple of things that had happened at work lately, and now she had a meeting with a security company.

"She can't stay," Lisa said. "Did you forget she's got that appointment the day after tomorrow? The one Armie set up because he's a crazy, paranoid freak."

Her stepmom's brow arched. "Like your husband isn't? Who do you think he called when he found out someone might be stalking his baby girl? Three answers, and the first two don't count."

"I don't think anyone is stalking me." She simply thought someone might be trying to get a look at her work. She'd mentioned it casually to her father and the paranoia had set in.

Lisa shrugged and ignored her. "I always knew Remy was crazy. Why do you think I married him? You, sister, were supposed to be the normal one."

Lila laughed at that one. "If I wanted normal, I shouldn't have moved to Papillon, where we have our very own gator mascot."

Sometimes she missed Otis. But she also loved living in a city. She loved having her own place and being independent.

Probably because only a few years before she hadn't thought that would be possible.

Her stepmother tucked a piece of dark hair behind her ear and gave her the look that let Noelle know she'd been thinking about a problem and was now ready to face it. "I know it feels like your dad is overbearing, but it's because he cares. You know he's worried about you, right?"

Noelle shifted in her seat, stretching her legs. It was a gesture she was well used to since her legs were so often the painful center of her universe. If she didn't get up and move soon, her calf might cramp. "I'm fine. I'm getting plenty of exercise. If I overdo it, I use my chair the next day. And I've got a great physical therapist in Dallas."

"I'm not talking about being worried about you physically," Lila corrected. "I was talking about the stress you've been under since your friend died."

Noelle shook her head. Had she not explained this properly? She mostly tried to be nice, but there was no way she was pretending Madison had been her friend. "Oh, she was not my friend. She was always trying to get me fired. It was weird since I'm super nice and everyone loves me. But Madison took one look at me and decided we were some weird enemies or something. I never figured out what I did to deserve that. We came in at the same time. We worked on the same kinds of projects. We were the only women on most of those teams. We should have been friends."

"Or she's one of those women who can't stand having other women around," Lisa offered. "I've known lots of those. Did she get along with the men?"

"Oh, yeah." She flushed as she realized how that could be misconstrued. "I mean she didn't date them or anything, but she was nicer to them. Only the ones in charge, though. She was pretty mean to the men who worked under her."

It was why the techs liked to work for Noelle. If they were given a choice between the chick who baked them cookies and the one who yelled at them and called them morons, they usually picked cookies.

"Lisa's right, and I should know. Women in STEM don't merely take crap from men," Lila explained. Her stepmom had worked in the medical field for years. She now ran Papillon Parish's only clinic. Noelle remembered how hard it had been on her in the beginning. "Women can be incredibly competitive and not nice about it. But I wasn't really talking about that. I want to make sure you're taking this seriously. Do you truly believe someone might be trying to get your research?"

She was desperately worried that what had been happening to her and what happened to Madison were connected, but she wasn't going to mention that part to her stepmom. Her parents were already freaked out enough by the fact that someone had stolen some samples from her lab, and she was almost certain someone had been on her laptop. They didn't need to know that she thought someone had murdered her rival. "That's why I'm going to meet with these people you want me to talk to. But I can't exactly afford a security team, you know."

She made good money, but she suspected she couldn't afford McKay-Taggart rates.

"I wouldn't worry about getting a bill," Lisa said. "Big Tag owes Remy. He's been doing side work for him for years. He's got his bodyguard unit built up again, but he still likes to send Remy out from time to time, and that means he's got to give us the family discount. Which means I'll send him some jambalaya. Don't discount that. Tag has like a hundred kids or something. It's a lot of jambalaya."

Lisa winked her way, reminding her of the secret they had between them. A discount on Big Tag's security services wasn't the only reason she would be meeting the McKay-Taggart crew.

She was starting a BDSM training class and she did not need her parents to know about it. She wasn't ashamed or anything, but her stepmom wasn't kinky, and her father needed to believe she didn't have sexual needs in any way. It had been Lisa she'd gone to about the possibility of visiting the club she'd hopefully join at the end of her training—Sanctum. Lisa and her husband, Remy, still went to Sanctum any time they were in Dallas, and Remy had done enough favors for his old boss over the years that Ian Taggart was willing to take her on as a trainee.

She started on Thursday, and going to the club was a big old bright spot in her life. Sex was hard for her, and she hoped this would help her find the ease with her body she dreamed about.

"Does Remy know who's going to be assigned to her case?" Lila asked.

"I don't know that anyone needs to be assigned to me." She sat up straight because her stepmom had the most serious expression on her face. It was the same one she had when she went into battle. Sometimes Noelle had been on the wrong side of that stare. She walked today because her stepmom was a warrior who never gave up on someone she loved.

"Of course they're going to assign someone." Her father stepped out onto the deck, stretching his big body and taking a deep breath. "Damn, that smells good. Remy, that new marinade smells like heaven."

Remy, joined her dad. "It tastes even better. I got the recipe from Big Tag's brother, Sean. You're going to love it."

Lila looked to Remy. "Do you know who they're assigning to Noelle's case?"

"I'd like one of the senior partners on it." Her dad was suddenly incredibly serious. He probably had a list somewhere, and whoever ended up with her case should understand that her dad would run a check on him. "Liam O'Donnell is a solid guy, and I like his partner, Erin Taggart. I would be comfortable with them. Or his brother, Theo Taggart. Any of the more experienced operatives would do."

"Good, then you'll be happy." Remy took a seat next to his wife, reaching for her hand as he usually did. "Hutch has been with McKay-Taggart for over ten years."

She had no idea who Hutch was. In her mind she pictured an older man, probably in his forties or fifties since he'd been with the company for over a decade, and from what she understood almost every employee at the company came from the military, mostly Special Forces, which meant they'd spent a lot of time in the military. She did the quick math. He could be early forties maybe, but probably with a wife and a couple of kids.

"Hutch, the horndog?" Her father's eyes had widened as he stared at Remy. "That's who Big Tag put on my baby girl's case?"

Remy gave him a seemingly apologetic wince. "He's the computer expert, man. Her problem is based around computers. Hutch is their go-to guy for tech stuff."

Her oldest brother was suddenly at their dad's side, pulling on his T-shirt. "What's a horndog?"

Noelle felt her face flush because unfortunately she understood her dad's completely outdated lingo.

"It's a particular type of dog who likes to sniff around women," her dad said. "I'm worried about him sniffing around your sister."

Her brother looked up, showing a heartbreakingly adorable grin. He'd recently lost his two front teeth. "Don't worry about it. Noelle always smells good. She always smells like cookies."

Only because she baked a lot. The only guys she attracted by smelling like cinnamon and sugar were kids who begged for sweets. She certainly wasn't going to have some beefy security guy panting after her. He would probably be some muscley dude who spent all his time in the gym and had completely cut out carbs.

"That does not help my case, Jason," Remy said under his breath.

That was the moment her dad took a Frisbee to the side of his head.

"Sorry, Dad. Kevin's got bad aim." Jason picked up the Frisbee and ran off again.

Her dad rubbed the side of his head. "Fatherhood wasn't this physically painful with you, Noelle. Though now I'm worried about Big Tag's choices."

"Armie, Hutch is the guy for the job," Remy explained. "He's been doing all the cyber work for McKay-Taggart since Adam Miles left to form his own company, and before you ask me about hiring them, I do not work for Miles-Dean, Weston, and Murdoch and you cannot afford them. Trust me. If Big Tag needs something from them, he'll call them in."

"Can't we get one of the married guys on this?" her dad asked. "You know how these things go. I swear the MT guys view their clients the way most people use dating apps. How many of those guys end up slipping into bed with clients?"

"Dad!" Her father still had the power to completely embarrass her.

Lisa shook her head and patted her round belly. "Nah, honey, he's right. How do you think I found Remy? And my sister Laurel ended up with Big Tag's lawyer when she worked for him, so it's not just the security guys. It's pretty much anyone in Big Tag's orbit. They get pulled into the whole love and marriage thing."

Her dad pointed Lisa's way. "Uh, uh. That's only some of the guys. What about all the women they went through first? Did Remy come into your marriage pure?"

Lisa snorted.

"I did not sleep with a bunch of clients," Remy argued.

"Just every Hooter's girl in Dallas," Lisa said under her breath.

Her stepmom frowned her dad's way. "Are you trying to say Noelle would be nothing more than a notch on this guy's bedpost?"

Noelle held up a hand. "I was planning on not sleeping with the guy who checks my computer for viruses and spies."

She would maybe though sleep with someone from her training class. Lisa had told her sex was common and that she'd had an amazing time with her training Dom. If they set out firm boundaries and she liked the man, it would be a safe way to indulge since the guy

22

would be highly vetted by a bunch of paranoid security experts.

But she wasn't mentioning that to her dad because…he was her dad.

"I bet Lisa wasn't planning on sleeping with Remy when he was her bodyguard," her dad said with an extra frowny frown.

"Oh, I planned to sleep with him. He played hard to get for years and all because he thought I looked too sweet for a guy like him," Lisa added. "So you're safe. If Hutch is anything like Remy, he'll stay far away because he'll think he's not good enough for her. Noelle, if he gives you trouble, show him your boobs. It worked for me."

Her stepmom choked on her iced tea, but her dad went pale.

"I'm not showing anyone my boobs." Well, not anyone she worked with. And certainly not some guy named Hutch. Who was named Hutch? He sounded like a refugee from a bad old TV show.

Lisa snorted, likely because she knew Noelle would be showing her boobs at Sanctum soon.

They were nice boobs. They weren't the largest, but they were perky. She would have to show her legs, too, and all her scars, but she'd decided to be okay with them. Anyone who didn't like them didn't have to look. She hadn't wanted those scars, but they were hers, and whoever she ended up with would have to tolerate them.

Her father sighed. "Just be careful. Like I said a lot of those men end up in bed with their clients. I've heard this Hutch fellow gets around."

"Well, maybe he did before and he'll walk in and take one look at how beautiful and smart and funny my daughter is and she'll be the one he marries." Her stepmom had stood, staring her dad's way. "Don't you forget you and I worked together, too. She is a lovely twenty-five-year-old woman, and any man would be lucky to catch her."

"What did I… I thought I was saying the guy's going to try to sleep with her." Her father scratched his head as though trying to figure out what he'd done wrong. "I didn't say she wasn't beautiful. She is. That's what I'm worried about. And it wasn't the same with us. I knew I wanted to marry you right away."

Lila nodded as though he'd made her point. "But Noelle isn't worthy of that from a man?"

"Of course she is but…" Her dad shook his head. "I'm going to get a beer."

Remy stood up, narrowly missing the Frisbee. "I'll go with you. It's going to be fine. Hutch is a good guy. He's even had a couple of girlfriends over the years. Well, one. Maybe two. Mostly he's a crazy hookup guy. Definitely not Noelle's type. I think you're safe."

Lila leaned over the table. "You're welcome. I've found the way to stop your dad's overly protective lectures is to challenge him in a stern voice. He usually backs down. Now he'll stop the 'no one should touch my precious baby girl' talk." She stood up. "Which is a good thing because we all know that's not true. You be careful at that club." She pointed her sister's way. "Laurel is still there, you know. So is our brother. He's on the board that approves new applicants. Did you honestly think he wouldn't call me?"

Lisa sat up. "Well, given that it's supposed to be a secret process, yes."

Lila's eyes rolled. "Like anything is really secret at Sanctum. They like to say they're all covert and mysterious, but when it comes to family…well, Will views Noelle like a niece and he wants to avoid her at all costs. Be nice to your uncle and don't do anything pervy around him. His club night is Friday. Maybe you could go on Saturdays."

She knew? Noelle felt her cheeks flame, but she straightened her shoulders anyway. This was her life. "I'm an adult…"

Lila put a hand on her head, smoothing her hair back. "Nope. No need to fight that fight with me. I meant what I said. You are smart and funny and beautiful, and you deserve everything you're brave enough to go after. I don't understand the whole submissive thing. I'm not wired that way, but if you are then there is no place I would trust more than Sanctum. After all, it's where my sisters and my brother found their loves. But do not tell your father. Not now. Maybe in ten years or so."

Maybe never. "Sorry I didn't talk to you about it."

Lila shook her head. "You talked to the best person you possibly could have, and when you get there, don't hesitate to talk to Laurel, too. I love you. I know we don't share blood and that you still miss your mom, but you're my daughter, too. I want the world for you.

You are strong and smart. If this Hutch guy is hot and seems like he'd be good for you, go for it. Even if it's only for a little while. Sex is good for you if you make smart choices about it. Never tell your father I said that."

She got to her feet and hugged her stepmom. Her mother had died so many years ago, but this woman had eased the blow. Lila had been everything she could have wanted in a mom, and she was grateful to be part of her family. "Thank you."

"Be safe out there." Her stepmom hugged her tight and then let go as something whizzed by her head. "I'm never going to survive those boys."

Noelle leaned over and grabbed the Frisbee. "I'll handle my brothers for a while if you want to have a glass of wine. That cake has to come out of the oven in about twenty minutes, but I can watch the boys until then."

"Cake. I'm up for cake," Lisa said with a grin.

Lila sighed and stepped back. "I'm going to miss you, Noelle. Remember we're always here for you."

Her stepmom walked back in the house, and despite the fact that she had some stress at work, she was hopeful for the future.

"That went better than I thought it would," Lisa said. "I'll be honest. I figured she would know sooner or later. Lila knows everything. Should Kevin be climbing the shed? God, please be a girl."

"Kevin! Get down from there." She picked up her cane and started for the stairs because her brother was trying to kill himself. Her stepmom's dog Peanut was whining as though he knew disaster was about to happen but couldn't figure out how to fix the problem.

Jason ran by her, grinning. "Throw it to me, Noelle. Throw it to me."

"I know Hutch," Lisa was saying behind her. "He's actually pretty cute, and I've heard he's good in bed."

Oh, that did not matter. She tossed him the Frisbee while she started to drag her other brother out of harm's way.

She kind of hoped Lisa had a girl, too.

And it didn't matter if Hutch was cute because she wasn't about to get caught in a trap. No way. No how.

* * * *

Dallas, TX

Greg Hutchins watched as his friends started to shuffle toward the door of Michael Malone's gorgeous high-rise condo that overlooked Victory Park. It was a far cry from the home Hutch had recently purchased, but in many ways he preferred his three-bedroom ranch in Chapel Downs. He never thought he would live in what was basically the suburbs, but when he'd gotten the chance to buy it from a friend, he'd taken it.

He'd moved in the month before, and the whole place pretty much consisted of a massive TV, a couple of gaming chairs, a folding table in the "dining" room, and his bed. He hadn't counted on how empty the place would feel.

Which was precisely why he'd been happy to get the invite from Michael to come to his place and watch an afternoon of college football. It had been good to hang with the guys instead of spending the entire weekend on his computer.

But now the game was over, and tonight was a play night at Sanctum. Most of his friends played on Saturday nights. He hadn't been in a few months. The club had lost something for him.

Like the rest of his life had lost… He wasn't sure what word he was thinking of. Spark? Adventure? Shine?

All he knew was that lately he'd felt like he was doing nothing more than going through the motions. Go to work. Go home. Eat dinner alone and sit in front of a screen of some kind. Wake up and do it all over again.

He felt a bit empty, and that wasn't what he'd expected since he knew what real tragedy was. He had most of what he needed in life, so why was there a hole in his soul?

"Are you not coming out tonight?" Theo Taggart asked, his keys in hand. "Case is in town, and he and Mia are letting the girls watch Heath. Although do not mention that to him. He thinks it's a hangout with his cousins. He doesn't know Tasha is getting paid. He's sensitive about the word *babysitter*. I'm not mentioning it to my eleven-year-old either."

Case and Theo Taggart were the youngest of the Taggart brothers. Fraternal twins, Case was a few minutes older than his brother. They were both solid guys. Hutch had worked with the brothers for years.

"Tasha's in charge of everyone?" Tag's oldest kid was very responsible, but there were a lot of kids in that family, and they were not known for their calmness. Tag alone had four besides Tash.

"Carys is there, too. Kenzie will be solid, and Kala will sit in her room and play on the computer." Theo frowned. "I hope that's what she's doing. I worry she's setting herself up for world domination or something. She spends way too much time with her Aunt Chelsea. Come with us. It'll be a blast. Case is only here for a week or two and then he's back in New York for the rest of the year. 4L is rolling out something big, and he's in charge of security around it."

It wasn't that he didn't want to hang with Case. It was that being in Sanctum reminded him how fucking dull his life had become. He couldn't put his finger on it, but somehow the things that used to hold meaning for him had faded. Somehow turning thirty had been a tipping point, and now playing video games all night with strangers across the globe no longer held appeal.

Which was precisely why he should go to the club, find a pretty sub, and pass a nice night.

Yeah, that had lost its appeal, too.

"Maybe I will come," he hedged because he didn't want Theo to think he was dodging Case.

Theo looked like he wasn't completely buying the words, but he nodded. "I hope to see you there. Michael, thanks for the hospitality. It was fun to spend an afternoon with the guys."

Because Theo rarely did it anymore. He usually spent his Saturdays at his daughter's soccer games or doing things with his son. He was a family man, and it was obvious that made him happy.

Michael Malone stood in his entryway and nodded. There was a smile on his face, but it couldn't hide the grimness in his eyes.

It hadn't been that long since Michael had called off his long-planned wedding, and there were still touches of his fiancée all over the condo.

The door closed behind Theo and he was left alone with Michael. They'd been friends for years. Over a decade. Hutch had been the tech expert on the CIA team Michael and the other guys worked for back in the day. Most of that same team now worked at McKay-Taggart, though they all found themselves at different places in life. Theo and Case had been married for years. Some of the other guys were in seemingly happy relationships. Some were single and mingling.

Hutch felt stuck, and he wondered if that wasn't how Michael felt, too.

"You going to Sanctum tonight?" Michael had been a regular when he'd been with his fiancée. Hutch still wasn't sure what had happened between the two, but Michael hadn't dated since the breakup.

Michael's mouth turned down in a frown. "I should, but I think I'm going to stay here and watch the late game. You're welcome to join me. I've noticed you haven't been going regularly."

Hanging out with Michael might be a better way to spend his evening. At least he wouldn't watch the scenes and the couples and try to figure out why he felt restless. After he'd broken up with Katy, he'd spent a lot of time at the club, but no time connecting with anyone. "It doesn't feel the same lately. It's weird. I can't seem to find my focus. I haven't found a scene partner I click with in a long time."

He'd only had a couple of women he'd viewed as anything beyond transitory partners. There were subs he would scene with when they needed a top, but none of them had been "his." His one foray into the vanilla dating world had been a spectacular disaster that led him to almost a year of celibacy, and he couldn't seem to get back into a routine.

"Give yourself some time. I know that breakup was hard on you," Michael said.

That was part of the problem. "It really wasn't. It was a relief."

Michael crossed to the bar and pulled out the good Scotch. "How so?"

"I didn't start dating Katy for the right reasons." He'd worked through all of this, but he wondered if Michael might be the one who needed to talk. "I did it because she made sense, and it felt like it was time to settle down. I kind of floated through it, you know. When I found out she was cheating on me, I wasn't even mad. She brought her new boyfriend to pick up her stuff from my place and I sat down and played a couple of rounds of Halo 7 with him."

Michael whistled. "You were not invested in that relationship."

He shrugged because he knew he'd been guilty, too. He'd made mistakes. "We weren't truly compatible, and I never felt a spark with her. But then I've never felt a spark with anyone, so I have to wonder if I'm just not that guy."

Michael offered Hutch a glass and held up his own. "You described my entire relationship with Tessa. Except for the cheating part. She's a good woman. I just couldn't love her the way she deserved. May they forgive us."

He would drink to that. Katy was a nice lady, but they were not meant to be. He clinked his glass. "May we forgive ourselves."

Michael chuckled. "You've been in therapy too long."

He shrugged and drank back a bit of the excellent Scotch. It burned in a pleasant way. "You can never get too much therapy."

Especially not when a person had grown up the way he had. Abusive father, check. Death of his mom. Check. Bad relationship with distant stepmother leading to life on the streets and then in and out of juvie. Check and check.

Sometimes he didn't even count that year he'd been undercover for an insanely criminal doctor who performed tests on soldiers. It was sad that the time he'd spent with Hope McDonald wasn't the worst of his life.

"I heard you're going out into the field." Michael settled on the barstool.

"Sort of. I'm not sure." It was still confusing. He wasn't the "field" guy. He was the guy who sat behind a computer, but he'd kept up the training McKay-Taggart Security required of all its employees. Even the receptionist had to take self-defense after that one time a CIA team had raided the office.

He'd been on the wrong side of that battle, but they'd all worked it out. God, that seemed like another lifetime. Everyone had changed, but he was stuck in the same place.

He didn't understand what Tag meant by going into the field since he could do almost anything he needed to do remotely. He didn't have to sit in front of a computer to hack it. Security had gotten better over the last couple of years, but so had his hacking skills. He was the dude who stayed in the background when the bullets started flying.

"What does that mean? I thought you were taking on that family case Tag was talking about," Michael said. "Something go sideways? I didn't get back until late Friday."

Michael had been on a case and hadn't heard the latest developments. "I was supposed to meet her two days ago, but something happened at her lab and she ended up going home for a couple of days. We rescheduled for Monday. The fact that there was an accident in the lab means Tag thinks I might need backup. He's paired me with a bodyguard."

Michael set his glass down. "Yes, I heard you're working with Kyle Hawthorne. He's…interesting."

"He's a walking time bomb, and everyone knows it." Unfortunately, he was also Big Tag's brother's stepson. If anyone needed therapy, it was Kyle Hawthorne. He'd recently left the Navy, and everyone thought he would go back to college. But instead he'd shown up at McKay-Taggart and went straight into the bodyguard program.

Things happened around Kyle. Dangerous things.

"Boomer went out on a job with him a couple of weeks ago," Michael mused. "He said Kyle was pretty solid in the field. He said Kyle watched his back when they got in some trouble."

Boomer had been on the team as long as Hutch had been. He was the group's firearms specialist. But he had his quirks. "Kyle probably bought Boomer a pizza and now they're best friends."

There was something dark in Kyle that made Hutch wary. It wasn't that he thought Kyle was a bad guy. It was that something simmered beneath his surface, and Hutch had learned that simmering tended to lead to exploding. He didn't want to be around when that man exploded.

"You could talk to Tag if you feel uncomfortable." Michael sat back. "He might send in someone else."

"I think Tag has his reasons." He trusted his boss. He was also worried there was another reason he was taking Kyle into the "field." "This is mostly a tech job. I'll still be behind a computer. Kyle will likely take point with the client. Reading the file, I'm not sure how much Noelle LaVigne truly needs a bodyguard. I get that her dad is nervous, but something feels off. Do you think this could be a setup? You know how Charlotte likes to play matchmaker."

Charlotte Taggart had matched up more than one of her employees, and sometimes she did it under the guise of "working" with Charlotte's choice of mate. He wouldn't put it past her or Big Tag to pair up their nephew with a family friend. Especially if they thought Noelle would be good for Kyle.

Michael's brow arched. "You know anything about this woman? I heard she's the daughter of a friend of Remy Guidry's."

He'd gone over the file on Noelle LaVigne several times. "She's super smart. She's heading a test team at the age of twenty-five. She was in a bad car accident when she was younger, and she had to learn to walk again. She still uses a cane or a brace, but she hasn't let that stop her. She grew up in a tiny town but moved to the big city, and she lives on her own."

Michael nodded as though Hutch was going down the right path. "So she's probably on the nerdy side, definitely likes tech. She's younger than you but not more than a couple of years."

Michael wasn't telling him anything he didn't already know. "Yeah. And Charlotte told me she likes to bake. So I might get some cookies out of it. That's a plus."

He wished he didn't still crave sweets, but he'd gotten to the point that he accepted it. He spent extra time in the gym, and it didn't show.

Michael stared at him like he was missing something. "So a cute woman who's interested in a lot of the things you're interested in and loves to bake comes along, and you think Charlotte is trying to pair her up with a dude who obviously needs therapy."

"Yeah, that's what I'm worried…" He could be slow about the emotional stuff sometimes, but the truth did hit him after a while. Like a sledgehammer. He sat there for a moment. "Shit. You think it's me?"

He hadn't even considered that.

Michael's eyes rolled and he chuckled. "Yes. I think the cute nerd who loves to bake probably fits better with the nerd who calls himself Candyman online. For one of the smartest dudes I know, you can be shockingly un-self-aware. Just remember the last man Charlotte set up."

That had been Michael Malone himself, and it hadn't worked out for him, though he and Tessa Santiago were still friends.

At least Charlotte hadn't set him up with a fellow employee. Michael had to see his ex every day.

He stopped. He wasn't going to let himself get set up. He was not that guy. Was he? It wasn't like he was great at picking his own women. But he wasn't that guy. "I'm not in a good place for a relationship."

"What place is that?" Michael asked.

He wasn't sure. What place was he in? A weird place where he wanted to date but he didn't want to date. He wanted what his friends had but didn't see himself there. He wasn't happy, but he wasn't sure how to be happy.

"No idea, man. I think that's the problem." He was ready and he also wasn't ready. He was still a big old mess, and that meant he wasn't good for anyone.

Still, she *was* pretty cute, and Charlotte was usually right about things. After all, she'd been the one to tell him she didn't think Katy could give him what he needed.

Katy had managed to give some dude named Bowen what he needed. Lots of times. Mostly in their bed, and he was pretty sure once in his car. He sighed.

"Come on," Michael said with a chuckle. "I think we should order pizza and watch the late game. Come Monday, you'll meet this Noelle and see if there's anything beyond the job."

"I am not being set up." He was absolutely certain about that. "I'm done with the vanilla world. I need to get back in the swing of things and find a sub and settle down."

Settling didn't seem like a terrible thing to do. It might be nice. And now he had a house to offer a woman. He had a good job and lots of friends who were like family.

"So you want to go to the club?"

No. He really didn't. Hutch groaned. "Nah. Order a pizza. Let's watch some football."

Mindless entertainment. That was what he needed. It would get his mind off the fact that he had an empty house to go home to, with no real prospects on the horizon.

Because he wasn't getting set up.

She was more than cute. She was smart, and she had to be tough to get through what she'd been through. He admired that.

He caught sight of a picture of Michael and his former fiancée. They were smiling and seemed happy.

Nope. He wasn't going there. He moved into the living room and found his seat, trying not to think about the fact that Charlotte thought the cute nerd might be a match for him.

He liked cute nerds.

But again, he wasn't going there. He sat back and tried to relax as the game came on.

It would be a long weekend, but they all kind of were now.

He didn't see that changing any time soon.

Chapter One

Hutch hustled into the McKay-Taggart building on Monday morning and groaned at the security line. Someone had set up two high-tech scanners and a barrier that would keep anyone from getting to the elevators without going through the tech. The scanners would not only detect weapons, they would also send facial scans upstairs to Miles-Dean, Weston, and Murdoch, who would weed out anyone who might be coming in to blow up the building.

He got into line because something had obviously happened since this wasn't normal security protocol.

A man stood in front of him wearing a dark collared shirt and slacks, his dark hair still cut in military style. Kyle Hawthorne had a soft leather briefcase in his hand. Hutch happened to know that particular brand was normally used to carry laptops and cell phones and tablets, but Kyle used it to carry around his personal tools of the trade.

Weapons. Lots of weapons.

"Any idea what's going on?" Hutch asked.

Kyle turned and nodded a greeting. "I think MDWM has some big politician coming in, and they're trying to make sure no one assassinates her on property. You should have heard the lawyers on ten arguing that they didn't sign up for this. Someone offered to let them talk to Big Tag and they got quiet quick."

It was good to know his boss was still feared by many. Or they knew Ian Taggart was an immovable object and they could get to work way quicker if they let security do its job. The company started by former McKay-Taggart employees was famous for working missing person cases and finding criminals on the run.

"I would bet all this security is also to protect Adam's tech." If someone from the government was coming in, they would be careful. The company worked with the government but hadn't shared their wildly successful software with them.

"Good for Adam." Kyle settled the long strap of his briefcase over his muscled shoulder. "He should protect himself because those bastards would steal anything he had and not blink an eye."

That was Kyle. He'd come into the company paranoid, and that was usually something that happened later. But Hutch was working with the guy, and that meant trying to get along with him. Kyle was an odd duck. He didn't spend a lot of time with the single guys, though they'd invited him to hang out plenty of times. He seemed to prefer the company of his brother and some of the guys who worked for Top, the restaurant his stepfather ran.

Something seemed to be happening up ahead in the line that had it at a standstill.

Hutch needed coffee. He'd overslept and barely managed to catch the train at the Royal Lane Station. Normally he rode in with Theo when he didn't drive in himself, but he'd woken up and realized he hadn't charged his freaking car. He'd let it sit for way too long, and now he was probably looking at battery damage he couldn't afford. So he'd taken the train. And that sucker had been packed.

It had put him on edge, and he needed some coffee with cream and sugar, and he prayed someone had brought muffins or something. Otherwise he would be eating his breakfast from the vending machines, and they were mostly fruit and protein bars since Charlotte was on a health kick.

His cholesterol hadn't come back bad. Why was he being punished for Big Tag's LDL levels, and he kind of hated the person who'd invented at-home blood tests.

"You read through the case?" Kyle asked.

He looked back up and the line had moved a bit. Kyle was slightly ahead of him, and there was a woman in front of Kyle. A woman with a nice shape to her. That was a pretty backside, and she had a ton of dark brown hair curling down almost to her waist. He forced himself to focus. "Yeah. It seems pretty straightforward. Chick works for high-end firm. It's a pretty impressive think tank. Her dad is a crazy, paranoid guy, and now we get to babysit."

Kyle frowned. "You're not taking this seriously, are you?"

"You haven't been around long," Hutch replied. "You don't know the signs."

"There are signs?"

He was going to have to explain and hope he didn't sound like a complete asshole. Kyle should know that this was a setup going in. He still wasn't completely sure which of them was the target. He'd had all day Sunday to wonder why Charlotte would think he needed a girlfriend—besides the obvious lack of companionship, lack of motivation, lack of dishes in his brand-new house. "This is a case Big Tag took strictly because he knows this chick's dad. He's some sheriff in a town where there's more gators than people. He's probably one of those people who thinks his baby girl will immediately be murdered when she steps foot in a city."

"I have known the type," Kyle allowed. "But that doesn't necessarily rule out a serious problem. He can be both paranoid and right. I've known that type, too."

Kyle kind of was that type. But he didn't understand Charlotte Taggart's hobbies. "Look, there's a reason we're on this case."

"Yes, you're here because it involves some high-tech stuff, and I'm good at not letting the people around me die," Kyle replied as they moved forward again.

"We're also single, and apparently this young lady is looking for a husband." He wasn't sure Noelle LaVigne knew Charlotte was setting her up, but it was smart to go into the situation thinking everyone else was in on it.

A brow rose over Kyle's eyes. "Seriously?"

At least he now had the man's attention. "Come on, man. You have to know Charlotte likes to play matchmaker."

"She does that at the club," Kyle replied. "She wouldn't do it in her professional world."

"Who do you think set up Michael and Tessa?"

Tessa was on the bodyguard team, so Kyle should know her pretty well. "Seriously? She thought Michael and Tess would suit each other? They're too alike. She needs someone...I don't know, lighter than Malone. I was actually thinking of introducing her to my brother."

He would never in a million years have thought that Kyle freaking Hawthorne was the kind of dude who would set up his own brother. "My point is this whole case is a setup. For one of us. I'm not sure which."

"She's pretty and smart. I can think of worse things," Kyle said. "Although I'm not in a good place for a relationship."

"You and me both." There was light at the end of the tunnel. Four more people and he could hop on that elevator and get his coffee, get to his meeting, and hopefully shut Charlotte's plans down. "I do not need to be set up with a small-town princess who probably caused this whole problem by leaving her laptop where she shouldn't. I do not need some paranoid sheriff begging me to date his daughter."

"My dad doesn't beg, I assure you," a feminine voice said. "And I keep my laptop close. He wasn't always a small-town sheriff. He was a detective in New Orleans. I spent most of my childhood there. But Dallas is a scary place for a hick like me."

Hutch felt his whole body flush.

And he also saw the first genuine smile he'd ever seen on Kyle Hawthorne's face. "Hutch, meet Noelle. She got here right as I did, so naturally I let her go ahead of me. I'm a gentleman. She brought lemon poppyseed muffins because she heard the big guy likes lemons."

"You're a massive asshole," Hutch said under his breath.

"Oh, I'm not the one who looks like an ass," Kyle shot back before focusing on Noelle, who was way prettier than her picture.

Her picture didn't show the way her eyes sparkled or the generosity of those lips of hers. In the picture the sun wasn't shining on her hair, bringing out the red and gold that threaded through the lush brown.

"Noelle likes to bake," Kyle added. "What do you say?"

"Baking is just chemistry but with a sweeter product at the end," Noelle replied. "And I did not realize everyone thought this was some kind of joke. I assure you I can handle it on my own."

Oh, he was going to get his ass kicked. Hard. By multiple people. "I'm sorry. It was pointed out to me that my boss might be trying to set us up. Or Kyle here."

She turned and moved forward. That was when he noticed the cane. She moved with it as she carried her tote bag that was full of what could have been his breakfast if only he'd kept his damn mouth shut. "Oh, yes, well that was part of the process. I got a big book to look through and pick my possible husband. I'll let Charlotte know she should send psych evals with the beefcake pics."

She smiled at the security guard and handed him her bag.

"Is she joking?" Hutch asked. "She's joking, right?" Because he was pretty sure he hadn't posed for pictures, but there were definitely nights that it could have happened.

Damn, but she was hot. And now angry with him. Like everyone was going to be.

"I think it's safe to say she's joking," Kyle replied. "And it's also safe to say you're about to be off the case. I'm sure MaeBe can handle it. She can go in the field with me."

May Beatrice Vaughn was another member of McKay-Taggart's cybersecurity team. In the beginning it had just been Adam Miles, and then Hutch had backed him up for a couple of years. He'd moved into Adam's old job when Adam had left, and over the years they'd hired a couple of specialists, including the perkiest of them, MaeBe Vaughn.

He and MaeBe were strictly friends. She was like a kid sister. But he also recognized that MaeBe was adorable and had a banging bod. "Did you do all of this to get MaeBe on the team instead of me?"

"Did I set up a scenario where the client showed up and you made an ass of yourself? No." Kyle pulled his briefcase off in anticipation of the search he was about to go through. "Did I see an opportunity and take it?" He gave Hutch a predatory grin. "Oh, yes. I'll take Ms. LaVigne upstairs. Don't worry about her."

But he kind of wanted to now. He glanced over and she was handing the security guard her cane. She seemed to brace herself and then walked through the scanner to the other side, where she stopped because the guard was examining her cane.

She didn't want to walk without it. In that moment he didn't see a potential threat to his own freaking loneliness. He saw a pretty woman who was vulnerable, who was trying hard not to show it, probably because he'd been such an asshole. A woman who'd gone through so much, who still carried the burdens of her past but could smile the way she did.

"Hey, Howard, it's just a cane." He knew the security guys. "She's a client of Mr. Taggart. I don't think she's got a cannon in there or anything."

Kyle was moving through the scanner. Hutch handed over his laptop bag.

"Never can tell these days." Howard gave Noelle back her cane. "And I don't know if we should let anyone take a bunch of baked goods up. There's a senator coming to meet with Mr. Dean. We were told to be extra careful. Miss, I'll keep these down here for you. If you'll fill out a form…"

"Do you want to explain to Big Tag why he didn't get the lemon muffins he ordered?" Hutch was not letting her bag of treats go. She'd made them and carried them all the way here. She got to keep them.

He knew he was doing an awfully fast 180, but he couldn't help himself. He'd said things she should never have heard, and he felt like crap about it.

"He didn't actually…" Noelle accepted her cane and seemed to figure out what he was doing. "They're a surprise. Mrs. Taggart ordered them for her husband. Should I call her?"

Howard immediately handed over the bag. "Nope. If Mrs. Taggart wants them upstairs, then upstairs they go." He frowned Kyle's way. "Do you need all these guns?"

Kyle shrugged. "They're my favorite accessory." He grimaced when the scanner turned red. "Sorry. I forgot about the knives. Give me a second."

He moved to the side, and Hutch hoped the man didn't have to undress to get through security. It gave him a shot at going first since he wasn't carrying. He stood still and let the scanner do its work. The second guard waved him on, and he grabbed his laptop and joined Noelle, who seemed to be waiting on Kyle.

"Could I carry that for you?" Maybe being a gentleman would

smooth things over. "I can walk you up to the office. I'm Hutch. Sorry about the joke I was playing on my buddy over there."

"Sure. You were joking," she said, not moving an inch. "Mr. Hutch…"

She had the sweetest accent. It was very Southern and polite. "Just Hutch. My name is Greg Hutchins, but I was named after my dad who was an abusive asshole, so I prefer Hutch."

"All right, Hutch," she replied evenly. "Let's not mince words. You don't want to do this job, it's fine. Kyle mentioned someone else."

"Kyle doesn't assign agents." Though apparently he liked to fuck them over.

"I don't want to cause trouble." She leaned a bit on the cane. "I'm fairly certain we're going to find out that this wasn't worth all the time and effort. If you've got a junior team member I can work with, I'll be happy to make the switch. I was told you're the top computer guy."

It was sometimes hard to believe but he'd been heading the cybersecurity unit for years now. "I'm good at what I do. I can figure out if you have a problem. So your dad did Big Tag a favor once?"

"The ties are more complex than that." She looked him up and down. "My Aunt Lisa said you were cute. She didn't mention how highly you thought of yourself."

He knew that name well. The Daley family had close connections to MT. "Lisa Daley?"

Noelle nodded. "She goes by Guidry now. She's my stepmom's sister, but I call her aunt anyway."

Kyle seemed to have gotten through, and he hurried over. "Yeah, it's weird, right? Like I don't have any blood relation to Big Tag or Charlotte, but they consider me family because Sean's my stepdad. It can be hard to figure out what to call those relationships when you're an adult. As a kid you call everyone aunt and uncle."

He kind of wished Kyle had stayed on the other side because at least then he could pretend Noelle had one of those faces that always looked a little frowny. Nope. She smiled Kyle's way and pretty much lit up the room.

"That's a lot of knives," she said. "I'm sure my dad would

approve."

Kyle knelt down and shoved one into his boot. "It's only three. And I'm carrying extra guns because I borrowed a couple to try out at the shooting range. I'm trying to find a good semi. Come on and I'll get you upstairs. I'm afraid we're late."

Hutch didn't like the "we" part. He moved to the other side of Noelle. "Tag will understand. He has to know what the situation is downstairs. I'd like to talk to you a bit before we go into the meeting. I've read through the files but sometimes talking it through can give me a better perspective."

"I thought it was all the overblown rantings of small-town hicks who think the big city is scary," she replied as they made it to the elevator.

"I might have been overstating that case," he admitted. "I'm really sorry you heard that."

"I'm really sorry you said it," she shot back.

So she wasn't the woman who would let a guy get away with shit. It did something for him. He hated it when a woman felt like she had to smile and forgive simply because the man who'd hurt her apologized.

He'd dug a deep hole with this woman, and it sucked because he was a nice guy. He was the guy who made sure everyone got home and who sat with his friends when they weren't feeling well. He was the caretaker of the group. He was the guy ladies slept with because he was safe and would be nice.

Naturally the one woman to spark his interest he'd been a jerk to.

Not that he was…

Screw that. He *was* interested, and there was no way Charlotte had set her up with Kyle. No way. That bit of sunshine had been meant for him. Had he been his normal, flirty, nice-guy self she might be eating out of his hand by now. And he would have her muffins halfway down his throat. Yep. It did not escape him that he wanted to taste all her sweetness.

The elevator doors came open and Kyle gallantly held it for Noelle.

He should have done that. Hutch sighed and got on the elevator. "I'm sorry I said it, too, since I know what it's like to be stereotyped.

41

It was a dumb thing to say and I apologize. I hope I can make you feel comfortable working with me."

"Or you can talk to Charlotte and get another agent on the case. Hutch is not the only tech guy we have," Kyle said helpfully. "There's even a lady tech, if you would feel more comfortable with a woman."

"Yes, she's on my team." It was time to take control. Kyle seemed more than willing to throw him under the bus. "I'm in charge of assignments when it comes to my team. Ian asked me to take this case because I'm the best."

"I thought his wife asked you because she wants to marry you off," Noelle quipped.

"Or it could be me," Kyle offered. "He said he wasn't sure. I am single, too."

Kyle was married to his weapons. Hutch shook his head. "It's me, and I still think Charlotte had a hand in this, but I was given the case and I'm keeping it. I'm also the senior agent. I'm in charge."

"I'm the client," Noelle began and then frowned. "Who isn't actually paying anything, so I'll take what I can get. You should know, Mr...Hutch, that I am not interested in being set up. I won't be throwing myself at you or expecting anything beyond your help in one specific situation. You're perfectly safe. Also, I think you'll find your part of the job is pretty simple. I brought my laptop with me. We might be able to figure it all out this morning and go our separate ways. I do think my dad's being paranoid. He also warned me you're a horndog and I should stay away from you."

"I'm a what?" He'd never heard the expression.

Kyle snorted. "From some of the stories I've heard, it's a pretty accurate description." The doors opened and there was the entrance to McKay-Taggart. "Come with me, Noelle. I'm more than happy to show you around while Hutch sets up our briefing. And those muffins smell delicious. Would you like some coffee?"

"I would love some. Thank you." Noelle completely ignored him as she walked off with Kyle. "It's a lovely office."

She had a lovely backside. And muffins. And she smelled like vanilla.

That was a good thing to remember. It hadn't worked with a

vanilla woman. He could have tons of vanilla sex, but it didn't fill his soul the way it should. He needed more control than most women were interested in handing over.

He took a deep breath and followed. Sometimes mistakes were made for reasons. He had to hope that was the case here.

And he had to figure out what a horndog was. He sighed and moved toward the office. His day was already going bad.

* * * *

Did he have to be so cute? Noelle sat across from the man her father had warned her about and wished he wasn't pretty much her exact type. If she was going to build a guy she found attractive, Hutch checked off all her superficial needs. He was gorgeous, had that strong jawline that made her heart go all girly. From the look of his forearms, he spent a lot of time in the gym. And he had beautiful eyes. He wasn't so big that he overwhelmed her, but he also looked solid. His emotions seemed to play across his face. In the short time since she'd met him, she'd seen what he looked like when he was frustrated, embarrassed, and angry. She'd caught sight of him grinning with some of his coworkers, and that smile of his lit up the room.

Why couldn't she like the Kyle Hawthorne, superhot and broody type? Any one of her friends would have taken one look at him and been a puddle at his feet, but she'd merely felt an artistic appreciation for the man's perfection.

She didn't like perfect. She liked laid back and fun. She liked a guy she could read, who didn't constantly hide everything he felt.

"So you work for Genedyne?" Ian Taggart's deep voice brought her back to the reason she was here, which was absolutely not to stare at Hutch while he stared down at the screen of his cell.

Her dad had told her Taggart had recently turned fifty, but he didn't look it. He was hot, too, though in the Kyle Hawthorne way. He looked like a man who regularly dodged bullets.

He'd asked her a question. It was a tribute to how flustered Hutch had her that she couldn't focus. She always had to focus. She had to be the smartest person in every room because not only was she a woman in a male-dominated field, sometimes her coworkers saw her in a wheelchair.

How to explain what Genedynamic did. "Yes, I hired on straight out of college. One of my professors had worked with Jessica Layne when she first started out. It's pretty much my dream job because Ms. Layne is known for funding some big ideas and letting her researchers kind of go wild. She's got several labs around the country, but Dallas is her base."

Her boss was a controversial figure in the scientific world. She was known for offering young women the kinds of jobs that tended to be reserved for mature men, but she was also known for loving publicity and suing the hell out of anyone who offended her. Oh, she called it protecting her patents, but some of those suits had little ground to stand on in Noelle's opinion.

"And what kind of projects do you work on?" Charlotte Taggart was a gorgeous woman, light to her husband's dark. She wore a power suit and some killer heels, her strawberry blonde hair in an elegant bun.

"I'm actually working on helium." She totally knew what came next. If she'd concentrated on a lesser-known element, she wouldn't always have to explain. If she told someone she was studying ways to make a stronger magnet by using neodymium, most people's eyes glazed over and they were back to talking sports or what movies they'd seen lately pretty damn quick. But everyone knew helium.

"Like balloons?" Kyle asked, his lips quirking up.

Hutch's eyes were suddenly on her, studying her intently. "Seriously? Are you looking for alternatives?"

"Alternatives?" Kyle asked.

"Is this about the helium shortage?" Big Tag proved he'd actually read up on her. Or he knew more about science than most people.

"Shortage is in the eye of the beholder," she said. "Some people think it's merely a break in the supply chain and the fact that the new big deposits have been found in countries like Qatar and Russia, and sales can be influenced by political situations. Every couple of years something goes wrong and anyone who requires helium to run their machines gets nervous. We're in one of those times when it's a bit of a scarce resource. The price has gone up significantly in the last few years. But the truth of the matter is helium is a nonrenewable and vital resource. You think peak oil is a problem, meet peak helium."

Kyle frowned. "Okay, I'm going to get the award for dumbest guy in the room when I ask this, but why are we worried about something we use for kids' birthday parties?"

Hutch shook his head. "It's way more than balloons. Helium is a cryogenic element."

She bit back a laugh at Kyle's expression, which told her Hutch was talking way over his head. But not hers, and she thought it was sexy that he understood what she was working on. It made her want to talk about gas chromatography and whether or not nitrogen was the solution. They could start slow and move on to more complex scientific conversations. But she remembered where she was and what she was doing. She also remembered he was kind of an ass. "He means helium is an element we can use to cool any number of systems. Helium has a low boiling point which means we can easily turn its natural gas state into liquid. Liquid helium remains in that state all the way to absolute zero."

Hutch sat up straighter. "That's zero on the Kelvin scale. It's more like negative 450 Fahrenheit. Should I explain why we would use Kelvin?"

Taggart shook his head like a father dealing with obnoxious kids. "We know you're a smarty pants, Hutch. You don't need to dunk on him."

Kyle ignored them both. "Does this have something to do with quantum computing?"

So Kyle kept up with the state of technology. "Among other things. Liquid helium is used to cool magnets in machines like supercolliders and medical imaging. It's important, and my lab is trying to refine a process that allows us to use less helium to do the same job. We're also trying new techniques to better recycle the helium we use. It's important to do that and to store it properly because if helium leaks out, it floats to the upper atmosphere and we have no way to recover it."

"So what you're saying is you're working in a high-tech field where your research could make people a lot of money," Kyle surmised. "Hence, you being worried someone might have accessed your laptop. You're worried about corporate spies."

"She should be worried about spies of all kinds. The technology she's working on is the kind governments would be interested in obtaining for themselves," Hutch added. "When did you first start to worry someone was messing with your computer? Is your laptop where you keep the majority of your research?"

"I have some of it on my laptop, but the majority stays on the systems in the lab. I've got a bunch of statistics and reports from the experiments, but they don't include the protocols on how we ran the experiments. The company wants to keep a lockdown on employees potentially selling sensitive data," she explained.

"I thought Ms. Layne did that by threatening to sue anyone who looks at her the wrong way." Charlotte sat back. "She's famous for it. Do you like working for her?"

Her boss was extremely litigious, but she also allowed a kind of freedom no one else in the business ever did. It was a bit like walking a tightrope. "I rarely see her. She's pretty hands off at this stage. If my research pans out, that's when I'll have more contact with her. The truth of the matter is if rumors get out that someone's had access outside the company to my research, it could be bad for me."

"She's sued former employees before." Hutch continued her line of thinking. "Mostly over loss of income due to the former employee not following security protocols. Did you sign an employment contract?"

"Of course."

"We should have legal take a look at it." Hutch's tone had changed as though he was shifting to a more…dominant role. "I'll run a search on your laptop, and I think we should also take a look around Ms. LaVigne's apartment and check on anyone who has significant contact with her. I'll need a list of everyone you spend time with. Have you had any new neighbors recently?"

She wasn't sure what her neighbors had to do with it. And he wanted a list of her friends? This wasn't what she'd expected. "Uhm, a new couple moved in two doors down from me last month. The woman who lives next door is pretty new, too."

Cara was a freelance journalist who'd moved in a couple of months after Noelle had. Noelle liked her and they'd become fast friends. They spent a lot of time drinking wine and bemoaning their romanceless lives. Still, she hadn't mentioned Sanctum to the other woman. No one but Aunt Lisa knew. Well, and her stepmom, but she tried not to think about that. She wasn't sure why, but it hadn't seemed like something to bring up with Cara. It was also a private club, and it seemed mean to talk about something she could never take her friend to.

Kyle had a notepad in front of him. "I'll need names, but then we should probably play it safe and run traces on anyone in the building, and also at least the employees who would come into contact with Noelle."

"Whoa. I don't think that's a good idea. I don't want to invade anyone's privacy." Somehow she'd thought they would look at her system, tell her she was being paranoid, and she would be on her way. She should never have told her dad about it. She should have sucked it up and gone to company security and taken her chances. "Look, I think I've made a mistake, and I am sorry for wasting your time."

She started to stand.

"Sit down, Noelle."

Noelle sat at the sound of that commanding voice. It did not escape her that everyone was staring, but oddly, not at her. They were staring at the man who'd ordered her to sit. She got the feeling they were all surprised those deep-toned words had come from Hutch.

"Dude, you sound serious. Good for you, man." Taggart nodded Hutch's way.

Why was she sitting? She forced herself to stand again and reached for her cane. "Thank you for your time. Again, I'm sorry for wasting it."

Hutch's eyes met hers, and she felt a bit pinned by them. "Ms. LaVigne, the only thing you're wasting is the unique opportunity to figure out if you truly have a problem. If you thought you could fix this some other way, you wouldn't be here. I assume you're going to ignore the problem now that you've decided we're going to be too much trouble. There's a reason you didn't in the first place. If you turn your laptop over to company security, what do you think is going to happen?"

"Hutch, perhaps we should…" Charlotte began.

Her husband reached out and took her hand in his. "No. I want to see how this plays out. You wanted him in the field. He's going to need to take charge. And possibly learn how to protect his balls. She looks like she knows how to wield that cane."

She did, actually. Her self-defense teacher had believed deeply in turning anything around him into a weapon. He'd been careful to teach her how to make that cane work for her in more ways than one. "I think it's not any of your business."

"Oh, but it is," Hutch contradicted. "Ian, you don't fully understand what's going on here."

Taggart's lips were turned up in a ghost of a smile, as though he loved the drama but wasn't going to make it too obvious. "Oh, I think I do."

"She's embarrassed and trying to find a way out," Hutch said, his expression grim. "I made an ass of myself because I thought this might be a Charlotte setup, and I hadn't gotten a good look at her, so I was an asshole."

"What is that supposed to mean?" Was he about to be an asshole again?

"It means you are the sweetest thing I've seen in a long time, and I regret the fact that I'm not going to get a chance to do anything but work with you. But you should understand that I believe you have a real problem."

She was not going to think about what those words did to her. "That's not what you said before."

"That's because I hadn't looked into the fact that someone recently died at your lab." He managed to make the words an accusation. "You didn't bother to mention that. You said there was an accident and the lab had to be shut down to ensure it was safe. You did not mention that one Madison Wallace died in that accident."

"I didn't think I needed to." She knew she should have, but the last thing she needed was her father to think she was in more danger than she was already in. He would have a bodyguard sleeping at her place, and that was not necessary.

"I think you knew exactly what you needed to say and you didn't," he shot back. "You don't want to be here. You don't want the disruption to your life. You don't want to acknowledge the problem might be bigger than you're willing to admit. And you're in a bind. You know something's going on at your office but your boss—while brilliant—is also vindictive and seems to genuinely enjoy firing people and creating as much drama as she can. No matter what they find on that system, you'll be under close scrutiny."

He wasn't wrong about that. "Well, I've got friends who are good with computers. They can look into it."

Did he think she wasn't connected? She literally worked in a lab. She was surrounded by people who were obsessed with computers.

Not once had she thought about going to one of them. Not once.

His eyes narrowed slightly. "I think you don't want to rock the boat with your father. I also think you're the type of woman who thinks she's smarter than everyone else."

"Hey," Kyle said.

Hutch held a hand out. "You are not the primary on this case."

"Well, we're not going to have a case at all if you keep talking," Kyle complained.

"I definitely think I'm smarter than you." He was starting to irritate her. And her heart was pounding because no one challenged her like this. No one. She was the sweet, innocent Noelle who couldn't walk as well as the rest of them. She was treated with a politeness no one seemed to understand marginalized her, too, because she wasn't allowed to be passionate. She could hurt herself. She was weak and fragile.

It felt good to snarl a little his way.

He stood, his palms flat against the desk, as though he didn't quite trust himself if he didn't plant them there. He stared at her, every lean line of his body predatory, and yeah, that did something for her, too. "You probably are, but I'm about to prove that I'm a better game player than you are because I've already hacked your system. I did it with my phone. With my phone, Noelle. That's how easy it was. You have spyware all over it."

She gasped at the thought. She wasn't bad with computers herself, but she'd had no hint that there was spyware. "But I have security on it."

"And whoever uploaded it to your system knew exactly how to get through," Hutch explained. "Do you know what else I found on your system? Because I can let you guess or I can send it straight to your father and let him handle the problem."

She felt her face flush because she thought she knew what he was talking about. It was habit for her to write down her thoughts. It helped her organize them. She had lists all over her system, but only one that Hutch could threaten her with. "You wouldn't. You don't have any reason to."

Kyle frowned. "I seem to be lost here. What exactly are we doing?"

"She believes someone murdered Madison Wallace, and she wants to find the killer." Hutch let the words sit there like a bomb that was definitely going to go off right in her face. "On her own. She's got lists of suspects. She thinks someone screwed around with the chemicals Madison Wallace was using. And somehow she's not connected the dots here."

"There is such a thing as coincidence." But now that he said the words out loud, she could hear how dumb she sounded. "I don't know why anyone would hurt Madison. Not for the same reasons they would hurt me. Everyone hated her, but she was a rock star. From what I can tell, she was on the verge of a breakthrough. We didn't work on the same projects, so I don't think my computer problems are connected."

"And I think they are," Hutch countered. "Who do you think your father is going to believe?"

He had her in check, but she still had a move to make. She turned to Charlotte. "Mrs. Taggart, I will do whatever you want me to do. I'll be a good girl and follow every protocol you think I need, but I would like another agent to work with. Kyle said there's a woman on the team. I would feel safer with her."

"Don't. I haven't done a damn thing to make you feel unsafe," Hutch argued. "I might have hurt your feelings, but don't push that shit on me."

"I'm feeling a little unsafe now because you're being very aggressive." He wasn't really. His words were, but she didn't feel physically threatened. He was, however, threatening her peace of mind because her heart was pounding, and she wondered what would happen if they were alone.

"Ian, do you remember that year of my life I spent being tortured so you could get your brother back?" Hutch said the words to his boss, but his eyes were steady on her.

Tortured?

"I do," Taggart said evenly.

Hutch's jaw went tight, straightening to a razor's edge. "I'm calling that in now. This op is mine. I am in charge. We do this my way or you get on the phone with Sheriff LaVigne because one way or another she's not going home alone tonight."

"I thought the cotton candy machine was the trade-off for a year in hell," Taggart said.

Hutch finally turned that stare his boss's way.

Taggart sighed and focused his attention on Noelle. "Ms. LaVigne, Hutch is the only agent available to work your case. In light of what he's found, I'm going to assume he'll want close cover, and he'll probably need to get into your office at some point. You'll have to decide how to integrate him into your life. And pretty quickly."

What did that mean? "Kyle has to come with me to the office?"

"No. I do. Kyle is strictly muscle, but he does have to stay close." Hutch straightened up, seeming to relax a bit. "You recently went home. Does everyone know you went home to visit your family?"

"Yes." She wasn't completely sure what was happening, but she was almost certain she'd lost control in a big way. "I mean they know I went home. I'll be honest. I've only been there for a year. I've got a couple of people I consider work friends, but I don't talk to them about my family. We talk work stuff."

Hutch seemed to relax a bit as though he knew he had her where he wanted her. "Good, then when you came back with a boyfriend, no one will question it. We worked out our relationship and we decided I should come to Dallas with you. Kyle is my slacker brother who needs a place to stay while he's looking for work."

Every syllable from his mouth horrified her. "No."

Kyle snorted. "Because I look like the slacker."

Taggart stood, helping his wife to her feet. "Excellent. It's all settled then. Come along, my love. It's lunchtime. Noelle, thank you for the muffins. They were delicious. I leave you in Hutch's surprisingly authoritative hands. Unless you'd like me to call your dad."

She was staring at Hutch like she could move him with pure willpower. "No. That won't be necessary."

"Hutch, see me before you go to check out Ms. LaVigne's apartment," Taggart ordered.

And then she was left with the man she would have to put up with. Well, and Kyle, but he seemed incidental at this point. Hutch had every bit of her attention.

Check and mate.

But their game was far from over.

Chapter Two

"Do I need to buy you a box of condoms?" Big Tag asked as Hutch closed the door behind him.

Unfortunately, they weren't alone in Tag's big corner office or he would have given the boss his happy middle finger. It looked like they were having a lunch party with Charlotte, Alex, and Eve all sitting around with takeout containers on Ian's sofas.

Like the security team version of the *Big Bang Theory*. He would bet Noelle liked that show as much as he did.

Their babies would be smart *and* beautiful.

Nope. They would be nonexistent because Noelle would barely look at him now. He'd felt her pull away and close in on herself, but he rather thought it wasn't in the obvious way. She wasn't protecting herself from the Big Bad Wolf. She was trying to figure out a way to take him down. She wasn't some wilting flower who would cry because a guy challenged her. No. She would retreat and rethink her battle plans.

He could offer her several scenarios that would have him on his back, but he was smart enough to keep quiet about that. "I don't think that's happening any time soon. I don't know if you noticed but the woman doesn't like me."

He'd dug a huge hole, and he wasn't sure he could climb out of it. He'd lost it in that conference room. He'd lost it by taking control in a way he almost never did. Except at Sanctum. He was careful around women because he'd seen how poorly it could go. He'd watched his father abuse woman after woman. He'd taken many a beating because he couldn't sit by.

But something about Noelle LaVigne brought out the beast in him.

"She might not like you, but she's aware of you, and sometimes that's just as telling as instant attraction." Charlotte put down her lunch. "I thought the two of you would get along. I didn't think you'd nearly set the conference room on fire."

"So this was a setup." He knew it. At least he could still trust his instincts. "And it was definitely me and not Kyle."

"Oh, she would not be good with Kyle. Kyle needs someone…well, Kyle needs to spend some time with Kai before he thinks about a relationship." Eve closed her takeout container. "He's hiding a lot of pain, and it's going to come out in some not healthy way if he doesn't deal with it. But that's not a professional opinion. I haven't had a session with him. It's merely observation."

They were all worried about Kyle, and now Hutch would be spending days, maybe weeks, undercover with the man. Noelle would be with Kyle, too. "Do you think he's a danger to others?"

"If she thought that, he wouldn't be working here," Big Tag said with a frown. "He's had a couple of sessions with Kai. Everyone has to in order to work here, but he turned down continuing on when it was suggested he should. I'll be honest. If he wasn't family I probably would have passed. He's good at his job, but I'm worried. Something happened to him during his time in the military. I can't figure it out, and my buddies who are still active tell me there's nothing in the records that make them think he's hiding something. That tells me one thing."

Kyle had been Special Forces. Unless a mission had been classified it should all be out in the open. Or… "How long did he work for the Agency?"

Alex sighed and sat back. "We don't know, and honestly, it's only a suspicion at this point. Sean thinks so, but we pretty much cut ties with anyone who would help us figure it out."

McKay-Taggart had cut ties with the Agency years before, and only recently they'd reupped that firm rejection after a CIA operative used Big Tag's teenaged daughter to spy on them all. Big Tag had not been amused.

"We did that for good reasons." Charlotte put a hand on her husband's thigh, a sure sign of her support for his decision. "The Agency has changed. We don't have anyone there we can truly trust, and to open the relationship back up means putting ourselves on their radar."

The Taggarts wanted some peace after years of dealing with the spy shit. They wanted to raise their unruly brood and enjoy their lives. He couldn't blame them, but Kyle was family, and now Hutch realized he'd been set up in more ways than one. "You want me to figure out what's going on with Kyle."

Big Tag shrugged. "I want you to guide him through his first major case, and if you happen to find out what those fuckers did to make him wake up screaming in the middle of the night, then I'll consider it a plus. His mother is worried about him. I am, too. We all told Grace we thought the military would be good for him. I think we might have been wrong about that."

Big Tag was capable of carrying the world on his shoulders. "I'll find out what I can. In the meantime, I heard Eve talked to Noelle this morning. I'd like to know what your thoughts are."

A smile broke over Eve's face. "I think she's lovely. She's been through a lot and she wasn't broken by it. She loves her family and her work. I would be cautious about underestimating her. She's intensely intelligent and far tougher than she looks."

"She's used to people underestimating her." She looked soft and sweet and vulnerable. "She'll find it annoying, and she'll also use it if she has to."

"Very astute. I concur with that opinion," Eve said with an encouraging smile. "You're attracted to her."

He shrugged. There was no point in denying that. "Yeah, but again, made an ass of myself. I'm not sure she'll give me another shot, but that's honestly for the best. I know Charlotte thinks the world should be all paired off, but I don't know that I would be good for anyone."

"Says the man who made sure he gets to live in her apartment and play her boyfriend for the next few weeks," Alex pointed out.

He'd been running on pure instinct, and that instinct told him he should stick close to Noelle. "She's not happy about that either. I'll have to watch her or she'll try to find a way to put me on the sidelines."

"Don't forget that this isn't merely about attraction." Charlotte toyed with the water bottle in her free hand. "She's in trouble. She's downplaying her original fears. It's like that sometimes, especially with intelligent people who've been taught to trust data instead of their guts. There's a reason she called her father. She was scared. Now she's got some time and distance and she's questioning those original instincts."

"I think it's worse than dismissing her fears." He'd seen her pale when he'd leveled his accusations against her. He'd made a direct hit. "She's playing detective."

"Her father was a damn good one," Big Tag pointed out. "Don't underestimate Armie LaVigne. If he thinks she's in danger and you're not taking care of her, he'll show up here and he'll take control."

Yes, that was a big part of what he had to overcome with her. He'd insulted her father, though he hadn't meant to. He'd been a dumbass playing to stereotypes. "I'll keep him as updated as I can without breaking Noelle's confidence. Armie might have called in favors with you, but Noelle is my client."

Big Tag nodded slightly, an unmistakable sign of approval. "Keep me up to date on everything relevant. Charlie's got some worries about this one."

Charlotte's lips turned down. "I don't like her boss. I've read up on Jessica Layne and she worries me. And it's not because she's a woman in tech. I get any female CEO is going to have to be tough."

"It's the crazy eyes," Big Tag offered. "She's somewhat hot and all, and she plays that up as much as she can. But it's all in the eyes. There's pure bugout crazy in those baby blues."

"I think you should be careful," Eve agreed. "And so should Noelle. I believe Jessica Layne is a narcissist, and potentially a malignant one. I've read her interviews and watched her publicity spots. She's as interested in her own image as she is in the science she backs or the money she makes. If you come into contact with her, do not challenge her view of reality."

"So don't call her on her shit." He'd known people like that. Of course they didn't usually have the same money and power someone like Layne did. "Or she'll sue me."

"The lawsuits are a way to break her victims," Alex explained. "You know she had a partner in the beginning. Another woman who insiders believe was probably the brains of Genedyne. At some point, Jessica decided to cut her out. Not only did she bury the woman in lawsuits, but she sent her social media followers after her. Oh, she said everything in public that she should have, but there's evidence she was manipulating things behind the scenes. Her partner was crushed on many sides and eventually took what the police called an accidental overdose of sleeping pills. Then Layne cried prettily on camera and made it all about her and how she'd had to survive a relationship with a person with mental illness."

Eve sighed. "She looks like a model, and she'll be good at putting the people around her at ease. She'll be charming right up to the moment she decides to devour you whole."

Alex stood and held a hand out to Eve. "Good luck, Hutch. I think you're going to need it. And keep us updated on Kyle. Also, try to remember that just because your past taught you how a bad relationship works, your present has a whole lot of good ones in them. I would hate for you to miss out because you're still worried there's a piece of your father in there."

He shook his head. "It's not that."

Eve started to lead her husband out. "Sure it's not. Come on, babe. I've got to go through about a thousand employee reviews before we can leave. The kids all have afterschool activities that include dinner of some kind, and we're not on carpool this week. We're picking up some Top and watching TV that includes actual human beings instead of cartoon characters this evening."

They were still talking about drinking wine and watching TV as the door closed behind them.

"Ah, that's the dream. All the kids out of the house for the evening," Big Tag said. "All my monsters are grounded after the whole 'let's play spies' thing. Do you know that kids get grumpy when they're not allowed to do anything but chores?"

Charlotte's head dropped to Big Tag's shoulder. "So grumpy. And Hutch, I really thought the two of you would get along. What I saw today makes me think I made a mistake. I'm sorry. I won't try to do it again."

"But you were right. We're definitely attracted to each other." He knew it was perverse, but he felt the need to argue with her.

"But there wasn't a lot of peace there," Charlotte mused. "It's good for sparks to fly, but that was more like war than 'hey, I just met my future spouse.'"

"When I met my Charlie and our eyes locked across the crowded dungeon, I knew," Big Tag said.

She snorted, but her lips were turned up. "That's why he promptly invited me to join him for a threesome."

He chuckled. "Foursome, baby. Give me credit."

She smiled at her husband, their faces close together. "I promptly got rid of all the other subs and started a fight that ended in butt plugs flying. All for your amusement. But I did know I wanted you in that moment. I knew, somehow, that you would complete me." She turned back to Hutch, and a sad expression came over her face. "That's why I'm sorry I set you up with her. I saw two people who should have had a lot in common, and I couldn't help myself. I was definitely meddling, and it didn't work. I won't try again. I promise."

Again, it was perverse, but he didn't like the sound of that. "I think if I were in a different place in my life, we would probably suit each other very well."

"I think she might have too strong a personality," Charlotte admitted. "I did underestimate that."

He wasn't sure how that was a problem. "She obviously needs a guy as strong as she is."

Charlotte nodded. "Yeah. I can see that, too."

"You are such a bitch," Ian said softly, though he was smiling in that way that told Hutch he wasn't getting their inside joke.

"She was attracted to me, too, you know." He'd caught Noelle staring at him, and it hadn't been with distaste. He'd actually been surprised because most women would have watched Kyle, but she'd seemed oddly unaffected by him. And she'd definitely sparked when he'd started talking about helium. He was a science junkie. If she wanted to throw down over some future tech, he could be right there with her.

Except she was a sweet lady from small-town Louisiana who had probably never once been tied up and had her tits clamped. She'd never cried prettily while her Dom fucked her ass with a plug.

"I don't know." Charlotte sounded uncertain. "She seemed annoyed. But it's okay because you don't want a relationship. Maybe *you* should be the brother."

"No." He wasn't going to let her play around with Kyle. He could be dangerous, and honestly, he and Noelle made more sense. "We're the more believable couple, and I need access to the systems. She's right. The company works on a closed system. I could hack them, but they have far better security than Noelle has on her laptop. Although, honestly, she's got pretty good security, which makes me think this is an inside job. I can't get into her lab as her boyfriend's brother."

"You could get a job there." Tag seemed more interested in his wife's earlobe than the discussion at hand. "I'll fire you right now. I'm a team player, man."

He'd been through this so many times. Ten years he'd been here, and he'd seen way too many times Tag decided to turn his office into a playroom.

God, wouldn't that be something? Having a woman to share all of that with. Having one soul in the world who meshed with his. Someone he could tease and have discussions with. Someone who would help him figure shit out.

He was getting tired of figuring shit out on his own. Or rather not figuring anything out and letting life flow by him, bouncing from one good time to another until they all felt hollow and meaningless. Maybe it was the fact that he'd bought a house from a man who for years had been a whole lot like him, a man who'd finally gotten his life together and moved into a future with the woman he loved and their kiddo.

God, did he want kids? No. He wasn't father material. His dad had been awful. But then he knew what not to do, and wasn't that part of the battle? Didn't he know exactly what he'd needed from his parents? He wasn't a bad guy. He constantly checked himself because he knew there was darkness in him.

"Do you think he's going to stand there and watch?" Charlotte's question brought him out of his thoughts.

"I think he's thinking, and I also think I don't care," Big Tag replied. "Hutch, I took the kids to church on Sunday and let my wife have a morning all to herself. She's about to pay me back with a midday blow job."

Hutch sighed. "I don't suppose the fact that I need guidance changes your mind."

Big Tag shook his head, a decisive no. "Church. Kids. I missed the first quarter of the Cowboys game. No. Also, I can give you good advice while I'm getting a hummer."

"He really does think better mid-sex," Charlotte added as she gracefully slid to the floor and found a submissive position.

"I think I'll go and make sure my client hasn't run." He'd told her to wait at his desk and he'd escort her to her office, pick up a key to her place, and then get them all moved in together while she worked.

"You sure you want to do this? Because I can still fire you and you can go the employee route," Tag offered as his hand went to stroke down his wife's head.

So Noelle could ignore him entirely. "I think I've got a handle on it. I'll call in with an update."

He practically ran out the door because those two weren't waiting. He almost bounced off Geneva Rycroft, Big Tag's long-time assistant. She was a lovely woman with dark hair and a ready smile. Another woman who'd been through hell and found her happiness on the other side in the form of a husband and two kiddos she adored. She was carrying a stack of files.

Hutch shook his head. "You should wait a while. Big Tag had to go to church."

Her eyes widened and she set the files down and picked up a single laminated sheet of paper that she often hung on her boss's door. It had one word on it. NOPE.

Genny had once told him she'd made the sign because Big Tag and Charlotte never locked the door. They liked the danger, they often said.

He often thought Genny had saved them many an HR complaint.

"Cool," she said. "I'll set this up and go take a coffee break. Maybe I'll go see what the bodyguards are up to."

She had a sparkle in her eyes because her husband worked in that unit.

Everyone was getting lucky today.

Except him. He would likely be sleeping on a couch tonight.

Genny had two muffins on her desk. Noelle's lemon muffins. She'd taken them to feed to Tag when he got snacky this afternoon. She did that a lot.

Well Big Tag could survive on one. Hutch grabbed one of the muffins and prayed it wasn't as good as it smelled.

He savored that tart and sweet piece of heaven.

He was in so much trouble.

* * * *

Noelle sat in a chair in Hutch's office and wondered about the man. The name plate outside simply said Hutch, Head of Cybersecurity. Not his whole name. Just Hutch. The office was surprisingly spartan given the fact that the man had worked here for a decade. That was what had thrown her off. Was he older than he looked? She thought he was likely in his early thirties. How had he gone from the military to college to head of a team for one of the world's premiere security firms in a little more than a decade?

The math did not add up.

She looked at one of the three framed pictures he had in his office. This one wasn't actually a picture. It was his degree from the University of Texas at Dallas proclaiming Greg Hutchins was a graduate with a Master of Science in Computer Sciences.

"He did that without an undergrad, you know," a feminine voice said. "That's why it's his only framed degree."

She turned and there was a young woman standing in the doorway. She was the quintessential geek girl in her miniskirt, black T, and combat boots, her purple hair in a high ponytail. There was a familiar laptop in the woman's hands.

"How do you get a master's without an undergrad?" She shouldn't have asked, but she was pretty much fascinated with Hutch.

Much to her own chagrin.

"You score so high on the GRE that they can't not take you," she said, walking into the office. She held out a hand. "I'm Mae Beatrice Vaughn, but everyone calls me MaeBe. And yes, I cringe when I say that sentence too. How that song is still popular I have no idea. I blame all the covers. Anyway, I'm working my way through the same program right now, though I do have an undergrad. I don't have Hutch's real-world experience, though. You must be the chemist. Nice system, though totally infected. Sorry about that."

She handed her the laptop she'd bought for herself when she'd gotten the job at Genedyne. "I didn't notice anything was wrong except that a file that I hadn't touched in a long time was showing up in my recents."

"Yeah, it's funny what can trip a hacker up." MaeBe leaned against Hutch's desk. "You open the files you're currently using by going to the recently opened folder?"

It was a habit. "Of course. What do you do?"

"I know where all my files are. I pull them up. I organize my own system," she replied. "If you didn't use the recents folder, you likely wouldn't have noticed anything at all. Unless you typically check the dates on your files, which I would bet you don't."

"No. I'm more worried about what's in the file than when I last used it," she admitted. "I don't think about security very much, but I noticed that file and thought it was weird. And there was a break-in at my building. The woman in the apartment underneath me got broken into, and the only thing they took was her laptop."

"Why would that make you worry?" MaeBe asked. "I mean besides the obvious that you don't want to get your stuff stolen."

She'd put this in the file. It was one of the things that truly worried her dad. "Because when I first hired on, I mistakenly put the wrong floor number on my HR paperwork. 515 instead of 615. I'd just moved from a building in Austin where I lived on the fifth floor and it was ingrained in my brain. I've fixed it but..."

"So someone could have mistaken that apartment for yours," MaeBe surmised. "Yeah. That doesn't feel coincidental."

"So now I've got a file I need to worry about. There was research on that one. I can see why a corporate spy would want to read it."

MaeBe waved a hand. "Oh, honey, it was all your files. Like every single one. I'm almost certain they duped the whole thing then went back through and fixed the metadata, but they forgot one. It was kind of a sloppy job. I've got a few thoughts on who it could be."

There was a brief knock on the door and then Kyle was walking in. He was all confidence and swagger as he looked Noelle's way. "Good. I was afraid after Hutch's performance that you would have run. He should be back in a few minutes and then we'll get you to work."

"Hutch performed?" MaeBe asked.

And then Kyle wasn't so confident. His eyes flared and then softened. "Hey. I didn't know you were in here. Uhm, everything okay this morning?"

MaeBe gave him a smile. "Yes. I'm good, and thank you for walking me to my car last night." She nodded Noelle's way. "I had a date go bad and he works in the building. He seems to think if he bugs me enough, I'll go out with him again. Big Tag has a bodyguard walk down with me. Kyle got the job last night, and lawyer dude did not show. I think after Jamal stood over the guy and told him if he ever saw him near me again, he would be the one who needed an attorney, he got the message. Jamal has a foot on him and way more muscle."

"I still think we should keep it up for a while," Kyle replied, his voice softer than before. "And you have my number. I'll be on a job for a week or two, but I still want a call if he bugs you again."

"Sure. It will teach me to date lawyers. My dad always warned me," MaeBe said with a grin that lit up her face. "I'm sticking to geeks from now on. If a guy can't speak computer or doesn't own a bunch of board games, this shop is closed. How about you, Noelle? You're a science girl. Do you date other scientists?"

Noelle was fairly certain MaeBe didn't notice the way Kyle's face had flushed slightly.

He liked the woman but he didn't think he was her type.

"I don't date much, but I think opposites can attract. I wouldn't want someone who was too like me, you know." Which was why she should stay away from Hutch. Why had he not gotten an undergrad degree? Why didn't he carry himself the way the other military guys did? "It's good to have someone in your life who can bring a different perspective. As long as that person is willing to listen to you as well. It's hard when you meet someone set in their ways and their views."

"Hutch called her a hick," Kyle said with a shrug.

MaeBe's eyes went wide. "What? Hutch wouldn't say that." She turned to Noelle. "I don't know what you heard, but Hutch is like the best. He's a great boss, and he's one of the nicest men I've ever met. Super laid back."

"He threatened Tag," Kyle continued.

MaeBe turned his way. "What? Dude, I need the lowdown on this meeting. What did Tag do? Did they fight over those awesome muffins? Did you try one or are you watching your carbs?"

"Watch my carbs?" Kyle frowned. "I don't have to watch my carbs. And Noelle brought them in."

"My Aunt Lisa knows Mr. Taggart from way back and told me the best way to soften him up was to offer him something lemony," Noelle replied. "I like to bake. I got it from my mom. I like to think that all those times we spent in the kitchen together were my first experiments. I'm glad you liked them. And I wasn't that offended by what Hutch said. It's not like I've never heard it before. I'm from small-town Southern Louisiana. I've been called a hick many times."

"I never used that word." Hutch was in the doorway, frowning her way. "And I've apologized. I know what it's like to be stereotyped, so I shouldn't have done it. Now, MaeBe, do you have our credentials?"

MaeBe stood up taller. "All done, boss. Anyone looks and you are from Papillon, Louisiana, by way of Dallas. You and your brother Kyle were born here in Texas. You moved to Louisiana when your dad took a job at a place called Beaumont Oil. I can't change your accents so you can't be born there. You met your girlfriend in high school. The rest of the story you two need to work out, but let me know if I can get you anything. You'll find you have a credit card, library privileges at the Papillon Parish Library, and a grocery store discount card. I also Photoshopped some pics of you and your bro there. And I hacked the high school archives, so there's some sweet pics of you and Noelle at senior prom."

What? This was all moving fast. "How did you do that? I didn't even know there was an archive."

MaeBe gave her a grin and brushed her electric pink nails over her shirt. "I'm just that good."

Hutch moved to his desk. "MaeBe is taking over some of our deep-cover logistics. She's good at making sure anyone who tries to do a trace on one of us sees what we want them to see. She's got a creative mind."

"She's thorough is what she is," Kyle corrected.

"*And* creative." MaeBe smiled and walked toward the door. "I take all compliments, thank you. I left packets on your desks. Let me know if you need anything else. I live two blocks from Noelle's building. Noelle, if they cuddle together on the couch, get me pics. Hey, boss? Where's my treat?"

Hutch chuckled and his hand disappeared inside a…was that a Star Wars cookie jar on his desk? It didn't contain cookies. He pulled out a small packet. "Mixed berry Skittles."

He tossed it and MaeBe reached up to catch the candy. "Thanks, boss. I love these. Y'all be good."

She practically bounced out of the room.

Were they really staying at her place? She hadn't woken up this morning thinking she would have two houseguests, much less two men she didn't know. Surely this wasn't what her dad had planned. "MaeBe seems competent. Are you sure…"

"She's not a field agent." Hutch sank down behind his desk. "She's only been with the company for the last year, and she's strictly behind a desk for now. She doesn't have the right training."

"And you do?" Kyle's brows had risen.

Hutch stared back at him. "I did a year in the Army."

Kyle snorted at that thought. "You did the bare minimum."

"And then I did time with a CIA team," Hutch said evenly.

"You sat behind a computer," Kyle challenged.

Hutch was quiet for a moment, and then the room felt charged with his words. "Do you honestly believe I can't do undercover? Because I promise you, I've done some of the toughest undercover work anyone has ever been through, and I knew how bad it would be when I went in. I did it for your family."

There was a subtext between the two men that she didn't understand. Oh, but she was curious. It was very much like what had gone on between Hutch and Taggart in the conference room.

Kyle sobered. "I know, man. I'm sorry. I'm giving you shit when I shouldn't. I'm not used to seeing you off balance, and I'm being an asshole." Kyle turned Noelle's way. "I have no problem with this man watching my back. He'll take care of you."

"I don't need taking care of." She hated those words. It was silly because she took care of the people around her, but it always made her think of that time after the accident when she couldn't walk, couldn't make herself try. When she'd been nothing more than some wounded thing to take care of.

"I'll watch *your* back, Noelle," Hutch said, his voice soothing. "You might not need taking care of, but we can all use a team around us. I've learned that over the years. You don't have to do this alone. You pick experts and you listen to them. I'm your tech guy. Kyle's the one who throws his ass in front of you when the bullets fly. It's okay. I'll be behind you, so Kyle will die first no matter what."

Kyle finally smiled. "Yeah, I get that a lot. You ready? We can get her to work and then we can pick up our stuff. Did you drive?"

Hutch sighed. "I forgot to charge my car. My battery's probably toast. I took the train."

"I did, too. The train runs right by my building. I don't drive much." She didn't have to because DART took her most of the places she needed to go. She could drive. She just wasn't comfortable doing it. "I don't need an escort. Surely I'll be fine on public transportation."

Both men stared at her. She knew that stare. She'd been around overly protective males many times before.

"You know I only have one guest room, and it's got a daybed in it." She wasn't giving up her perfectly comfy bed. She leaned on her cane because her right leg was starting to ache a bit. "And I've got a class I'm attending on Thursday, and I'm not canceling it. If you insist on staying close to me, you should understand that I'm not going to change my whole life because the two of you take your jobs too seriously."

"Hopefully by Thursday we'll know more." Hutch closed up his laptop. "We should get going. Kyle, looks like you're driving."

"Uh, I don't actually own a car right now," Kyle explained. "I

66

gave mine up because I didn't want to have to store it. I haven't replaced it since I came home. I got a ride in with Jamal."

"So we're three Gen Zs with a single car between us at the moment and only two beds." Hutch sighed. "Yeah, we're not telling Tag that."

"Agreed." Kyle shook his head. "I have no idea how my stepdad survived growing up with him. You want to rock-paper-scissors for the bed?"

"Is the bed in front of the door? Where the bodyguard should be?" Hutch was a wily one.

Kyle growled a little. "Fine. I need a sleeping bag." He brightened slightly. "Hey, MaeBe's got a car. She can drive us. I'll go ask her."

"He definitely has a thing for her." She was aware she was now alone with Hutch. In his office that she'd been exploring before he'd walked back in. At that time it had seemed pretty big. Now it was way too intimate.

"Really?" Hutch stared at the door like he'd never thought about it. "He's definitely not her usual. Her usual is all piercings and tats and shouldn't we look up his arrest record. Kyle's a little all-American for her. Your muffins are fantastic."

It took a moment for her to realize he was talking about baked goods and not some body part. What would her muffins be? Boobs? She probably had a muffin top, but she wasn't wearing jeans, so he shouldn't be able to see that. It was the way he said it. Low and sexy, like he was thinking of something that brought him great pleasure. Yep. He was talking about the muffins she'd brought. "Thanks. I've been perfecting the recipe. I like to bake. But I don't cook a lot. I usually pick up a sandwich on my way home. I've got some frozen dinners."

"Aren't you in luck then because I'm a halfway decent cook. I learned young."

"Did your mom teach you?"

"No, my mom died, and my dad wasn't big on doing things he considered feminine tasks. I learned to cook, or I didn't eat." He sat back, his chair moving with him. "I'm not a brilliant chef, but I have some skills. I'll stop by the grocery store before Kyle and I head to your place. Anything you don't eat?"

He slipped that tragedy in like it didn't matter, like it was nothing more than a factoid on a report. She wasn't sure what to say so she simply answered his question. "I eat pretty much anything." She felt horrifically awkward. Moments before she'd been angry with him, and now she wanted to ask about his childhood. It was better to focus on the job. "Do you really think this is necessary?"

"Can you honestly tell me you weren't going to investigate the accident in the lab?"

"I don't like to ask for help." She didn't like to feel small. She'd felt it much of her life, had learned exactly how fragile it all was at a young age. She'd also learned that the minute she asked for help was the minute everyone around her started thinking she needed it all the time.

"I can understand that. I need you to understand that despite my earlier impression, I don't tend to underestimate people. I don't judge a book by its cover, though the cover might be awfully pretty."

He'd obviously decided to go the charming route. It wouldn't work on her. "Sure. The first thing anyone notices about me is that I'm pretty."

"Well, if I'd noticed the cane first, I wouldn't have made an ass of myself," he pointed out. "So you need to understand that you probably manipulate a lot of men with those eyes of yours, but it won't work on me."

Outrage sparked through her and then she caught a ghost of a smile on his lips and realized the jerk was fucking with her.

No one fucked with her. Not like teasing. No one in her world treated her with anything but the utmost respect. Except Madison. God. Was that why she wanted to investigate? Because Madison had at least respected her enough to play rough. Madison was the kind of woman who would have ignored her utterly if she hadn't felt threatened.

This man already zeroed in on a weakness Noelle herself hadn't realized she had.

"I'll remember that." She wasn't going to give in to the need to spar with him.

The grin disappeared. "I know you're independent and that's

important to you, but someone absolutely is spying on you through your computer. I found some sophisticated software that was uploaded five days ago. What else happened that day?"

A chill crept across her skin. "Madison died. All right. I can make connections when they're that obvious. So I'm supposed to tell my coworkers we're high school sweethearts who reconnected and now we're together again?"

"How close are you to your coworkers? Have you talked a lot about your past?"

She could lie and tell him this plan of his would never work. She should have told him she already had a boyfriend, but she'd lost that chance. And yet she found herself leveling with him. "I've got a couple of people I have lunch with at work. Sometimes we go to happy hour. I've spoken very little about my past. I find coming from a small town puts me in a box with a lot of people in my industry. I talk about my time in Austin. I talk about the awards I've won and the papers I've written."

"So they don't know much about your life," Hutch mused. "I promise I can handle this. I can handle your friends and make them believe I've cared about you for a long time. I can make them comfortable, and I'll make you comfortable, too. I'm sorry we started off the way we did."

Something about the words put her on guard. "I'm not looking for a boyfriend."

Hutch shrugged. "And I'm not looking for a relationship either, so we're good."

"But you're flirting with me. I don't like it." It threw her off. No one in her life flirted with her. She got asked out from time to time, but the men who asked her always seemed serious. Hutch was different.

"It's a part of who I am," Hutch conceded. "I'll try to not do it outside of our cover. I'm sorry. I think flirting is a coping mechanism. I spent a lot of years surviving by making people like me. I did some time in foster care and on the streets as a teen. I'm only telling you because you should get to know me. I'm not trying to get sympathy."

"Yes, you are."

The slight grin was back on his face. "Is it working?"

"Is it true?"

The smile faded again. "Oh, yes. I don't lie about my childhood. My scars are all on the inside, but they're there, and they affect every part of me. I'll lay it on the line. I'm a man who's been in therapy for a decade. I go almost every Thursday. My therapist is on vacation right now, but I have an appointment next week. Unless it's dangerous for me to leave you, I'll make that appointment."

"You don't have to justify your therapy. It's good and healthy, and I'm happy it works for you. I've done some myself. After the car accident. I still struggle to drive. Anyway, your healthy attitude toward therapy is okay with me." More than okay. He'd been vulnerable in the last couple of minutes, and she had a hard time shutting him out. They would be working together for a little while. "Do you want to start over? Like pretend the whole morning didn't happen?"

He stood, his eyes warm as he held out a hand. "I'm Hutch. It's nice to meet you, Noelle."

She took his hand, and she could have sworn she felt freaking sparks. Warm and true. He enveloped her hand and she had to remember to breathe. "It's nice to meet you, too."

"Hey, MaeBe says yes. She can take us. I call shotgun." Kyle was smiling and looking way less broody than he had before. And younger.

She felt younger standing there looking at Hutch like he was the lead singer in a boy band. She forced herself to take her hand back. "We should go then. I'm late."

She would focus on work and not the man waiting for her at the end of the day.

He wouldn't be there for long. That was the truth she had to remember.

Chapter Three

Twenty minutes later she made her way to the parking garage, Hutch at her side. She'd noticed he'd matched her stride, which was much slower and shorter than his. It was only polite, she supposed, but there was something nice about it. Often she felt like she was holding people up, but Hutch seemed perfectly comfortable with the slower pace.

"Do you know what Madison was working on? And I'd love to see any kind of reports on the accident in her lab."

While they'd waited for MaeBe and Kyle to text them that they were ready to go, they'd talked about the case. He'd gone over how a hacker could get into her system, patiently explaining the methods and answering her every question.

He'd also offered her candy. He had a surprising amount of candy on his desk.

"She was working on something top secret. I think it's some kind of biochemical experiment," she replied as they stopped on the ground floor of the garage. "She had every technician who worked with her under some hard-core NDAs."

Everyone signed a nondisclosure agreement when they started work at Genedyne, but Madison had her own to cover her specific lab.

"So you work on whatever you want to?" Hutch had a bag in his hand. Apparently he kept a spare set of clothes and a toiletry bag at the office in case he got stuck working late.

"Consider Genedyne as something of a think tank combined with a university, but making money like a corporation." It could be hard to describe the way these new firms worked. "They're all about the patents they potentially get coming out of this."

"So you do the work and the company gets the patent, and the patent is what makes money. Doesn't seem fair to me, though I know it's how the system works."

"If I was at a university, they would own my research. I honestly wouldn't *have* research if I didn't have company money backing me up. I get a generous salary, my name on everything, and bonuses if the idea works out." She loved her lab. "If I hadn't been hired by Genedyne, I would probably be working in some company on someone else's research. I'm female and young, so getting to do my own work is a miracle."

"How did you get hired?"

"The normal way. Everyone knows once you get hired there's the internal fight for a private lab. I liked the fact that ideas were more important than past experience at Genedyne. Not that I would have kept my lab if I screwed up. Jessica is quick to hire and even faster to fire," Noelle explained. She didn't talk about the fact that an employee who got fired was lucky to merely slink away. Sometimes the employee got fired or accused of trying to steal company property.

"And Jessica Layne's reputation didn't bother you?" Hutch asked.

"Do you know what it's like to be a woman in a man's world? Of course you don't. She has to be tough or they'll eat her alive." She knew the rumors, but she was giving her boss a chance. "Look, I'm careful. I want to stay off her radar as much as possible, but I also recognize the amazing opportunity she's given me. I know a lot of what she does is theatrical, but it's how she gets attention for the company. She's always been considered an innovator. Is she perfect? Of course not."

"Hey, it's not like there aren't many controversial tech figures. They kind of try to be controversial, so I understand the marketing play," he replied. "I work for Ian Taggart. Trust me. When I first met the man, I'd heard lots of rumors about him."

"From the CIA?" She couldn't help it. She was curious about Hutch. She wanted to ask him what exactly he'd done that shut down everyone the minute he mentioned his "sacrifice." He was an incredibly handsome man, but he didn't look like a guy who'd been in the Army and the CIA. Of course, according to most people, she didn't look like a badass scientist, and that's exactly what she was.

"Yes. I was working with a CIA team when I first met the Taggarts," Hutch explained. "The first time I ever went into this building we were raiding it."

"Raiding it?"

He nodded and pointed up to the ceiling. "We came in on a helo, landed on top of the building, and came in through the front door with flashbangs. Shock and awe did not work on McKay-Taggart."

"Okay. The last time I checked, the CIA was concerned with foreign countries. I know Texas sometimes seems weird, but it's still America." She had a million questions, and there was a flutter in her stomach because standing here with him, talking to him, felt good.

His lips had turned up in a wistful smile, the memories seemingly fond to him. "Well, my boss at the time had embedded his sister here at McKay-Taggart. She was Agency, too. Big Tag finds out he's got a plant but doesn't realize she's CIA, and definitely doesn't know she's my boss's sister. Big Tag wants some help figuring out what intelligence agency she's from and mouths off about taking care of her. Hence the ex-Special Forces team raiding an American company. The worst part was they were having a baby shower that day. Our asses run in expecting to find some kind of torture going on and it's all punch and cake and pregnant ladies."

"What did you do? I mean everyone must have been terrified of guys with guns coming into their workplace."

"Yeah, we had guns, but we were ordered to keep the safeties on. We were never going to shoot anyone. My boss wanted to easily extract his sister. Also, fear wasn't the emotion I would say was riding high that day. They were pissed, and one of the pregnant ladies caught one of our guys, and she did not have the safety on her gun. We decided then and there to lay down arms and all have cake." His eyes closed briefly. "It was this Italian Cream Cake with the best icing. Just a little granular. The texture was perfect."

He was speaking her language. "I love that kind. I know everyone talks about creamy, but that hint of texture is my favorite. But it's such a fine line between perfection and the icing getting lumpy. It's usually because you start with the ingredients being too cold."

His eyes were open again. "It's all about the chemical reaction, right?"

Those eyes were too blue, too warm.

"That's what baking is," she replied. "I'm afraid you'll find I bake a lot. I take most of it to my lab."

"Oh, I'm not afraid of that. You should be afraid that you won't have much to take to your lab after I steal your cookies."

Her heart rate had gone sky high, and she appreciated MaeBe's timing as she chose that moment to drive up in her Prius. She had the new compact model, and unfortunately, she did not have a compact man in the passenger seat. Kyle Hawthorne looked hunched over, and she would bet he had that seat all the way back.

This was not going to be a comfortable ride.

MaeBe put the car in park and both she and Kyle got out, MaeBe bouncing from her seat with a smile and Kyle unfurling his body, wincing the whole time.

"I'm getting a car this weekend. I swear," Kyle said. He looked her way and visibly noticed her cane. "I'll take the back seat."

She felt a flush go through her. "It's fine. I'll fit better."

Kyle shook his head. "No. I wouldn't dream of it. You'll be more comfortable getting in and out if you take the front."

"Yeah, I don't care about Kyle's comfort. I'm actually interested in seeing if he and Hutch can fit back there." MaeBe seemed amused.

They wouldn't fit at all, and she would. It might not be the most comfortable, but she was pretty sure MaeBe was the only one tiny enough for this car. "I'll be fine in the back."

"Absolutely not," Kyle insisted. "I'm not going to take your seat."

But it wasn't hers. She knew he was trying to be polite, but all she could hear was she couldn't even sit in the back of a car. Yes, she used a cane, but getting into that car would be awkward for anyone.

"She said she would be fine in the back. Why do you think she can't sit in a back seat?" Hutch asked, his eyes narrowed.

Kyle's gaze went right for her cane. "I'm trying to help her out, man."

Hutch walked to the car and opened the door, reaching in to drop the seat forward. "She knows what she can and can't do. You seem to be the one who doesn't because there's zero shot at you fitting back here. Noelle, do you mind sitting in the back so the big guy's spine doesn't crack?"

God, that was refreshing. "No problem."

It was totally awkward getting into that car, but she managed it and then scooted over when Hutch got in after her. His knees were practically up to his chin, but he settled in.

She heard the trunk open and then close as Kyle put Hutch's duffel in, and then he climbed into the front. "Sorry. I was trying to help."

She knew he was, but she preferred Hutch's method. He hadn't told her what her limitations were, hadn't expected that because she used a cane she couldn't see someone else had a greater need. "It's okay, but I'm actually pretty flexible. I know the cane throws some people off, but you should see me do yoga."

"I've been meaning to give that a try," Hutch said. "Maybe you can teach me some moves."

"I'm the one who's going to need it," Kyle complained.

"Don't be a baby. This car is excellent. It meets all the new standards." MaeBe started out of the parking garage, turning onto Pearl Street. They moved from the gloom of the garage and into the brilliant light of day. "And I told you it was small. I named her Tiny."

"Well, I thought that was one of those names that was the opposite. I was expecting an SUV or something." Kyle seemed to be fiddling with the seat.

Hutch's hand came up. "No. You are far enough back. And seriously, you thought the chick with the nose ring and purple hair drove a massive SUV?"

"I thought we weren't stereotyping today." Kyle's head brushed the top of the car.

"MaeBe could drive an SUV if she wanted to." Noelle had put

her cane on her left side, but now she wondered if she shouldn't have put it between her and Hutch because there was pretty much nothing to stop their hips from brushing together.

"I like Tiny. She's got character," MaeBe said.

Their hands brushed, and when MaeBe turned again, she was knocked into Hutch. "Sorry."

His arm had gone behind her, steadying himself. "It's okay. It's close quarters. And it's not a bad idea for us to get more comfortable with each other. You know, for our cover."

Their cover. "I don't think we'll need it all that much. I thought it was just to explain why I suddenly have two men living with me."

"Oh, no. I'm going to need to get into that building at some point. You're allowed visitors, I would assume." His arm was still around her seat. Of course if it wasn't, it would be cradled to his chest. He might not be as massive as Kyle, but he was still a big guy.

"Sure. I have to log you in and out. There are cameras everywhere. I'm not sure what you can do."

"Take over the CC cams, hop into the system, and take a look around. Trust me. I'll handle the security stuff. You save the helium," Hutch replied. "But I can't do what I need to do unless your coworkers buy that I'm your boyfriend. And someone you've known for a while. I would bet you're careful about the people you date."

She kind of liked that he used the word people. Again, not putting her in a box, but she was in this particular box due to her biology. "Oh, it's men."

"Do the people at work know that?" Kyle asked. "Because you and MaeBe would be pretty cute together. Hey."

His seat had jerked, probably because Hutch had punched it.

"I don't date much, but I did go out a few times with a guy from another lab." It had been weird and awkward, and she kind of thought he'd been looking for information about her research. "I think Madison set him up because she did that a lot. She had this group of guys who did a bunch of her dirty work."

"Dirty work?" MaeBe asked.

"Oh, yeah. She was one of those people who felt like she wasn't getting ahead unless she was stepping on someone. Literally, at times. She used to step on my feet and then call me clumsy. I'm not all that sad she's dead, but I have an intellectual curiosity about her death, if you know what I mean."

"You think she sent someone to ask you out so he could watch you?" Hutch's question was quiet but there was an edge to it.

He didn't like that thought. It was subtle, but there was a distaste she recognized. "She did. He was a lab tech, but he wasn't a good spy. He asked way too much way too fast. I didn't fall for it. And honestly, there was zero chemistry there."

But she was starting to worry she had lots of chemistry with Hutch. Despite how they'd started, she was beginning to like him. She liked the fact that he had a drawer full of candy, and he seemed to know all the kids in the on-site daycare. It had been sweet to see how his face had lit up when a four-year-old boy holding a young woman's hand had knocked on the door and asked to see him.

Hutch had gotten to one knee and talked to the kid before offering him a small piece of chocolate.

Her heart had kind of melted, and she got the idea he did that a lot.

"Don't worry about anything, Noelle. I can handle this," he promised.

"I read that Jessica Layne throws some crazy parties. Any of those coming up? Because I wouldn't mind getting a look inside that penthouse of hers," MaeBe admitted. "Do you get to go to the parties?"

Noelle had skipped out on the last big party she'd been invited to. Jessica only invited higher-ups in the organization. When Noelle had been granted her lab, she'd gotten her first invite. She'd heard the rumors about what went on at them and had decided it was better to stay home. It was an annual celebration and she'd heard they partied with lots of booze and bed hopping. There was talk of a whole lot of swinging going on with the married executives.

"I don't go to the parties," she admitted. "I've heard it's a lot of weird sex and designer drugs. It's not my scene."

Sanctum was hopefully her scene.

Did Hutch go to Sanctum? From what she understood a lot of the McKay-Taggart guys did, but not all of them. It was a private thing, so she wasn't going to ask him.

His arm came back from around her seat and he tried to put some space between them.

He was being polite, and again she should be grateful. She was such a flipping weirdo that she wished he hadn't done that, wished she could still feel his forearm brush the nape of her neck.

Kyle cleared his throat. "Yeah, we should all steer clear of the weird sex stuff. Is that the building?"

MaeBe seemed to take that as a command to turn right as absolutely quickly as she possibly could. The car swerved and the motion sent her knocking into Hutch. She slammed into him and his arms went around her, keeping her from crashing back.

"Sorry," MaeBe said.

"You are a terrible driver," Kyle complained.

"Am not. I get distracted. I also have some depth perception issues," MaeBe admitted. "But we're here and everyone is mostly whole. Any chance Jessica Layne comes in late? That's a sweet Maserati up ahead."

"That's hers, but it doesn't mean she's in it. She often leaves it in front of the building in case she decides to go out. She doesn't like to have to wait." Noelle righted herself and smoothed her blouse down. "Thanks for the ride."

She'd given Hutch everything he would need to get into her place and the keys to her car. It would be more comfortable, and she would be happy to let him drive. Keeping her foot on the gas for longer than a few minutes made one of the muscles of her calf tighten up.

Kyle got out and pushed the seat forward to allow Hutch out.

"MaeBe, could you..." Noelle began.

"Nope. I'm well trained and he wants to help you," she said in a voice above a whisper. "It's got nothing to do with your legs and everything to do with the whole top thing. Go with it. It'll make him feel good. I assure you it was hard for him to let you sit in the back even though he sounded like he handled it well. He's just that guy."

A gentleman. No. That wasn't what she'd said. Top. Well, that answered one question. He definitely hung out at the club, and MaeBe did, too. He'd likely been going for years, so they wouldn't mix or anything. She was only in training and wouldn't actually be in the club for at least a month.

And she might not like it. She might not enjoy being taken care of for a reason that had nothing to do with her legs. She might not like being able to drop all of her control and let someone else take over for a while.

Hutch's arm came back, offering her a hand out.

She shouldn't take that hand. She should stumble and fall and force her way out because that hand was warm and strong, and it didn't mean what she might want it to mean.

She reached out and let him steady her as she wriggled out of the car that definitely could use another door. She lost her balance, but Hutch caught her, his free hand going around her waist and pulling her against him.

"You okay?" He was staring down at her.

She nodded.

"The whole building is Genedyne, right?" His voice went low and she heard a vehicle coming into the entrance circle in front of the building.

"Yes." She wished she didn't sound breathless.

"Okay. Can I kiss you?" Hutch asked. "There's a big group getting out of a van right behind us, and I would like to start to cement our cover."

He wanted to kiss her? No. He didn't want to kiss her. He wanted to give credence to their cover because there were a bunch of her coworkers hopping out of that van, likely coming back from lunch. Was she doing this? If she didn't, she'd have her dad sleeping on her couch instead of a hunky guy. Yes. She was doing this. She went up on her toes and gave those gorgeous lips of his a peck.

Behind her she could hear someone asking if that was LaVigne. They were definitely watching.

She dropped back and Hutch gave her an amused expression before his hands came up, cupping her face right below her jaw. "Yeah, that's not how we're saying good-bye."

His head dipped down and his lips brushed against hers, gently at first, like a butterfly sweeping by as it flew. Then he kissed her again and she felt fire in her veins. He controlled the kiss, and all she had to do was follow his lead. Her hands went to his waist, feeling the lean muscles of his torso. The world seemed to drop away as he kissed her, and it was a shock to her system when she heard a whistle.

She stepped back and saw a group of the techs standing there watching her. She gave them her best stare. "Don't you have something to do?"

There were a whole lot of *yeses* as they turned and started to walk in the door.

"LaVigne, I didn't know you were seeing someone."

She stopped because she knew that deep, whiskey voice.

Hutch was already in motion. He moved away from her, holding out a hand. "Hi. I'm Hutch. I'm Noelle's boyfriend from back in Louisiana."

He was doing a fairly good accent. It was subtle, like he'd spent a lot of time there but wasn't completely a local.

Jessica Layne was standing next to her candy-apple-red Maserati dressed in her signature all-white power suit, her blonde hair cut in a chic bob. She looked Hutch up and down like he was a meal she was sizing up. She held out her manicured hand and shook Hutch's a second too long for Noelle's liking. "Jessica Layne. I'm Noelle's boss."

Hutch pulled back and had an arm around Noelle's shoulder in a heartbeat. She could feel the slightest tremble in his hand, though his voice was completely steady, his expression pleasant. "Of course I recognize you, Ms. Layne. It's an honor to meet such an iconic figure in our world today."

He was nervous. She wasn't sure how she knew that, but she did. She was so certain that she wound her arm around his waist not for cover, but to comfort him. "Sorry I'm late today. I'm afraid I brought back some souvenirs from home. Hutch and I were high school sweethearts. We reconnected a couple of months ago and he's moving up here. With me. In my place."

"Yes, I rather thought that was what you meant." She'd caught sight of Kyle and MaeBe, whose eyes had gone wide. "Did you find this one there, too?"

MaeBe looked like she was staring at a rock star. "I'm from here. From Dallas. I'm such a huge fan."

Jessica ignored her. "How about you, gorgeous? I know you don't work for me. I would recognize you."

Kyle looked like a deer caught in some bright headlights. "I'm Kyle. I'm his brother. I don't have a job."

"He's staying with me until he finds something," Noelle explained. "He recently got out of the military and didn't want to work on an oil rig or haul tourists around to look for gators. That's about all we have in our town."

It wasn't, but it was best to not have long explanations. This was absolutely the longest conversation she'd had with Jessica since she'd hired on. She was ready to head back to her lab.

"Well, you should see about applying here, Kyle." Jessica's expression softened. "There are lots of good jobs here."

"Oh, I'm not good with science. I've got an interview at this restaurant that hires ex-military guys," Kyle said quickly. He nodded MaeBe's way. "My girlfriend set it up. She lives here. We met online."

MaeBe hesitated as though she couldn't quite believe she'd gotten pulled into this crap. Then she smiled and leaned against Kyle. "Yep. I'm glad to have him here so we can figure out if our relationship works."

It was time to end this uncomfortable meeting. She turned to Hutch. "I need to get inside, and you need to get your brother to his interview."

He leaned over and kissed her again. "I'll pick you up at five thirty."

She started to say she would take the train, but she'd given him the keys to her car for a reason. "Will do. Have a good rest of the day."

He squeezed her hand before turning away. "Ms. Layne, again, a pleasure to meet you."

"The pleasure was all mine. I expect to see you around, and Kyle, think about my offer. There are good jobs right here." Jessica looked at Noelle. "I should check in on you. You're running the helium project, right? Interesting work. Maybe we'll have lunch sometime and you can catch me up."

She watched the woman walk away, perfectly steady in her sky-high heels.

She was on Jessica's radar now.

"Hey, you did great," Hutch said. "Go to your lab and work like it's any other day. I'll be here this evening and we'll talk some more."

She nodded, took a deep breath, and got back to work.

* * * *

Hutch stood in front of Noelle's building, still thinking about that moment he'd seen the cold gleam in Jessica Layne's eyes. He'd been quiet on the drive over, letting MaeBe blow off some steam about how no one should ever meet their idols because they turn out to be man-eating tigers who ignored other women when a hot guy was in the room. Kyle seemed to have found his feet again because he sounded confident as he joked about how hard it was to look so good.

"Do you blame her? I work for all this," Kyle was saying.

But Hutch didn't feel like joking because he'd seen that look in a woman's eyes before. He'd seen it in a man's, too. It was the look of a person who didn't really see other people as anything but toys for their own amusement.

He'd looked into those eyes and seen Hope McDonald's. Jessica Layne had touched his hand and he'd remembered how McDonald would put her hand over his chest and call him one of her pretty boys.

Kyle whistled, his head turned up. "Dude, the girl does well."

"She's a chemist working for an incredibly successful company." MaeBe had a bag of groceries in her hand. She'd driven her Prius from the office to Genedyne's soaring glass building downtown, then to a Whole Foods, and finally this building in Victory Park. They weren't far from Michael Malone's place, and he had oil money. Oh, he didn't dip into his trust fund often, but he lived like a millionaire in that gorgeous condo. Noelle's digs looked a little less crazy wealthy than that, but it was still nice.

Jessica Layne was the type of woman who could take it away from her in a heartbeat.

Kyle stretched and grimaced. He'd complained a whole lot about how small that car had been. "I should have spent more time in school."

He hadn't even been stuffed in the back of that tiny car the way Hutch had. Kyle had been in the front. Hutch had spent the whole ride with his knees almost to his chin.

And he'd been shoved in with Noelle, so close that he could smell her. She smelled incredible. He wasn't the guy who went around sniffing a chick's hair. That guy was a weirdo. That guy was a perv.

But then he'd never smelled Noelle's combo of laundry detergent and lemon muffins.

When she'd snuggled against him as he'd talked to her boss, he'd found a strange comfort from that smell.

Fuck, but he wanted to eat her alive. She'd tried to keep herself from bouncing into him, but the close quarters had meant they kept brushing against each other.

And then she'd talked about weird sex and how she wanted to stay away from it.

Yeah, he'd backed away. But not for long. Noelle was a treat he wasn't sure he could afford.

"Isn't your brother a professor or something?" MaeBe started for the lobby. They had a keycard to get into the building, and a key for Noelle's apartment.

"Yeah, he's got a doctorate, but not Noelle's kind," Kyle explained. "David's an associate professor of history. He can barely afford his shitty townhouse. It's in a crappy neighborhood, and I'm pretty sure it's going to collapse soon. I love my brother, but I do not get his obsession with dusty old books. Of course I don't get Noelle's with all the science stuff."

"That's because you're a Neanderthal and you're only interested in beer and football," MaeBe said with a prim wrinkle of her nose.

She walked ahead.

Hutch leaned in and whispered Kyle's way. "A Neanderthal is..."

Kyle gave him a Neanderthal-like frown that let Hutch know he was probably close to being clubbed. "I know what a Neanderthal is. And I like more things than beer and football."

Yeah, he liked MaeBe, and that wasn't going to happen for him. He felt for the guy. MaeBe was a cutie, but Hutch had always viewed her as a little sister. "She likes board games. Obviously she likes computers, but your way in is board games. She hosts a game night. Get invited and you can get to know her."

"Games? Like Monopoly?"

Hutch groaned. "Nope. It's way more complex and much cooler. You know our receptionist isn't dating anyone. Maybe you should ask her out."

Yasmin was lovely and funny and not anywhere close to as quirky as MaeBe. She was seemingly the better fit for a guy like Kyle.

Kyle settled his duffel over his shoulder. "I'm not interested in dating. I just got home. I need time to settle in. I'm living in my brother's office."

"Doesn't your mom have a big old house here in town?" They weren't all that far from Top, Sean Taggart's original restaurant. If he was right, they could walk there for dinner. He wondered if Noelle had been.

"My mom also has a whole new family," Kyle said with a sigh. "I love my mom. I love Carys and Luke. Hell, I love Sean. But I can't handle the happy family thing right now. You know what I can do? I can sleep on a cot in my brother's musty office, work, and go to the gym. David's researching some book. He barely notices I'm there. My brother lives like a monk. It's kind of peaceful."

This was part of his job. No one had gotten close to Kyle. He'd been a closed book for the month he'd been with the company. He didn't come to guys nights or hang out after work at the bar across the street. He didn't go to Top when they had special nights.

David Hawthorne wasn't the only one living like a monk.

Hutch was tired of living like a monk. He hadn't dated since he'd broken things off with Katy. He'd gotten involved in work, and hookups in coat closets didn't hold the same appeal they once had.

He looked ahead and MaeBe was standing in the lobby talking to the security guard. It was good to know they had one.

"Is she flirting with that guy?" Kyle was back to frowning.

So Kyle was the jealous type. "Somehow I doubt it."

There was something about the man MaeBe was talking to that sent alarm bells through Hutch.

MaeBe smiled Hutch's way. "Hey, guys. This is one of the building's security guards. He said he didn't realize anyone was coming to stay with Noelle today. Mr. Taylor, this is Noelle LaVigne's boyfriend and his brother. She should have sent the building a notification."

"I was unaware she had someone moving in with her," the guard said. He was an oddly familiar-looking man. He looked to be in his early thirties, likely close to Hutch in age. He was roughly six foot two and looked like he spent a lot of time in a gym. "We have protocols in this building. I can't let you up without written consent."

"Have you checked in the last hour?" Hutch thought fast. "We were supposed to get here this evening when Noelle would have been home to let us in. I couldn't wait. I took an earlier flight."

Kyle seemed to pick up on his play. "He is one over-eager dude, if you know what I mean. When he found out we could get here a couple of hours early he hounded me. I barely packed. He's lucky my girlfriend could pick us up or we would still be sitting at Love Field."

"We called Noelle on our way over," MaeBe said, huddling close to Kyle. "She gave Hutch a key this weekend. Do you think she forgot? I can call her again."

"I'll go check." The guard stared at them all as though memorizing their faces. "I just came on shift and haven't checked the mail. You'll have to fill out some forms if you're staying more than a week or two. Please wait here until I can clear you."

Hutch watched as he strode away. "Why does he look familiar?"

MaeBe moved away from Kyle, leaning toward Hutch. "Because he's DPD. I'm almost sure of it. I think his name is Chris Taylor. I saw him speak at one of the conferences we went to. He seemed like kind of a big deal. Why would he be working here?"

"Lots of cops moonlight," Kyle said. "And they typically do it in the security field."

He knew lots of beat cops who did, but detectives? "Are you sure?"

MaeBe shrugged. "I think so. I didn't actually meet him, but I enjoyed his lecture on what it means to work major crimes."

"I'll have Tag see what he can find out." The idea that there was a cop working at Noelle's building made him uneasy.

Before he could say anything else, the big guy was walking toward them again.

"She has sent the proper paperwork," Taylor said, a bit friendlier now. "Sorry. Ms. LaVigne is a nice lady, and we've had some trouble lately. I had to make sure you were legit."

"Yeah, I heard there was a break-in." Hutch took the opening. "Is that something I should worry about? Do I need to get Noelle a better security system?"

Taylor waved that off. "No. Not at all. It was a complete fluke. The whole building is smart. Truly state of the art and integrated. Everything from the security system to the entertainment systems and lighting to the fridge is smart."

"Then what happened?"

"I have my own theory, but it's up for debate," Taylor allowed. "Our security is pretty tight. There's always at least one guard on duty. Residents have a keycard to get into the building. As you learned, if a guest comes in without a resident, they have to check in and are logged into the security roll. We have cameras in every hallway. The parking garage is secure, too."

"Then how did someone get in?" MaeBe asked.

Taylor shrugged. "Possibly came in with a resident. Maybe even with the resident herself. She has a lot of people over, and at odd times. She claims she locked the door and when she came back it was unlocked and her laptop was taken. That was the only thing they took. The place wasn't trashed or anything. Now the odd thing is we've got nothing on camera. I think she might be committing insurance fraud. I think she either lost it and doesn't want to admit it or she wants her renter's insurance to pay for a new computer. It wouldn't be the first time."

Or there were blind spots in the system, and someone knew where they were. He was still curious.

He heard the sound of elevator doors opening behind him. It was time to get upstairs and start figuring out how to shut down all that smart tech because that smart tech could be used to watch them.

"I appreciate the information. I feel better about having Noelle here," Hutch said. "And if you'll get me the paperwork, I'll fill it all out. I'm moving in with Noelle permanently. My brother is only staying with us until he can convince his girlfriend here to let him move in."

Hey, Kyle had done that to himself by introducing MaeBe to Jessica Layne.

Kyle stopped staring at him, but MaeBe immediately moved to Kyle's side, threading her arm through his and cuddling up.

"I'm a little wary. He's like the best, but are we there yet? I don't know. I think we need a couple of weeks." Perhaps MaeBe was way more ready to be a field agent than he gave her credit for. "He could be a crazy dude."

"I am not a crazy dude." But Kyle pulled her close.

The woman who'd walked out of the elevator stopped. She was probably thirty and strode forward with confidence, her reusable shopping bags in hand. "I'm sorry. Did you say you were Noelle's boyfriend? Because the last I checked she didn't have one."

Ah, the one friend she'd made here. This was the only person in Noelle's life he was worried about. On the car ride over, he'd questioned her thoroughly on everyone she was close to in the building. She'd only really spent time with one woman—her next-door neighbor, who'd moved in after she had. After Noelle had taken a serious job tackling an important scientific issue in a lab that could potentially solve it.

Cara Dover was a pretty woman in a yellow sundress, a pair of sandals on her feet. According to Noelle, she worked as a freelance journalist. That word *freelance* always made him suspicious.

It was a good cover for a spy. It was one he'd used before when he'd been with the CIA.

It was the cover he'd used to make his way from Africa to Europe on the most dangerous mission of his career. God, today he'd thought too much about Hope McDonald and the torture he'd endured to bring her down.

He gave her his best smile. "You must be Cara. Noelle told me all about you. She said you were her closest friend here."

He was pushing a narrative he hoped she picked up. He knew exactly what he looked like. Blandly handsome. All-American good looks. Muscled but not threatening. He used his relative pleasantness to his advantage as often as he could.

The same way Noelle did. Even if she didn't realize that was what she did. She coped. She found value in what most people would consider weakness.

Cara stopped, considering him. "Yes, I am, and I'm confused. I saw her when she came back from visiting her dad. She didn't mention you at all."

Yes, he'd thought this could be a problem. "I didn't fly back with her. We made the decision for me to move in over the weekend, and I had some loose ends to tie up."

She still looked suspicious. "I would think she would say something if she was moving her boyfriend in."

"I've known her since we were young." He was riffing now, but it felt oddly personal. It felt like he was talking about the woman he'd always wanted. That best friend he'd searched for, the one who'd stood beside him so he'd known he wasn't alone. "My brother and I moved to the town her dad lived in. She was in New Orleans with her mom, but we lived close to her dad and spent a couple of summers together before she ended up moving in with her dad."

He'd learned a lot about her in a short amount of time.

"You're from Papillon?" Cara asked, her eyes narrow on him.

He gave her his most charming smile. "I was her high school boyfriend. She kind of left me behind because she's the smartest thing in the world. She went to UT and I had to go to community college before I made it to a four-year school."

"You did a great job, brother." Kyle stepped up beside him. "We always knew you two would find your way back to each other."

Cara stared for a moment. "I didn't know she had a boyfriend at home."

He shrugged. "We haven't been close in a couple of years, but she came home before she took this job and we've been talking ever since. She came home this week and sparks flew again. I've got a job interview up here. Noelle and I are going to try to make a go of it."

Cara's head shook. "She's never mentioned you."

He held a hand out. "I'm Hutch. This is my brother, Kyle, and his girlfriend, Mae."

"I'm going to find a job here, too," Kyle explained. "We recently had our third hurricane of the season, and I'm freaking tired of cleaning up downed trees. It takes a lot out of a man, you know."

Kyle was good at playing the brainless hottie.

MaeBe sidled up to Kyle. "I bet you look good cleaning things up. Do you take your shirt off?" She turned to Cara. "We met on the

Internet. He's got great abs."

She ran her hand from Kyle's shoulder to right above his waist.

"Ms. LaVigne emailed earlier and put these people on her list," Chris explained. "I was about to show them up."

"Well, it's an interesting turn of events. I wouldn't have thought Noelle was capable of keeping a secret like that." Cara's hand tightened around the bags she was carrying. "It was nice to meet you. I guess I'll see you around."

She walked off, her free hand reaching for her cell phone.

He would really like to know who she'd called. He would get MaeBe on her as soon as possible because something about the way she'd reacted had him thinking.

Chris had his hands in the pockets of his jacket. "Ms. Dover is usually more friendly than that. I think you'll find the whole building is pretty nice. And despite the one problem we've had, it's extremely safe." Chris strode to the elevator. "I'll take you up to her place and make sure you get in all right. You'll need your own keycard to move through the building. We have several shared spaces."

Chris started talking about the gym and swimming pool as they all entered the elevator. The doors closed, and Hutch was forced to contemplate the fact someone who worked for the police, someone who knew a lot about security, was working in the building where Noelle lived.

If someone planted DPD here, Noelle LaVigne could be in big trouble, and this op had just turned more dangerous.

Chapter Four

Noelle tried to focus on the screen in front of her but the events of the day weighed heavily.

She usually worked late because all that was waiting for her was a frozen dinner and the next episode of whatever show she was streaming.

Except tonight there would be two guys waiting for her. Did she have three frozen dinners? She hadn't bought groceries lately. She had some protein shakes. That might work for Kyle, but she got the feeling Hutch wasn't a protein shake guy.

He'd kissed her. God, he'd kissed her and she'd melted. It wasn't like she'd never had sex. She'd had a couple of college boyfriends. But she'd never melted for a guy.

For a guy who was also a Dom.

She wanted to call her Aunt Lisa and ask if this whole body going gooey thing had happened to her. Maybe it was just that he'd been so commanding. Except he hadn't. Not in the beginning. He'd even asked for her permission to kiss her.

She should tell him it was okay and he had blanket permission. For the cover, of course. The man shouldn't have to ask every time he thought they should be affectionate to keep their cover up.

The idea of Hutch kissing her often held way too much appeal.

She was horny. That was all. She was a healthy, horny young woman.

A cup filled with Frappuccino was set in front of her and then Pete Moore was settling himself into the chair beside her. Pete was the lead engineer she was working with, an affable man in his late thirties with a husband, two kiddos, and the most adorable Maltipoo. "Hey, I heard you came up with the big boss after lunch. Are you okay? Did you actually go to lunch with her? I didn't think she ate anything but the beating hearts of her enemies."

She'd met Pete when she'd hired on and had started working on another doc's project. He'd helped her write up the proposal that had gotten her this lab. Pete had been fought over by all the lab leads. When she'd won her lab, she'd offered him the job as her head engineer. What she hadn't known until later was that several others— including Madison—had offered him a job, too. There had been a lot of bitterness tossed her way.

Actually, after seeing all the camaraderie at McKay-Taggart, she was starting to wonder if her office wasn't a toxic cesspool.

"No, it was nothing more than coincidence. We happened to be walking in at the same time." It had been an awkward trip up to her floor. She'd actually slowed her stride to give Jessica Layne every opportunity to race ahead of her, but she'd been standing in front of the elevator when Noelle had made it there.

She'd asked a lot of questions about Hutch and Kyle.

"I thought she closed down the elevator when she was in it," Pete said.

She'd heard that rumor, too. "She invited me in. It was weird."

"Yeah, I've heard a lot of weird things today. Tommy from the battery lab said you were making out with some hottie in the parking lot." Pete took a sip of his drink. "He didn't actually call him a hottie. He said it was some dude. I went and looked at the security cams. He's a hottie. Like both of them. Where the hell did you pick up two Greek gods?"

"I told you about my high school boyfriend, right?" She knew she hadn't. She rarely talked about her hometown except to say she missed it sometimes.

McKay-Taggart had reminded her of the sheriff's office back in Papillon. She'd answered phones there as a part-time job for years. It had been fun because of how laid back it was. Her stepmom would sometimes show up for lunch and they would sit on the grass under the big oak tree and talk while they ate po' boys and drank sweet tea. Her dad would bring the family dog up and Peanut would walk around looking for a pet. Everyone acted like family.

"No, you didn't."

She sighed like she hadn't expected the response. "Huh. I guess I didn't realize how much I missed him until recently. His name is Hutch. We went to high school together." She was actually a couple of years younger than him, but he had a baby face. And according to MaeBe, he also had a fake birth certificate that showed the proper age. "We broke up when I went to college. He came up here for a job interview, but he's going to stay with me. We're going to try to make it work."

"Who was the big military-looking guy?" Pete knew his guys.

"His brother who recently got out of the Navy," Noelle replied. "He made a big impression on the boss. She's pretty aggressive. His girlfriend was standing right there and Jessica pretty much hit on him."

"That doesn't surprise me. That woman goes after what she wants." Pete stood again with a sigh. "Well, I'm going to check on some tests I've got running. I tweaked some things on the MRI and I'm happy with how fast we're hitting the right temps."

She glanced at the clock and hadn't realized how late it had gotten. She still hadn't asked some of the questions she was curious about. She'd tentatively broached the subject of Madison's lab with Jessica, who had deflected and turned the subject back to Noelle's fake love life. But Pete might know some things. "Did you work on the biotech lab last week?"

"Do you mean ground zero?" Pete asked with a shake of his head. "Yeah, after the police were done and the biohazard unit left. You should be glad you weren't here last week. It was bizarre. At first we had DPD all over the place, and then they were gone and men in biohazard suits were cleaning stuff up."

"Did you read any of the reports?"

Pete chuckled like she'd asked a naïve question. "Honey, no one has. Jessica locked everything down as quickly as possible. I've heard the police report is calling it an accident. Supposedly OSHA investigated, but I don't know anyone who talked to them. They're blaming it all on Madison. She was up in the lab after hours, and the rumors are she was taking some pretty stiff pharmaceuticals. Not the legal kind."

She had a hard time believing health nut Madison had a drug habit. She didn't even touch alcohol. "Do you know if they did an autopsy?"

"I would assume so." Pete stopped and his gaze became wary. "Why? I didn't think you two were friends. She was always such a bitch to you."

Noelle glanced around to make sure no one was listening. It looked like most of her team was cleaning up and finishing their daily reports in advance of quitting time. She leaned over and dropped her voice. "Don't you think it's weird?"

"That a young, intelligent woman blew herself up in a lab?" Pete asked. "Yeah, I do, but she was working with some pretty unstable chemicals, from what I heard. She had ammonium perchlorate in her lab. If she was playing with that while she was high, we're lucky she didn't blow the whole floor up."

That was another mystery. "She was working on a biochem experiment. Why would she have a chemical used as a rocket propellant in her lab? Have we seen her inventories?"

Each lab kept a careful inventory that was tied to the budget system since each lab had a different budget. Madison's would have been large. Noelle's wasn't. Madison had run a lab with ten techs and a medical doctor on staff. Noelle had three techs and Pete. She had to do her own paperwork, for the most part, and there was a ton of paperwork.

They had reports for everything. Shouldn't there be one for the accident?

"The word is Jessica locked everything down pretty fast," Pete explained. "Legal was definitely all over the place last week. I know all of Madison's team spent time with them. Besides a couple of the engineers, the building was empty of regular employees with the exception of legal and Madison's team."

"Who cleaned up the lab?"

"She brought in another firm. I was only allowed in to test the remaining equipment and to walk through with a structural engineer to make sure the building is okay and the fire didn't damage the safety equipment." A shudder went through him. "I'll be honest. It was creepy. There was something off about those cleaners. You know most teams that work biohazard are usually jokey. I mean it's all dark stuff, but they usually talk a lot. These guys said nothing. I mean nothing. They were perfectly silent as they worked. At least they were any time someone from our company entered the room."

She wanted to know the name of that company. Maybe Hutch was right and she did need to be able to bring him in the building. She hated to admit he was right, but she'd had an awful feeling all day every time she passed Madison's lab. The area was still locked down. "I know she wasn't a nice person, but I still have questions."

Pete sighed and put a hand on her shoulder. "Honey, I'm going to give you some advice. Don't ask those questions. Forget them and do your work. The woman upstairs doesn't like to be challenged, and this incident is something she wants us all to forget. I am almost positive it's because she knows Madison's parents are going to sue. That's probably why legal worked so fast to get everyone on the same page. She also wants to keep the press off the story. Right now it was reported as a tragic accident and they've moved on. If a reporter looks more closely and suddenly we've got stories of drug culture at Genedyne, the investors are going to have questions. She'll pay off Madison's parents and move on."

Or she would drag Madison and her family through lawsuit hell. That was the more likely outcome. She was getting all her ducks in a row and then she would shoot them all in neat order, declare victory, and life would move on at Genedyne.

"And if you get in the way of her plans," Pete continued, "I worry for you. You're doing a fantastic job with this project. I've worked a lot of these. I think in two years you will have everything you need to prove your thesis and your procedures. You'll write up your research and you'll be a rock star in this world. You'll be able to write your own check wherever you want. Sit tight. Focus on your work and you'll be out of here in the blink of an eye. Hopefully you'll take your friend Pete with you."

It was probably good advice, and she would have to think about it. "Thanks. I'll get this stuff done and go work out before Hutch picks me up."

There was a nice gym on the seventh floor, and at this time of day it was quiet. Almost everyone worked out in the mornings. By five o'clock she was left with one or two people sharing the space.

"I expect you to introduce me to your boyfriend." Pete started to back away. "Maybe you two can come out and have dinner with Jimmy and the kids."

Hutch was good with kids. "Sure. Let me know when."

He nodded and she decided to finish up her day. She closed down her laptop and grabbed her bag, heading up to the seventh floor. She felt like she was on autopilot as she changed into her gym clothes, locked up her stuff, and hit the treadmill. The news was playing on the screen overhead, but she wasn't listening. Her mind was on what Pete had told her.

She was still thinking about it when she finished up and walked back into the locker room. She'd lost track of time and was going to have to skip the shower she would usually take. It wouldn't normally matter. She could simply take a later train to get to her place, but she thought Hutch might worry.

Hutch, who would sleep in her apartment tonight. Who would wake up in her apartment tomorrow. Who would figure out she was going to be a trainee at the club he went to. Would that be weird? He wouldn't have anything to do with her training class. She wouldn't have to see him in the club until she'd finished, and that was six weeks away.

By then maybe she'd find out she'd been freaky paranoid about this whole thing and life would go back to normal. It was entirely possible that her computer problems were caused by some weird virus while watching dog rescue videos.

That was when she realized her locker door was slightly ajar.

A chill went through her because she knew she'd locked it. She'd tested it before she'd walked away.

Someone had been in her locker. Someone had gotten through the combination lock and opened it. They'd probably tried to be quiet, and that was why they hadn't quite closed it again.

She went to it, opening the locker door and checking the bag she'd placed in there. Her laptop was still in its case.

A little sound made her stop, fear shooting through her because she'd thought she was alone. "Hello?"

She listened, the sound of the air conditioner blowing making an eerie soundtrack. But something told her she wasn't alone. Someone was with her. It might be strictly fear at work, but she would have sworn she could feel someone staring at her.

She didn't have her phone. She never brought it with her to the gym because she wore a smartwatch and had wireless earbuds. The phone would have been one more thing to carry when she was already attached to her cane.

Her hand tightened around it. Her leg ached a bit, but it always did after a workout. She'd stretched, but it wouldn't be until she'd gotten in the shower and let the heat sink in that her muscles would truly relax.

She was being silly. All that talk with Pete had set her on edge and she was paranoid. She reached for her phone. Hutch had put his number in. She would text him and tell him she was running late.

Maybe he would spank her.

Or she would turn over her laptop again to see if anyone else had been on it. Maybe something had happened with the security system on her locker. Like everything at Genedyne, it was on the cutting edge of technology, and sometimes it needed work. Were any of the other lockers open? When she'd signed up for her gym privileges, she'd been assigned a locker.

There was one slightly open. The one directly behind hers. The one Madison used to have.

She could tell herself she worked out in the evening because it was easier, but Madison was the real reason. Madison had constantly asked about her scars and if they bothered Noelle. Because they would certainly bother her. Madison had once left a tube of scar cream on the bench in front of her locker with a note that promised it was for Noelle, but it was also for everyone in the locker room who had to look at her.

She really hated that woman. She moved toward the locker, expecting it to be empty. Surely they would have cleaned it out. It was empty, but Noelle inspected it anyway.

There was nothing left, as she'd suspected.

A shadow moved out of the corner of her eye, a fear she couldn't quite process. Instinct made her bring the cane up like a bat.

"Who's there?" If no one said a word, she would know for sure. She could understand not hearing her the first time, but this question was asked in a loud, firm voice.

If no one replied, she would know she had to fight because there was no way she'd imagined that big shadow.

She heard the sound of a door slamming shut. Had someone left the locker room? She moved to the end of the lockers, checking the door to make sure whoever it was had run away. Of course she should also consider the fact that whoever it had been had simply walked away, not wanting to deal with her.

Or someone had made the sound as a fake out to get behind her. An arm came around her throat and she suddenly couldn't breathe.

She tried to kick back, tried to get her cane back far enough that she could hit him with it. Whoever was behind her kicked it away, and she felt her knee buckle. Her muscles, the ones she worked so hard to keep strong, failed her.

The arm tightened and her head was light. Panic threatened but she couldn't do anything about it.

The world went dark and she was sure she was done.

* * * *

Hutch glanced down at his watch again. It was a smartwatch that connected to just about everything, a true tech-junkie's watch, but right now all he needed from it was the time.

Noelle was late. A full ten minutes late.

He'd texted her when he'd reached the building and pulled into a parking space. He'd kind of thought she would be waiting in the roundabout, not wanting to give him another reason to get his hands on her.

That would be a smart move on her part. He would take any excuse she gave him because he'd thought about that kiss all freaking day.

It was stupid. It had been a kiss. It hadn't even been real since he'd done it to establish his place in her life for the op. Yeah, he was going to keep telling himself that.

She'd been ridiculously soft in his arms, and he would bet a lot that somewhere in the middle of that kiss, she'd forgotten why they'd been kissing. She'd forgotten they had an audience and she'd let go. He'd felt the second she'd truly given herself over to the moment, and she'd responded to him in a way no woman ever had before—openly and with a pure need that called to his own.

His whole body had been on edge since that kiss, but not in a bad way. He'd enjoyed the ache he'd had all day. It meant he wanted something. Her. He wanted Noelle.

And he'd decided to have her.

He could play it vanilla. He didn't need to tie her up and clamp those pretty tits. He didn't need to see her laid out over his lap, feel her squirm while waiting for his hand to land on that spectacular ass of hers.

Nope. He could do it.

But she had to come down for him to start his very vanilla seduction. He'd already prepped because he had everything ready for dinner. After thoroughly checking her place for any listening devices, he'd marinaded some chicken breasts and put together a salad. While MaeBe had taught Kyle how to properly shut off some of the functions on Noelle's smart TV and her smart speaker systems, he'd gotten a couple of potatoes ready to bake.

He'd thought about telling Kyle he was on his own. It would be nicer to send Kyle out to find his own dinner while he fed Noelle and got time alone with her. There was a fast-food place within walking distance. But he had to play the nice guy here. And Noelle hadn't been interested in hunky Kyle. She'd been interested in him.

"Did you call her?" Kyle strode up. He'd been much happier in Noelle's sedan, but much grumpier the minute MaeBe had left to go home. "She's late."

He managed to not give Kyle a childish "duh." He actually

wasn't a bad dude, and he had better taste in women than Hutch would have given him credit for. Kyle seemed fascinated with MaeBe. It was a good thing because he wasn't going to let the guy get close to Noelle.

Damn. He was getting possessive fast. That didn't happen. He was laid back. He was live and let live. He wasn't the guy who thought someone belonged to him.

But maybe he hadn't met the woman who belonged to him up until today.

She was also the woman who was making him nervous because she wasn't replying to his texts. "I'm going to call."

"Have you thought about the fact that she might not have her phone?" Kyle asked.

"She's got her watch. She can reply with her watch." She'd told him she worked out after she finished up in her lab. She could be in the shower.

He didn't like it. She would have texted him if she was going to be late. She was a careful woman, and a woman who tried not to cause trouble for others. He'd read back through her file again, and simply looking around her apartment told him that. She had a calendar on her bar where she reminded herself to call her family and friends on certain days. Her mail had three charitable donations waiting to be sent out. She wasn't a woman who kept others waiting.

"I'm going in." He started for the front of the building because her phone was going straight to voice mail.

They were going to have such a talk about following his very reasonable requests. She was in potential danger. She should keep her phone or watch on at all times. She should answer his every call because he was the man watching out for her.

"Are you sure she's in there? She might have gone to happy hour." Kyle followed behind him.

Except he was supposed to be the man working the technical aspects of her case, and Kyle was the bodyguard. He should be back at her apartment studying up on Genedyne and trying to figure out who wanted onto Noelle's system. He hadn't been able to send Kyle out alone. "I've been tracking her phone. You should do that, too, since you're the bodyguard."

"When did you do that? Doesn't she have to give you permission?"

Not when he could easily get into her phone and give himself permission, but he'd asked. He pulled his phone out, making sure she was where he thought she should be. "She did. It's part of the job. She's in the building, but I can't tell what floor she's on. Her phone is active and so is her watch. She should be answering."

When did Genedyne lock their doors? The office hours were done, but he would bet a lot of employees stayed late. He might need to take another tactic. "Follow my lead."

There was a security guard at the desk. He wore a uniform and seemed to be checking the security cameras. Hutch hustled up to the desk. "Excuse me, sir, but my girlfriend is having a medical episode. She works at Genedyne. She was supposed to meet me downstairs over thirty minutes ago and she's not responding to calls or texts."

The guard was an older man who sighed as though this wasn't the first time he'd had to deal with a situation like this. "Are you on the guest list?"

"Greg Hutchins." She'd been given instructions to get him on the visitor list. It wouldn't give him free entrance, but it would make it easier to find her. He intended to make it a clear choice for the man in front of him. "My girlfriend is Noelle LaVigne. She's…"

"Are you talking about the young woman who uses the cane?" The guard was on his feet now.

In this case, he would let the man in front of him think whatever he wanted to think. He wasn't going to point out how strong she was. He would use that cane and what it meant to so many people to remove the barrier between them right now. "I'm worried she's fallen or something happened. She could be in trouble. She's had some heart palpitations lately. Please let me get up there to look for her."

The man whose nametag proclaimed him to be *Ernie* stood and picked up his walkie-talkie. "Scott, we might have a medical emergency on six. I'm going up. We have a couple of guests I need you to watch after."

Damn it. "Please let me come with you."

Ernie shook his head. "I can't. The building is technically closed. We have protocols to follow. Scotty should be down soon. You stay here and I'll go up and check on her."

That was not happening.

His heart rate ticked up, adrenaline priming his system. It was a good thing he'd kept up his workout routine. He mostly did it because if he didn't Big Tag pointed out his soft middle, and it was irritating to always be the paunchiest guy in the room.

And he remembered a time when there had been pain and punishment involved in letting himself go even the tiniest bit.

"Of course." He managed to get the words out like a man who actually meant them. "I'll keep trying to get her on the phone."

Ernie nodded. "She's probably in her lab. Sometimes those labs can be hard to get a signal in depending on what they're working on. I'll be back with some news."

He waited until the guard was out of sight and then took a quick look-see at the system sitting on the security desk. There were monitors and a laptop. And manual releases for both the outer doors and the first floor stairwells. Thank god for fire codes.

Hutch pulled the wireless earbuds out of his pocket and shoved them in his ears as he dialed MaeBe's number. One of the things they'd done earlier was to set up how this op was going to work. "Kyle, when I'm close to the stairs, you hit that stairwell button to release the lock and then keep the other guard off my back. Don't let him watch the security cameras."

Kyle frowned his way. "What are you... This is a tech thing, isn't it? Go. I'll handle things down here."

"Hey, boss. What's up?" MaeBe asked.

"I need you to walk me through the Genedyne building." He didn't wait for her to pull up the schematics. He needed to go. "I'm starting in the west staircase. I think I need to get to the private gym."

He started up the first flight. Ernie would head for her lab, probably stopping to talk to whatever guard worked that floor. He was sure they had some serious security. He prayed the gym wasn't at the freaking top of the building.

"It's on seven," MaeBe announced.

He could handle seven. That was a painful but doable number of stairs. Still, he was going to spank Noelle if he ran up seven flights of stairs only to find her drying her hair. Or fixing the world's helium problems. Yep, he'd spank her for that, too. Hard. She would cry and beg forgiveness and he would think about it. Hard.

Sprinting upstairs was fucking hard.

"Okay, I've got them up on my tablet." MaeBe's voice was steady in his ears. He'd made sure she had the schematics to the Genedyne building and to Noelle's apartment building just in case. "Are you going through security or trying to avoid it?"

"I'm going to break down a fucking wall if I have to."

"All right. The easiest way there is to take a left when you hit the seventh floor. The gym isn't far, but it's got keycard access into the locker rooms. The locker rooms open to the gym. The women's locker is on the right about halfway down that first hall."

In the background he could hear the sound of MaeBe's microwave pinging. At least she was home and was working on her own system. That meant she would have access to some of Noelle's data. "I need you to get into her smartwatch and tell me if you see anything weird."

This was the part he hadn't exactly told Noelle. When she'd given him permission to track her phone, he'd kind of let himself in the back door to pretty much everything in her cloud. He could see every piece of data her phone and watch collected, and it was a shocking amount.

"I think you're right about her being at the gym. She logged thirty minutes of exercise about fifteen minutes ago, but then it gets weird. Her heart rate goes crazy up, like way more than the exercise, and then it drops."

He upped his pace even as his quads and hamstrings started to burn. The smartwatch had health components and tracked the user's heart rate and minutes of exercise. "What do you mean by drops?"

"I mean her heart rate was in the seventies and then it shot up to almost a hundred and thirty, and now it's sixty. And all in the course of two minutes."

Shit. "But we're still getting a heartbeat?"

"Yes. It updated thirty seconds ago. Now it's fifty beats per minute. I would bet she's not conscious," MaeBe said, tension coming into her tone.

He hit the seventh floor and blasted through the door. The

hallway was quiet, almost eerily so. "I'll call you if I need anything else. Keep monitoring her."

Before she could reply, he shut the phone down and dialed Noelle again. "Come on, pick up."

Panic was starting to get to him as he reached the women's locker room door and was confronted with the first security he'd had to get through. He didn't have a keycard. He didn't have his kit. He should take the box apart and connect to it, but he didn't have what he needed and there wasn't time to MacGyver anything.

"Hey, you okay?" A tall man walked out of the men's locker room, a gym bag in his hand. "Aren't you the guy Noelle was with earlier?"

"I think she's in trouble." He didn't care who this guy was. If he'd been in the locker room, he had a keycard. "Can you get me in?"

A brow rose but he seemed to get that this was an emergency. "Uh, sure. What's going on? I saw her in the gym a couple of minutes ago and she was fine."

"I know this sounds crazy, but I monitor her smartwatch and her heart rate dropped. Like a lot."

The man moved forward quickly, pulling his card out and swiping it. "Here you go. I work in her lab. I hope she's okay."

He was in the minute that door opened. He slammed through and didn't care that he might walk in on a bunch of women changing. They could scream at him later.

Then nothing mattered but the fact that Noelle was on the ground. She was still dressed in her gym clothes, her hair in a ponytail. She was limp on the floor of the locker room, her face away from him. He dropped to his knees as he heard the man behind him start to dial 911.

He reached for her arm, needing to feel her pulse.

Her eyes fluttered open. "Hutch?"

Relief flooded his system and he clutched her hand. "It's okay. You're okay, but we've got someone coming to check on you."

"Pete?" She started to sit up, but Hutch settled her back down.

"I've got an ambulance coming," the man named Pete said. "I'm going to meet them. I'll bring them up as quick as possible."

He ran out of the room.

She started to try to push up again.

"No. You are staying down until the EMTs get here." He moved so she could rest her head on his leg.

Her eyes closed again. "I'm glad you're here."

And Hutch was left holding her hand as he started to sort through what had happened.

Chapter Five

Noelle sipped her tea and tried to wrap her head around the fact that she'd been choked out.

Choked out. That was the term Hutch had used.

It was also apparently why he wanted her to be careful about what she said.

"This is something the police do? My father has been a cop all of my life and I've never heard anyone at the station talk about choking someone out." The mug warmed her hands, but nothing had made her feel safer than looking up and seeing Hutch's blue eyes staring down at her. She'd started to panic as she'd come back to consciousness, but then she'd felt his hand in hers, seen his eyes, and known she would be okay.

He was a rat fink for not bothering to mention that he could now tell when her heart rate went up or down and how much exercise she got, but she wasn't even going to argue. He'd been able to find her. He'd known she was in trouble and he'd come for her.

It made her realize how alone she'd felt for the last year.

"Not anymore." Hutch was pacing the floor of her living room. "The practice was outlawed completely a few years back, but that doesn't mean they don't still know how to do it. It's not something you learn in a typical self-defense class. I would bet this guy is either a cop or former military."

"Did you get any kind of look at him?" Kyle asked. "There were mirrors in the locker room. Did you see him?"

"It could have been a woman. She was in the women's locker room." Hutch walked ten steps to the left, taking him past her dining room table.

She thought about the moment she'd realized she was caught and there wasn't anything she could do. She forced herself to take a long breath. "No. I didn't get a look. I knew someone was in the room with me. I saw my locker was open and a minute later I lost consciousness. I think it was a man. I was pulled back against a muscular chest. He was definitely taller than me."

"You're five foot two, sweetheart. Everyone is taller than you," Hutch pointed out.

"I still think it was a guy." Something about the way he'd smelled. She'd been going over and over it. "He smelled like…sandalwood. That doesn't tell me a lot, though. It's the smell of the soap they have in the men's locker room. The women's is lavender. We voted."

"So we think at some point he took a shower that day." Hutch seemed to mull that over. "In the men's locker room. I need to see a list of everyone who used a key to get into that locker room. Better yet, I saw a security cam on that hall."

"I'm sure we can probably figure out a way to get a copy," Kyle said.

"Oh, I'll get whatever data I need." Hutch started to pace again.

There were some problems with that scenario. "I don't know that it will help. First of all, at least half the company uses the gym at some point of time in the day."

"But I'm only interested in the hour around the attack on you, and I'm interested in who was in the men's locker room," Hutch pointed out.

"The locker rooms can be opened by any key," she explained. "It was why Pete could get in. So a man could use his keycard to walk in, but I doubt he would use the hallway entrance. It would be simple to enter through the men's locker room and then come around to the gym entrance. You don't need a keycard to get into the locker room from the gym."

"Would there be a record of who came in and out of the locker rooms?" Kyle was seemingly calmer than Hutch. He'd come up with the EMTs and Pete, who'd hovered around, too. Pete hadn't left until the EMTs had.

"I would bet my life there's a record for who went in," she replied. Genedyne was big on records. The one place they didn't have security cameras were the locker rooms.

"Let's not joke about that right now since you almost lost yours." Hutch had his hands on his hips and looked as prim as a really hot guy could manage.

From what she could tell it hadn't been all that close. Yes, she'd lost consciousness briefly due to her carotid artery being squeezed, but all of her vitals had been stable and she felt perfectly fine now. Physically, at least. Emotionally she was kind of a mess. "All I'm saying is the keycard would tell you when a person went in, but it doesn't keep track of people going out. There's also the possibility that whoever did this was smart enough to enter with another employee. Then his keycard wouldn't show him going in. And the EMTs said I was all right. I didn't even need to go to the hospital."

Hutch had argued with her over that call, but she'd done everything else he'd asked her to do. She'd kept her answers short when she'd talked to the police, who didn't seem all that interested. She'd stayed close to Hutch, letting him hold her hand while they'd talked to both the cops and security.

She'd told the police she thought someone was trying to steal from the lockers. She didn't mention any of the other odd happenings because Hutch had explained that he was worried about the police. He was concerned about the guy who sometimes worked the second shift here at her building. He'd freaked out even more when she'd told him Chris had been hired on only a few weeks before.

"It would have been better if we went to the hospital," Hutch insisted. "It would make things easier when I walk you up to work tomorrow and start getting people used to seeing me around."

"Or I could take the maneater up on her offer." Kyle watched Hutch as though trying to figure out exactly how to deal with him. "I could potentially be in that building with a keycard all of my own in a couple of days."

Hutch shook his head. "I don't want anyone close to that woman. Especially not you. I saw how she looked at you."

"Jessica pretty much looks at every hot guy that way, from what I've been told." She'd heard the rumors about Jessica's men.

Kyle gave her a smooth smile. "Thanks for the compliment."

"She said Jessica Layne thinks you're hot. Not that Noelle does," Hutch complained. "And you shouldn't view it as a compliment. From what I've read, Ms. Layne never keeps a man for long."

"I mean he's hot," she heard herself saying. "In a purely aesthetic way. But Hutch is right. Jessica isn't like looking for a long-term thing. And Kyle is her type. She likes the all-American beefcake guy. She's not into..." How did she put this nicely? "I mean she's really looking for men who don't work in the tech industry."

"Or the medical industry or legal," Hutch continued. "She likes himbos, Kyle. Are you a himbo?"

Kyle shrugged as if he didn't care whether someone thought he was all abs and no brain or not. "Depends on who you talk to. My brother would definitely say yes. But you two are acting like I'm going to sleep with the woman. I'm not. However, I can use the attraction to get me where we need to be, which is in that building. Noelle, we haven't talked about why you were attacked. I understand why Hutch wanted you to be careful around the cops. We're both worried that a DPD officer showed up in your building a few weeks before we think someone screwed up a break-in."

"But Chris would have my accurate address." She didn't understand why a guy working a second job was such a concern. "He knows where I live."

"I'm not at all saying he would have done the break-in himself." Hutch stopped in front of the mantel over her fireplace, his eyes seeming to catch on the framed picture of her and her stepmom and dad. It was a graduation photo, and she was in her cap and gown. She was also in her old wheelchair.

"We're more worried that he's here to facilitate someone Ms. Layne or someone in her organization might hire." Kyle crossed one muscular leg over the other. As wound up as Hutch seemed, Kyle was the opposite. "We'll know more when we talk to some people we trust at DPD tomorrow. We have some questions they may or may not be willing to answer."

Hutch turned, catching Kyle's gaze. "Yeah, I'm worried about that, too."

They seemed to know something she didn't. "Worried about what?"

Hutch's arms went over his chest. "I'm worried that we either found a guy who's on Layne's payroll or we walked into the middle of an active investigation and you're part of it."

She felt her eyes go wide. "I'm not part of any investigation."

"You wouldn't know you're a part of this investigation because you're a potential target." Kyle made the pronouncement like he was talking about how nice it was outside.

Was he talking about a criminal investigation? "Why would I be a target? Why would Dallas police care about me? And for that matter, why would they care about Genedyne?"

"Because it's a big tech company that has rumors around it. You've heard some of them, right?" Hutch asked.

"We do not have labs where anyone experiments on people. Not in a non-FDA approved way." She'd heard the urban legends. "We're basically a big old think tank where a crazy, rich lady funds our wildest dreams."

"One person's dream can be another's nightmare." Hutch started moving again. "There's also rumors that her finances aren't as good as she says they are. Genedyne is her most famous business, but she's had others."

She probably didn't know as much as she should about her boss. "I still don't see what that has to do with me. I study helium."

"You run a lab at Genedyne. You knew the woman who recently died under what some people would call mysterious circumstances," Kyle mused. "If I was running an investigation into Genedyne, I would put you under surveillance."

"Someone's been watching me?" She could feel panic start to surge.

Hutch stopped in front of her, his expression softening. "Hey, it's okay. From what I can tell, there were no bugs in this apartment, no hidden cameras. We went over every inch of this place and you're good. If they are surveilling you, I think they're doing it to figure out where you fit into the picture. The truth is we don't know what's going on, but I'm going to figure it out. You're going to be okay."

She wanted to reach out and touch that strong jawline, run her hands over the scruff that hadn't been there earlier in the day. That face of his was a work of art. And she was honest enough to know that she wasn't even close to being in his league. That knowledge didn't make her stop remembering how good it had felt when he'd hugged her. The whole time with the EMTs and Pete and security asking her questions, Hutch had played the boyfriend role to perfection. He'd held her close and made sure she was comfortable. He'd been the one to find her cane.

She would have to use her braces tomorrow. She could feel it. There were days she needed more support than others, and typically they came after a fall. She could already feel the ache in her hips from hitting the floor of the locker room.

She forced herself to give him a smile she hoped portrayed a confidence she didn't feel. "Thanks."

"We have to deal with the fact that someone needs to be in that building with Noelle," Kyle said, breaking the odd connection she'd felt. "After today, you can't deny that."

Hutch stood again, his hand raking over his golden brown hair in obvious frustration. "Agreed. But I'll do it. I didn't like how she looked at you."

"Ah, but it was the way she looked at me that means I'm the one who can get in," Kyle replied softly. "If you try to hire on right now, it could take weeks."

He was right about that. "I don't think we're hiring in tech support. I did hear something about security needing a couple of guys."

Kyle stared at Hutch. "Hiring you on will take too long, and she basically offered me a job on the spot. I know I'm not the tech guy, but you can teach me what you need me to do and I'll be there if Noelle needs someone. She already thinks I'm your brother. It won't be odd for me to walk my brother's girlfriend in and out of the building."

Hutch's phone pinged and he sighed. "I've got to go down and get the pizza. I'll be right back." He frowned Noelle's way, a deeply forbidding look. "Don't go anywhere."

Where would she go? "All right."

He'd obviously had a day. Perhaps he was the one who needed a big hug, but that look had told her he didn't want it from her.

The door closed behind him and she turned to Kyle. "Is he mad at me for getting attacked?"

Kyle sat back. "Nah. He's mad because his dinner date got canceled."

"He had a date?" Wow. She didn't like how that felt. He hadn't had pictures of a girlfriend in his office, but then he hadn't had framed pictures at all.

"Yep. He had it all planned, and I'm almost certain he tried to figure a way to cut me out. He was eyeing that fast-food place pretty closely earlier," Kyle replied. "Lucky for me MaeBe picked up the chicken breasts and bought three, or Hutch would have used that as an excuse to shove me out the door."

She was confused. "He was bringing a date here?"

A brow rose over Kyle's eyes. They were a brilliant green, the most striking feature on the man. "Come on, smart chick. You can do this."

She couldn't help but roll her eyes. She wasn't about to believe that. "He was only making dinner. That wasn't for me. I bet he took one look at my sad refrigerator and decided I can make nothing but cookies and cinnamon rolls. He realized if he didn't want frozen lasagna, he had to do it himself."

Kyle's eyes were gorgeous, but she preferred Hutch's. There was a warmth to Hutch's eyes, a pull to his stare that dragged her in even when he was frowning at her.

"Trust me. Hutch has eaten MREs that would make that sad lasagna look like a four-course meal. Nah, he was trying to show off," Kyle replied. "And then he realized how late it was, and that was why he ordered the pizza on our way back here. He's going to have to call Big Tag and tell him he almost lost you, and Big Tag can be a lot to handle. I also think meeting Jessica Layne freaked him out a bit. But mostly it's about not getting the time he wanted with you, and you should think about that."

She shook her head. "He's being nice to make up for being a jerk in the beginning."

"I don't think that's what he's doing. I think he's attracted to you, and this is his way of making a play. Again, you should think about whether you want him to do that because he's got some baggage, and he's proving that right now. I'm going to take that job whether he wants me to or not, and he's going to flip his shit. You should stay out of that fight when it comes, by the way."

"Why?" It made sense to her that if they could get one of them on at Genedyne, they should. "Why will he be angry? I know Jessica has a bad rep, and she's earned it on some level, but I don't think she's going to assault you. She might objectify you."

Kyle's lips curled up. "Yeah, I think I can handle that." He sobered. "Hutch can't, and you should understand that. He would never play a chick for information, and he wouldn't do it to make your working relationship easier. Ever. Believe it or not he's actually trying to protect me by not letting me take the job and I find that…oddly refreshing. I'm not the dude most bosses think they need to protect."

"What does he think Jessica will do to you?"

Kyle seemed to think about that for a moment, probably deciding how much to tell her. "About ten years ago Hutch went through something pretty awful. I wasn't around at that time, but I've heard the stories and I know what Hutch did for my family. I think he should tell you what he wants you to know, but understand that he doesn't play around with a woman's feelings. Ever. And he's not smooth enough to think feeding you might make the job go easier. He's apologized and you accepted. For him that's over and done with, and now he can move on to what he wants next."

"And what's that?"

"Again, use that big old brain of yours."

She huffed. "He does not want me. That's ridiculous."

Kyle shrugged. "You can believe me or not, but watch him over the next couple of days. See how he treats you. He could have come back and done his dinner thing, but he was worried it would take too long and you would get hungry. You mentioned you felt a little weak. He chucked all his plans and got food here as quickly as possible."

He'd been at her side the entire time, not letting go of her hand. He'd even insisted that Kyle drive while he'd sat in the back with her.

It had been easy to let Hutch take over. She was still scared, still confused, but there was a core of strength she'd found because she hadn't been alone. He'd taken charge and she'd let him. And she'd stood up to him when he'd wanted her hauled to the hospital.

Her mind went back to that moment in the parking garage when Hutch had made Kyle back off. Wasn't that what she'd been looking for? It was hard to find a guy who didn't see her as weak but also acknowledged she needed help from time to time. One who let her set the pace she was comfortable with, but also challenged her when she needed it.

"So give it some thought. Like I said, he's a good guy, but he's got some issues." He sat back again. "When are you going to tell him where you're going on Thursday? Unless you've changed your mind about Sanctum's training program?"

She glanced at the door, hoping Hutch wasn't close. "How do you know that?"

"I'm supposed to start on Thursday, too," he admitted. "If you're still going, I can go. If not, I'll join the next class, no problem. Naturally, I snuck a look at the list. Your name is on it. If you're interested, they did not put the two of us together. You're with some dude I don't know named Jeff."

She felt an odd rush of relief. A man named Kai Ferguson put partners together. She'd had an interview with the man who ran the Ferguson Clinic, a therapy and wellness center that was next to Sanctum. The way the process had been described to her, she would be placed with a Dom in training and they would go through the course together. They could have as much or as little physical contact as they liked, but sex was absolutely not allowed in the club until the process was done. Nothing said she couldn't see him outside the club. In fact, they would have homework they would have to do together. Her aunt had talked about how much fun she'd had during those weeks—though not around her husband because he had not been her training Dom.

Suddenly that didn't seem like something she would likely do. Only the night before she'd been lying in bed thinking about the fact that she might be attracted to her training Dom and they might agree to sleep together for the training period. Just have a good time and explore the lifestyle. It wouldn't be a big deal. It wouldn't be some crazy love affair. It would be sex and fun and mutual interest.

How could she possibly entertain the idea of sleeping with a guy when she was interested in another man? Or maybe she should realize that feeling this close to a man in such a ridiculously short period of time was a big old red flag.

Hadn't her dad known pretty quickly he was crazy about Lila Daley? It hadn't taken more than a couple of weeks for him to ask Lila to marry him. Shouldn't she give that a chance?

Or she should accept that she was lonely and he was lovely and kind and he made her feel safe when she'd so recently found out she was in danger.

She couldn't trust this feeling. Not at all.

"So you're not going to tell him?" Kyle's question reminded her she wasn't alone.

"He'll find out soon enough." Or maybe he didn't have to at all. "Why does he have to go with me? If you're there he doesn't have to. I certainly don't expect him to spend every minute with me. He should have a life."

"I think he's going to want to go."

The door came open and Hutch walked in carrying a large pizza. "All right we've got half meat lovers, and half sausage with peppers and onions. There's a salad in the fridge. The chicken will keep until tomorrow night. There's wine, too. I didn't know if you would like red or white. Unless you don't drink."

Kyle groaned and pushed himself out of her comfy chair. "I'll drink whatever she doesn't."

She could use some wine. She stood and her back seized up. Before she could fall to her seat, Hutch was there.

"Hey, you okay?" He balanced her, one hand in hers and the other on her back.

She was being ridiculous. She should have gotten in her chair the minute they'd made it home, but she'd pushed it because she didn't want him to see her in it. That was stupid. She needed a wheelchair from time to time. It made her life easier, and she was grateful for it.

A few hours off her feet and a couple of days with her braces and she would be fine with the cane again. Anyone who didn't like it could bite her butt.

"I should use my wheelchair for the rest of the night. I have to rest my muscles when they get like this." Tight, painful, but the pain reminded her that once she hadn't felt anything at all. If she had to spend some time in a wheelchair, she was cool with that.

"It's in her bedroom against the east wall," Hutch said.

"I'm on it." Kyle strode off.

"It's weird that you know that."

"I had to go over the place with a fine-tooth comb." Hutch showed no signs of stepping away. He stayed right there with her. "Listening devices can be anywhere. They're tricky suckers."

"You went through my place?"

"That's what I meant when I said I was going to make sure it was secure."

"I thought you would check my locks." She hadn't considered the fact that he would look for listening devices. "I mean, you looked on the walls and stuff, right? Maybe checked the lighting fixtures?"

A slow smile creased his face. "Are you asking me if I found your body wand?"

She wasn't going to be ashamed of that either, but she still flushed and was absolutely certain she was a bright shade of red. "You honestly thought there could be a listening device in my nightstand?"

"I'm a thorough guy. And it's pretty standard. I think every woman I know has one. Here you go." He turned her toward Kyle.

Silly man. He absolutely shouldn't have looked in her nightstand. Also, she was a bit resentful about the "standard" comment. Did he think she couldn't be kinky, too?

Would he be surprised when she changed into her fet wear on Thursday?

He helped her ease down into the small chair she used around the house. Once she'd been in a much bigger one, but this one was easy to maneuver. It was the speedster of wheelchairs. She strapped in and backed up, giving Hutch her sauciest grin. "Well, then I'll have to hope you didn't get into the tote bag in my closet because that's where I keep the fun stuff."

The sexiest grin lit his face. "I sense a secondary search coming on."

Kyle sighed. "Can I eat before you two do the sexual tension thing? It's upsetting my stomach. Sorry. I've spent a lot of time with Big Tag lately."

She wasn't sure what that had to do with anything.

"Yeah, because watching you flirt with MaeBe was the highlight of my day," Hutch groaned. He looked down at her. "You got this or you want a ride?"

Her father would have simply started pushing. The last man she'd dated hadn't liked to be around her when she was in the chair. He'd pretended it wasn't there.

She liked Hutch's approach so much more. "Nah, I'm pretty speedy, but I wouldn't mind a glass of white wine."

He stepped back and gave her room. "I'll get it for you."

"I wasn't flirting with MaeBe," Kyle insisted.

He and Hutch started to argue, and the smell of pizza hit her, making her stomach growl.

She settled in at the table. It was nice to have company.

She let go of her worries for a time because she was going to enjoy the moments she had with him.

* * * *

Hutch stepped out on the balcony, giving up any actual hope of getting sleep. It was way past midnight, and he'd already given the guest room to Kyle since he'd known he would be awake for a long time reading up on the woman named Jessica Layne and trying to figure out what she could be investigated for.

A lot. A whole freaking lot, if his instincts were right. He took a deep breath. At some point a mild cold front had come in and the heat of the day had broken, bringing some relief to the night around him. It would blow in and out quickly, and tomorrow would be right back to oppressive heat, but for now he enjoyed the breeze and wondered if Noelle was sleeping. The big balcony overlooking the park opened from both the living room and the master bedroom. The bedroom was dark. She was probably sleeping away.

Or using that body wand of hers and finding some relief that he wasn't going to find.

He stared out over the quiet park, a Red Vine in his mouth, dangling like a cigarette. When he got insomnia, he tended to chew on a Red Vine. Or when he was thinking. Or playing games.

He pretty much just liked Red Vines.

A soft sound drew his attention behind him as the sliding door to the master bedroom came open and Noelle was suddenly standing there wearing a pair of pajama shorts and a T-shirt that proclaimed she was Ready to Snooze. Her hair was up in a messy bun on top of her head and she was soft and sexy, and he bit down on that damn candy.

"Hey, are you all right?" Noelle asked, stepping onto the balcony.

Her balcony was like an outdoor living room, complete with a couple of small rattan sofas and a coffee table he'd been using as a desk for the last hour. "Yeah. I'm good. Sorry if I woke you."

"You didn't. I wasn't sleeping. Too much on my mind. I was going to sneak out for a snack, but I was afraid I would wake up Kyle."

He could help with that. As long as she wanted to snack on Red Vines. "I've got extras. Or you can go to the kitchen without worry. I gave Kyle the guest bedroom. I knew I would be up working late. I came out here for some fresh air."

She stepped onto the balcony, her hand going to the back of the nearest sofa, and he realized she'd arranged the furniture so she would always have something to hold onto. She wouldn't need her cane or the braces in her closet out here. She'd made a space where she could move easily.

Noelle LaVigne adapted.

Could she adapt to him?

She took the piece of candy he offered her and unwrapped it. "Do you always carry a bunch of candy around? Are you always ready to offer someone a sweet?"

"Well, that makes me sound like a perv."

She blinked up at him as she took a bite. "I was just asking. I don't know many guys who have candy on their desks or in their pockets."

"It's in my bag. I get snacky from time to time, and my snacks resemble a five-year-old's. I am a walking, talking example of what happens when you're too rigid with kids. I rarely got candy when I was young. My dad liked to control pretty much everything in our lives, and diet was part of it." He felt the need to explain so she wouldn't think he carried around candy to tempt kids or something. "The rare times I got to see my grandma, she would sneak me candy."

He missed that smiling old lady. She'd been his mom's mom, and when she'd died a light had gone out in his life.

"Your dad was hard on you?"

His nightmarish relationship with his father would be difficult to explain to someone whose dad had loved her, still loved her. It could be tough to make someone with a functional family understand what it was to be truly alone in the world at such a young age.

"My father was an abusive prick who broke my mom's spirit until one day she took a tumble down the stairs. I often wonder if she fell because of the sprained ankle she was nursing or if she stood there at the top of the stairs and realized nothing would get any better and let herself go." He took a deep breath. "I'm sorry. I'm weirdly contemplative tonight."

Normally he would be sitting in front of a monitor playing online games with his buddies.

"Because of Jessica?" She sat down on the sofa across from him. "Sorry. Kyle mentioned something about her being a trigger."

He chuckled, but it wasn't an amused sound. "I hate that word. Trigger. To some people it's come to mean a person's not strong enough to handle life. I've often found those people haven't had much trouble with life, though they think they're tough. It's funny. When Tag asks me if something's going to trigger me, he's the one sarcastic asshole in the world who isn't being a jerk. He knows what a trigger is and that even when we don't mean to pull it, we still do so much fucking damage."

"I'm sorry. I didn't mean it in a bad way. If there's anyone who understands what a trigger is, it's me. I still freak out in storms sometimes. Especially if I'm driving and it catches me unaware. It's one of the many reasons I don't like to drive." She looked up at him, her eyes shining in the starlight. "I would never make fun of anyone who gets emotional because of something that happened to them. I got caught in a storm driving from Papillon back to Austin a couple of years ago. I got so scared I blacked out. I apparently managed to get to the side of the road and park the car, but I swear one minute I was driving in the afternoon and the rain started to fall, and then I heard the thunder crack and I was fifteen and sitting next to my mother watching the lights come at me and feeling my body break."

He moved closer to her. "It was a car accident?"

She studied him for a moment. "You didn't ask about why I can't walk?"

"You can walk."

She sighed. "Why I can't walk properly?"

Did she think he was playing around? How often did she have to justify her existence to people who thought the word *normal* meant anything at all? He'd learned *normal* was a word humans tossed around to describe something that didn't exist.

"You walk the way you walk, Noelle. There's nothing proper or improper about it." Except the way her ass swayed. That gave him perfectly improper thoughts. "Your walk is a part of you. I didn't ask why because it doesn't matter."

She stared at him for a moment. "I can't quite believe you're real. Of course it matters."

Hutch didn't see why. "Would my knowing why change my acceptance of you? Would it be different if the reason you walk the way you do came from a congenital defect? If you want to talk about it, I would love to. I would love to know how any incident you want to talk about affects you, but it doesn't change the fact that there's nothing wrong or damaged about you."

"Hutch, I assure you I was damaged," she said. "I couldn't walk for a long time. I probably wouldn't walk today if my stepmom hadn't come into my life."

"All right. Then how about I say it's typical to be damaged. Being human and damaged go hand in hand. I assure you I'm as damaged as a person can be."

Even in the low light he could see her eyes roll.

"Yes, you look damaged."

He would love to have the right to put her over his knee for all that sass. "Most of mine is on the inside. My dad was good about not leaving scars. A good punch to the gut can put a kid out of service for a while without a ton of visible damage."

"I'm sorry," she sputtered. "It's just you're so comfortable talking about it. I still don't like to."

"I've gone through ten years of weekly therapy. I've learned that I can talk about it or I can let it eat me up inside. I ended up on the streets when I was a teen. Oh, there were group homes I could have gone to, but I rather enjoyed finding my own space. I got into a lot of trouble. I ended up meeting a man who I think saved my life. Tennessee Smith. He's the reason I went into the Army and joined the Agency and eventually landed where I am. Big Tag pretty much chucked my ass into therapy after a particularly long op, and I learned how to talk about my feelings." He knew there were guys out there who would call him weak, but he knew how strong a base knowledge of his own soul made him.

It should make him strong enough to walk away from her.

"Was it something about your childhood that made you worry about my boss?" Noelle asked.

He sighed and sat back. "There are lots of reasons I'm worried about your boss. I don't believe in coincidences, not at this level. I could buy that someone tried to get on your laptop and there was an accidental fire in a lab. Tie that together with a DPD detective in your building and someone attacking you and it's a pattern I haven't identified yet."

"You didn't answer my question," she pointed out softly.

Yeah, he'd wanted to avoid that. "It was a shitty time of my life. I avoid talking about it with anyone but my therapist, but as it's the reason I can't sleep tonight, hell, why not."

She crumpled the empty Red Vine wrapper in her hand. "You don't have to."

He didn't want this moment to end. He got the feeling the intimacy between them would be over if he let her go back to bed. "If I talk, I want something from you."

She sat back as though she was happy to have a reason to stay. "What?"

He'd never felt this comfortable with a woman before. Maybe comfortable wasn't the right word. In synch was better. "Whatever you're willing to give. A story about your childhood or some of your cinnamon rolls. A list of your favorite songs and why you love them. It's up to you. I only want it to be something you don't mind giving me."

"All right," she agreed. "I know I should tell you that you don't have to talk, but I want to know the story."

Because she felt what he felt. She felt the pull of whatever this thing was between them. "Okay. Then I'll tell you why Jessica Layne bothers me. It's not that I have a problem with powerful women. I work around a whole bunch of them. I would let Charlotte or Erin Taggart watch my back any day of the week. I've witnessed a wealth of kindness from my friends' wives, and there's power in that, too. But I was held captive by a woman who called herself a doctor."

"Held captive?"

It sounded like the plot of a bad action film, but it had been his life. "Yep. I was held hostage for my computer skills. Hope McDonald was working on a super-soldier program that included being able to wipe her subjects' memories. She kidnapped soldiers and intelligence employees. She took one look at Theo Taggart and decided he would be her greatest soldier. It didn't matter that he had a girlfriend. She went right for him."

Noelle nodded. "Like Jessica flirted with Kyle."

He'd seen the look on the tech guru's face and been right back to that time in his life when Hope McDonald ruled everything. She'd made his father look like a great and loving papa. "Yes, though McDonald was even more aggressive. No one thought anything of it at the time. We joked about how Theo had a stalker and generally gave him hell about it. And then she took him and erased his memory, and for a long time we thought he was dead."

She gasped. "She really erased his memory?"

"Yes, she did. She was brilliant. She was known as a wunderkind, much like your boss. She was also a sociopath. She took a lifetime of memories and replaced them with perfect obedience to her. She beat her subjects, gave them days of pain if they stepped out of line. She forged them into perfect soldiers. I was on the team that found Theo, but it went wrong and instead of me capturing Theo, my dumb ass was captured *by* Theo. Thus began my year in Hope McDonald's tender care."

She was on the edge of her seat, her hand coming out to cover his. "How did you get your memories back?"

He wanted to flip his hand over and thread their fingers together, but she didn't know the whole story yet. "Oh, she didn't take mine. You see, muscle memory is a thing. She could erase a soldier's memories and the ability to fight, the training they'd had before, was still accessible. But kicking ass wasn't what I was brought in to do."

"They wanted your skills as a hacker," she surmised.

"And my connections to the hacker world, and after a couple of what felt like years of torture, I gave them to her. You should understand that, Noelle. I've been broken. I've had my soul stripped down and seen who I am at my core, and I was broken. I did what she told me to do." He sat back, drawing away from her and picking up a fresh licorice. It was a weird emotional crutch that went back to those days with his grandmother. "One of the things she did was put me on a diet. I went in at a pleasingly plump one eighty, and when I came out I was one hundred fifty pounds of pure muscle. Two percent body fat because if I got above that I was beaten and didn't eat for three days. It took me a year to be able to eat anything sweet after I got home. I hated the fact that this thing that gave me comfort and reminded me of the one good thing about my childhood was suddenly another means of torture."

"Anyone would break under those circumstances."

That's what he'd been told over and over again. "When Big Tag came to rescue us, I stayed in the plane. I actually walked back on the plane because I'd been taught whenever something was going wrong to go back to base. It took me a good ten minutes to make the decision to break free."

"But you did. You did break free."

"And then I went back in."

"What?" Noelle asked on a gasp. "What do you mean you went back in?"

It had been the hardest decision of his life. And oddly, the easiest. "I mean the night we were rescued Big Tag came to me and asked me to go undercover. He asked me to make my way back to McDonald. I knew there were more men under her control. I'd seen evidence of it, though at that time she kept me away from her other bases. I was the only one who could do it."

"He asked you to go back in?" The question came out on an outraged huff.

"He did, and then he had to pretend I'd defected because we couldn't be sure that Theo was solid. The training…"

"You mean brainwashing," she corrected.

He supposed that was a good term for it. "Yes, the brainwashing was effective. In some ways I was almost relieved because I didn't have to try to be the me I'd been before, if that makes sense."

"It does. You didn't want to have to face the fact that you'd changed. You didn't want to look at the people who'd known you before and disappoint them because you couldn't be that person anymore."

She did understand. Their traumas had been different, but they were both survivors. "I feared standing in front of my brothers and feeling like I didn't belong there more than I feared the pain that would come from going back to McDonald. Obviously they weren't my blood, but the men I served with, I worked with, they were my brothers. When I joined that CIA team, it was the first time I felt like I had a family."

It had taken him a while, but they'd gotten to him. Those men had accepted him and joked with him and invited him to their family gatherings when they'd realized he didn't have anyone. He'd spent Thanksgivings with the Malones and Christmases with his buddy Deke and all those sisters of his. Lately they all went to the big Taggart family holidays.

But at the time all he could see was how he'd failed. "I had to go back to find myself again, and it was a close thing."

"You thought about staying with her?"

He shook his head. "No. I thought about disappearing. I thought about walking away from all of it and never showing my face again. But I knew those men were in hell. I'd been in hell and I couldn't leave them there. It was like penance."

"You had nothing to do penance for. It wasn't your fault."

"But I needed it," he explained. "I needed to walk in there willingly, to sacrifice. In some ways, it was the turning point of my life. I'm stronger now. I broke, but I put myself back together. Well, with lots of therapy."

"I've been thinking about seeing one myself," she said. "So you're worried Jessica is going to be another Hope McDonald, and that's why you're trying to protect Kyle."

"And you." He stared right at her, giving her all the honesty he had. "And not strictly because you're the client. So that's my sad story. I've got completely unsupported emotional concerns about a woman I don't know. And I've got real concerns, too. I've spent a lot of my evening researching her, and she's dangerous. I think her corporate structure is sketchy, too. I think there's a good chance she's under some kind of investigation, and you're going to get dragged into it. Is there any way you could take a couple of weeks off?"

It was the conclusion he'd come to. He would feel safer if she didn't go back into that building again.

She shook her head. "I can't. If I leave, I leave my research behind, and I'm close. If I prove my processes can work I'll be able to hire on anywhere, and that would be remarkable at my age."

Well, it was the answer he'd expected. "I want you to keep your eyes open and call me the minute you feel like anything's weird. Trust your instincts." He let out a breath and admitted the answer he'd come to. "I'm going to let Kyle go in with you tomorrow."

"Good, because I have it on the highest authority he was going to take that job anyway."

It was good to know he was in charge. He closed the screen of his laptop. He should go to bed and let her have some peace. She had to be at work early in the morning. He would lay on her couch and stare at the ceiling.

He was about to stand when Noelle beat him to it. "Hey, you didn't get your prize."

"Prize?"

"That's kind of what you wanted, right? I'm supposed to give you something for opening up to me."

"I wasn't thinking about it as a prize, though I can see where you would." He wanted to explore this thing between them, and having her talk to him or tell him something important about herself would do that. But he wasn't going to push her. "You don't have to if you don't want to."

He was going to go slow. He was going to get to know her and ease into a friendship that could become something more. He had to be patient.

"I want to." She crossed the space between them. "I want to give you this."

She had another Red Vine in her hand. He'd wanted something personal from her. Something that would let him know this woman better. He got his own candy back. Story of his life. Still, he gave her what he hoped was a game smile and reached out. "Thanks."

She pulled her hand back before he could take the candy. It wasn't even a full one. It was the last little piece of what he'd given her.

"I want you to take it from me." She licked her lips and put it in her mouth.

He was fully awake now, and about three thousand reasons this was a bad, bad idea went through his head.

It was too soon. She was sheltered and inexperienced. He was not. He had needs that would shock her. She'd literally said she didn't do weird sex stuff. He did. A lot of weird sex stuff.

He should wait because she wasn't doing this because she was in love with him. She was doing it because they had wild chemistry and she couldn't help herself. He should be the senior partner and end this experiment of hers.

She settled on his lap, right over his dick, which had come to full and complete life the minute she'd gotten close. He was suddenly hard as a rock, and every muscle in his body was tense and waiting to see if she was doing what he thought she was doing.

"Noelle?"

She lifted her face to his, offering that last bit of sugar, and he gave up the idea of waiting.

Chapter Six

Noelle could taste the candy on her lips and prayed Hutch wanted her as much as she wanted him. She would look like a moron if her seductive act went wrong and he was one of those totally normal people who didn't eat candy that had been in someone else's mouth.

What had she been thinking? Was she insane? She'd just met this man and...

One strong hand pressed against her back, moving her close, and his mouth met hers, tongue dragging across her lips before he bit down on that candy, taking half.

It was the single sexiest thing that ever happened to her, and that included full-on sex.

This was why she'd taken the chance. She was tired of not taking chances, and she had to know what making love with this man could do for her.

No one had ever affected her the way Hutch did, and she wanted to see where this road led.

"What else are you offering me, Noelle? Or was that sugar all I get from you?" His voice had gone deep and something had changed. The laid-back guy was gone, and in his place was someone darker, more commanding.

The Dom. She'd known he went to Sanctum, known he was a

top, but now she was facing the Dom and he made her heart beat faster. The fact that there was such a difference did something for her.

"It depends on how much you want from me."

His other hand moved to her thigh, pulling her legs closer and caging her in. "I want it all, Noelle. I want to eat you up. Let me. Let me carry you to your bed and stay there all night. You won't regret it."

She might. She might regret it when this was all over with because she already felt too much for him. It was important for her to acknowledge what this was. "I want you. You need to understand that I'm not asking you for anything but tonight."

The hand on her back moved up to cup the nape of her neck, tightening slightly in a way that sent heat through her. "Then I'll have to make you want me again tomorrow."

Even his voice was deeper when he was in this place. He hadn't acknowledged it—hadn't told her he wanted to top her—so she didn't say anything. But the difference was right there. She would know where she stood with this man.

After the story he'd told her, she believed Kyle. Hutch wouldn't manipulate her with sex. He would be open and honest about what he wanted.

His lips teased at hers, gentle at first. They coaxed her to play, to let him suck her bottom lip between his teeth and teasingly bite down. His tongue then ran over it before he started the game all over again. He took his time.

He'd told her he wanted to eat her up. She was ready to let him do it.

His tongue surged in and she couldn't think about anything but how good he felt, how incredible it was to have her body respond the way it should. So often it felt like her body failed, like it didn't work the way other's did, but now every inch of her seemed to come to life and it didn't matter that her legs didn't always work normally.

Her legs would spread fine, and she had a feeling her clitoris was about to get a workout like it had never had before.

This could be just sex. It didn't have to tear her heart up. They would be together for a while. They could explore this and enjoy it and be okay at the end.

This time she could protect herself.

He kissed her for the longest time, making her feel like she was the sweetest treat he'd ever been offered. His tongue coaxed hers in to play, sliding and teasing and finally dominating in a way that had her primed and ready.

She'd never been this ready for sex.

"Tell me how long it's been for you." The words were whispered against her ear right before he nipped her earlobe, sending a delicious shiver down her spine.

She couldn't think when he was this close. "What?"

"Sex, baby," he replied, licking the shell of her ear. "How long? I don't care if you had sex last night, I just want to know how slow I should go. I can go slow and make this last for hours, or I can fuck you right now and then turn around and fuck you again fifteen minutes from now. It's up to you."

Fucking sounded perfect to her. "Yes, please."

His hand cupped her breast. "You didn't answer my question. How long? I'll tell you how long it's been for me. It's been three months."

She got the feeling if she told him the truth he might stop altogether. She wasn't a virgin, but she'd been focusing on her career for the last couple of years. "About the same for me."

He had her flipped up and over his knee before she could take another breath. She was suddenly staring at the outdoor rug she'd bought when she'd moved into this place. Was he going to…

Spank her. She wanted him to.

He stopped and she heard him take a deep breath. "I'm sorry I did that. It was habit… That's sounds bad, too. Let's get you up and I'll explain. You should know a few things about me before you make this decision."

Yes, she definitely needed to make a decision. He sounded unsure, like he thought she would reject him. How many times had she been in that place? So many. "Hutch, my Thursday appointment is to start the training class at Sanctum."

She felt him go still.

"You're training at Sanctum?"

"Yeah. I probably should have told you."

His hand moved over the curves of her ass. "Noelle, you need a safe word. Right now."

She bit back a whimper because he was making her crazy. "Why?"

"Because I'm on the edge. Because I've spent all this time thinking I was way too dirty for someone as sweet as you. Because you said you were horrified at the idea of weird sex stuff."

Huh. She guessed she had. It wasn't like she'd left him waiting too long, but she thought she probably shouldn't point that out. "Well, I was talking about orgies and swinging. Not BDSM. I've spent tons of time in physical therapy, so the torture that leads to something good doesn't seem weird to me at all."

She could feel his cock under her belly. It was thick and hard, and she wanted to see him naked. Want. Need. She was filled with it, and it felt good. She'd lived in her head for years now, ignoring her physical needs. All she'd cared about had been her research and building her lab. Just as she'd decided to make a concession to her other needs, she'd met this man and he was rocking her world.

His hand came down on her backside, a sharp shock to her system. "Noelle. Safe word."

"Chuckles." She shot that sucker out of her mouth fast because maybe she wasn't...it had hurt, but now, not so much. It hadn't taken more than a few seconds for heat to spike through her, and she was now in a weird place where she both dreaded and anticipated the next slap of his hand. But her safe word wasn't sexy. Should she have picked a sexy one? "Sorry. It was the name of my childhood dog. We named him that because he had the weirdest bark. It sounded like a laugh. I can pick..."

Another smack shut her mouth because she had to concentrate on breathing.

"You need to learn focus," Hutch proclaimed. "Oh, I'm sure the science whiz kid knows how to focus on a problem, but when we're alone together you're going to focus on me, and I'm damn straight going to focus on you. We're on the same page now. You're interested in the lifestyle, and I've been in it for a long time. Though you should understand I'm not even close to being full time. I like to play."

That worked for her. "The couple I know are pretty much play partners in the bedroom only. Though Remy will get bossy from time to time."

That big hand kept moving over her skin, stroking her. "I'll have to thank Lisa the next time I see her because I had no idea how I was going to play this vanilla. Now be still unless I hurt you or scare you."

"You're not going to scare me. I want to explore this, and you are so not scary." He was adorable and hot and sexy and…

She bit back a shriek because he'd meant business with that slap. It had been hard and sharp and sent a bolt through her system.

"That's right," he said, his voice going low. "Keep quiet or your neighbors are going to wonder what's happening. Do you think they'll be surprised that the sweet, innocent genius next door likes to get her ass slapped? Do you think they'll be horrified when they find you out in the open with a man fucking you with his fingers? Eating your pussy on your balcony in the middle of the night? Because I intend to do all of those things. If you don't stay quiet, I can always find a gag for that pretty mouth of yours. How scary am I now, Noelle?"

She thought about starting a lecture on how she was only beginning to explore and wasn't all that interested in gags of any kind, but his hand was right there, and Lisa had told her that there came a point in time when a sub had to indulge the Dom. "Very scary. Why don't we go to the bedroom?"

She had lots of neighbors. Sure it was dark out, but there was the possibility that someone had binoculars and happened to be up at this time of the night.

"It's too late for that." He pulled at the waist of her pajama bottoms and exposed her ass to the cool air. "Fuck, you're pretty."

He was looking at her ass. Staring at it and likely ignoring the fact that she had a bunch of scars. Some from the initial accident and many from the subsequent surgeries. She'd seen them in the mirror, contorting herself so she could get a glimpse after she'd been able to stand long enough to manage it.

But if he was saying he thought she was pretty, why shouldn't she believe it? His cock hadn't wilted at the sight. A woman didn't have to be perfect to be beautiful.

She felt…sexy.

She wriggled on his lap, trying to make him as on edge as she was.

He slapped her cheeks again. "I'm going to start your training, brat. Do you know what a brat is? I'm not talking about some nasty, snot-nosed kid. I'm talking about a cheeky little sub who gets her ass smacked and then fucked. Now answer my question because you forget I've done my homework on you. You haven't had a boyfriend in months. At least that's what your friend told me. How long has it been?"

How could he expect her to talk when she was bare ass and over his lap? "A long time. I don't remember the exact date or anything, but at least two years. I broke up with my boyfriend to concentrate on finishing my grad degree, and then I was starting my lab and I didn't…damn it, I didn't want anyone until I saw you."

"That makes me happy. Not the 'you haven't had sex' part. Like I said I wouldn't care if you'd had someone last night. I'm happy you want me because I took one look at you and lost my damn mind." His hand moved over her cheeks and then lower. "I asked because I want to take my time if it's been a while. I'll be honest. I pretty much want to take my time no matter what. Tell me your pussy's wet."

Her pussy had become the center of her whole world because his fingers were close. He hadn't pulled her pajama bottoms and underwear all the way down so they trapped her legs. Like he'd tied her up. "I'm very wet."

She could feel how wet she'd gotten. She wouldn't be able to sleep in those undies.

She gasped when she felt his finger slide between her thighs and over her labia. He was touching her. She was over his lap and his fingers were playing in her pussy and they were sitting on her balcony where anyone could see them.

It made her hotter than she'd ever been before.

Her initial observation had been correct. She was a little freaky.

She held onto his ankle as he gently pressed a finger deep inside her.

"You are going to feel like heaven around my cock," Hutch said on a groan. "I need you to tell me I can have you tonight. You can stop me at any point, but I need to hear you say yes."

He was killing her. That finger of his dipped in and teased, and then she felt him brush against her clit and she had to grit her teeth or Kyle might run out on the balcony with a gun in his hand. "I already said yes."

"You said yes to hopping on your bed and riding my cock to a mutually nice evening. I'm now asking you to say yes to me doing some filthy things to you, to me taking control and bending you to my will. My will includes a lot of bending, baby. I meant what I said. I'm going to lay you out on this couch and shove my face into your pussy, and if you say yes you'll spread your legs and let me. You will thank me for how well and thoroughly I'm going to devour you, and then take my cock in whatever position I want you in."

"Yes." She didn't even think about saying no. That word wasn't a blip on the radar because she wanted every dirty fantasy this man could give her.

She wasn't this girl. She wasn't the adventurous chick who had sex in crazy places.

Or maybe she was and she needed to accept it. She didn't have to be one thing, didn't have to pick between smart scientist and woman with a good sex life. She could be both.

And that meant she could have him. At least for tonight. She couldn't expect him to stick around. Their lives were far too different, but she could have him tonight.

His finger pressed in. "You're going to be fun to spank. You tell me if I do anything that makes you uncomfortable."

"I'm uncomfortable right now. You should press harder."

He smacked her cheek with his free hand. "Like I said, you're going to be a brat, baby. I can already tell. Lucky for you I quite like a brat."

He pressed on her clit, making her eyes close so she could concentrate on the feeling. He rubbed a circle with what felt like the pad of his thumb while another finger foraged deep.

He fucked her with that finger, all the while manipulating her clitoris with an expert hand. Every time she thought she was going to go over the edge, he drew back and made her groan.

"Oh, does my pretty sub want to come?"

This apparently was the frustrating part of D/s. She'd been told there were some aspects that would make her clench her teeth, and that getting a nasty Dom who liked to keep a sub on the edge was one of them. Lisa had told her that truth one day while sitting on the patio at Guidry's and frowning at her husband.

She'd then told Noelle that nothing in her life felt as good as the moment her Dom relented.

She hoped Hutch wasn't patient. "I'm willing to take whatever you want to give me, Sir."

"Fuck, this is going to be good." He pulled his hand from between her legs.

Well, that wasn't what she'd wanted. Before she had a chance to protest he stood, picking her up like she weighed nothing at all. He eased her back down, flipping her so she was sitting up. With a twist of his hand, he pulled her panties and PJ bottoms off and tossed them aside before dropping to his knees.

"I want your feet on the coffee table." He was standing so close she would have to spread her legs wide to obey that command.

That was what he wanted—her spread out so he could do anything he wanted to her.

She looked up at him. Even in the dark she could see the way his eyes ate her up, how rigid his every muscle was. He might be a hot nerd most of the time, a thoughtful, sexy man, but in this he was a predator, and she thought being Hutch's prey might be the most pleasurable experience of her life.

She forced her legs to work. There was still a bit of stiffness from what had happened earlier. She would be using braces for days when she needed to walk more than a few steps. But she could do this.

She felt exposed as she found the edge of the table with her feet and showed Hutch her pussy.

He was staring down at her. "I'm only going to say this once and I expect you to remember it. I never want to inhibit your pleasure or make you feel like you can't explore this to the fullest, but if I do or ask you to do anything that hurts…"

"I'll let you know." There was something sexy about a man who didn't treat her like an invalid, who didn't worry he was going to break her. She trusted him to stop if she asked him to, but it was good to have someone who trusted her to know her own limits.

She didn't want there to be any limits with this man.

"You do that," he murmured as though happy to get that out of the way so he could move on to what he wanted. Her. He dropped to his knees.

It was deliciously dirty. She was spread wide and not even completely naked. He'd managed to put her in a position that had a plump pillow to rest her lower back against. It was a position she would sit in and watch the city while she had her morning coffee. Except totally perverted because there was a dark head between her legs, the warmth of his mouth hovering over her.

And she didn't care. She wanted this, wanted to feel like nothing mattered in the whole world except Hutch's mouth on her pussy.

She watched as he started to move, felt the first long drag of his tongue against her tender flesh, and had to bite her lip to keep from crying out. It felt so good. It put her right back on the edge. He gave her everything he'd said he would—his lips and tongue and the sexy scrape of his teeth. He speared her, lapping up her arousal like it was the best dessert he'd ever been offered and then going back for more.

When he sucked her clit between his lips, she couldn't hold out a second longer. Her heart threatened to pound out of her chest as the wave of pleasure crashed over her.

Hutch surged up and captured her lips, kissing her and giving back her own taste. His tongue rubbed against hers, breath mingling as though he could absorb some of the pleasure he'd given her.

"Tell me yes one more time, Noelle."

Did he think she would start telling him no after that? "Yes. Yes, Sir."

There was no going back, and she didn't even want to try.

* * * *

Hutch was fairly certain he would come in his freaking jeans if he didn't get inside her soon. The good news was Noelle didn't look like she would care if this first session wasn't the longest.

She had a dreamy gaze in her eyes. He'd put that look there. He'd made that gorgeous, unbelievably smart woman forget everything but how hard he could make her come.

He glanced to his left and realized they weren't alone. Kyle was standing back from the sliding glass doors with a frown on his face and a gun in his hand, reminding Hutch that the man was here to be a bodyguard. One of the things they'd discussed was the balcony and how Kyle didn't want her out there alone. She hadn't been alone, but he would bet Kyle wouldn't consider him a good guard.

Kyle rolled his eyes and pointed around as if to show him all the places a sniper could be waiting to take Noelle's head off, and could he please fuck the client somewhere safer next time? Kyle proved he was able to get his point across with a couple of rude gestures.

It was a good thing because it calmed his dick down a bit. He gave Kyle a shrug and was grateful Noelle still had her eyes closed because while she'd been open in the moment, the idea that someone had actually watched her would likely have her closing off real fast.

He didn't want that. He certainly didn't want to explain to her that Kyle was only doing his job and they were lucky he hadn't opened the door and taken a position in front of them.

She probably also didn't want to know that when he'd tossed aside her bottoms and underwear, they'd gone through the railing of the balcony and were probably six floors down by now.

Yeah, he wasn't going to mention that either. He wanted her far too much, and now that he knew she was interested in D/s, he meant to have her as often as possible.

This was what he'd been waiting for—this feeling, this connection to a woman. He'd been drifting forever, and it felt good to have something ground him. He could focus on her, give her what she needed.

He knew he was already in too deep. It was too much and too fast, but he didn't care. For once in his life he wasn't going to overthink it. He was going to follow his instincts, and they had all flared to life when he'd gotten close to Noelle.

Her eyes finally came open and he realized he had a small window before her brain took over again. He didn't want that to happen. He scooped her up and started for the door that led back to her bedroom.

Noelle's arms wound around his neck. "I've been carried around a lot. No one ever made it feel sexy."

He started to close the door and heard a decisive click. Kyle was being an ass, reminding him he hadn't locked the door on his side. He clicked the lock closed and started for her bed. It was covered in a fluffy white comforter that she'd thrown back when she'd gotten up.

"Carrying you around should always be sexy. You are the sexiest thing I've ever seen," he replied as he set her on the bed. He wanted to see more of her. "Give me that shirt and let me see your breasts. The rest of you is fucking perfect. I want to see every inch of you."

She'd responded beautifully. Like she'd been made for him.

He could still taste her on his lips. He might go to his grave remembering how she'd tightened around him, how she'd come all over his tongue.

She'd liked it—all of it. She might only be starting to explore the lifestyle, but he would bet she'd found a bit of subspace in having him take control. Her job was all about her mighty brain. He would bet she forgot she had a body, too—a body with needs that he intended to take care of.

She pulled the T-shirt she'd been wearing over her head and tossed it aside. "Do I get to see you, Sir?" She frowned. "Do you like Sir?"

He wasn't going to talk about protocol right now. He moved in and kissed her again. "I like you. Tonight you can call me anything you like." Tomorrow they could talk about a contract. They could talk about him taking over her training and everything that would come with it.

When he thought about it, taking Noelle as a sub would make it easier to keep track of her. Yeah, that's what he'd tell the guys. What he'd tell her was the truth—that he was crazy about her.

He stepped back and decided to give her what she wanted. He tugged his shirt off and was really glad he hadn't given up his workout routine. His abs were one good thing that had come out of his time with McDonald. He stared at her for a moment, taking her in. "You're fucking perfect."

"And you are blind, but I'm okay with it. You know I'm never this comfortable with a guy. It's weird, but I knew these scars wouldn't scare you off."

She had a few scars on her lower back and a couple on her legs.

They showed how serious that accident had been, but he wasn't a man who worshipped perfection. She was beautifully Noelle, and the scar across her shoulder didn't detract from that. He reached out and touched it, brushing his fingers over the line that went from her shoulder blade to right above her breast. "Was this part of the accident, too?"

She nodded, her eyes on him. "The car flipped and there was jagged metal where I pulled myself out. It's the one that bugs me most."

Because it was the one she had to see in the mirror every day. He had one of those, too. He took her hand in his and brought it to the left side of his body, below his ribs. "This is the one I have to look at every day. It was a knife wound."

"From that woman who took you?"

Her fingers moved over that ancient scar, and he had to bite back a groan. He wasn't sure what magic this woman worked on him, but when she touched him his body came to life in a way it never had before. "No. She was actually excellent about not leaving scars. She had other methods of punishment for me. No. This is from when I was on the streets. I was sleeping in an alleyway and woke up to a guy with serious problems trying to gut me. I still dream about it from time to time, but I don't wake up fighting or anything. You're safe to sleep with me."

That time seemed so long ago. A complete lifetime. He wasn't alone now. He had a family, though they didn't share blood. It struck him how far he was from that lonely, scared boy. He was in a warm place now, and it was made infinitely warmer by her.

"Take off my jeans." He wanted to be skin to skin with her, wanted to get in that bed and mold his body to hers, wanted to sleep wrapped around her.

But first he wanted to know what it was like to be deep inside her.

She moved to the end of the bed, seated in front of him, and her head tilted up as she undid the fly of his jeans.

She licked her lips, but he wasn't sure he could handle that. He would come far too soon, and he couldn't wait another moment to fuck her. They had days and days to play. He would take her to

Sanctum and start her training. He would let her explore everything, but tonight he had to have her.

He stepped back and shoved his jeans down. "I don't trust myself to let you touch me too much."

Her lips curled up in the sweetest grin. "Do you think you'll like my touch?"

"Way too much." He kicked his jeans off. His boots were in the living room, so he moved toward her completely naked and comfortable being that way with her. He put his body between her legs and dropped his head down to meld their mouths together.

He loved kissing her. Her mouth was soft and yielding, her tongue sliding along his. He let his hands sink into the silk of her hair, and he gave over to the sensation of being surrounded by her. Her hands stroked down his back to cup his ass. His cock brushed her belly and started an insistent pulse that could only end one way.

And then he remembered that he wasn't exactly prepared. He hadn't shoved a condom in his pocket or anything. He hadn't started the day thinking it would end this way. He cupped her breast, feeling her nipple against his palm. "Noelle, baby, do you have some condoms?"

Her eyes came open. "What? No. I don't."

"I'll be right back." He might have one in his bag. Might. Fuck. He needed to be way more prepared.

His bag was on the sofa. Hopefully Kyle had gone back to bed. He opened the door and had no such luck.

Kyle sighed, shook his head, and handed him a line of condoms, proving he was better prepared than Hutch. "Dumbass." Kyle turned and started back toward the guest room. "I left the military for this job."

Yeah, Kyle should get used to shenanigans because they went hand in hand with being a McKay-Taggart employee. No shame washed through Hutch, just a deep gratitude that someone had condoms. Otherwise he would be running into some 24-hour store begging.

Noelle had gotten into bed and covered herself with a sheet by the time he came back.

That was not happening.

He gripped the sheet and pulled it back. "Don't cover yourself when we're playing. I want to see every inch of you. When we're playing, you're mine. If you want to stop, that's fine, but I don't think you want to."

He pulled off one of the condoms, placing the rest on her dresser. He ripped it open and found her staring at him.

"I think you're perfect, too," she said quietly.

He was far from, but he would take it. He stroked himself as he stared down at her, getting himself hard and ready. She watched him, her eyes on his cock. She bit her bottom lip, and her nipples were a deep pink and stiff. She still wanted him.

He laid himself out, wanting to give her the control in this case. Later, he could turn her and twist her and fuck her any way he wanted. But this first time he wanted her to go at any pace she liked. He'd eaten her pussy in an attempt to make sure she came, but he wanted to watch her come again, wanted to see the look on her face, know they were together in this moment.

"I want you on top. I want to watch you," he said, offering her his body.

"You want to push me." She pressed up off the bed. "I've never been on top."

He shook his head. "I want to watch you. Why wouldn't you..." Was it hard for her to be on top? Did the position hurt her in some way? "I want to give you what you want."

She smiled and moved over his body. "I like the fact that you don't immediately think of my legs and whether or not they work. I don't know how this is going to go. Let's find out."

She was awkward and gorgeous as she straddled him and took his cock in hand. He bit back a groan as he felt the heat of her pussy start to surround him.

He let his hands find her hips. "You're the sub, baby. You're the only one who gets to tell people what your limits are, and we can explore them all. In that, yes, I do want to push you and I want you to push me, too."

But right now he wanted her to fuck him. His eyes threatened to roll to the back of his head as she started to lower herself onto his cock. He watched as she gasped and adjusted to take in every inch. He tilted his hips up, wanting there to be absolutely nothing between them.

"I think I like this," she whispered as she started to move. "It feels really good."

It felt like heaven.

He glanced up, and there was a look of wonder in her eyes that had his hands gripping her harder as though she might disappear if he didn't hold on to her.

"I like this a lot, Hutch. It feels different." She moved up and then back down.

It took her a minute to find a good rhythm, but he helped her. He thrust up, every muscle in his body tense and wanting. "You feel different."

Different than anything he'd had before. He matched her, finally synching up and letting himself go. He let go of anything but how good it felt to be here with her. Her head dropped back and he felt her tighten around him, sending him straight over the blissful edge.

She dropped onto his chest and he wrapped his arms around her, perfectly content that he was still inside her.

"I think you could push me a little more, Sir," she whispered in his ear.

He flipped her over and kissed her.

He intended to push her all night long.

Chapter Seven

Hutch finished up the toast and stretched, pure satisfaction running through him. He couldn't remember the last time he'd slept so well. He'd wrapped himself around her and slept like a baby.

He'd thought about waking her up with sex, but decided to prove he could feed her other hungers, too. She had to go back to work, and he was going to make sure she was ready.

Damn, but he was in a good mood this morning.

"Is any of that for me?" Kyle was already dressed, wearing slacks and a button-down shirt. He looked smooth and polished.

It was a good thing his Noelle seemed to prefer scruffy with a hint of nerd. Hutch was still all comfy in pajama bottoms and the T-shirt he'd worn the day before. "I was getting ready to cook the eggs. Scrambled okay? There's coffee in the pot."

"Excellent. If they're good, I might forgive you for what you put me through last night." Kyle reached for a mug. "I've seen far too much of you."

Hutch shrugged because he wasn't about to feel bad about that. It had been one of the best nights of his life. "Get used to it. I heard you're in the training program at Sanctum. You'll see a lot of everyone once you get on the dungeon floor."

"Yeah, not sure that's going to happen. Not at Sanctum." Kyle took a sip of black coffee. "I'm in this training program because The Club doesn't have one."

The Club was another BDSM club run by a man named Julian Lodge. Lodge was one of the richest men in Texas, and he'd supplied much of the seed money for McKay-Taggart. In a lot of ways, The Club had been where Ian Taggart had learned how to run Sanctum. "Why would you play there?"

"Uh, I love my mom. I do not need to see that or hear about it or even be in the same space where it happens." A shudder went through Kyle. "Dude, I know that lots of siblings play in the same club, but this is my mom and stepdad. It's not happening. Julian is offering me a membership because he understands that as some of the kids grow up, they're not going to want to play where their parents play, so he and Tag are switching off where they can. My brother's thinking about doing it too."

Hutch snorted. "Don't expect those kids to go to Julian's. I can see where that would work for you and David, but I don't see it happening with the younger set. Nah, they'll start their own and scare the shit out of their parents."

"My sister already scares the shit out of me," Kyle admitted. "Carys is fifteen and basically dating two guys, and we all ignore it. I'm convinced my stepdad genuinely thinks she's simply hanging out with two guy friends—who buy her things, and when they think no one's looking, hold her hands. Both of them."

He didn't see what was wrong with it. After all, Carys had two hands. "It works for Tristan's parents."

Tristan was Jake, Serena, and Adam's oldest kiddo. He and Liam's son, Aidan, had been trailing after Carys since they were all babies. Hutch thought it was sweet. And it really did work for Jake and Serena and Adam. They'd been married for fifteen years without much drama. The threesome still played every week at Sanctum. Serena seemed perfectly happy to have two men holding her hands.

"Yeah, well, Carys is in high school. It's not known to be the most accepting place," Kyle explained. "From what I can tell no one's outed them yet because Aidan goes to a different school, but at some point, it's going to come out and my sister will bear the brunt of it. No matter how confident Carys is, that's going to hurt."

He didn't like to think about that. He'd watched those kids grow up, and now they were old enough that the world was going to start biting at them, taking its share of their souls. "I'll take care of anyone who hurts her."

"I think that's my job," Kyle replied. "And trust me, Sean can take care of her, but this is something we can't fix. Maybe I'm wrong. Maybe kids these days will shrug and threesomes will become a thing, but I worry. I'm also worried about what happened last night. Did you two talk about how this is going to work now?"

They'd talked about important stuff, and this evening they'd talk some more. "I'm going to write up a contract between us. And I promise to always carry a condom from now on. Don't tell Tag about that."

The big boss had a thing about condoms. Probably because he had five kids.

A devilish grin came over Kyle's face. "I'll probably get a raise for saving you." He sobered. "Seriously, have you two talked this out? You started a sexual relationship last night, and while you might be accustomed to one-night stands, she is not. You've read the reports on her. She hasn't even dated in a couple of years. I seriously doubt she's been tearing through guys. It's not going to help us protect her if you break the client's heart."

"Why would you think I would break her heart?" He cracked a couple of eggs into a bowl. Then he looked at Kyle and cracked five more. He was a big dude. "I'm serious about her."

"You're serious about a woman you met yesterday?"

He shrugged, a light feeling coming over him as he beat the eggs and added some milk before pouring them into the pan. It didn't seem like it was just yesterday. The morning before seemed light years behind him. "What can I say? When you know, you know. I'm not saying we're getting married or anything." That would be crazy, so he wasn't going to say it. Not out loud, but some instinct told him Noelle was the one, the magical stupid one his married friends talked about. "But we're together. Don't worry about me hurting her. I'm going to take excellent care of her."

Kyle's expression told him he still wasn't sure. "See that you do. You need to check your texts. Big Tag wants you in the office this morning. I'll take Noelle to work and see if I can't get a job."

He wanted to argue, but sometime in the night he'd decided Kyle was right. He had the best in, and he should take it. "You're sure you can handle undercover? Jessica Layne is smart, and she'll see through you if you aren't careful."

"I think I can handle it," Kyle said with the confidence of a man who'd done undercover. Though the files on him didn't report he had. He'd been a Naval officer. The longer Hutch was with him the less he seemed like an everyday military guy. "I'm not going to forget that this is an op and we've got work to do."

Hutch turned back to the eggs and hoped Kyle wasn't the reason he was being called into the office. If Kyle expressed his worries to Tag, there could be trouble. He wasn't about to allow himself to be pulled off this case.

"Say hi to MaeBe for me," Kyle said. "Tell her it took a while, but my spine is finally straightening out."

It was good to remember he wasn't the only one who'd chased after a woman the day before. "Are you going to ask her out?"

Kyle seemed flummoxed at that question. He stopped and went still for a moment.

"It's not a hard question." Hutch watched him. It was odd to see that deer-in-the-headlights look on the tough guy. "You like the girl. You ask the girl out. You see if the girl likes you."

He shook his head. "No. I'm not in a good place for that. I was just…I had fun with her yesterday. It's been a long time since I was around someone as carefree as MaeBe. I don't like her that way. Does anyone else think I like her like that?"

There was an odd, almost panicked undertone to his question. "I don't think I've heard any rumors about you."

Kyle's face smoothed out, and he was back to the neutral expression he usually wore. "Good, because while I enjoyed spending the afternoon with her, we're not compatible."

Hutch kind of thought they were. MaeBe and Kyle had been in synch in a way he rarely saw two people who didn't know each other be. They'd smiled more in each other's presence. He'd caught MaeBe looking at Kyle when he turned away.

Something about Kyle's obviously emotional response made

Hutch think.

Then he wasn't thinking about anything but Noelle because the door came open and she walked out wearing a pretty green dress and leaning heavily on her cane. She smiled brightly until she caught sight of Kyle. Then she gave him a polite nod, as though trying to hide the fact that they'd gone at it hard the night before.

"Good morning, Kyle, Hutch. I hope you both slept well," she said.

"It was hard to sleep when you two were..." Kyle began.

Hutch snatched the coffee mug out of his hand. "You can get your own, asshole."

Noelle had gone the sweetest shade of pink as she approached the bar. "I thought we were quiet."

"I'm your bodyguard." Kyle got a mug and simply poured another cup. "I don't sleep deeply when I'm on assignment. I woke up when Hutch went onto the balcony. I was willing to let him die, but then you joined him. Could the two of you find a place that isn't out in the open with at least five sniper perches available? Don't blush, Noelle. Or maybe do. Get it all out of your system because on Thursday, the freaky stuff starts."

She hauled herself up on the barstool. Had he been too rough with her? She'd been through a lot the day before and he'd spent the whole evening twisting her around so he could get his dick inside her.

He got her a cup of coffee and her sugar jar and put it in front of her. "Do you want some cream, baby?"

Her eyes widened slightly, as though she was surprised by the affectionate name. Well, she'd better get used to it.

"No. Just sugar, thank you. And thanks for making breakfast. I usually skip it."

Not while he was taking care of her. "No problem. Breakfast is my specialty. I'll make some pancakes tomorrow."

"That might make up for what I went through last night," Kyle snarked under his breath before sitting down next to Noelle. "So are you going to call Kai and tell him or should Hutch do it?"

"Tell Kai what?" Noelle asked.

Hutch plated her eggs and gave her a piece of toast, sliding it in front of her before plating his and Kyle's.

"I'll deal with Kai." He wasn't going to make her explain to Kai, who would likely tell her she was moving far too fast.

He took a bite of his toast and thought about trying to move them all to her dining room table. There was a spot for him at the bar, but he liked sitting across from her.

"Why would you deal with Kai?" Noelle stirred sugar into her coffee before reaching for the toast and butter. "I've had all my appointments with him."

There was a lot of butter in her fridge. Salted and unsalted, and a crock on the counter. She also had a ton of baking ingredients. They would make an excellent team. He would make dinner and she could be…make…nah, no matter how he looked at it, she was dessert.

"To let him know you don't need the training class," he explained. "It's okay. You can train with me in private and get the same certification you would at the end of the class. It'll be fun."

She went still for a moment, and he got a sinking feeling in the pit of his stomach.

"Hutch, I'm not leaving the class," she said quietly. "I want to take the class. I've been looking forward to it for a long time, and I'm not giving it up. I don't know why you would think I would."

Kyle hopped off his chair, taking his plate with him. "And I'm out of here. I'm going to finish getting ready and we'll head into the office."

Hutch ignored Kyle. Maybe he wasn't understanding her. Or she wasn't understanding him. "You agreed to be with me last night."

"Yes, last night." She carefully enunciated the words. "I didn't think that meant I had to quit my class. I don't see what the two have to do with each other."

Good, this was merely a misunderstanding. He could fix that. "You're not quitting. You're taking a different route to get to the same place. It's okay. I can give you the same training."

She shook her head. "But you can't. It's not the same at all. I want to go to the class and be with other people who are starting out. You know everything already. The relationship would be totally different. And honestly, I was looking forward to making some friends. I enjoyed last night, but I didn't think you were offering me anything permanent."

And it struck him suddenly that she didn't *want* anything permanent.

How had this gone so wrong? He'd looked at her and thought this was a woman who would need some permanency. "I was offering to take care of you the way I would a sub."

"But I'm not a sub yet," she corrected. "I haven't taken the class. I can't know for sure."

She thought a class could tell her that? He already knew the truth. This was a woman who would enjoy being sexually submissive, and honestly, who could use a partner who would top her from time to time in real life. "Trust me, you're a sub. It's okay. I told you I would take care of you and I will."

"I'm taking the class." A stubborn look came into her eyes. "I'm sorry if that upsets you."

She wanted to take a class where some other Dom would put his hands on her body? She wanted to take a class where almost everyone fucked their training partner. God knows he had.

She didn't want him to train her, didn't want him to be her Dom. The truth slowly dawned on him. He'd seen what he'd wanted to see. He'd fallen fast and hard for the first time in his life and couldn't bear the idea that it wasn't reciprocated. Hadn't he learned?

She'd wanted a fuck and he'd been willing to give it to her.

And honestly, why would he think the incredibly smart scientist with the perfect family would want him for anything but sex? Her dad was a sheriff and his dad had been an abusive asshole. Her stepmom was some kind of medical superhero. His stepmom had chucked him out on the street. Her father would figure out how much time Hutch had spent in jail.

"I'm not trying to hurt you," she said, sounding uncertain for the first time.

He turned away and put his plate close to the sink. A numbness had descended and his appetite was a hundred percent gone. "No problem. I misunderstood."

"I think you might be misunderstanding now. I'm not saying I don't like you. I really do. But I want to take the class."

"Cool. You should."

He heard her sigh. "I'm not sure what's happening here. Last night was great, but I didn't think you would stop going to Sanctum because we spent one night together. I thought we might see each other there after I finished the class."

He thought he'd go to Sanctum with her. He hadn't wanted to go lately, but last night had given him fresh energy. And now it was all gone. He rinsed off the skillet he'd used. "Good. I tend to play on Saturdays. Kyle can watch you then. I'm sure by the time you finish the training class, we'll have cleared up your security problems." He turned. "I'm going to go take a shower and get ready for work. Kyle can drive you in."

"You're not coming with us?" She turned and looked so vulnerable and sweet that he wanted to carry her back to bed and convince her that he was a better bet than he was.

But it was time to be realistic. It was time to save whatever dignity he had. "No. I have to go into the office. I don't know how late I'll be."

"I feel like I'm not explaining well enough," she began.

He held a hand up because he'd gotten the message loud and clear. She might be willing to sleep with him, but she wouldn't change her plans for him. She wasn't going to consider getting serious about him. He didn't need to hear all her reasons. He knew them by heart. "It's cool. What happened last night was nice. I thought it would be fun to continue that while we were working together."

"I never said I didn't want that."

She wanted the sex, but she was going to keep her options open. Yeah, he'd heard that before. He wasn't anyone's serious guy. He was the dude who kept candy at his desk and got the waitress off in a broom closet. Noelle was the woman who might win a Nobel Prize one day.

"We'll take it as it comes," he replied because even though she'd broken his heart he wasn't sure he would be able to resist if she invited him into her bed again.

He would have to remember what it was. Sex. Temporary sex.

That was all he was worth.

* * * *

She'd seriously fucked things up with Hutch, and she wasn't sure what had happened. She sat next to Kyle, who was driving her sedan, and kind of wished she was on the train and they'd left the car for Hutch. He was going to have to switch a couple of times to get to the McKay-Taggart building. It was a straight shot to Genedyne. One train, three stops. It was faster on the train because they didn't have to deal with traffic, but Kyle had insisted. Something about it being easier to watch her in a car than on a train.

And Hutch had agreed. He'd nodded and given her that pleasant smile that didn't come anywhere near his eyes.

He'd made breakfast for her and she'd kicked him in the gut.

"Should I turn on the radio?" It was so quiet that it was awkward.

"I'm fine." Kyle kept his eyes on the road, which wasn't hard because they weren't actually moving. They were sitting. Like she'd warned him about.

She fell back into silence as they moved two car lengths before the light turned again.

"Why did he think I wouldn't go to the training class? We hadn't talked about it at all so I'm confused on why he thought I would cancel." She asked the question out loud before she could think better of it. She didn't have many guy friends, didn't have many friends at all when she thought about it.

Kyle finally looked her way, his mouth in a deep frown. "Uh, what station do you want it on? Yeah, we should turn on the radio."

Coward. She knew she should go back to her inner monologue now, but Kyle had kind of already put himself in the middle of this. "Did you watch me have sex on my balcony last night?"

"No. I watched the area around you to make sure no one was pointing a red dot your way," he corrected.

"Do you know what I look like when I don't have panties on?" She wasn't letting him get out of this one. He was her best resource— her only resource. She didn't know any of Hutch's other friends. If MaeBe had been here, she would have asked her, but that wasn't how her morning had gone.

First there'd been the horrifically awkward fight with a man she might be crazy about. Then there had been the notes posted to every door in the building reminding tenants that throwing items from the balcony was a fineable offense. She'd shaken her head and wondered what asshole had done that only to walk outside to the scene of her underwear being picked out of an oak tree by one of the landscape guys.

So no. No, she wasn't giving in for Kyle's comfort.

"I got a glimpse, but it wasn't a perverted thing," Kyle insisted. "It was very professional. When I go into professional mode, I don't see things the way I normally would."

"It's good to know my hootch was a mere distraction. I'm glad to know it. Why did Hutch act like I kicked his favorite puppy this morning?"

Kyle sighed. "I don't know Hutch all that well."

How to make a man talk? Maybe she should go back to her teenaged years. "Well, I should change the subject then. You know, I thought I felt some PMS cramps coming on, but let me tell you, there's nothing like a good orgasm to banish them completely. My cramps can be…"

Kyle groaned. "Do you women take a class on this shit?"

Oddly, she rather thought if she wanted to talk about her period with Hutch he would listen. "I can keep it up for days. Do you know how hard it is to use a tampon when you're in a wheelchair?"

Kyle talked and fast. "He's jealous. He's painfully and obviously jealous. And the fact that you didn't get that makes me feel real damn sorry for the dude. I'm going to be honest. I gave him a lecture this morning on not breaking *your* heart."

"Why would he break my heart?"

"Because you seemed like the kind of chick who couldn't sleep with a guy just for sex. Not that there's anything wrong with that, but you seem like…" He stopped as though realizing he was about to say something insulting.

"Just say it, Kyle." She'd rather know the truth.

A low grumble came out of him, like a cranky pit bull. "Fine. You seemed like you might be clingy. Turns out Hutch is the clingy one."

She didn't like the sound of that. Clingy reminded her of how she'd been when she'd first left the hospital. She'd clung to her father for years, clung to that stupid chair because she'd been afraid she wouldn't be strong enough to do what she'd needed to do.

Later, when she'd reflected on that horrible year between the accident and her stepmom coming into her life, she knew what she'd really been doing by refusing physical therapy. She'd been punishing herself because her mother had died and she'd lived. She'd been in shock, and only her stepmom had been strong enough to risk everything to drag her out of it.

She didn't want to be clingy ever again.

"I don't think he was being clingy," she said quietly. "I think we made a nice connection. I think the sex was good." That was an understatement. It had been the best sex of her life, and she wasn't sure why she'd been cool this morning. Perhaps because she'd woken up and wanted nothing more than to walk right out and coax him back into bed.

She'd wanted to cling to him. Yes, that was why she'd put a bit of distance between them. She'd dreamed of him, and it was all happening way too fast. He was already important to her, and she didn't think that was such a good idea.

"Oh, he was clinging hard, but I think you managed to detach him." Kyle made it through the light this time. "He was thinking you'd settled something the night before. You hadn't. You set him straight, and now you can both move on."

She didn't want to move on. She barely had time to understand there was a place to move on from. "I only wanted to go to the class. I wasn't trying to break things off with him."

Kyle chuckled. "But he understands the class, and that's why he's all jealous and shit."

"I'm not walking in and immediately having sex with my training Dom," she said with a huff. She'd thought about it, but she hadn't even met the man yet, and if she was exploring a relationship with Hutch, she certainly wouldn't cheat on him.

"Most people do by the end because it's an intimate experience," Kyle pointed out. "And that's what you want. At least that's what I heard when you talked about it. You want the experience, and Hutch knows what that means."

She did want the experience. She wanted what her aunt had found at the club—a network of friends who were also counted as family. If she let Hutch train her, she would always be Hutch's sub. She wouldn't simply be Noelle. She wouldn't find her own friends, and she couldn't count on the man forever. The most likely scenario was that they'd had an odd bonding experience when she'd been attacked the day before, and it had led them to an intimacy that wouldn't hold up in the real world. They would sleep together during this crisis, and then it would fall apart when they went back to their own spaces.

And she would be devastated because Kyle was right about the fact that she usually felt something for the men she'd slept with. She felt so much for Hutch. If she let herself, she could fall in love with the man.

She'd hated that look in his eyes, like she'd killed some light there.

"He'll get over it," Kyle said as he finally turned down the road that led to Genedyne. "And hey, who knows, maybe when you're done with training you'll want to play with him. If he ever goes back to the club."

"MaeBe told me he was a member there."

"Yeah, but from what I understand, he hasn't been going regularly." Kyle pulled into the parking garage, and the monitor overhead picked up the sticker on her windshield and let them in. "He's been…I don't know…looking for something lately, according to his friends. But don't worry about it. He's a good guy. He'll find it someday. He was moving way too fast with you."

She'd felt it, too. "We made a connection."

Kyle seemed to think about that for a moment. "What you have is insane chemistry. It happens sometimes, and it feels like the best thing in the world. It's incredible and addictive, and it doesn't mean you're in love. It means some people fuck together better than they do with others. Sex isn't love. It's a biological function we're taught to pretty up so we forget we're animals at the core."

Well that had gone dark fast. "You don't believe humans can love each other?"

"Of course I do. I don't think that sexual chemistry equals love, even though it can feel like it," Kyle insisted. "I think love is more than passion. Love is about the quiet times, being comfortable. It's about friendship every bit as much as it is about sex. You can have the best sex in your life and if the person you're having it with isn't good for you, it's not love, and no amount of trying to make it love will fix things."

He pulled into the parking spot reserved for her. It was one of the best spots in the building. This row was close to the elevators, the spaces larger than the tiny ones on the floors above. It was another perk that came with being the head of a lab, one she rarely used, but when she'd offered to let Pete use it, he'd paled and said no one wanted Jessica to catch a non-lead using the spots.

She wasn't trying to make last night into some kind of love thing. It was what it was. Good sex, and she liked Hutch. Really liked Hutch. "Should I talk to him?"

"Yes. *Him.* You should talk to him." Kyle suddenly sounded enthusiastic. He put the car in park. "You should have talked to him before you slept with him. I'm sorry. I'm putting that on you when it should be on Hutch. You were looking for a good time. He was looking for something more. He should have talked to you and figured out you weren't on the same page."

"I wasn't looking for a good time." She slid out of the car and grabbed her braces. She hated using them, but the cane wasn't going to do it after what had happened in the locker room. It would be days before she would be back on her cane.

Hutch hadn't seemed to mind.

"It's okay." Kyle shut the door and hit the button to lock it up. "You don't have to make excuses. Sex for sex's sake is normal and healthy. But I would suggest you think about it before you hop in bed with him again. He's looking for something you're not, and you could hurt him. And I say that knowing I'm going to get kicked out to the couch again. Did I mention your couch sucks? It is not comfortable."

"Yes, it is." She sat on that couch and watched TV all the time. Sometimes she fell asleep when she didn't want to go to bed.

Hutch had been the best body pillow ever. She'd wrapped herself around him and slept like a baby for once.

"You ever laid your six-foot-three-inch body out on that sucker?" Kyle stopped as a familiar Maserati pulled up and the driver's side window rolled down.

"Hey." Jessica looked Kyle up and down like he was a glorious package wrapped up for her. "Long time no see."

Kyle gave her a smooth smile. "You said something about a job. I want to get off my brother's girlfriend's couch."

Jessica's perfect red lips parted. "Excellent. Meet me up in my office. I'll get your paperwork started." She turned slightly Noelle's way. "LaVigne, I need to see you, too. I'll come down to your lab this afternoon."

Her stomach did a flip. That didn't sound good. Maybe the job Hutch was doing would be over way sooner than she'd dreamed. "Of course."

Jessica winked at Kyle and then her tires squealed as she took off.

"What's the female equivalent of swinging a big dick?" Kyle asked.

She didn't know, but it might be every single thing her boss did. "You should go on ahead. I'm moving slow today."

Kyle's eyes rolled. "Yeah, I'm eager to get up there and fend off Lady Ten Hands. Nah, it's better to keep her waiting. See, Hutch should have kept you waiting."

She frowned up at him. "I can't decide if you're telling me I should stay away from him or trying to make me feel like crap so I try this thing with Hutch again."

A wistful smile crossed his handsome face. "I don't know. Maybe both. I feel for the guy, but you're smarter than he is. You don't really know him. I would say try again, but it's hard to go back. I've found you get one shot at doing something right."

And she'd blown hers. They'd blown theirs by going too fast.

Her heart felt heavy, but she couldn't throw herself into a relationship with a man she barely knew. She just couldn't.

She followed after Kyle and hoped the day didn't take a worse turn.

Chapter Eight

"Thank you for joining us, Señor Grumpy Face." Big Tag sank into his chair at the head of the conference room table.

Right back where he started. Wasn't that the story of his life? One step forward, two steps back and shoved to the street.

He was in a fucking mood. He glanced around the room. Big Tag was there, but Charlotte was not. In her place sat Adam Miles, and that meant something serious had happened. Adam didn't work for McKay-Taggart anymore and hadn't for years. He was the head of his own firm. The two companies worked closely together, though, and Adam was always around to help with a crisis.

Just what he needed.

He slid into a chair as the door opened again and MaeBe walked in. Today's outfit consisted of bright green tights and a black skater dress that went oddly well with her combat boots.

"Good morning, boss. Morning, big boss." She waved Adam's way. "Mr. Miles."

Adam gave her a friendly smile. "It's Adam, MaeBe. I'm just a guy."

He was a guy who'd built an insanely successful company that had changed the industry. Adam had gotten used to the techies of the world kind of worshiping him.

"She's calling you mister because you're old, not because she respects you," Big Tag said with a roll of his eyes.

Big Tag and Adam had a weird thing that had been going on for as long as Hutch could remember. They played pranks and gave each other shit more than any of the others.

"I'm not old," Adam insisted.

"She's twenty-five. To her you're old as dirt," Big Tag explained.

"Uhm, I totally respect you, Mr. Miles. You're a giant in my world." MaeBe settled in beside Hutch. She leaned in. "Did I do something wrong?"

He shook his head. MaeBe had only been around for a year and had yet to get a full dose of Big Tag and Adam's unmistakable chemistry. "Nah, it's the way they flirt."

Adam coughed, nearly spitting out the coffee he'd been drinking.

Big Tag simply laughed, proving he was perfectly comfortable with himself.

"We do not flirt," Adam corrected. "He's an asshole and I have to defend myself."

Big Tag gave him a once-over. "If I swung that way, it could happen. He'd be a good sub after some proper training."

Adam pointed a finger Big Tag's way. "I am not a sub."

Big Tag shrugged. "In some weird parallel universe, I would bet you are, and trust me, you wouldn't be bottoming for Jake. MaeBe, you got any idea why Hutch stalked through the office like Godzilla earlier? He made small children cry."

"I did not." He might not be in a good mood, but he wasn't a monster.

"Yasmin said you didn't even say hello, and she had her daughter with her, and yes, she did cry," Big Tag insisted.

"I have no idea what you're talking about," MaeBe replied with wide, innocent eyes. "He seemed perfectly normal to me. And Yasmin's little girl was crying because she wants a puppy. Like real bad. There's an adoption drive in my neighborhood this afternoon, but Yasmin doesn't have any personal days left."

Big Tag made a gagging sound. "Not only did you cover for your boss, now I have to lose my receptionist for the afternoon so she can pick up some sad-sack dog who will poop on her floor. You're working reception."

MaeBe sat up straighter. She never seemed to mind covering the phones. "Absolutely, boss."

Excellent. Everyone was getting what they wanted except him. "Why am I here?"

He wasn't sure he wanted to be back at Noelle's, but he knew he didn't want to be here. He should go to his place and work from there, but he'd stopped by before he'd come to the office and been struck by how little warmth there was there. Unlike Noelle's, which was covered in pictures of her family and friends, his house had blank walls and utilitarian furnishings. It felt empty.

Like his life.

Adam nodded Ian's way. "Yeah, I see what you mean."

He wasn't playing around right now. "I have work to do. I'll be in my office if you need me."

"You're not going anywhere." Tag shifted from mildly amused to that blank expression that let Hutch know he meant business. "We've had a couple of developments in Noelle LaVigne's case."

His gut tightened because whatever Tag was about to tell him wasn't good, and if Adam was sitting here rather than running his own company, then it was probably bad. "What is it?"

"First of all, I ran a check on the security guard you asked me to look into. He's definitely DPD," Tag explained. "Brighton told me he couldn't work with us on this one, and that tells me we're caught in something serious."

"Chris Taylor is a veteran detective who moved onto a major crimes task force six weeks before he took on this second job of his." Adam rested his hands on the table as he talked. "Brighton might be loyal to his department, but we can always find someone willing to give up some intel."

"Brighton would talk in a heartbeat if he thought someone was in danger. Brighton's unwillingness means that Chris Taylor is working something serious. One of the things he's known for is working well with the feds," Tag explained.

The knot in his stomach got tighter. How serious was this and how was Noelle involved? "So we think we've got feds on this?"

"That's what I want MaeBe to figure out." Big Tag passed her a folder. "I need you to do a deep dive on Genedyne and Jessica Layne. I want to know everything about this woman, including all the nasty rumors about her on the Deep Web. You know they're out there. I want to figure out who's looking into her and why. Check into Chris Taylor, too. I'd like to know if something in his background makes him suited for this particular job. If there is, it might give us a clue about what he's looking into."

MaeBe nodded, taking the file. "Will do. The rumors about Jessica Layne are numerous."

"I want to hear them all." Now that Kyle was moving into the woman's circle, they needed to know everything about her. "I've got some contacts who might be able to help."

He kept up with his old group of hacktivists. Most of them were married with families, but a few were still active. He could throw out a couple of lines and see if he caught anything. The Deep Web thrived on rumors and gossip.

"Do that, but we've got something else we'd like you to check into." Tag looked to MaeBe. "I'd like something on Jessica Layne this afternoon. Thank you, MaeBe."

She stood, taking her tablet and the folder with her. "I know when my clearance level has been reached. Fine. But it will be hard to do since I'm covering the phones."

She didn't even flinch when Tag grunted, proving she'd been around long enough to speak Tag. That was his you-got-yourself-into-it grunt.

The door closed and Tag's attention was once again on Hutch. "She was a good hire. She didn't even tell me you're upset because you slept with the client and then apparently got the cold shoulder from her."

"Seriously? Damn. I didn't expect that," Adam said. "Are you sure? Isn't Hutch usually the one who slips out the door before his lady love awakens?"

"You've been reading too many of your wife's books. Hutch doesn't have to slip out of the door. Well, not out of the door of like an apartment or a house. He's slipped out of lots of closets. You know his upper body strength must be off the charts," Tag mused. "Some of those closets are small. He's got to be picking them up."

"I was thinking he's super stretchy," Adam countered.

He managed to tamp down his irritation. "I take it Kyle's been talking."

Big Tag's jaw went tight, and he sat back. "He writes a detailed report, and he's sending them to the head of his department every morning. Fisher thought I should see this one since it involved a developing relationship. That was how Kyle put it in his report. I read the subtext. I'm right about you sleeping with Noelle?"

"It's okay because I apparently was neither stretchy enough or upper body strong enough for her." He wasn't going to let the humiliation get him down. It was his old friend. "So it's not going to be a problem."

It was good to know Kyle was a tattletale. Although at least he'd been somewhat discreet. Big Tag could read between almost any line though.

"She told you she didn't like the sex?" Adam asked.

"I am not doing this. I made a mistake. I'll fix it." He'd thought about it a lot. There was a simple solution, and he thought Noelle would appreciate it. They didn't need another awkward encounter. "The truth of the matter is it's not necessary for me to stay at Noelle's. Kyle is the bodyguard. I can come and go as needed."

"That would have been an option had you not introduced yourself around as her boyfriend," Big Tag shot back. "I think there would be a bunch of questions if you left and your so-called brother was living with her. Unless you haven't met any of her friends yet. How did you introduce yourself when you went against Genedyne security and found Noelle in the locker room?"

"I suspect you know exactly how many people I've met." Kyle seemed thorough. So his plan to drop all the in-person work into Kyle's lap seemed like a long shot now. Or a no shot. Like his relationship with Noelle. "I'll handle it."

"See that you do," Big Tag intoned. "So I sent MaeBe away for a reason."

Now they would get to why Adam was here. Everything he'd heard so far would have been handled by McKay-Taggart. "All right. Is this about the case? Because I trust MaeBe implicitly."

"Not about this you won't." Tag nodded Adam's way.

"Yesterday Jake met with a member of the Senate about the search for her missing daughter," Adam explained. "Julia Ennis was reported missing in Hong Kong, where she'd been working with the American embassy there. That was three months ago. The government hasn't been able to find her. Her mother is frustrated."

Adam passed him a folder.

Hutch pulled it toward him. Almost everything they did now was done on tablets. If Adam was giving him a hard copy it was because whatever was in that folder was sensitive enough, he didn't want any chance of it getting hacked.

He opened the folder and saw a picture of a stunning woman with long blonde hair and green eyes. She stared at the camera with a ready smile, but there was something cold about her. "This is the daughter? And you said she was working with the embassy, not at the embassy?"

"Yes. She actually works for a large conglomerate. She speaks three different languages and has a business degree from Yale. She's in charge of coordination between the arms of the company, and apparently that means she travels a lot," Adam explained. "From what we've been able to put together, she was on the road roughly thirty weeks last year alone."

"What does this have to do with my case?" Hutch asked.

"You've gotten impatient." Tag took over. "You know I've tried to stay out of the spy shit for the last seven years."

Hutch sat up straighter because that statement was correct. The last seven years had been peaceful in their way. Tag had told the Agency to fuck off, and he'd concentrated on the Dallas and London offices and his family. It had been ages since Hutch had found himself in the middle of an international conspiracy. "You think she's a spy? Why would a missing woman drag you back into Agency business?"

"I think she might be trying to bring back an old enemy. She's visited ten of the most important CEOs in the world over the course of the last year, and I'm seeing a familiar pattern," Tag said, his tone grave.

A chill went through Hutch. "The Collective broke up a long time ago."

Adam sighed. "As they might say in royal circles, The Collective is dead. Long live The Collective. They might call it something else, but eight of those ten she visited were suspected Collective companies back in the day. The daughter of a senator would have a lot of opportunities a member of The Collective could use. We suspect she's brokering between the companies."

"And none of that would be my business because I'm not going to work with the Agency again." Tag's fist clenched. "But they found a way to drag my ass back in. Turn the page, Hutch."

Hutch turned the page and realized the one thing that could drag Big Tag anywhere he didn't want to go.

Family.

There was a collage of photographs showing the same young woman, but this time with a man. A couple of the photos looked like they'd been taken from CCTV, but some were definitely from a personal camera, one with a long-range capability.

Kyle Hawthorne. The man in the photos holding hands with the lovely and probably deeply corrupt woman was Kyle.

Kyle, who had maneuvered himself into a situation where he had access to one of the most influential CEOs in the world.

"I can't tell Sean because he'll have to tell Grace," Ian admitted, his eyes on the table in front of him. "How am I supposed to tell my sister-in-law that her son might be working for the same organization that tried to kill her and her whole family?"

"Or he's investigating them." Despite his tattletale ways, Hutch couldn't see Kyle as a man who would betray his family like that. "Does Kyle know the story? Does he know what happened to his mother?"

What had happened to Grace Taggart had been getting shoved off a building by a rogue CIA operative after watching the same man nearly kill Sean. He'd read the files on those dark days and struggled to see how Kyle would reconcile working with people who could hurt his family.

"At the time he didn't. We told Kyle and his brother, David, that what happened to Grace was an accident, but he could have found out if he was working with the Agency the way we suspect he was," Adam explained. "There's a report on why I believe Kyle at the very least worked with the CIA on several occasions. His military records don't match up with my facial recognition. I can place him on different continents from where the military records put him."

The facial recognition software Adam had invented was the centerpiece of his investigative empire. It was likely why the senator had come to him.

"Did you ask the senator if her daughter had a boyfriend?" Kyle looked awfully cozy with the blonde.

"They hadn't talked in the six weeks before her disappearance," Adam explained. "Jake is getting more information from her, but she seemed to genuinely not know anything. She's worried about her daughter. I had Eve work up a profile on her and she suspects if the daughter is doing something criminal, the mother isn't aware of it."

"I asked them not to show the senator the pictures of Kyle," Ian admitted.

Because the last thing they needed was pictures of Kyle leaking on the Internet or the senator wanting to make him a suspect in her daughter's disappearance. "Have we thought about asking him what's going on?"

"Do you think I didn't put him through a lot of talks before he hired on?" Tag asked. "I asked him flat out if he'd worked for the Agency. He said no. Should I believe him when he tells me no, Uncle Ian, I'm not using your company to get to your corporate clients? Shortly after Julia Ennis went missing, Kyle left the military, and a shocking amount of cash showed up in his accounts. Yeah, he hasn't told his parents about that either."

"We're worried that Kyle took Julia's job." Adam got to the heart of the matter.

"I'm sorry, Hutch. I was worried about him lying to me about working with the Agency, but I did not have this intelligence in front of me when I gave you this job," Tag said. "I would never have sent him out knowing what I know today. I have to decide what to do."

"You let me do my job." Hutch closed the folder and handed it back to Adam. "I can't take this with me. We're going to be in close quarters, and if he finds it on me, he'll figure out I'm watching him."

"I know I joke about what a dipshit you are," Tag began.

Hutch held up a hand to stop him. "Sarcasm is a part of who you are. We both know how good I am at this type of undercover. You don't have to tell me." But he'd had a day. "Or you should. Go on. I could use some praise."

"It's because the chick didn't like the sex," Adam whispered.

Adam was a dick.

Tag ignored him. "Hutch, you're one of my best agents. I don't send you out in the field often because you're brilliant behind a computer, but when I needed you, you came through in a way few people ever do. I trust you to handle this."

And that was why he put up with Big Tag's shit. Because at the heart of it Big Tag was the best father figure he'd ever had. He would never say that though. The dude had gotten sensitive since he turned fifty.

"You should know that Kyle is meeting with Jessica Layne right now about a job." Hutch might not be on the Kyle-is-bad bandwagon, but he wasn't going to hide anything from his boss. "You should also know that I tried to talk him out of it and he was incredibly insistent. He wants to be in that building."

Tag nodded. "Understood. Watch that relationship for me. I need daily communication, Hutch. To me. No one else. If you need Adam, call him. He's going to keep us up to date on the Julia Ennis case."

"It's a thrill to be back to dealing with politicians." Adam understood the language of sarcasm, too. He stood and grabbed his tablet and the rest of his things. "You coming down for lunch? Phoebe ordered pizza."

Tag nodded. "Charlie and I will be down shortly. I'm going to finish up with Hutch."

Adam snorted. "He's going to ask if you wore a condom."

Well, at least Kyle hadn't told that story. "I did."

He'd gone through all three Kyle had given him. He'd mentally put *box of condoms* on his shopping list as he'd lain beside her the night before. That was one errand he didn't need to run now.

The door closed behind Adam, and Ian sat back.

"You are also one of my more careful employees," Ian said with a sigh. "I know you have your reputation, but in this case I don't think you would have slept with the client because you found her hot. You slept with her because you felt something for her."

"I did." There wasn't a point in lying to Ian if he wasn't going to lie to himself. "I felt more for Noelle in a day than I've felt…in my life. She didn't feel the same way about me and so we're moving on."

Tag's eyes narrowed. "Moving on?"

Hutch nodded. "Yes. She made it clear that if the mood strikes her, I might be welcome back in her bed, but she's not interested in a relationship."

"Maybe she's not in a good place for one," Tag said pointedly.

Hutch huffed. "Yes, I remember saying it. I know. Karma's rough."

"So you're moving on," Tag reiterated.

He wasn't sure where Tag was going, but he needed to make it clear to the boss that there wouldn't be trouble. "Yes. I'm not going to bother her again. We can have a professional relationship. Moving on."

"You do that a lot, you know."

Hutch shook his head. "I do not need some session with you. I have Kai for that."

The corners of Ian's lips curled up in a hint of a smile. "But you don't see Kai until next week, and you'll have ruined everything by then. You like her."

Hutch sighed and sat back. "I do. I screwed up with her, and I wonder if that's why she's not interested. Maybe a bit of revenge."

Tag seemed to think about it for a moment. "I doubt that young woman is capable of revenge, but she might be incredibly capable of questioning her own feelings. She's an intellectual."

"She's super smart. You know, I'm not exactly a dummy." He'd worked hard for his graduate degree. He still studied. He still kept up with new tech and science.

"That's not what I meant. You're smart, but I wouldn't call you an intellectual. After all, you hang out with Boomer."

Boomer was a nice guy, but he wasn't the brightest bulb in the box. "You think she wouldn't like my friends?"

"No. I'm saying she's got a different mindset than you, and that can be a good thing for a couple later on. In the beginning, it can be rough. You trust your instincts. You've pretty much never had anything but your instincts *to* trust."

He hadn't had a functional family until he'd joined McKay-

Taggart. He'd been on his own for much of his young life. "That's a fair assessment."

"But Noelle was raised by two loving parents who divorced and then questioned their every feeling for each other," Tag explained. "From what Remy tells me it wasn't exactly an amicable divorce. Then there was the car accident and numerous surgeries. Her trauma was different than yours. She might be more cautious about relationships than you are."

"I moved too fast." Yeah, he got that now, but damn it, she'd been there with him.

Tag shrugged. "So slow things down and show her who you are."

This was not the advice he'd expected from Ian. "I thought you would tell me not to fuck the fucking client."

He hadn't been there when Ian had told Adam those words, but they were pretty legendary around the building.

Now Tag smiled, a genuine expression of pure amusement. "Yeah, if I did that there would be way less kid drama." He leaned in. "Charlie is usually right about these things. I know your history has taught you that if someone rejects you, it's time to walk away. But sometimes the right one is worth fighting for. You're a good man, Hutch. You are solid and true. Do you think she's worth risking some heartache for? By the way, the heartache will come one way or another. Even in a good marriage. Even in a marriage that works in every way. There are little hurts and heartaches because we're human."

"Are you and Charlotte…" He couldn't even stand the thought.

Ian shook his head. "We're the parents of five kids. Sometimes we have to focus on them and put our marriage in that second-tier spot. I know that intellectually. The rest of me gets jealous even of my kids, who I adore. Don't worry. I have plans to show Charlie she's still my sub. What I'm saying is you already made a decision about Noelle."

"And she made one about me."

"Did she?" Tag asked. "You said she still wanted to sleep with you."

She'd made herself plain. "She wants to use me as stress relief or something."

Big Tag's head fell back and he groaned. "God, I should have let Theo take this one." He looked Hutch's way. "Dude, this is not the time to clutch your pearls. You've trained for this moment. You've seduced woman after woman after woman, and many of them in places that go against all standards for comfortable fucking. This is your time, Hutch. Wrap that well-trained dick of yours and get on the field because it's go time."

He was confused. "You're telling me I should have sex with her."

"I'm telling you to fuck her until she can't possibly fuck another man because you make her so happy, she wouldn't think of it. She's smart, but women think with their nether regions, too. Make her pussy happy. Don't be a super douche outside the bedroom. Be better, hotter, cooler than her training Dom."

The idea of her having a training Dom at all was enough to make his fists clench. He wasn't used to this feeling. "I offered to train her privately."

Tag pointed his way. "Ah, you were a jealous asshole. That's cool. I get that. Shove it to the side because it's not going to help your case. You two had a fight about this?"

"I don't know that I would call it a fight." He'd gone into retreat mode pretty damn quick.

"Good. Then when you see her tonight, tell her you want what's best for her and you moved too fast. Tell her it's great to be friends. Then be the best boyfriend she's ever had. She'll figure it out if you give her time and don't let your butt hurt too much."

"So lie to her?"

Tag's eyes rolled. "It's not lying. You're going to be friends with her. You're also going to be sneaky and slip in under all those careful walls she's built. This is a mission, brother."

He was getting hyped up. What Tag was saying made sense. Noelle was guarded, and he hadn't taken that into account. "Okay. A mission."

"You are going to get in there and convince that woman that against all odds and all her very real concerns, she should jump into a relationship with you. Because you're Hutch and you can not only fix her computer, you can fix her pussy."

"Uh, I don't think there's anything wrong with her pussy,

actually." It was kind of his favorite pussy of all time, and he already missed it.

"Oh, yes there was," Tag corrected. "It was empty, and you are the horndog who can fill it."

He groaned and let his head hit the desk as Tag continued on like a BDSM coach facing the Super Bowl of submission or something.

But Tag was right about one thing. He was giving up too easily.

Noelle was worth the work.

And he couldn't leave her alone with Kyle. He might have to protect her from his own partner.

* * * *

"You feeling okay?" Pete asked.

She looked up from the latest data and saw that hours had passed. It was almost time to go home. She'd been able to lose herself in an experiment and the gold mine of data she'd gotten from it. She'd briefly forgotten about the horrible morning with Hutch. But she wasn't about to get into that with Pete. He'd done enough for her in the last few days. "I'm great. How about you?"

He stared pointedly at the black crutches she was using today. Her cane was often a neon blinking sign that said I'm different, but the heavy crutches really got the point across. "You sure about that?"

"I tweaked my back. I'll be fine in a day or two." She hoped she was okay by Thursday night. She hated the thought of joining her class like that.

Like what? Like herself? The cane and crutches and chair were a part of her. People would either accept her or they wouldn't.

Hutch had seemed to accept her. He'd been the kind of Dom her aunt talked about. The lifestyle, according to Lisa, was open to all types of people, and no one would blink at her cane. It wasn't like a trendy nightclub where only pretty people were welcome.

That wasn't supposed to be true at Sanctum.

Hutch seemed to think she was pretty.

Seemed? He'd told her time and time again the night before that he thought she was gorgeous.

She had to stop thinking about that man. He'd made it plain this morning that they were over since she wasn't willing to drop her whole world because they'd spent a night in bed together.

The best night. A night she was never going to forget.

"I'm glad to hear it." Pete sat down beside her. "I spent some time with the legal department."

"I've got a meeting this afternoon." It was only to be expected. She had to file paperwork about the incident with several of the departments. She'd already talked to security and then HR. She hoped Jessica herself forgot about wanting to speak to her.

"You know they're going to want you to sign away your rights to sue," Pete pointed out.

The legal department of Genedyne worked a lot of overtime. "I thought I did that when I hired on."

"She'll want more. She'll want you to say you took the chance, and she's not responsible for anything."

She shrugged. "I don't know that I can blame her for this. I don't think we should change the gym protocols or anything. It would suck to have to key into the locker room from the gym. And honestly, whoever it was likely would have found a way. I'm not sure it was about me. I think I might have been in the wrong place at the wrong time."

She didn't truly think that, but she and Hutch had decided to play it this way. She didn't want to draw more attention to herself by being the chick with all the conspiracy theories.

Especially since she was starting to believe at least one of them was true.

Whoever had been in the locker room had only looked through two lockers. Hers and Madison's. What was the connection? She was missing something, but she couldn't figure out what. All the pieces were there, but she couldn't make them fit yet.

"Well, it's definitely her responsibility that the security cameras were out," Pete mused. "I find that very convenient."

She did, too, but there was nothing she could do about it at this point. Hutch might be able to tell if someone deliberately turned them off or if they failed, like she was being told.

"Well, I was glad I was there to let that man of yours through," Pete admitted. "I think he would have kicked the door in if I hadn't.

Why was his brother up in the executive offices earlier? That was his brother, right? I met him last night."

"Kyle, yes." She understood the story she was supposed to tell. "He's recently out of the military and came up here to look for work. Jessica took a liking to him."

"You mean Jessica got a look at him," Pete corrected.

She gave him a faint smile. "Yes. I'm afraid she did."

She couldn't laugh about it after the stories Hutch had told her.

Except they weren't stories. They were his life. He'd had to survive all of it. He'd survived a lot in his life, and he still seemed open and happy. Until she'd told him she was taking that class. Then he'd looked hurt, and he'd shut down to the point that they'd barely spoken again.

Would he even be there this evening? Or would he leave her with Kyle and go on about his life?

"Well, I can't blame her. He's hot. Have you warned him that women can be sexual harassers, too?" Pete asked.

"I think he's going in with his eyes open," she replied. She glanced over, and her whole staff seemed to be standing at attention. Her science geeks who usually were hunched over their laptops or peering at their ongoing experiments were standing tall.

"This the new data?" Pete looked at her screen. "Damn. That's an excellent save ratio. That's ten percent more than standard now."

She nodded, her eyes on the room outside. This part of the lab was separated by floor-to ceiling glass walls. It was all very modern and allowed her to see over the whole space without being distracted by chatter. "Yes. It's promising."

She was about to turn her attention back to him and start the discussion of how to replicate those results with other devices when she caught sight of why her techs looked like a bunch of deer in the presence of a lion.

Lioness.

Jessica Layne strode through the lab, her chic, icy blonde bob barely moving, as though her hair knew to behave or else. She wore a designer sheath that showed off how toned she was and heels that brought her to the same height as most of the taller men around her.

She ignored all the techs gawking at her and seemed to be

looking for someone.

Noelle.

And Jessica wasn't alone. Kyle walked behind her, his shoulders straight and eyes taking in everything. He had a Bluetooth device in his ear.

Well, that hadn't taken long. Jessica was normally accompanied by a bodyguard or two. Noelle noted that her normal bodyguard was standing right outside the lab. She wondered if he minded being replaced by the brand-new guy.

Kyle nodded her way as Jessica reached the door. He moved in front of his new boss, opening it for her, and she breezed in.

"Hello, Noelle." Jessica glanced around the lab as though taking stock. "I was hoping you had time for a brief chat. Peter, you are not needed here."

Yep, that was her boss. Always a charmer.

"Of course." Pete slid his bag over his shoulder and gave Noelle a look that told her he wished her good luck. "See you tomorrow."

The door closed with Kyle on the other side.

So they were alone. It was disconcerting, and she realized how much she'd longed to avoid this. She'd never wanted to be a rock star like Madison, who'd partied with the big boss and got a bunch of shout-outs on socials from her. Nope. Noelle had been more than happy to keep her head down and play with her helium.

"Ms. Layne," she replied.

"Please, call me Jessica. We're all friends here at Genedyne." She moved in and looked down at the laptop and then back up at Noelle. "Are those numbers right?"

She didn't need to get ahead of herself. "It's the first data we've got with the new procedures. I need to replicate it about a hundred times before I can write it up."

Jessica was back to staring at the data. "I'm going to need you to forward your protocols to me. You can start writing it up now. I know you won't publish it until we've got all the backing data, but I want to get ahead of this. There are a couple of people working on something similar, and I want the patent first."

Of course she did because whoever got that patent controlled the tech and reaped the benefits. Jessica would make sure that was

Genedyne. Noelle would get the credit and a nice bonus, but more importantly she would get the reputation she needed to move into a slower-paced university setting. She didn't like how cutthroat the corporate world could be. "Sure. I've got enough notes that I can write up something pretty comprehensive this week."

"I want it by Monday." Jessica stood back up. "This is impressive, Noelle. I know it's not as showy as some work being done here, but this is a moneymaker, and I like a moneymaker. You make this work and there's real potential for you to move up and fast."

She'd moved up as high as she wanted to at Genedyne. People who found themselves in executive offices soon learned all that luxury came at a price. Still, she wasn't about to tell her boss she was using this highly sought-after job to find one many people would consider lesser. "That would be great, but I want to make sure everything is solid first."

Jessica leaned against Noelle's desk. "Of course. We can't cut corners, but we do need to ensure that we're first in line." She gestured back to the door. "I think your boyfriend's brother should be out of your hair soon. He said he was staying at your place."

"Yes. He and Hutch came back from Louisiana with me. Hutch already has a job, but Kyle was looking. I take it you hired him."

"Oh, on the spot. He's exactly what I'm looking for in a bodyguard," Jessica replied. "I've got an interview with *Rolling Stone* next week. They're writing an article about the new goddesses of the tech world. Kyle will look good in the background. He won't actually start getting paid for two weeks, but after that I'll show him around, help him look for a place."

She bet Jessica would. "Good. I'm sure he'll appreciate that."

"So, I heard something went wrong last night in the locker room." Jessica's gaze focused on her, eyes going steely. "Any idea who wanted to hurt you?"

The question came as a surprise since she hadn't told the security team she thought the attack was anything but a botched robbery attempt. She'd been specific in telling them she thought it was a random thing. "I don't think anyone wanted to hurt me. I think whoever it was wanted to rifle through the lockers. I know some people keep things in there like their handbags and jewelry. Some people store wireless earbuds and personal equipment."

"I specifically tell people not to keep any valuables in there," Jessica shot back. "I'll have to reiterate that. So you didn't think it was odd that the only other locker that appeared to be touched was Madison's?"

Why had Jessica read the reports? Also, Noelle hadn't mentioned that she'd recognized that the locker that was open was Madison's. She'd left that out, only talking about her own.

But someone had noticed.

"Was hers gone through? I thought it was only mine."

Jessica stared at her for a long moment as though trying to discern whether or not she was lying. "Well, I suppose you were flustered at the time. No. From what security was able to tell, the two lockers our attacker was interested in were yours and Madison's. I should have been able to immediately find out who the fucker was, but something happened to my CCTV cams. They managed to go out on that floor for ten whole minutes. The outage affected the floor above and below. Security tells me they can't even be sure who went up or down the stairs. I've got a list of people who were still in the building, but it seems like an odd coincidence."

"Yes." She couldn't disagree with her. "Whoever was in that locker room obviously took out the cameras."

"See, that doesn't sound like someone looking to steal some AirPods or trying to slip a twenty into his pocket. That seems more serious to me, Noelle."

She felt like she was walking through a field covered in land mines. "I can see why it would, but I have no idea why anyone would go through my locker, much less Madison's. I thought it was cleaned out after the accident."

"It was. Every place Madison Wallace touched has been thoroughly cleaned out. I wouldn't want to be accused of holding anything back from the investigators." Jessica sighed. "I'm going to tell you something in confidence, Noelle, and I need you to understand that it should stay between us."

Yep. She was close to one exploding in her face. "You don't have to tell me anything."

Jessica ignored her. "Madison was a corporate spy. She was working with someone on the outside to steal our research here. I was too kind to her. I got close, and she even stole some of my own research, and I believe she was planning to pass it off as her own."

This was new information, though certainly not the first time Jessica had accused another researcher of attempting to steal her work. It made Noelle real damn happy Jessica wasn't a chemist and didn't do any research in that area. "I'm sorry to hear that."

"You can see why we've kept pretty quiet about her death," Jessica replied. "It's being investigated thoroughly by the authorities because I suspect Madison was trying to auction off my research and got into trouble."

"You don't think it was an accident?"

Jessica shrugged as though they were talking about something meaningless and not a potential murder. "I think Madison was sloppy, so it could have been exactly that, but we have to make sure there wasn't foul play. Did she send you anything before she died? There's some evidence that she knew we were onto her and that she might have tried to smuggle the research out in different ways."

Noelle shook her head. "Oh, Madison and I were not friends. In any way. She was a bully and I was one of her favorite victims, but that was the extent of our relationship."

Jessica frowned. "Why would she bully you?"

"There was a wealth she chose from. The cane and crutches. The extra five pounds I carry at all times. She didn't like the way I dress."

Jessica shrugged. "You could stand to wear some more color, but I'm sorry about the rest of it. She was always nice to me. I thought that was how she was to everyone. I can be naïve at times. I want to see the best in people."

Yes, she could see how this Jessica could be dangerous. She seemed friendly.

Jessica's tone went low, almost sympathetic. "She was probably jealous of you."

"I don't see why she would be."

"Because she knew you're going to make bank for this company. She might work on flashier projects, but everyone knows it's minds like yours who bring in investors, who fuel the other projects. You might not change the world with the helium project, but you're going to make it easier for doctors to use the diagnostic machines they need, to pay for that use. You're making a real difference," she said.

Yep, now she remembered why she'd been excited in the beginning. She'd seen only this side of her boss. "Thank you. I'm grateful to have the backing of Genedyne. But to your question, no. She didn't send me anything. Our lockers were across from each other. Maybe they got confused."

She doubted it. But she also didn't understand why anyone would think Madison might leave her something.

But she might have been setting her up to take a fall.

That thought sent a chill through her, and she had the sudden and deep desire to talk to Hutch. Her father would immediately panic and make a move to protect her at all costs. If she talked to Cara, she would probably be told she was being paranoid.

Hutch would talk to her. Well, he would have talked to her. This was about the case, though. Perhaps he would have to talk to her, and she could come to some understanding of why he'd gotten upset.

You know why he got upset. He got upset because he felt what you did, and he wanted to go with it. He wanted to go all in, and you couldn't trust it.

She still couldn't. This wasn't a feeling she could trust. She was in danger and he was safe. He was pretty much her perfect man, and she hadn't even realized what she wanted until she'd met him.

No one fell for a person this quickly. It never worked.

"I need you to let me know if anything else happens," Jessica was saying. "We need to keep everything quiet because the last thing we want is publicity. You understand that we need our investors to know we're a solid company."

"Of course." She needed to think about everything that had been said. There was something more going on here. "We are a solid company."

Jessica's smile went bright, and she stood again. "We are. All right. You can meet with legal tomorrow. Why don't you head home and get some rest? I'm excited about this new experiment." She turned to the door. "Are you sure you want the geeky one? Don't get me wrong. He's cute, but his brother is divine."

She followed Jessica's gaze and then her heart skipped a beat because Hutch was standing in the outer lab talking to Kyle. He was wearing jeans and sneakers and a T-shirt that said something snarky, she was sure. His hair was a bit long and he brushed it back, showing off those ridiculously strong arms of his.

He might not be as showy as Kyle, but she'd seen him naked and knew how demanding the man could be in the best of ways.

His eyes caught hers, and a stunning smile crossed his face.

"Nope. He's the one I want," she said, wishing that she could actually have him. But she wasn't stupid. They came from completely different worlds. Maybe somewhere down the road they would find themselves at Sanctum and she would be ready for someone like him.

Of course, he would have moved on by then.

Jessica waved him in. "Well, I suppose I should be grateful for that. Kyle, I'm going back up to the office. I've got a date tonight, so you can knock off early. Bentley can take me upstairs."

Hutch walked straight up to Noelle, his eyes warm on hers. "Hey, baby. I missed you all day. I hope you don't mind me coming by. I wanted to head home with you."

She would have said something, but his hands were on her and then those lush lips of his were covering her own, and he wasn't holding back. The night before rushed into her brain in vivid clarity, and every hormone in her body flared to life. By the time he stepped back, she was completely breathless.

"Okay, maybe I get it." Jessica winked her way before turning. "Don't forget that report."

The door closed and Hutch's face fell.

"Hey, I'm sorry. I thought I should..." he began.

It was for their cover. Of course. It was all for their cover, and at least now she knew he wasn't going to leave her high and dry. "It's okay. I understand. She was watching."

"Pretty much everyone is watching," Kyle said with a frown. "So could we not fight again?"

Hutch gave her a sad smile. "We're not going to fight at all. Noelle, I'm sorry for how I acted this morning. I...turns out I'm fond of you and far more capable of feeling jealousy than I thought I was. I moved too fast, and I hope you can forgive me and we can be friends."

Wasn't that exactly what she wanted? So why did the idea of being friends with him feel like a letdown? "Of course. I would like that a lot."

"Good. Then maybe the third time will be the charm."

Third time? She supposed it was. "Friends then."

"I'll believe that when I see it," Kyle said under his breath.

Hutch gave her a nod. "Friends. Now kiss me again, friend, because we've got a fake relationship to maintain. Let's head back to your place and I'll cook us all some supper and we can talk about what we learned today."

She glanced over and most of her techs were staring into the room as though they couldn't quite believe what they were seeing. Didn't think she could get a date, huh? Well, she mostly couldn't, but she'd gotten Hutch. She wished there had been a way to keep him. She brushed her lips against his and then put her laptop in her bag.

Hutch picked it up. "I'll take this. And I think I saw some chocolate chips in your pantry. Any way I could convince you to make some cookies? I've got a sweet tooth."

What else are you offering me, Noelle? Or was that sugar all I get from you?

She forced herself to smile. "I would love to. And thanks for making dinner. I appreciate it. I have a lot to tell you."

When he handed her the braces, she took them and he fell into step beside her with the ease of a man used to measuring his gait, to adapting to the people around him.

Could he adapt to her?

He moved ahead to get the door for her, and she wondered if being friends with Hutch wouldn't be even worse for her heart than being nothing at all.

Chapter Nine

Hours later, Hutch set the glass of wine in front of Noelle and looked to Cara, who had shown up shortly after dinner and who might be the damn reason he didn't get cookies tonight. "You two need anything else?"

Cara was sitting across from Noelle on the couch and shook her head. "No, just some privacy, please."

She did not like him. Noelle looked his way, though, her cheeks a bit flushed.

"Sorry."

He leaned over and laid a kiss on her forehead. "It's not a problem. I'm going to take that bottle of Scotch I bought and sit out on the balcony with my brother. He had a big day."

That flush on her face had deepened, likely going from being embarrassed to a little aroused. He should be pissed that Cara had shown up, but it gave him a chance to kiss her. He'd had to pull back when the three of them were alone, had to play the nice guy instead of the ruthless Dom who'd found his sub and meant to make her his.

She nodded his way. "Thanks for dinner. It was delicious, and I'll get those cookies going as soon as possible."

He winked. "I look forward to some more of your sugar, baby."

Yep, it was definitely one of the two—arousal or

177

embarrassment—because the blush rushed down her neck, spreading almost to the tops of her breasts. "You're a terrible man."

Arousal won. She'd said the words with the sweetest smile that let him know she wasn't thinking about cookies.

Nope. Tag had been right. This was far from over. Their chemistry was off the charts and still quite alive, despite Noelle's trepidation. She didn't think she could trust this crazy first-sight thing, so he was going to give her a whole lot more time to make the right decision. This war wouldn't be won by him retreating.

Not that Cara looked like she was willing to come down on the side of quickie commitment. That woman was still staring a hole through him as he grabbed the Scotch and two glasses and walked to the balcony.

"He should be careful out there. I heard someone is now throwing clothes off their balcony," Cara huffed. "There was a pair of underwear in the oak tree. What is this place coming to?"

He managed to not snort as he heard Noelle sputter. He quickly slid the balcony door closed and joined Kyle, who was leaning against the balcony railing.

"Hey, I have good news and bad news." Hutch set the bottle on the table.

"Oh, I always want the bad news first." Kyle stared down at the street before.

It did not surprise Hutch in the least that Kyle was a bad-news-first kind of guy. "Cara apparently hates the two of us, me in particular."

"That's not bad news."

Hutch had more. "And our downstairs detective is probably working undercover with the feds."

That got Kyle to turn around. "Are you serious? Shouldn't that have been the lead, man? You've had hours to tell me that and you spent it cooking and seducing a woman you've already been to bed with?"

Well, he had to seduce her if he wanted to get back into bed with her. There was a logical reason he hadn't mentioned what Tag had uncovered to Noelle. "Taylor's investigating someone, and I can't be sure it's not Noelle."

Kyle's arms crossed his chest. "If that woman is…" He sighed and shook his head. "No. I'm not going to say that. She could be bad. Anyone can be. She could simply be excellent at covering and a good actress. I'm impressed with you, Hutch. I would have thought you would be that guy who told her because you have feelings for her. I didn't suspect you would know how to play the game so well."

Oh, he knew how to play the game, and he knew when someone had no idea any games were being played at all. "Noelle is innocent. I didn't tell her because I don't want her to worry about some federal investigation that might or might not be real. Now don't you want the good news?"

Kyle huffed, a predatory sound. "The Scotch, I assume."

Hutch poured out two fingers each. He'd started as a beer guy, but his appreciation for a 12-year single malt, as many things in his life, had been taught to him by Big Tag. He'd choked it down the first time and had only tried it again because Tag had seemed so pleased to share it with him.

He was right back to Ian being the father he'd never had. Now he had to navigate this tricky situation for the man. He had to start to get a real handle on who Kyle Hawthorne was.

"Of course." Hutch passed him a glass. "This is an excellent Scotch."

Kyle took a long swig. "Yeah, I hear that from my stepdad a lot. He's all about the Scotch. I can't tell the difference between Scotch and whiskey. Or bourbon, for that matter. It's all one long burn to my belly. So, you are a naïve idiot when it comes to women. Crazy doctors aside, of course."

Most of the military guys saw him that way. He was the funny one, the one who looked younger than he really was, the computer geek. "I'm not naïve. What I am is pretty damn good at figuring out who will hurt me and who won't. I learned that while I lived on the streets, and then I learned it in prison. I learned it when I was on a CIA team."

"Then you should know that you can't be sure of anyone."

"Of course I can. You're sure about your family, right? No one could ever say anything to you that would make you doubt your mom?"

Kyle sank down to the sofa. "Of course not, but they're my family. I've known them all my life. This isn't the same thing at all. My mother and my brother are above any suspicion."

Hutch noted that he'd left an important person off that list. "You don't trust your stepfather?"

Kyle shook his head. "Not true. I trust him in a lot of ways. I trust him with my mother, with my brother. With my life. But Sean's a hard guy still in a lot of ways. I don't think he trusts me entirely, and that means I can't totally trust him."

"Why do you think he doesn't trust you?"

"That's a longer story than I'm willing to get into with you because despite your penchant to go deep as fast as you can possibly go, I don't swim that way. I don't know you, Hutch."

He found it interesting what Kyle wasn't saying. He trusted Sean with everything but his secrets. He wanted to press but he was good at this, was good at sensing when to take a step back. This was as far as Kyle was willing to go on this subject. "No problem. I'm cool not talking at all. When Cara gets through telling Noelle whatever important information she needs to tell her, we can all head our separate ways for the night."

Kyle sat for a moment before reaching out and refilling his glass. "What game are you playing with her?"

"Game?"

"Yeah, with Noelle."

Hutch shook his head. "I'm not playing a game. I'm into her. Way into her. I had all day to think about it and while we moved too fast, I don't see why we can't be together at the end of this. So I'm showing off my boyfriend skills."

A brow arched over Kyle's eyes. "Are you serious? Because that sounds…"

He honestly didn't care what anyone thought. Another lesson he'd learned from Tag. The most badass thing he could do was be himself with zero apologies. "It sounds like what, Kyle?"

Kyle seemed to realize he was about to say something offensive and backed off. "I don't know. It doesn't sound… Whatever."

He was not letting Kyle off the hook so easily. "Are you trying to tell me I'm not being masculine?"

Kyle shrugged. "I'm trying to figure out a way to express that without fucking up too badly."

He could only imagine how a guy like Kyle would handle the situation. "I suppose you would club her over the head and drag her back to your cave."

"Nope. First of all, I wouldn't have decided that she was mine after a single night. Second, if she'd turned me down, I would have walked away with some dignity," Kyle replied.

"Then you haven't met a woman you truly care about yet." Hutch wasn't going to argue about the value of dignity. Or the meaning of the word. He wasn't sure how fighting for the woman he wanted meant he lost his dignity.

"Or I've done the head over heels love thing and realized what a lie it is." There was no way to miss the bitterness to Kyle's words. "What you call love...it's nothing more than lust. It's a biological imperative to breed, and when you wake up you're going to realize you don't know this woman at all."

Oh, so Kyle was projecting. Hutch had to wonder if this bitterness was coming from Kyle's most recent relationship. "So my wanting Noelle is nothing more than my primal need to mate kicking in? Do you think Noelle is giving off hormones or something to attract me? I've had a lot of sex. I wonder why I'm desperate to mate with only her."

Kyle's eyes rolled. "Don't be a dick. I'm serious. The love thing is bullshit."

"Or you found the wrong one and you're letting a bad relationship ruin any good ones you could have?" Hutch had been in therapy long enough to know a few things. "Your mom had two good marriages, right?"

He'd spent some of his afternoon studying up on Kyle Hawthorne. He'd been fifteen when his father had died in an accident.

"Sure, but that's different," Kyle countered. "My mom and dad were good partners, and she and Sean are similar. I don't know that I would call it some great love story. I mean I know they have a good sex life. I wish I didn't, but I get that the lifestyle stuff works for them. But what really works is that they have a great partnership. I would bet my mom and Sean never once had a real fight. She met him, realized he would be a good partner, and the rest was history. Sean is the same. He's a solid guy. I would bet a lot he never lost his head over a woman."

Hutch would totally take that bet. It answered one question. Kyle had no idea what his mother had gone through all those years ago. And he'd been through something rough with a woman. Had that woman been Julia Ennis? "I am going to ask the obvious question. Who hurt you, Kyle?"

He asked it with a twist of humor, though damn, he was interested in the answer.

"It doesn't matter. All that matters is I learned my lesson," Kyle replied, sitting back. "The question is how have you not been hurt enough? After everything you've been through, why are you so willing to throw the dice again?"

He could tell Kyle the truth he'd learned about the world, but he wouldn't want to listen. He'd learned that often the adults who had the most heartache and trouble were the ones who'd never dealt with it as children. Kyle had lost his father, and that had surely been terrible, but he'd had a loving mother and brother to help him through. The real question was why wasn't he leaning on them now. "I guess I'm an optimist."

Kyle studied him for a moment. "Yeah, I don't understand that either. You know you only have two days, right?"

"Two days to what?" Hutch was pretty sure the case wouldn't be over in two days. Between what Noelle had told them about Jessica's suspicions and the possibility that Chris Taylor was working a federal investigation, they weren't about to clear this up in a couple of days. This might be a long-haul case, and he welcomed it. It could take a while to break through Noelle's reservations.

"Two days until she joins the training class and plops down on her training Dom's lap."

The thought made his fists clench, but he had to deal with it. If Noelle fell for her training Dom, or even if she simply decided she wanted the other man, he would have his answer. But she needed to understand that she had a choice. "Noelle wants to take the class. I have to hope her training Dom is unattractive but nice. Maybe an older dude who can view her as a daughter."

Kyle's lips quirked up. "You want her to call him Daddy?"

Hutch groaned. "No. I would prefer she have a friendly relationship with a nice Dom in training who just wants to learn with her."

"Who wants to learn how to spank her naked ass?" Kyle held up a hand as though staving off a fight. "Sorry, man, but I think it's kind of fucked up. If it helps any, Noelle doesn't understand what's wrong. She wanted to talk about it this morning on the way to work."

He bet that had been fun for Kyle. "How can she not understand?"

Kyle shrugged. "I don't think she truly gets how intimate this is going to be. She thinks she's going to put on some fet wear and fill out a couple of worksheets. I worry that she's going to balk when she gets to anal plugging 101."

"She can always put that down as a hard limit. She'll go through all of that on Thursday when she's in class." He didn't think it would scare her off. Not the idea of taking a plug. He kind of hoped in a couple of weeks when they got to that part she might not want another Dom's hands on her. In the beginning it would be an introduction to contracts, a whole lot of talking, and getting used to the equipment.

Why did she need to go through the class? Lots of people didn't. Lots of Doms found their subs in the vanilla world and vice versa. They went through private training. He'd heard some talk that the board of Sanctum was discussing starting a new program where long-term couples mentored new ones or couples with problems.

Noelle didn't want that. She wanted the class where she didn't know anyone.

"I guess you have to hope she gets a training Dom with zero desire to fuck her," Kyle said with a tip of his glass. "Good luck with that. She's pretty cute."

She was gorgeous and sexy and strong. She'd been broken and come through it with all of her light intact. He wanted that light.

That was what he'd decided this afternoon after his conversation with Ian. She was worth the potential heartache. "I want her to get everything she needs. I don't understand why she feels like she has to take this class, but I'm comfortable taking the risk." It was time to move on. "Speaking of risk, how much of one are you taking with

Jessica?"

Kyle frowned. "Like am I risking falling in love with her? Dude, no."

It was Hutch's turn to roll his eyes. "I was thinking more about your body. Are you going to sleep with her? The way she was looking at you, I think you could easily slip into her bed."

"I'm going to avoid that if I can. I don't like the idea of fucking for information, and honestly, I don't think sleeping with Jessica would buy me much," Kyle replied. "I think I actually get more if I play it cool, let her chase me for a while. I also can't protect Noelle if I'm sleeping somewhere else."

"I can handle Noelle," Hutch promised. "I know I'm not in the bodyguard unit, but I can shoot."

"I think I would prefer to handle that part of the gig." Kyle got up and stretched his long limbs. "All of that said, I do believe taking that job is already working. I can buzz you up whenever I like. Like I did today. I'm going to see if I can get you a badge."

That would be helpful. "How close is she keeping you and what have you learned about the security system?"

Kyle seemed more comfortable talking about the case. "I sent you the name of the system, but that's building security. Jessica's office has its own system, and I couldn't find any identifying paperwork when I went through the system manual. I suspect it's something she's put together herself. Or had custom made. Once you get into her office, there's more security. Her desk itself has a biometrics component."

So she was paranoid. That was good to know. "How about her laptop?"

Kyle shook his head. "I didn't get a good look at it. She doesn't leave it on her desk when she's not in the office like a lot of people would. She locks it up."

"I would bet it's not connected to the building's network. It makes me suspicious about what she keeps on it."

"My job is going to be in-building security for now. She's got two bodyguards she uses outside the building. From what I can tell at least one of them has been with her for years. The other has changed every couple of months. I think she hires someone she thinks is attractive, plays around with them, gets bored, and she lets the dude go."

"The bodyguards are all men?"

"Yes. I'm going to quietly get as much info on the security systems and her personal laptop as I can. Anything else you want?"

"Eventually I'll need access," Hutch explained. "I need to get in that building when there's not hundreds of people there. I can't hack her security without being there, and I'm going to need to take out the CCTVs to do it."

"Noelle works later from time to time," Kyle mused. "I overheard Jessica talking to her CFO about how much money she thought they could raise off Noelle's experiments."

"Raise? That's an odd word to use."

"It's how she put it. Maybe she meant make, but I heard raise." Kyle put his glass on the table. "The CFO didn't blink, just asked how fast they could get the word out. She's expecting Noelle to get her initial results soon. I'm saying that because it wouldn't be shocking for Noelle to work late and her boyfriend to bring her some dinner."

It was a good plan and one he'd thought about himself. "I'd like to go in knowing a little more about the systems. I'd also like to figure out what we're looking for. If the feds are involved, we have to be looking at something that crosses state lines, maybe some kind of fraud."

"Give me a couple of days. From what I can tell Jessica isn't careful about who she talks around. Not when it comes to her bodyguards. She thinks we're something pretty to look at and that she can intimidate anyone with her lawyers."

"Yeah, I'm going to do a deep dive into her legal activities. MaeBe's working a dossier on our cop. Hopefully we know something more tomorrow." Hutch glanced back into the apartment where Noelle and Cara sat. Noelle's back was to him, but he could see the tight set of her shoulders. "Maybe we need to do a deeper dive on Cara, too."

"That's your business," Kyle conceded. "But mine is to ensure the client's safety and yours."

"I can watch my own back."

"Perhaps I should be more precise. Hutch, I don't think you

should tell Noelle the specifics of our operation."

"What is that supposed to mean?" Hutch asked.

"It means she doesn't need to know you plan on getting into Jessica Layne's office. She doesn't need to know you're going to use her as an excuse to do it. In this case, I'm protecting McKay-Taggart, too."

Hutch didn't like the sound of that. "She's our client."

"Her father is our client, and he's not a client at all," Kyle pointed out. "He's a friend of a friend, and we don't truly know any of these people. What we do know is that there is likely a federal investigation, and the cop isn't hanging out at the Genedyne building. He's here. He's watching Noelle."

The thought didn't sit well. "She's not involved."

Kyle sighed. "If you can't even entertain the idea, then you shouldn't be working this case, and I'm going to make that note to my boss."

"Feel free to report whatever you like." Hutch wasn't concerned that Ian would take him off the case. Not when Ian had spent much of the afternoon game-planning on how Hutch would get his girl. And Kyle didn't know there was a secondary mission. But Kyle did have a point. "I'll think about it, but I'll consider keeping her in the dark about the logistics. I don't want to make her anxious, and it's best she doesn't know the exact plans."

She was nervous enough as it was. She didn't need the added pressure. Besides, she wasn't a spy. She wasn't trained, and she could give them away.

"That's all I'm asking." Kyle turned and went back to staring out over the street below. "Be careful with her. You think you know someone, but they can turn on you."

"I'll keep it in mind." Noelle wouldn't turn on him, but she could break his heart.

He had to make sure that didn't happen.

* * * *

Noelle held the glass of wine Hutch had given her, grateful she had something to hold or she might have reached for his hand. He looked so good, and the last couple of hours had been easy and peaceful. She'd expected him to be difficult, to avoid her at all costs. That hadn't been the way the evening had gone. He'd focused on her, and that had caused her to focus on him, on how thoughtful he was, how nice he could make her feel, how freaking hot the man was in a pair of jeans. "Thanks for dinner. It was delicious, and I'll get those cookies going as soon as possible."

She wasn't feeding his ego or being nice. The chicken breasts had been delicious, and he'd made an actual salad. He'd cleaned while he'd cooked, leaving her with only the plates to wash after. Even then he'd moved next to her and dried and put away the dishes.

It had been way too nice and far too comfortable to work beside him. Like they'd done it forever. Dinner talk had been half about the case and half about her research, with Hutch asking thoughtful questions and showing an ability to truly talk to her about science. They'd decided to play a game after dinner. She owned a couple of fun ones. Ticket to Ride might be easy to teach Kyle. She thought he might think it was weird to play a game where cute animals built an economic system and bought and sold commodities. Naturally when she'd mentioned it, Hutch had told her Raccoon Tycoon was one of his favorite games, too.

He was practically perfect.

She'd almost forgotten Kyle was there until the doorbell had rung and he'd answered it. It had been Cara, determined to talk.

Hutch winked down at her. "I look forward to some more of your sugar, baby."

Heat flashed through her. She'd thought after this morning that there would be a distance between them, a coolness. Nope. There was warmth, and it was more than sexual. If it had been merely sexual, she could have ignored it. Probably. This crazy mix of lust and longing was threatening her resolve. "You're a terrible man."

He gave her a sexy smile and retreated to the balcony. The one where he'd made love to her with his hands and tongue. Even thinking about it made her body go hot with arousal. She was going to stay in her room tonight. Lock the door. Could she lock the door so she couldn't get out?

Cara watched him walk away. "He should be careful out there. I

187

heard someone is now throwing clothes off their balcony. There was a pair of underwear in the oak tree. What is this place coming to?"

"No idea," she managed to sputter before trying to get back on track. "What's up? You sounded upset. I'm sorry I hadn't called you back. It was a whirlwind day."

Cara turned her way. She'd left two voice mails before simply coming over and knocking on Noelle's door. "I wouldn't call it upset. Confusion is a better word. I thought we were friends. You never even mentioned you were dating someone, and now you have two guys living with you? It's not like you. Did you run that past management?"

She didn't have to. "I have two bedrooms. I can have up to four people stay for six weeks. By then Kyle will have gotten his own place, and all I have to do in order to be in compliance is put Hutch on my records."

"You never even mentioned his name before." Cara seemed to relax, the brittle look on her face softening. "We've talked a lot."

They'd talked about work and movies and the way the guy in 408 shouldn't wear a speedo. She wasn't comfortable with lying. She kind of hated it, but she'd agreed to keep their cover. "It was hard to talk about Hutch."

No lies there. She wanted to call her stepmom and talk about him, but she was worried her dad would overhear and go into protective mode. Of course she was also worried her incredibly sensible stepmother would tell her she'd been reckless when she'd fallen into bed with him.

"Because you were so close?" Cara asked.

Maybe she could get something out of this. She couldn't talk to her family, and she hadn't made friends at the office. Cara was way more experienced than she was, and she seemed level-headed. "We were high school sweethearts, but we've changed a lot. It's been years since I really spent time with him."

Cara studied her for a moment. "So you do know him. You've known him for a long time. He's not someone you recently met?"

Now she did have to lie. "We met in high school, but even then it was pretty fast. I met him and we clicked."

Cara's eyes narrowed. "See, I thought you told me you didn't date a lot until college because of the accident."

She wasn't good at this. "Like I said, it was hard to talk about him. I cared about him and he was a good boyfriend. I left him behind when I went to college and it seemed better to concentrate on my studies. I missed him, but we were young. Those relationships, well, I watched one of those relationships disintegrate. My mom and dad were high school sweethearts, but they grew apart over the years. I used to look at pictures of them when they were young and they looked happy. I don't remember those times. I remember fighting. I remember my mom hating moving out of Papillon and to New Orleans for my dad's job. And then refusing to leave New Orleans because she would never move back to a small town. She changed so much over the years that they didn't fit together anymore."

"We make a lot of mistakes when we're immature. I think it can be a terrible idea to get too serious when you're young. But sometimes the heart wants what it wants, if you know what I mean," Cara replied with a sigh. "I think you were smart to choose your career."

She'd pursued her dream, and it had been easy because she hadn't been leaving her dad alone. He'd married Lila by then. He'd been old enough to know what he truly wanted, and she was sure this time was forever for her dad.

Had he felt a deep need when he'd met her mom? Like the one she felt for Hutch? She was fascinated by him and yet also comforted by his presence. Had it been the same for her parents? How long had that feeling lasted before it had died out? Before they couldn't even stand to be around each other anymore? They'd both loved her. She'd never had a doubt in her mind, but they hadn't even liked each other at the end.

"I couldn't stay home. I love Papillon, but I couldn't do the things I feel like I was born to do there." And she wouldn't have met Hutch. She wouldn't have found out that sex was so much better when the man was focused on her, devoted to her pleasure. When her lover didn't treat her like she was something he could break.

"So you went home this time and reconnected with him?"

This was where Cara's advice might help. "Yeah. We were both at the same restaurant my first night in town and we ended up sitting at the bar together. I went back to his place. It was like a flash fire. It was like no time had passed at all, but it was also different."

"It was hotter because you're both older and more experienced."

Noelle nodded. "Yeah."

Cara gave her a smile. "So the sex is good."

She sighed, a sound of pure longing. "It's amazing."

Cara's gaze went to the balcony, her nose wrinkling. "Really? He seems like a nice guy, but a little on the nerdy side. Don't get me wrong, he's adorable. But I'm surprised you're with him instead of Kyle. I guess I like them hot and broody."

"Hutch is totally hot. Trust me. If you'd ever had that man's mouth on you, you would know how sexy he is." Undercover sexy. He made her dinner and treated her like a princess and then spread her legs and fucked her like his favorite sex toy. He talked science and computers and board games and ordered her to ride his cock until she couldn't take it anymore and she called out his name while she came.

Was she making a terrible mistake? Should she throw out the whole training class thing and give him what he wanted? She got the feeling if she was willing to give up the class, he would give a relationship a try.

Cara smiled. "Okay. I've known the type. Is he better than he was in high school?"

Noelle shook her head. "We didn't have sex then."

"Ah, this is a one-that-got-away situation. That can be intense," Cara conceded. "But why the quick move in? You seem so careful. I'm sorry I came on strong, but I'm worried about you."

"Worried?"

"You have a lot of pressure on you right now. I mean between that fire at the lab and your research, you've got a lot on your plate," Cara pointed out. "They haven't figured out what happened in Madison's lab, right?"

She'd talked to Cara a lot about her situation at work. "It was reported as an accident. That's how the authorities are treating it."

"Yes. I find it interesting that they filed the paperwork and closed the investigation so quickly."

"How would you know that?"

Cara shrugged. "Noelle, I'm a reporter and your friend. I know you've been worried about how Madison died. It's so typically Noelle that you would worry about a person who was terrible to you."

"Jessica told me Madison was careless."

"From what you've told me, she was working with some highly unstable materials," Cara pointed out.

"She was, but she knew how to work with them." It was what didn't make sense. All the rumors she was hearing lacked logic for her. "Madison was mean, but she was smart. She wasn't a careless person. Discipline was a big thing with her. She had a schedule and she kept it to the point of dropping out in the middle of a meeting because she went to the gym every single day. She never missed a workout or was late to a meeting. She ran her lab like a well-oiled machine. Probably better than I do because I let my techs manipulate me with sob stories I know can't be true. Billy can't have had the same cat die four times."

Cara gave her a smile. "You've got a soft heart."

"Madison didn't, but if there was one thing she deeply believed in it was her own self-preservation. She wouldn't do anything that would cause her to gain a couple of pounds, much less do an experiment alone in a lab that normally requires at least two extra sets of hands." She'd gone over all of this with Hutch, who'd had her write down the questions she had about the accident. He'd told her not only would it help him but that it might calm her mind to actually write them down. It had. She'd spent time writing up her questions and her thoughts about Madison. Madison had been a careful woman, organized to the point that her lists had a list. "I also find it odd that she was there so late at night."

"And that she managed to turn the security cameras off around her lab." Cara crossed one leg over the other, a thoughtful expression on her face. "That's what the reports said. She used her own passcodes to override the system."

Suspicion sprang up in Noelle's head. "How do you know all of this?"

"Like I said, I'm a reporter," Cara replied. "And this is an interesting story. Also, I'm worried that you're getting pulled into it. Look, I know we haven't been close for long, but I really like you, Noelle. Something is off about this whole thing. You have to understand that the authorities closed the investigation in a week. That should have taken months."

Noelle could think of a couple of reasons why they'd rushed a report. "Jessica's got pull. She told me today that she's worried about how a long investigation might upset investors."

"Did she tell you if she bribed them? The police? OSHA?"

"Whoa, she didn't say anything of the kind." She'd told all of this to Hutch and Kyle. "She told me she was happy they'd cleared it up quickly. I guess it was plain that it was an accident."

Cara stared at her and Noelle could see the reporter in her friend. "But I thought you said it wasn't plain to you."

"I didn't know you were looking into it. I guess now I feel kind of weird talking to you about it." She wasn't sure what Hutch would want her to say.

"I didn't mean to make you feel awkward," Cara offered. "I'm trying to look out for you. I hope you know that. I don't have many friends. I might be a little abrasive."

"No, you're not." Cara was aggressive sometimes, but it came with her job. "I like you, too. But I don't think you have to worry about me."

"I would worry about anyone close to Jessica Layne," Cara admitted. "While you were in Papillon, I did some research on her. More than the usual surface stuff. There are some people who think she didn't earn her degree. She was set to graduate with a business degree and then in the course of two semesters made the switch and suddenly had a bachelor's in science."

"She's got a genius-level IQ."

"I think that might be another of her myths," Cara argued. "She's excellent about building a narrative around herself and her company. Up until now you've flown under her radar."

"Why wouldn't I continue to?"

That seemed to make Cara stop. "I guess you could. I guess that's what I'm saying. She's dangerous."

That's what everyone told her. "I'd like to see your research."

Cara nodded. "Good. I'd like to share it with you. Maybe we can have dinner and go over it Thursday night."

"I can't. I've got a thing Thursday." She still wasn't willing to share the Sanctum part of her life with her friend. She wished she hadn't been forced to share it with Hutch. It should be private until she decided she knew what she was doing. Still, she would need a good excuse. "We're all going out on Thursday to meet a friend from home. She's coming up to a conference and that's the only night she's got for dinner."

Cara finished her glass, setting it down on the table. "Well, then maybe we can do it some other time." She stood up. "Just know that if you want to talk about anything, I'm next door. I hope you know what you're doing with this guy."

Cara held out a hand, not asking Noelle to get up. Cara seemed good about knowing when she wasn't feeling great. One of the things that made her like the woman was the fact that she didn't make a big deal out of it. Cara, like Hutch, treated her like a normal person.

Because she was normal. She could hear Hutch in her head. She was a perfectly normal Noelle, and that was all anyone could expect of her.

It was good to be reminded from time to time.

"I do, too." Noelle squeezed Cara's hand before she let it go.

She was going to hold the line. She didn't know Hutch and couldn't trust that anything between them was real. If she threw herself into a relationship with a man she didn't know and tossed out her chance to explore something she thought could be good for her, then she would be the fool. She'd seen how that could work out.

Of course, she'd also seen how fast her dad had fallen for her stepmom. But they were older, they'd made all their mistakes and were ready to truly commit. How many of her friends had she seen get their hearts broken because they'd picked the wrong guy? Even Cara admitted she'd had a bad breakup.

"Do you ever think of him?" Noelle asked as Cara started for the door.

Cara turned, her hand on the knob. "Of my ex?"

"You were supposed to get married, right?"

"Yeah. I took a job he wasn't happy about," Cara admitted. "He couldn't handle the fact that I switched companies. Uhm, newspapers. He was a reporter, too, but he preferred to stay and write about local stories. I was more ambitious, and he thought that made me a bad person. Like I'm supposed to stay loyal to my team at all times."

"There's a difference between loyalty and accepting good opportunities. I mean you didn't step on anyone's toes, right?"

Cara shook her head. "I didn't. All of our friends were happy for me. That's the sad part. He was the only one who didn't understand. Be careful with your guy. He might seem great now, but you're going places, Noelle. Guys can have fragile egos about things like the women in their lives making more money and being more respected than they are. Jessica Layne at least has one thing right. She said she wouldn't ever marry because she wouldn't find a man who could handle her ambition and drive. At the end of the day, they all still want a woman who cooks and cleans and takes care of them. Call me. Maybe we can have lunch. I missed you while you were in Louisiana."

She nodded again and then Cara was gone and she was left with a whole lot to think about.

The door to the balcony came open as she started to get up. She needed to lock the door.

"Hey, I'll get it." Hutch hurried to turn the dead bolt. "You okay? That looked intense."

It had been for a moment, but now she felt a sense of warmth because she'd missed Cara, too. "She's researching Jessica. She's worried about me."

"Or she's working on a story." Kyle closed the balcony door, the bottle of Scotch and a glass in his hands. "I want to look into her."

"You do that." Hutch sat down on the couch across from her. He didn't look Kyle's way, though the words were meant for him. "Now, I think it's late for you to make cookies, but I did pick up some gummy bears, and I've heard they go with that wine."

Damn, but he made her smile. "You're an expert on wine now?"

He shook his head. "Not at all, but I do candy pairings. Let's put our feet up and watch some TV. I sat in a chair all day, and I honestly think Kyle's head is too thick to learn a board game tonight."

"You know I went to college, right? I'm not dumb," Kyle complained. "I can win games. But I would rather work. Are you two doing it tonight or do I have to sleep on the couch?"

Noelle felt her face flush.

Hutch stood. "I'll sleep out here. Grandpa Kyle wants to go to bed, and I'm not sending us all to sleep because he needs his beauty rest. There's a new *Star Trek* on tonight."

She loved the new *Star Trek* show. Naturally he was a *Star Trek* guy. But she didn't want him to give up his room. "It's okay. I can watch it online."

Hutch shook his head. "Kyle's already gone. I won't get that space back. It's okay. I don't sleep much anyway. All right. Let's eat some gummy bears and watch some *Trek*."

It was only later, when she was in her lonely bed, that she realized Hutch had suggested they stay on the couch because he'd figured out her back had ached from all the walking, that sitting in a chair and playing a game might stress it further.

She didn't get much sleep that night either.

Chapter Ten

Hutch looked up from his laptop. He sat in one of the comfy chairs in the men's locker room at Sanctum. Years ago, Big Tag had turned the communal space into a massive man cave. There were three different TVs that usually played various sports. There was a fridge that was filled with water, soda, and beer. He would often walk in and find his friends playing video games. Like Theo Taggart and Michael Malone were doing at this moment. They were happily shooting each other in the latest sci-fi game.

The locker room was buzzing for a nonplay night. Some of the more experienced Doms had come to help with the first night of training, and some had simply come to check out the dumbass newbies. The Doms, that was. There would be a hell of a lot of ribbing going on.

Wade Rycroft was currently helping his youngest brother, though he was sure West Rycroft could put on a set of leathers without the help. Wade was the head of the bodyguard unit at McKay-Taggart. He used to run Sanctum, but he'd given up that job years before when he took over the unit and needed more time to spend with his wife and daughter.

"I'm good, brother. I didn't need you to come down here," West insisted.

"It's not a problem," he heard Wade reply. "I'll introduce you around and get you familiar with the place."

"I thought that was why I'm taking the training class. Also, the tops went through orientation last week. The big guy showed us around and pretty much threatened to murder us if we did anything wrong."

Ah, some things never changed. Sanctum ran one or two training classes a year, and Big Tag loved to fuck with the baby Doms.

West Rycroft rounded the corner, followed by his brother. The big cowboy had moved to Dallas recently. He was six foot three and all muscle, with longish sandy hair and a handsome face. He was all masculinity. He probably didn't cook or play board games or watch *Star Trek*. He lassoed things, and women thought he was manly because of it.

Was West Rycroft what Noelle was looking for? Was he her training Dom, and she was about to lose her mind over her gorgeous, masculine partner?

The friend zone sucked, and he was pretty sure that was where he was now.

Hutch glanced up at Wade. "Do you want me to take a picture? Baby Boy's first day at Dom school?"

Wade snorted, but West shook his head vigorously. "Don't even tempt him. I swear he's hovering over me like a mother hen or some shit. I'm a grown-ass man. I can handle a damn training class. I do not need my brother to hold my hand."

Wade stared at him pointedly. "I'm here because you forgot your kit."

Theo chuckled and then sighed because Michael murdered him on screen. He turned West's way. "Don't even bother, man. Older brothers can't help themselves. And whatever you do don't get yourself kidnapped and mind wiped. I swear you'll never hear the end of it."

West shook his head like he was trying to figure out if Theo was joking. "I'll remember that."

Hutch could have told him Theo wasn't joking at all, but he kind of liked having the other man a little off-center. "You should understand that if Noelle LaVigne is your training partner and you hurt her, your brother won't be able to save you. It's nothing personal. It's a lecture I'm giving every single one of you. Welcome to Sanctum."

West's eyes rolled. "Yeah, like I'm afraid of tech support."

Wade's hand came out and smacked the back of his brother's head. "First of all, don't think he can't kill you. He's been in and out of the field for years and you're brand new. Secondly, he's been through more dangerous shit than you could believe. Third, he won't merely beat the crap out of you. He'll wreck your life with a couple of keystrokes. You want to be put on a no-fly list? Because he can do that."

West put a hand to the back of his head. "I was joking. Damn, man. I thought that's what everyone did here. Sorry, Hutch. I'll look out for your girl."

"Ah, that's the problem," a familiar voice said. "She's not his girl and it's made him cranky."

Kyle leaned against the lockers. He, too, looked all big and muscley in a pair of leathers. Still, Noelle showed no signs of having a thing for Kyle, so he kind of hoped the gods had put them together. He didn't see Kyle making a move on her.

"She's my friend and I care about her," Hutch explained.

That got Michael's attention. "Dude, are you fucking the client? Did you miss the lecture? Big Tag puts it in all the training materials. *Thou shalt not fuck the client.*"

"Oh, he's not fucking her now," Kyle replied with a smirk. "He's cooking dinner for her, making her lunch, watching TV with her, and he sleeps on her couch."

Michael winced. "Sorry. Wow. So you slept with her and now you're still working with her but she's about to meet her training Dom, who is not you. That is some serious awkward."

Said the man who still worked with his ex-fiancée. "Pretty much."

He'd honestly thought Noelle would invite him back to bed. That first night after they'd sat up watching TV, there had been a moment when the world seemed to still and he could feel the air crackling between them. He'd known he was going to kiss her.

She'd said good night and run to her bedroom.

He'd sat on the balcony for the longest time, but the door hadn't opened.

Still, he caught her looking his way, and it wasn't with distaste. Would that change when she met her training Dom? Would all that sweet feminine energy and smarts be directed the new guy's way?

The only time he managed to get his hands on her was when he showed up to take her to lunch. Kyle had started driving her to and from work.

"I told you I'll look after her." Kyle pushed off the lockers. "She'll be fine."

"I thought we weren't supposed to sleep with the clients," West said, his voice hushed but absolutely audible to everyone in the damn room. "Not that I want to. The one client I've had was an old dude."

"Yeah, it's going to stay that way until you've completed your training." Wade put a hand on his brother's shoulder. "Come on. I'll walk you out."

They strode out of the room.

Michael looked at Kyle. "How did you manage to avoid your stepdad showing up for your first day of school?"

Kyle shuddered a bit. "Sean and I have decided to completely avoid even talking about this subject. Look, I know some of you have brothers and sisters who play here, but she's my mom. My mother. I do not need to know anything."

"You know moms can have sex lives," Theo pointed out.

"Do you want to see your mom get spanked? For that matter, do you want to see her in a thong?" Kyle replied.

Theo grinned. "Absolutely not, but I will say yours looks spectacular."

"I might need to vomit," Kyle said with a groan.

Hutch looked up at him. "Anyone else back there?"

"Are you asking me if there's anyone else you can threaten?"

"Yup."

Kyle shook his head. "Nah. It's almost time. I think we missed the first couple. And West isn't her training Dom. I might have taken a look-see. Noelle's paired with a guy named Jeff."

Theo frowned. "Jeff? Are you talking about Jeffrey Sinclair?"

Kyle shrugged. "That sounds right."

"Huh," Theo began. "I'm surprised. I didn't like him during the orientation. He was in the group I oversaw."

Hutch didn't like the sound of that. "What was wrong with him? He's not an employee."

"No, he's a favor for a friend of Tag's. Not a friend, exactly," Theo explained. "But his dad has done some big favors for the company, and he thinks his son needs to learn discipline. He got through Kai so he must be solid."

It was Michael's turn to frown. "Kai didn't have time to pair up this group. He let one of his partners do it because he and Kori are on vacation. They went out to see Jared and Sara for their little girl's birthday. They go every year. Kai did the psych evals, but the new counselor did the pair ups."

"She's the family counselor, right?" Hutch didn't like the idea that Kai hadn't paired up the partners. Kai Ferguson had been in charge of that for years. It was important to pair up training partners properly.

"I'm sure she knows what she's doing," Michael assured him. "She would take into account what the trainee says she wants out of the class. I remember my training partner." A smile hit Michael's face. "I'm pretty sure we both said something about wanting to explore the lifestyle through tons of fairly casual sex. We were perfect together. She would high-five me after an orgasm. Sometimes I miss her."

"You are not helping," Kyle admonished. "Hutch, I think you're fine. I've been hanging with her all week, and she talks about you constantly when you're not around. She's cautious. Keep up your I'm-the-best-boyfriend-in-the-world bit and she'll come around. Now I would like to feel like I'm not stuck in a bad rom com, so I'm going to head out. You guys dry his tears, get him a glass of Chardonnay, and convince the man to chill. She's still into him. I'll make sure her training Dom isn't too big of an asshole."

"I'm not in tears, and at least you'll know a big old ass when you see one," Hutch shot back.

Kyle's lips tugged up as he opened the door that led out to the hall and the stairs that would take him up to the dungeon level. "It takes one to know one."

"Hey, she's using her heavy braces." He hadn't even thought about that. "Can you make sure she gets upstairs okay? She might not want to use the elevator because no one else will."

Kyle sobered. "Yeah, I'll make sure she's okay."

"Thanks." He hated the thought of her standing at the bottom of those steep stairs and wondering how she would get up them. She might not know where the elevator was. Subs didn't get the same orientation that the Doms did. There was a reason for that. Doms were supposed to conduct a tour for their subs. It was a test to see how they treated their partners and how seriously they'd taken the initial class.

He wouldn't be the one to show her around. He would be the dude she saw across the dungeon one day months from now. He would be the guy she waved at before going back to her friends.

He realized the room had gone super quiet, and when he looked over Theo and Michael were staring at him like he'd grown two heads.

Had he thought having a bunch of brothers would be a good thing? Because right now it kind of sucked. "I'm not going to cry."

"I don't know. You kind of look like you're going to," Michael said, a note of horror in his tone. "I'm wondering if I can flee the room before the first tear falls. If I make it out before it hits his cheek then I'm not it, right?"

Hutch flipped Michael the bird. "Asshole. I'm not crying and I'm not sitting around listening to sad love songs in my car and then saying it's all a mistake that the freaking love station is programmed into my satellite radio."

Michael frowned. "It came with the car."

Theo put down his controller. "Sure it did. Look, don't worry about…it's Noelle, right?"

Hutch nodded. "Yeah. She's got some mobility issues, and getting attacked in her place of business didn't help. She usually uses a cane, but she's been in forearm crutches for a couple of days until her muscles chill out. Normally I wouldn't worry at all because Noelle's adaptable, but she doesn't know this place."

Michael turned Theo's way. "Who is he?"

Theo sighed, a long-suffering sound. "He's who you should have been if you wanted your relationship to work."

"Ow." Michael put a hand on his chest as though Theo had wounded him. "But maybe fair. I wasn't as thoughtful as I should have been."

"Because you weren't in love with Tessa and she wasn't in love with you," Theo replied. "You were both impatient. You see your brother with his wife and two kiddos and you want that for yourself, but you can't force it. The same way Hutch can't force Noelle to see that he's right for her."

"I'm not trying to force her to do anything." He hated this, hated that she was out there and probably looked gorgeous, and he wouldn't be the man who greeted her. He wouldn't be able to make sure the man who did treated her with respect. He didn't have any rights at all where Noelle was concerned and that hurt.

He was a man who'd avoided responsibility for the most part, and now that he wanted it, he couldn't have it.

"You can't force her to do anything, but you can make her world so comfortable she doesn't remember how she got along without you," Theo advised.

"That's what I'm trying to do. Kyle's right. I feed her every day. I watch TV with her. I rub her feet, and every night she runs to her bedroom."

"She runs to it?" Theo asked.

Hutch nodded. "Yeah. I think she's afraid I'll do something I shouldn't."

The idea that she might be afraid of him hurt more than anything.

"Or she's scared she's going to jump you," Theo offered. "Does she seem comfortable around you before it's time for bed?"

"Oh, yeah. She has no problem hanging out with me until Kyle is solidly in his room. Then it gets weird. Even though Kyle pays little attention to us at night. He comes and goes between the living room and his room." Kyle wasn't impressed with their taste in TV. He ended up watching sports on his laptop, and Hutch had heard him mention several times that this was a boring-ass assignment when he talked to his brother at night.

Boring was good. Boring was safe. Boring meant no one was shooting at them or choking out Noelle. Boring gave them time to research and try to understand why anyone would want to hurt her.

"Then Kyle's right and you should be patient. She's not going to take one look at this Jeffrey guy and forget you exist," Theo said. "You need to give her a couple of days. The class is once a week, and there won't be a ton of homework tonight. And hey, you'll be right there when he comes over to do homework with her. You can scare the crap out of him then."

Actually, that wasn't a bad idea. "What am I supposed to tell him? If he comes to her place, we risk him running into the people in the building who believe I'm Noelle's boyfriend."

Michael seemed to think about the problem. "This doesn't work. She can't take the class while she's the object of an active investigation. I don't know what Tag was thinking."

He could shut this shit down right now. He could claim it was far too dangerous, and she would have to wait until they had another class if she insisted on doing this with a group. And then Noelle wouldn't get what she needed. He didn't understand it, but she seemed to need to be here. She needed to do this on her own terms. "I'll make it work. I'll ensure all the homework is done here at the club, and Noelle and I will come up with something to tell him. Maybe we can let him know I'm investigating something for her."

"Big Tag might not like telling this guy anything at all," Michael pointed out. "You shouldn't say a thing until you run it by Tag."

"Then I should talk to Noelle because we didn't discuss this before." He stood up. Why hadn't he thought of this problem? Because he'd been too busy denying that she would actually go to the class. Because he'd been thinking of himself and not the case at hand.

"You've still got about ten minutes before they start the class." Michael picked up his controller again.

"Don't fuck it up," Theo advised. "When you come back we can order some pizza and play some more, if you want. Back when I was chasing after my wife, it always helped to take out my frustrations in video games."

Hutch wasn't sure he would be able to concentrate on a game right now, but it wouldn't hurt to hang out with friends and get through the next couple of hours. He rushed out. He would find Kyle and Kyle could talk to Noelle so she didn't feel like he was trying to disrupt her class.

It would be better if he didn't look at her because then he wouldn't be able to think about anything but her boobs. They would be gorgeous in a corset, and he hoped she was wearing a miniskirt because if this Jeff asshole saw her in a thong he would likely be hard to lose.

He took the stairs two at a time and then realized he was going to be lucky for once on this shitty day. Kyle stood just outside the dungeon talking with the Domme who now ran Sanctum—a lovely woman named Lea—and a dark-haired man in leathers Hutch didn't recognize.

"What exactly are you saying, Jeffrey?" Mistress Lea's voice had gone icy cold, and it stopped Hutch from calling out to Kyle.

Something serious was going on.

"I'm saying I didn't sign up to coddle some disabled chick," the man said, pointing back toward the dungeon space.

Kyle looked up and caught sight of Hutch. "Fuck. Lea, we have a problem."

"Why is she here?" Jeffrey asked, ignoring Kyle. "What can she do? She couldn't even get up the stairs without help. I'm not spanking some girl who can't even walk right. No way."

"Hutch," Kyle began.

But Hutch wasn't listening. Hutch saw fucking red and the rest of the world fell away.

* * * *

Noelle couldn't stop looking around Sanctum. It was crazy that she was here, and she was wearing a purple corset and a miniskirt, and there was a human hamster wheel that supposedly lit up when a sub was running on it.

It was crazy and she was stupidly excited.

Only one thing held her back from one hundred percent bubbling over with enthusiasm.

Hutch.

He'd stood outside the women's locker room when he'd dropped her off and given her the saddest smile.

I hope you have a wonderful time tonight. Whoever they put you with…he's so lucky, Noelle. Don't forget that.

Then he'd turned and walked into the men's locker room across the hall. She wouldn't see him again until the class was over and she'd gotten back into her slacks and blouse and she looked like regular old Noelle again. It felt like she was withholding something from him, but that wasn't what she'd meant to do.

Would he like the way she looked now? Would he stare at the way the corset forced her breasts up and how small it made her waist look?

"Did you find the elevator?" Laurel Daley Bradford was dressed in a crimson corset and tiny shorts. She was her stepmom's sister, and apparently she'd taken on a teaching role at Sanctum. A long-time sub, she had a son with her husband, Mitch, who practiced law here in Dallas.

"Yes. Erin showed me." She'd been greeted by Erin Taggart, who'd explained she was acting as a mentor to the new subs along with Laurel. She'd also been cool about whatever Noelle wanted to do with the stairs. When Noelle had chosen the elevator, Erin had sighed in what seemed like pure contentment and gone up with her, cursing her brother-in-law because he'd never had to go up those suckers in a pair of five-inch heels. "I can make it up if I'm on a cane, but these babies make it a little more awkward. I should be back on the cane next week."

Because Hutch was taking such good care of her. He made sure she rested but somehow managed to not make her feel self-conscious about it. He never demanded. He persuaded, like if she would let him do this thing for her, it would make him happy.

Going to bed without him was getting harder and harder to do.

But she knew what he wanted. He wanted her to give up the class and focus exclusively on him, and then she wouldn't have this crazy, excited feeling that she was going on an adventure, that she was exploring with people like her, people who didn't know everything, who were on her level.

"No one's going to care if you're on your cane or you need to use your chair," Laurel explained. "This is a place where we take people as they come. It's also a place where ex-soldiers come to play. You will see a whole lot of prosthetics here. It's fun to figure out how to use the equipment. Kinksters can be incredibly inventive."

She could see Hutch plotting and planning how to make every experience good for her. She would have trouble with some of the apparatuses because it would be hard for her to stay in position for a long period of time. But Hutch wouldn't let that stop him if he wanted to spank her on it. He would adapt it to her needs.

Some of her excitement faded because she wished he was standing here beside her.

"Hey, sweetie, I'm not joking. This is a good place," Laurel was saying.

She shook her head. "I wasn't worried about being accepted. I met several of the other subs in the locker room and they seem great. I was thinking about something else. Someone else." She shouldn't have said that. "Please forget I mentioned it. I'm excited to be here. I was telling Erin how much I've been looking forward to taking this class."

"Someone?" Laurel's eyes went wide even as her voice went low. "Do you have a boyfriend? Lila didn't mention a boyfriend. We should think about this if your boyfriend isn't into the lifestyle. I know you don't have to have sex to practice D/s but, honey, there's going to be sex."

Noelle shook her head. "No. I don't. No boyfriend."

But she had to admit that she might want one. The days with Hutch had been a revelation. They had pointed out how nice it was to have something beyond work to look forward to. He was even starting to charm Cara. He'd invited her to dinner the night before and then they'd played games. At the end of the evening Cara had grinned and told her she took back saying Kyle was hotter than Hutch.

Because Hutch was so much hotter, and it had everything to do with how he could make her feel.

"But there's a guy you like," Laurel prompted.

She wanted to talk, but Laurel was her stepmom's sister, and her younger one at that. She'd come to realize Lila ruled the roost in the Daley family dynamic. Her younger sisters came to her for advice, and they would definitely report back to her if they thought something was up. Lila considered Noelle a daughter, and she would definitely want updates. "It's someone at work."

"It's Hutch." Erin moved in beside Laurel. "At least I hope it is because Hutch is acting like a mopey bitch, and everyone at the office knows it's about his client. Well, most of us do. Li and I were talking about paying her to do Hutch so we can get him to do work without the sad puppy eyes. I asked him to run a couple of traces for me on a business guy in San Francisco named Noel and I swear he sat there and stared at the work order and actually touched the name on the page. It was the saddest most Hallmark shit I have ever seen. Please do Hutch, Noelle. Please."

She felt her cheeks flame. She'd known he was going into the office while she and Kyle were at Genedyne, but he didn't talk about it much.

Laurel sent the redhead a dirty look. "She's new. You do not have to expose her to the sarcasm level at this stage."

Erin shrugged. "She should get used to it. And seriously, it's Hutch she's thinking about." Erin frowned suddenly. "Unless she's into Kyle. Damn, girl. I don't know that's a good idea. Hutch is a great guy and he's totally solid. Like we know Hutch isn't going to explode at any moment."

"It's not Kyle," she spat out and then realized what she'd given away. Well, there was nothing for it now. "I like Hutch, but I don't know that it's real. He's intense, and I worry that he'll figure out it can be hard to be around me."

"Hard?" Laurel asked. "What does that mean?"

"It means I can't take the stairs most of the time. It means I have to plan how I'm going to get around. I can't simply walk into a building and go wherever I want to go. I know it seems like an easy thing to deal with but it's not. What you take for granted, I have to spend time planning." This wasn't exactly why her other relationships hadn't worked, but it was a part of it. There had been other factors, but somehow her legs exacerbated things.

Except Hutch didn't seem to care. When they'd had sex, he hadn't treated her like she was fragile. He'd fucked her hard and trusted her to tell him what she wasn't comfortable with.

"I'm married to a dude who forgot most of our lives together at one point. He didn't remember how our son was conceived," Erin replied. "He's still got long-term memory issues. I know it's not the same, but when you find the right one, you do what you need to do. You also find a rhythm, you know? Like what seems odd in the beginning is perfectly normal ten years down the line."

"Erin's right. I married a guy with a whole bunch of issues, and we found our way through. I still have to work around the fact that it's hard for Mitch to deal with his environment changing, but we get through it," Laurel admitted. "You can't know until you try, and Hutch is a great guy. He's such a sweetheart and he's good around kids."

All around her the other women were gathering. She'd expected they would all be her age, but there were a variety of ages and races and yep, there was a pretty woman there with a prosthetic arm.

The men were showing up, too, and like the women there was a glorious diversity to them. Big and scarred or a little on the softer side, the men all looked excited to be here, too.

"I know he's a good man. But I want to take this class, and that seems to be a real sticking point for him," Noelle admitted.

"Oh." Erin looked to Laurel, who nodded as though she understood. "He's worried he's going to lose you in all of this."

"Training is pretty intense," Laurel acknowledged. "The good news is it's not forever, and you could get through it and still want to see him on the other side."

Would he still want to see her? Or would he resent her for going through with the class? Would he always wonder if she'd slept with her training Dom and let jealousy come between them? She'd known guys like that.

"Hey, Noelle." Kyle strode up beside a stunning man with vibrant green eyes and black hair. He wasn't as big as Kyle, but he was fit. "I wanted to introduce you to your partner for the class. This is Jeff. Jeff, this is Noelle."

Jeff was drop-dead gorgeous, but there was something cold about him. She'd placed her right crutch against the wall after she'd gotten to the dungeon floor. She could make it with one on the even surface. She held out her hand. "It's nice to meet you."

He shook it and gave her a smile that didn't quite reach his eyes. "You, too, Noelle. I look forward to getting to know you."

"I look forward to getting to know how Kyle got hold of the

partner list." Erin stared a hole through Kyle.

Kyle gave her a grin that made him look younger. He almost always seemed serious, but every now and then he'd smile and it lit up his face. "I wouldn't be good at my job if I couldn't even figure out where Kai's group keeps their lists, would I?"

Laurel shook her head. "Make sure Mistress Lea doesn't find out or you'll be on that hamster wheel."

Kyle merely slapped his perfectly muscled abs. "I can handle it. The way Hutch and this one here cook, I'm going to be pudgy if I don't watch it. Noelle makes the world's best chocolate chip cookies. Do not tell my mom. She's proud of hers, but Noelle's are better."

Kyle really could eat. Hutch could, too. The last few days she'd gone through most of the dough she'd frozen thinking it would last her for a couple of months. She'd made chocolate chip and peanut butter cookies, and she was planning on orange rolls for Saturday morning. She loved to bake and had forgotten how much fun it was to watch someone enjoy the fruits of her labor.

The sweets. Hutch thought she was sweet.

Jeff backed away. "I guess I'll see you soon."

Noelle nodded and watched as he walked away.

"He's hot." Laurel was watching him, too. "No wonder Hutch is worried."

"Hutch doesn't know," Erin insisted. "And I'm going to talk to Grace about not spanking her boy enough. That one is going to be trouble. I should go and make sure the sample contracts are ready. Noelle, if you have any trouble at all, feel free to talk to me or Laurel. Even if you just get a bad vibe off someone."

She wasn't sure what Erin was talking about, but the woman was still watching Kyle and Jeff as they approached the tall Domme who was teaching the class. Mistress Lea wore her chestnut brown hair in a severe bun. She also wore some spectacular stiletto heeled boots that came up over her knees and made her legs look a million miles long.

"I'm going to make sure everything's ready, sweetie." Laurel stepped back. "And I won't tell your mom about Hutch. Sorry, stepmom. I really do think of you as family."

Noelle had to smile. "You, too, Aunt Laurel, but we're a weird family because you're now my kink aunt, too."

"Just know that Uncle Mitch will be avoiding you at all costs." Laurel gave her a wink. "Have fun tonight."

Laurel walked off and Noelle said hi to a couple of the women she'd met in the locker room. They were all buzzing, talking, wondering which of the yummy Doms they were going to get paired with and how fantastic the Mistress looked.

But the gorgeous Domme had moved her talk outside. She watched as Mistress Lea took Kyle and Jeff out of the dungeon and toward the stairs. There weren't walls around this part of the dungeon so she could see them talking.

And then she could see Hutch coming up the stairs. What was he doing here? Had he come to make one last plea for her to not take the class? That was a pretty arrogant thing to think. He hadn't mentioned it again after that first night. He'd likely given up on her and was doing all the things he did because he would do it for anyone in his circle. She was in that circle right now, but when the case was over, he would move on and find someone who did what he wanted her to.

Hutch's whole body went stiff and then he sprinted across the space and attacked Jeff.

For a moment Noelle felt like her feet were glued to the floor.

Everyone moved around her like they were magnetically attracted to the fight that was now going on.

What the hell did Hutch think he was doing? Did he think he could get her kicked out of the program? Or if he took her training Dom out, maybe she would leave with him?

She hadn't expected this of him. She grabbed her left crutch because she might need to use one of them on Hutch's head.

"Kyle!" she shouted as she moved through the crowd. "Make him stop."

Kyle was standing back, Mistress Lea at his side. "If I make him stop, I might have to start."

Mistress Lea sighed. "As much as I'm enjoying watching Hutch take him apart, Jeff is one of Tag's favors to a friend. Kyle, if you would please get Hutch."

"Seriously?" Kyle's eyes had gone wide. "You want me to take the psycho while you get the crying baby who can't throw a proper punch?"

Lea's lips kicked up. "Ah, the privileges of being the Mistress of Sanctum." She glanced over at the other Doms. "West, help Kyle. Someone go and find Erin and let her know we need a first aid kit."

Noelle managed to make it to the front of the pack. She was horrified at the sight. Hutch was basically taking Jeff apart. "Hutch!"

He stopped and looked up at her, shock in his eyes as if she was the last thing he'd thought he would see standing there. His hands dropped to his sides and his face fell. "Noelle. Noelle, I'm sorry."

"You think you're sorry right now, you fucking psycho." Jeff backed away, pushing himself off the floor. "Wait until I'm done with you."

Hutch started to take a step toward her.

Noelle shook her head. How could he have humiliated her like this? How could he even expect her to look at him after this?

Erin came running in, her now bare feet pounding on the dungeon floor. "What the hell?" She looked from Jeffrey to Hutch and then back to Jeffrey, who'd gotten to his feet. "What did you do?"

"It was Hutch." She couldn't let Jeff take the fall for this. That was probably exactly what Hutch had planned on. Had he been trying to get Jeff thrown out? What happened to a sub without a partner? She would probably be told she needed to wait until the next class.

How could she have been so wrong about him? God, her heart actually ached because she'd thought he might be the kind of man she could honestly count on. She'd thought he was like her dad. But Hutch was selfish.

"Jeffrey said…" Mistress Lea began.

"Nothing." Hutch looked back at the Mistress. "He said absolutely fucking nothing. I didn't like the way he looked at me and don't take shit from baby Doms. You should all understand that."

"You attacked me for no reason." Jeff touched his busted lip. "Is this how I'm going to be treated here? I want your fucking name, asshole. Because you better believe I'm going to take everything you have."

"How could you?" Noelle ignored Jeff because Hutch was the only one who mattered. How could she stay now? How could she go into a training relationship with a man he'd beaten the crap out of? Jeff would find out about her relationship with Hutch. How could he

211

go on and train with her? How could she even stay? Hutch had caused this drama and that's all anyone would remember about her.

Hutch's whole body seemed to sag. "I'm sorry. I...damn it, Noelle. I don't know why I did that."

"You did it because he said he wouldn't coddle a disabled chick and said he wouldn't touch her." Kyle's words sent a shock through her. "You did it because you care about her and you won't let anyone talk about her that way. Ever."

Hutch's body was tense again, and he looked like he was ready to take on Kyle, too. "I didn't want her to hear that."

"She should." Kyle's eyes found hers. "She should hear it because she should know why you lost your shit. She should know the reason why her training Dom is leaving right fucking now."

"I'm not leaving." Jeff turned her way. "Look, it's cool that this club wants to let someone like you in, but you're going to make it hard on the rest of us. I came here to have fun, not to babysit."

She wasn't going to cry. Except she'd already started. She couldn't help the tears that filled her eyes. "I wouldn't work with you if you were the last person on earth. Hutch...I need to be not here but I can't..."

She didn't even get the request out of her mouth before he was there, picking her up and letting her crutches fall to the side. He hauled her up and cradled her against his chest.

She'd accused him, denied him, and he didn't hesitate to be there when she needed him.

"I'm taking her downstairs, but she'll be back for the beginning of the class. He better not be here, Lea." Hutch started for the stairs.

"The class begins now," Lea called out.

"No, it doesn't. It begins when she's in her seat and you've taken out the trash," Hutch replied without looking back.

But Noelle could see the whole group over his shoulder. She saw the way Mistress Lea smiled as though she utterly approved of the way things had gone.

"Have her back in twenty minutes, Hutch," Lea ordered.

She wouldn't go back. She watched as Laurel walked in, picking up Noelle's crutches and talking to Erin. She would get the whole sad story and then her stepmom would call and tell her all sorts of inspirational bullshit. All of the trainees would be talking about her, feeling sorry for her. Or maybe some would agree with Jeff. Maybe some would see her as holding the class back.

Hutch strode down the stairs, taking her away from that horrible scene.

She wasn't going to cry. Not the way she wanted to. She was going to suck it up and get through the next few moments, and then she would ask him to take her home and she would never try this again. Never.

Hutch now knew exactly how humiliating her life could be. There was always a Jeff out there, waiting to take her down a notch for inconveniencing him.

He kicked the door to the women's locker room open. "Anyone here? I need the room."

No one replied. The room was completely silent. He moved into what Laurel had described as the salon portion of the locker room. It was a big, lovely living area where the women of Sanctum relaxed before and after their playtimes.

She wouldn't enjoy this space. She wouldn't sit in here making herself pretty for her Dom and talking to her friends.

"You can set me down." She'd been impulsive. She'd been weak. She should have left on her own two feet.

"I can't. I can't because I'm afraid if I do, I'm going to lose you." He sank down on the sofa, his arms tightening around her. "Please forgive me, Noelle."

Forgive him? "There's nothing to forgive. I'm sorry it happened, but I can't be mad at you for defending me. Though it's not…"

His head shook and his jaw went mulishly stubborn. "Don't you even finish that sentence. I'm on edge and I didn't get to do what I wanted to, so please don't push me by telling me you don't need me."

Emotion swamped her, and she wasn't even sure which one was hitting her the hardest. Humiliation, pain, self-pity was in there. But so was gratitude, and now empathy because he looked lost. "Don't need you?"

"I know you don't feel the same about me, but I can't stand by and let someone treat you like that. I can walk away when I know you're safe, but don't make me walk away knowing you didn't need me. Even for a little while." He dropped his forehead against hers. "Don't let this hold you back, baby. You belong here. He doesn't. Every single person in the club will support you, and if they don't, they won't be a member of this club for long. Big Tag owes me and I'll call in all the favors to make sure you have a good training experience. I'll find you the best newbie Dom I can, and I'm going to kick Kai's ass for letting anyone else do his work. I promise. I'll ask Kyle about his brother. David's a nice guy, and he's been thinking about taking the class. I'll make this work for you."

The indignity Jeff had heaped on her melted away in the face of Hutch's caring. She'd given him every indication that she didn't care about him in a boyfriend way, but damn he was acting like the most caring boyfriend ever. He was giving her everything she wanted merely because she wanted it.

She cupped his cheeks and threw away the humiliation and self-pity because there wasn't a place for either when she was with him. He could chase both defeating emotions away with a mere smile, and she was done denying him.

She didn't need the perfect training experience. She needed to experience it with him.

"Hutch, will you teach me?"

He went still. "Baby, you don't have to do this. I'll get you what you want."

He didn't understand. Her reluctance had done a number on him, but it stopped now. "I only want you."

He started to argue but she stopped him with a kiss.

"Don't," she ordered. "Don't waste more time. I know what I want and I want to be with you more than I want this class. I was afraid if I didn't take it, I would always be Hutch's girl and not just Noelle. But I can make my own friends here. I can do it without the class, and honestly, being your girl is not such a bad gig. Don't fight me on this. I'm not walking away because of that giant ass. I needed a moment to process, but I'm okay. He's not the first guy to insult the hell out of me and he won't be the last. Unless the word gets out about how good you are in a fight. He's bigger than you, babe, but you were well on the way to taking him apart."

He'd gotten angry because he cared about her. They would have to work on that, but in this one moment it gave her some peace. It let her know someone was willing to fight for her. Since she'd moved to Dallas, she'd had to fight for herself so often she was tired.

"I wanted to kill him," Hutch admitted with a sigh and then his mouth hovered over hers.

How had she gone from the depths of despair to wanting his kiss more than her next breath? The rest of the night didn't matter because she was done fooling herself. She wanted to be with Hutch. "Tell me you want me."

The smile that came over his face lit up the night. "I want you, Noelle. I want you in a way I haven't wanted anything in a long time. Not since I was a kid."

"What did you want then?"

"Safety," he replied simply.

He'd been a little boy with no power for much of his life. And then when he'd found his power had he wielded it simply to show he could? No. He'd saved his brothers, put his life on the line.

Why had she waited? "You're safe with me."

She brushed her lips over his, pouring everything she felt into that kiss. His hand moved along her thigh and up to her waist.

"You're safe with me, too." Hutch breathed the words against her lips.

She was. "Let's go home."

She knew she should say *her place*, but living with him for the past week had made that apartment feel more like a home.

"But then we'll miss your class," he said, and he picked her up again, making her feel petite and cared for. He stood up with her in his arms like she weighed nothing at all.

"My class? I told you I don't want another training Dom." She was sure David Hawthorne was a great guy, but she'd made her choice.

"And I told you I would make sure you have everything you want." He started for the door. "So I'll be your training Dom. I'll go right back to Dom kindergarten and do it all over again, and baby, you should understand I'm going to take homework seriously."

"But I thought it was against the rules." She'd asked about it. She'd asked Kyle and he'd explained that the training class was for newbies only.

"Rules are made to be broken." He pushed through the door and started for the stairs. "And like I said, Tag owes me and I'm calling it in."

She settled against him and suddenly was perfectly content with how her night was going.

Chapter Eleven

Kyle pulled Noelle's sedan into the parking space she'd been allotted and put the car in park. "Okay, we need to talk, you two."

Hutch didn't want to talk. He was way too busy kissing Noelle. He'd started the minute they'd gotten into the car and hadn't stopped the whole way back to her building. He'd helped her into the back seat and followed right behind her.

She was his sub. He was her training Dom. They were doing what they were supposed to do. Exploring the lifestyle. One kiss at a time.

He was ready to explore her body again. It had been far too long.

"Did I mention how freaking hot you were tonight?" He probably had, but it should be said about a thousand more times because she'd taken his breath away. "We're going to get you so much fet wear."

She grinned at him. "I can't wait to see you in a set of leathers, Sir."

He kissed her again, letting their tongues tangle as arousal pulsed through his body in a pleasant fashion. He hadn't changed into leathers, and Mistress Lea had allowed it for the evening, but she'd also used him as an example of how no one should be topping a sub while wearing a Spiderman T-shirt.

He could top Noelle in any number of geeky shirts. He had a

never-ending supply of them.

He was *not* sleeping on the couch tonight.

She felt so fucking good in his arms. When he'd carried her back up to the dungeon and sat down in one of the trainee chairs, she'd sat on his lap and Lea had simply sighed and begun the class. He hadn't even asked what they'd done with Jeffrey, though he'd been told he had a meeting with the lawyers in the morning. Erin would have taken care of that asshole, and now he could take care of Noelle. That was how his team worked. Even when they weren't at McKay-Taggart.

He was oddly excited to go through it all again. With her. The first time he'd gone through training, he'd done it because his friends were all doing it and it seemed like a good way to fit in. Only later had he realized how much he'd needed it. Only after he'd gotten home from his enforced time with Dr. McDonald. Then he'd needed to be in control.

It felt different this time, and not simply because he was experienced. It felt fresh and new because he was with the right person now.

"I think we're home," Noelle said between kisses.

"Yes," Kyle affirmed from the front seat. "And we should talk about what that means now that the two of you have canceled your membership to the lonely stares club. I never thought I would miss all the longing looks, but I think your fuck-'til-you-drop stage is going to be even worse, and that's why we need to set up ground rules. I have to live here, too."

He wasn't listening to Kyle. He needed to get his pretty sub upstairs and start her real training. Oh, they would go through everything the class at Sanctum did, but he was going to be a stern mentor. And a playful one. And he was definitely a horny one. Fet wear would have to wait. "We're going upstairs and you're going to get naked for me."

"See, that is exactly what we need to talk about," Kyle continued.

"I will." Noelle seemed perfectly willing to ignore Kyle, too. "But you have to be naked this time. I didn't get to see you the other night. Not the way I wanted to. I think you're beautiful."

He wasn't, but he would take her taste in men as a lucky break. "Deal."

"No deal. Look, I can handle a pretty naked sub walking around the apartment. That's cool. I've never lived that lifestyle, but it works for me in theory. But I draw the line at seeing Hutch's junk on a daily basis. I am not getting paid to see that." Kyle opened the car door.

"Do you think he didn't like Elisa?" Noelle whispered, mentioning the name of the woman Kyle had been partnered with.

"I think he's jealous." He kissed her again. He didn't care what Kyle thought. He'd barely noticed Kyle was around, though he'd been happy the guy was there to drive them home so Hutch could focus entirely on Noelle.

"*He* thinks Elisa is perfectly nice, but *he* is not planning on handing over his balls to the first sub he sees." Kyle sounded awfully proper for a dude who'd been wearing leathers an hour before. "*He* is going to view this not as a love connection but a certification. *He* is not going to forget that he has a job to do and part of that is making sure our client stays safe, and I do not deem this parking lot to be safe. Let's get a move on."

Kyle was right about that. He needed to remember that she was still in danger. He kissed the tip of her nose. "Let's do what Grumpy Dom says. That's his nickname now."

The rest of the class had gone off without a hitch, and all the subs had gathered around Noelle at the break to offer her support and denounce Jeff the Jerk, as they'd called him. She'd seemed to make a couple of connections, and he'd realized why she'd wanted the class.

She wanted friends. She wanted to belong on her own so if anything happened, she wouldn't be left out. Noelle wanted to be more than merely his sub. He wanted that for her, too, so he'd decided to stand back and let her fly whenever they were in class. He wouldn't crowd her or be overbearing, but when they got home, then he would be all over that sub.

"That is not my nickname," Kyle groused.

"He doesn't have to worry about Elisa falling in love with him." Noelle let him help her out of the car before settling into her crutches. "She told me she's gay. But she didn't want a female partner because she said she doesn't want any temptation. Just the class. She works in the DA's office and there's a woman she's interested in, but she's a top. She wants to make sure she enjoys the lifestyle before she pursues the relationship."

Wasn't that interesting? Because he was fairly certain Kyle was doing the same thing before he decided if he was going to chase after MaeBe. No matter what denials were about to come out of his mouth.

"So we're the perfect pair because I was very plain that I did not want a relationship at all, even a temporary one." Kyle engaged the alarm system and started for the lobby door. "Back to our actual important discussion. We were talking about safe places to indulge yourselves. Do you know what I deem as a safe place? Her bedroom, with all the doors closed and the windows shut. You could even lock the doors, maybe barricade yourselves inside so there is zero possibility that the doors come open and I have to see something I shouldn't have to see."

He was too young to be the old dude yelling at the kids to stay off his lawn. Kyle was also forgetting an important part of club life.

"How are you going to survive the class?" Noelle proved they shared similar minds as she asked the question he'd been about to pose. "I looked at the curriculum and talked to my aunt. I think there is definitely nudity coming up soon."

"Ah," Kyle began. "You obviously do not understand the value of compartmentalization. There's the club, where nudity among friends is acceptable. The locker room? Acceptable place to see your friend's junk. Waking up and walking into the kitchen? Not acceptable. I did not sign up for that risk. I will jump in front of a bullet for either of you. I fully expect to die on this assignment because it's been that kind of year. Honor my future sacrifice by not forcing me to die with the sight of Hutch humping seared into my brain. Lock the door."

Hutch rolled his eyes as Kyle strode up the stairs. Hutch followed Noelle to the ramp. It was easier on her than the stairs right now. When she used her cane the stairs here were manageable, but the crutches made things harder on her. He'd spent days watching her, learning how she adapted to her environment and filing it all away to make things easier on her.

He stopped as emotion threatened to swell again. He cared about her and she was vulnerable. She was smart and capable and still vulnerable. He fucking wished he'd had more time with Jeff. He'd barely managed to make the fucker bleed, though he'd gotten a couple of excellent gut shots in that the asshole would hopefully feel for days.

"Hey, it's okay." Noelle was standing in front of the door. "I'm okay. I'm tougher than anyone thinks, and I've already let it go."

Kyle held the door open, frowning. "What are we talking about now?"

Noelle's eyes never left Hutch. "He's still angry about Jeff and his rejection of me, but I need him to understand that I've moved on and would prefer to concentrate on him and locking that door to my bedroom for the night."

"Okay." Hutch let the anger go because she didn't need it. What other people thought didn't matter, and he'd handled the situation. It was time to let it go. He moved up the ramp to join her. "It's done."

She lifted her face up to his, a glowy smile on her lips. "I'm glad. I love that you fought for me, but I need you to understand that it will happen again, and I don't want you to punch everyone who insults me."

He stared at her. She couldn't believe he would sit back and let someone treat her like crap.

She stared right back. "I mean it."

"I reserve the right to defend you, but I'll think about it before I lose my shit," he promised and dropped a kiss on those pretty lips of hers. He could quietly take names and make them pay for it later.

"I do not understand you two," Kyle said with a sigh. He walked through the door.

"Thank you." Noelle grinned before turning and starting inside.

Kyle didn't understand how they could get each other. Noelle had known exactly what he was thinking. Hutch had never been so in synch with a woman.

He was going to get his hands on her again. He was going to turn the lights on and caress every inch of her skin. He wouldn't give a flying fuck what Kyle thought, though he would definitely close the door. What happened tonight was going to be between the two of them. It was the real start of their relationship because they were both on the same page now.

He was falling in love with Noelle, and it felt good. And he didn't care that his friends would make fun of him. It didn't matter. He was going to understand why Big Tag still smiled when his wife walked in a room. Why Sean and Grace still held hands after all these years.

"Are you hungry?" Noelle asked. "I could make us some grilled cheese sandwiches."

She stopped because Kyle held up a fist. It was a military gesture that let anyone who understood it know to go silent. It was a gesture that had his heart pounding for a completely different reason than it had two minutes before.

Hutch stood in front of Noelle, who seemed to understand what Kyle wanted. Hutch moved his hand to the back of his jeans where his Glock 22 was secure in a holster under his shirt.

"You can't come in here and expect me to take care of you." A deep voice spoke out of Hutch's sight. Masculine.

"I don't know. You seem to be doing pretty well."

This voice was familiar and feminine. He recognized it from the night she'd spent at Noelle's dinner table.

"Is that Cara?" Noelle whispered the question.

Hutch nodded. It sure sounded like her, and he thought she was talking to the second shift guard. Chris Taylor. Chris Taylor, who was also DPD and perhaps working with the feds.

What was Cara doing talking to Chris Taylor at almost eleven o'clock at night? Had she had a security problem? It didn't sound like it. There was a hushed tone to her voice that spoke of some kind of intimacy.

"I'm not going through this again with you," Chris replied. "You can't take what you want and then leave me."

"You know I don't have a choice." Cara sounded angry for a moment and then she sighed. "Come on, babe. I don't want to fight. It's been a long night. Can't we enjoy the now?"

A deep chuckle came from Chris, an unamused sound. "You would like that, wouldn't you? You would love it if you could use me and discard me as often as you liked."

"That was never my intention. The last thing I expected…" Cara stopped.

Then suddenly there was the sound of footsteps on the marble floor of the lobby and then Chris was moving into view. He wore his night guard uniform, but all Hutch could see was the police officer.

"Ms. LaVigne." His shoulders didn't relax, though he sighed as if relieved. "Welcome home."

"Noelle?" Cara put a hand over her mouth. "Oh, my god. I thought you were out for the evening."

"I was," Noelle replied. "It's late. We're just getting back. Are you all right?"

Cara's hands had a fine tremble to them. "I'm fine. What did you hear?"

"Nothing." Noelle was a terrible liar.

Cara started crying, tears rolling down her cheeks. "I'm sorry. I should have told you that Chris is my ex."

Chris's face went a nice shade of pink. "I didn't feel like an ex thirty minutes ago."

Cara gasped, a shocked sound. She turned on her ex, her fists clenched. "Are you kidding me? God, you're such an ass." Her attention refocused on Noelle. "Please don't tell anyone. I'm not this woman. At least that's what I tell myself. I keep going back to him when I know he's bad for me. I got him this stupid job and I should have known it was a terrible idea, but he needed the cash."

Hutch watched the pair. He was good at reading body language, and every line of tension in their bodies told him they'd been on the cusp of something sexual. They were also shocked to be found out. This wasn't the place to question them. He needed to think, to go over any possible connections between the two of them. How deeply had they vetted Cara? "Hey, it's none of our business."

"Is he bothering you?" Kyle looked Chris up and down as though assessing him as a threat. "I can make a call to management."

Ah, Kyle was making the play to see how far he could push her, how far she would take it. It was a good play because if they could get Chris fired, he wouldn't be close to Noelle. Of course, it wouldn't be a move Hutch would make since the authorities would almost surely send someone else in, and they would have to figure out who.

It was a good play if Kyle wanted to bring in his own person to watch her, to back him up.

Chris took a step forward, an obvious aggression. He was

sexually frustrated and wouldn't mind taking it out on Kyle. "I'd like to see you try."

Cara put herself between them, one hand going to Chris's chest. "No. He didn't do anything I didn't ask him to do. Please. I'm sorry. I'm embarrassed to get caught. I was down here and we fooled around. After we were done, I felt bad and we got in an argument. Please forget you heard anything. Like I said. I'm not proud of myself, but I've been lonely."

"It's okay." Noelle moved toward her friend, empathy plain on her face. "I can understand. I didn't know you knew him. You acted like you didn't."

Cara's jaw tightened, and she wouldn't quite meet Noelle's eyes. "I didn't want anyone to know. We were engaged at one point in time, and it blew up pretty badly. I don't like to talk about it."

"You blew it up, Cara. Put the blame where it belongs. I was perfectly happy. You were the one who let me know I wasn't enough for you." Chris took a long breath and backed off. "I'm going to do my job before you blow this up for me, too. Ms. LaVigne, I assure you I won't let her affect my performance again. I hope you have a good night."

He turned and stalked back into the small security office.

Cara's eyes were bright with unshed tears. "I'm sorry you saw that."

"Do you want to talk?" Noelle offered.

Damn it. He could see his whole perfect night turning into a long session where Cara cried and Noelle held her hand.

Cara shook her head. "No. I'm going to do what I should have done. I'm going to bed and when I wake up in the morning, I'm going to make better choices. I'll see you then."

She practically ran to the stairwell, eschewing the elevator that would likely have had them all going up together.

"What the hell was that?" Kyle whispered the question.

Hutch shook his head. "Not now. Cameras."

"I think it was obvious. Cara's sleeping with the security guard, and they have some kind of history." Noelle's eyes were still wide. "I'm so surprised. She mentioned an ex, but I didn't imagine he worked here. I've never seen her this upset."

"Well, now we know she's human." Hutch leaned over and kissed her, his voice going low. "Let's go upstairs to talk about this."

She nodded and followed when he started for the elevator.

"Like we needed more drama tonight," Kyle complained, sounding tired. He yawned. "First, I had to watch the two of you make out all night, and now I've got an image of Cara and the guard in my head. I need to find my own place and fast."

Good. Kyle was good. He'd moved into his role with no effort at all. He'd given no signs that he believed that fight they'd overheard was anything but a lover's quarrel. His face was bland, and that was all the camera would see. He didn't give up the fact that it was a lot of coincidence to think Cara had a connection to the man who might be watching Noelle.

Kyle was a pro.

It was easy to forget the secondary mission. Kyle was unassuming. He did his job, played around on his computer, talked to his brother most nights. He'd called his mom twice and made plans to have dinner at her place as soon as he could get free. He was a working guy. Nothing more.

Which was exactly what he should be if he was spying on all of them.

Still, Hutch took the cue because Chris could be monitoring them from that station of his. "Buck it up, brother. I've got the prettiest girlfriend in the world, and you just have to deal with it."

When the elevator doors opened, he walked inside and gave Chris something to watch. He backed Noelle to the corner and kissed her all the way up to the fifth floor. She'd been briefly surprised, but then her lips had opened and she'd seemed to forget about everything but softening for him.

Kyle simply groaned and grumbled the entire time.

Before too long the doors opened and he escorted Noelle to her apartment, no sign of Cara. Kyle shut the door and turned the lock.

"I don't think I'm hungry," Hutch announced. He wanted to get her into bed as soon as possible. They could talk in the morning. For now, he wanted to spend time with Noelle and when she was asleep, he would consider everything that had happened. "I think I'd like to head to bed. If you're hungry, let's get some snacks and lock ourselves away for the night."

"I think that's going to have to wait." Kyle crossed his arms over his chest. "We need to talk about what happened. I have a couple of thoughts."

Hutch was about to argue, to beg Kyle to wait for the morning to debrief because he was horny and he'd spent days sleeping on a way too short for him couch.

But he stopped because there was a red light on the bottom edge of her TV screen. A light that should have been off because he'd made sure that smart TV wasn't so smart. It shone in the low light from the living room, proof that something had gone terribly wrong. That light was on because in the last thirty minutes someone had turned on the monitoring capabilities of the TV. He'd studied up on the model and that indicator light stayed on for thirty minutes after the monitoring function was engaged. He watched as it blinked off, but that didn't mean they were safe. It merely meant that they'd been lucky enough to get that important clue. If they'd been a few minutes later, whoever was watching would have gotten away with it. He wouldn't have checked again because he'd turned the sucker off. Someone had accessed Noelle's system.

Someone was watching them.

His night had gone straight to hell.

* * * *

Noelle glanced around the three-bedroom ranch house and wondered why Hutch hadn't bothered to decorate. He'd explained that he'd recently bought the home from a friend of his who'd moved to Colorado, but he didn't have much in the way of furniture.

In the spacious living room there were a couple of lounger chairs and a big screen TV that apparently didn't scare Hutch the way hers had.

"Yeah, we're at my place," Hutch was saying into his cell phone. "Kyle is paranoid as fuck and he's doing a sweep. I think we'll be okay here for the night." He paused. "I thought about getting her out of there. I know. Ian, I know. No, I didn't panic, but she's not a damn spy. She wouldn't be able to monitor what she was saying the way the

226

rest of us would, and it's not fair to ask her. Of course I gave myself some cover. I faked a call from my cousin who told me my mother was in an accident. We packed up quickly and stopped to let security know we were going to be gone for a while. It should buy us a couple of days."

Kyle strode into the living room from the back of the house. There was no way to miss the big gun in his hand. Kyle had been tense since the moment Hutch had pointed to that red light on her television. She'd tried to tell him it was normal. She'd seen it before. He'd shushed her and then he'd faked his phone call and she'd realized he thought someone was listening to them. Or watching them. He'd been careful to put a wall between himself and the TV.

It sent a chill down her spine. She'd thought he was paranoid before when he'd explained he'd turned off all the monitoring functions of her home hub. She knew in the back of her mind that the virtual assistant "listened" and learned. It was how it knew her voice commands and anticipated certain needs. One of the reasons she'd selected her apartment building was how high tech it was, and it offered a wide range of innovations in smart home technology.

Now she wondered who'd been watching her before. How long had she had eyes on her? How long had the mysterious "they" listened in on her conversations?

"Yes, I'm sure," Hutch continued. "I'm sure because I'm the one who went in and turned them all off. I turned off the monitoring functions on every smart appliance she had. They were connected like a smart house should be. It's how her hub system can control everything from the lights to her streaming services to filling out a grocery order for her. No, yours is not the same. I hooked up yours myself and I built in a code that lets me know if anyone fucks with it. I swear, Ian, it's fine. I'm not coming over to do something that I already did. Yes, if someone has hacked your hub, you can absolutely pull my lower bowels out and feed them to your dog. I'll help you."

Noelle gasped. "Who the hell is talking that way to him?"

Kyle seemed to relax, putting his gun down on the TV tray that sat between the two loungers. He sagged down onto one. "Ah, that would be my kindly uncle Ian. You met him, right?"

She had, but she'd spent most of that time thinking about Hutch during her meeting with Taggart. "I don't like the way that sounds."

Hutch had moved into the kitchen, and she couldn't hear him anymore.

"Don't worry about Ian," Kyle assured her. "His bark is worse than his bite. He's softened up with age and a whole bunch of children. Once he was a pretty ruthless bastard. He was a legend."

"In the security business?"

"In the…military," Kyle replied. "He was in the Army. I was in the Navy, but we still knew about him. Mostly because his brothers, Case and Theo, were in the Navy, too. But like I said, he's not the same Ian Taggart. Hutch is calming him down. He can get upset when things don't run smoothly. You understand what happened, right? Hutch used a whole lot of professional terminology. I didn't get about half of it, but I do know the basics."

She'd gotten the gist. "Someone turned on functions of my smart home that Hutch had turned off. They were the functions that allowed the system to monitor things. Someone could watch me through the TV."

"Not just the TV. Pretty much anything with a screen," Kyle corrected. "And that includes your fridge. They could watch and record."

"Why would anyone want to watch me?" It was what she still hadn't figured out. She was boring. Even her research was considered boring.

"Because you work for Jessica Layne, and I fear she's involved in some dangerous things," Kyle replied.

"Like what?"

"That's what we're trying to figure out."

"What could she possibly be involved in?" Noelle sank down to the seat beside Kyle. She sagged back because it was pretty comfy. "I know she's harsh and she's quick to sue, but she's had to be. It can be hard to be a woman in STEM, much less a woman at her level."

"There are plenty of women in STEM who don't screw over everyone that they come in contact with. You heard the rumors about her former partner, right?"

"Of course. And I don't agree with how Jessica treated her, but I figure it's a lot like Jobs and Wozniak. Jobs screwed over his chief engineer so he could take control of the company." The fight for control of Apple was legendary in the world of high tech. "That's what Jessica did. It's not right, but it happens all the time in business."

"I don't think that's what's happening here," Kyle admitted. "What do you know about Jessica's plans to take Genedyne public?"

"I don't think she wants to. She's got investors, but it's not the same as having a board to answer to. If she went public, she would have far less control."

Kyle nodded and sat back. "Well, we know something's happening there, and you're involved in some way. You said she's now interested in your research?"

"Yes." She had a lot of work to do. She hoped Hutch didn't think she was going to be staying home for a few days. "Jessica got a look at my initial results. They're promising. She can raise money off it if I can reproduce the results."

"Did she raise money off Madison's research?" Kyle asked.

"Of course. Madison's research was flashier than mine. She talked it up all the time."

"And Jessica's still got that research?"

"Some of it, certainly," Noelle replied. "I'm not sure how much was lost in the fire, but she had backups for the initial research. She should have almost everything up to the night of the fire. But I do know the experiment Madison was working on was lost during the accident. So anything she tweaked that night would be lost."

"How much do you think Jessica raised on the hope of that research?"

Noelle didn't pay much attention to the business side of things. It was one of the reasons she wanted that sweet tenured position at a university someday. She loved science. Business was the awful part of her job. "No idea. Though I do know she had investor meetings about it. The rumor around the office had Madison on the cusp of a breakthrough."

"One has to think losing the head of the research would upset the people who invested because of it," Kyle mused. "I would really like to see the financials on Genedyne."

"I don't think she shares that with anyone except maybe her

CFO. I'm not sure. I don't spend a lot of time in the upper levels." She liked her lab, and now she had to wonder if she would see it again soon. "Does this mean I have to call into work?"

"No," Kyle said.

"Of course it does." Hutch was standing at the edge of his kitchen, his phone in hand. He put it back to his ear. "Yeah, do it, Ian. I've got a problem. I'll talk to you tomorrow. Fine. Tomorrow night. Yes, I'll come to the club."

He slid the phone into his pocket.

"What's Ian doing?" Kyle turned the chair around, showing it could swivel fully.

"Running some more reports on Cara," Hutch explained. "And I think it's best if Noelle takes time off work."

"I can't. My research is in a delicate phase. I actually need to work this weekend. My boss is expecting a full write-up on Monday." A bit of panic started. "Hutch, I can't miss work."

"You can write up your research here."

She shook her head. "No, I can't. A lot of my data is on the internal server, and I can't take that home with me. I also need to run the experiment again and then again and again to make sure it's not a fluke. I can't miss work."

"Chris believes we're heading back down to Papillon," Hutch pointed out. "So does Cara, since we had Noelle text her."

"I don't care what they think." She couldn't lose her job. "I'll get fired and I'll lose control of everything I've worked for in the last few years."

Hutch's eyes narrowed. "You could also lose your life."

"If they wanted to kill me, they could have done it in the locker room," she pointed out. "Kyle will get fired, too. I don't understand. Do you think Cara is watching me? Why would she do that? I don't understand how she would know I didn't go back home like I said?"

Hutch and Kyle shared a long look before Hutch finally answered. "She might not be who she says she is. We have to consider that she might be the person who's monitoring you."

She couldn't see Cara being a bad guy, but then she wasn't the spy. However, Hutch was ignoring a very important detail. "Then she already knows I didn't go to Papillon and it doesn't matter."

"She's got a point there." Kyle stood again. "I didn't see anyone tailing us, and if Cara's half the reporter she says she is, she'll probably find out we aren't who we say we are. She might already know."

He'd placed a slight emphasis on the word *reporter*. "You don't think she's really a reporter?"

"I'm worried she might be like Chris Taylor," Hutch replied. "I'm worried they're the ones who turned on your monitoring. She knew we weren't going to be in tonight. She asked about it. Chris can get into your apartment. If they're working together, then it's best we hole up someplace else."

Kyle put a hand on his shoulder. "I get it, man. You're worried about her, but she can't go on the run without even knowing what she's running from. We need to figure this out, and that means we might have to reach out to Taylor."

"We don't know who he's working for." Hutch's jaw clenched in unmistakable frustration. "It would be one thing if we were absolutely certain he's undercover for DPD, but we're not sure."

"Well, we'll find out real fucking fast if we do question him," Kyle replied.

"Or we'll end up in jail if he's working with the feds, or maybe dead if he's working for someone else," Hutch shot back.

Kyle went tense. "Who do you think he's working for, Hutch? I thought we agreed he's DPD and potentially working with the feds. You seem to have changed your mind about that but you haven't talked to me."

"He could be working for Jessica," Hutch replied. "You've read her file. It wouldn't be the first time she's hired someone to watch her employees."

"Why? If she's worried about my research all she has to do is pull it off the server." None of this made sense to Noelle. Neither did the odd tension between Hutch and Kyle. They were looking at each other warily. "She has no need to search through my laptop."

"Then we should still consider that Chris is working for DPD," Kyle said. "And if he hasn't approached us, he's not worried. We go to work. We come back here. We keep the peace and get our jobs done. Noelle is right. If whoever is watching wanted her dead, the locker room was the perfect place to do it. We need more data. You know this, Hutch. The only way to get it is to be in that building, to let me poke around."

The thought of Kyle getting caught made Noelle's breath hitch, but she knew he would be careful. She forced herself to her feet. "If you get caught, I lose everything."

"I'm not going to get caught," Kyle promised. "Half of what I'm doing is listening carefully. I'm supposed to accompany Jessica to a party tomorrow night. I've figured out there are going to be investors there. We need those names, Hutch. And Noelle needs to work this weekend because Jessica is talking her up. You understand that if she gets fired, it's not as simple as her losing her job."

"I lose my research." The thought brought tears to her eyes. "She might even bring legal action against me. I know I make good money, but I can't fight her in court."

Hutch seemed to think about that for a moment and finally he nodded. "All right. We should get to bed. Noelle, you can use my room for the night."

"You're not staying with me?" She blinked in an attempt to keep those damn tears from falling. The evening had been an emotional roller coaster, and the thought that she wouldn't end it with him felt like the worst rejection of all.

"I don't think it's a good idea." Hutch wouldn't look at her.

"I'm finding a corner to curl into so I don't have to watch the rest of this melodrama," Kyle said on a groan before pointing Hutch's way. "You are a dumbass, and this is absolutely a clusterfuck of an assignment. Decide, man. This wishy-washy shit's going to fuck with her brain. Call me if someone needs shooting. Noelle, that includes Hutch."

Kyle stalked off, and she was left alone with the man she was pretty sure she was falling wildly for.

"Noelle, I am not rejecting you," he said quietly. "I'm in a position where I feel out of control, and I don't handle that well. I'm angry, and that means I shouldn't touch you."

"You're angry at me?"

"No, I am angry at the situation. I'm angry at a world that won't seem to let me find some peace. I'm angry at fucking Jeff and angry at Chris and Cara, and I kind of want to punch Kyle now, too. I'm angry because I should have met you at a coffee shop and we should be going to see movies and having dinner dates instead of hiding out from whoever wants to hurt you."

He was angry, but the root of anger was almost always fear. He was afraid of what could happen. "I'll be as careful as I can be. I promise I want to come out of this alive, but my job is important to me. I've been working for this for all of my life, Hutch. I thought this dream was dead after the accident, and I spent a year having to figure out that I was the only thing holding me back. I worked hard to get here. I can't give it up."

"I know, and I'm going to spend tonight trying to figure this thing out so you never have to."

"I would rather you spent it with me."

His fists clenched at his sides. "Like I said, I need to calm down. Why don't you go to bed and I'll have a drink and chill and I'll join you later."

She reached for her right crutch and stood. He wouldn't join her until he was sure she was asleep, and they would have lost something precious. She wasn't ending this evening sleeping without him. The question was how to make him see reason. "Hutch, please."

"Noelle, I've given on the important thing."

Yes, and he was punishing himself over it. Still, she had to consider the fact that her pushing back had made him change his mind about her. "Do you not want to sleep with me because I'm not doing what you want me to do?"

His eyes finally came up. "I'm not sleeping with you because I want to eat you up, Noelle. I want to fuck you so hard you won't be able to walk tomorrow without feeling my dick inside you. I want to dominate you, need it to feel like I control one fucking thing in my life—the best thing in my life. I want to tie you up and do whatever the fuck I want to you, and you are not ready for that."

Oh, she felt ready for that. "Okay."

"No, you took your first training class tonight. I'm not going to throw you in the deep end."

"But my Dom swims so well. I can understand not trying things if you weren't already good at them, but you need something and I'm willing to give it to you. I'm eager to give it to you."

He shook his head. "No. I'm not going to risk it."

He wasn't trusting himself, but she had faith in him. Now she just had to push him to make him understand that she could handle what he needed, that she trusted him implicitly. She couldn't prove that if they were sleeping apart. They were at a crossroads. That idea struck Noelle forcibly. What happened tonight would set them up for a good long while. She could be his trainee—treated gently but held at a careful distance—or she could be his lover.

Being his lover might require some manipulation.

"Is it because I'm fragile? Because you got a good look at my legs tonight and you've changed your mind?" She knew it wasn't true, but she was willing to give his anger somewhere else to go.

Because she trusted him with her body and her heart.

That got his eyes to flare, and he crossed the space between them. "What did you say?"

Yes, now she had his attention. "I stated aloud my worry that you no longer find me attractive. Also, that you think I'm too fragile to have sex with."

His hand gripped the back of her head, tangling his fingers in her hair and giving her a tease of pain. "I've already had sex with you, Noelle. So either you're manipulating me or you don't understand me at all, and I don't believe that. I think you get me like no one ever has before."

"And I think you don't understand how far I'll go to comfort you," she whispered back. Because she did get him. She was rapidly discovering that he was part of her soul. "I know you're nervous about me going back to the office, but I'm going to be okay. We're going to get through this, and you'll be stuck with me because you decided to be my training Dom. No matter what happens you're stuck with me for six whole weeks."

That big hand of his tightened, lighting up her scalp. "You know damn well I'm stuck with you. And you know you're gorgeous."

"I know you think I am, and I'm grateful for that," she corrected. "I also know you think I can't handle what you need. You think you're pushing me by pulling my hair, but it's doing nothing but getting my nipples hard and making me wish you would kiss me."

He loomed over her. "You don't know what you're asking for."

"I know that there's more boiling under your surface than what happened tonight. It's all coming back. All of it. Being out of control. Being a victim. You're worried that's what's going to happen to me and you'll lose me. And tonight you're worried that the D/s you need to feel in control will hurt me like your dad hurt you and your mom, but it won't because it's not the same. It's something we both need to feel whole and complete, and that makes it beautiful. That makes it a part of what it means to be us. I'm asking you to share that part of yourself with me. I thought this was happening too fast between us, but I'm done pushing you away. So take me. Show me. Teach me. Above all, be with me. In this moment and every moment we have from now on."

His head dropped down to hers and she knew she'd won this fight.

Chapter Twelve

Hutch let go of any notion of not having her tonight. She was a little brat who desperately needed some discipline and a whole lot of pleasure.

She was a brat who was going to save him from his own misery. He couldn't sink into that dark place that found him from time to time when she was willing to drag him back into the light.

Emotion warred with arousal. Or maybe it was simply mixed in there—the natural combination that came with actually making love. He rubbed his forehead against hers. "You're killing me. I do not deserve you."

"I'll remind you of that when we do actually go to Papillon and you meet my dad," she promised.

He was not about to let her father's distaste for him be a wall between them. Nope. He'd faced down worse enemies, and he knew what to do. He tugged on her hair, forcing her head back and looking down into that gorgeous face of hers. "Your dad will love me. I'll fix his computer and end up being his personal IT guy. Now take off your clothes. You're going to leave them right fucking here. That way Kyle knows this is a naked zone and he should stay out of it."

Kyle was half of his problem. He wanted to trust the man, but Kyle seemed willing to put Noelle in harm's way so he could keep his position with Jessica Layne.

Hutch had to watch the man who was supposed to be watching their backs.

"You think I'm pretty." She kicked off her loafers.

He understood that she'd been manipulating him before, but there was still a hint of insecurity in her words. The first night they'd slept together the lights had been low, and they were fully on now. Did she think he'd forgotten an inch of her loveliness? Did she imagine he hadn't studied her scars and found them every bit as beautiful as the rest of her?

"I think you're gorgeous, and I'm going to show you. I scare you and you say the word yellow," he instructed. "I push past your comfort zone and you say red. Otherwise I'm going to do what I want, when I want, and for however long I want. Do I make myself clear?"

"Yes, Hutch."

He untangled his hand from the silk of her hair and stepped back. This was his time. She was the brilliant scientist whose work would change the world someday during the daylight hours. But at night, she would be his. His woman. His lover. His sub.

His to play with and adore and fuck.

Noelle let the crutch she'd been leaning on sit back against the chair. She felt steady on her feet and started to unbutton her blouse. She kept her eyes on him, offering him another connection.

"Who helped you with your corset?" He'd sat in the men's locker room and wondered who was taking care of her. He had no doubt she'd learn how to deal with the intricacies of fet wear in no time at all, but she'd admitted this was her first time in a corset.

"Elisa. She has the locker next to mine. She was the first of the trainees to introduce herself."

"Did she?" He couldn't help but grin at that thought because he was pretty sure Elisa hadn't minded helping her at all.

His inuendo did what he'd hoped it would. It had Noelle rolling her eyes and grinning before she let the blouse drop. She wore a pretty pink bra that showed off the tops of her breasts. "She's not interested in me."

"Oh, if she likes women, she appreciated how pretty you are." He needed to make her understand that it was all okay in the confines of the club. With the exception of that fucker Jeffrey, she could trust the men and women of Sanctum. "It's all right at the club. That's the beauty of Sanctum. You can walk around naked all day and unless you want someone to touch you, they won't."

She unclasped her bra and let it hit the floor.

And proved she hadn't been lying about her nipples. They were hard as rocks, and his fingers itched to touch them. But he was in control again, his fears pushed down in favor of taking care of her. He would get his hands on those luscious breasts, but it would be on his time. She unbuttoned the top of her slacks and slid the zipper down.

"Keep going," he commanded. He wanted her to make the decision to be naked in front of him.

His dick tightened, arousal flooding his system in the most pleasant of ways. She pushed the slacks down and caught the waistband of her silky undies, pulling them along and leaving herself naked in front of him.

She was even prettier in full light, and he was going to have her naked as often as possible.

His cell buzzed in his pocket letting him know the text he'd been waiting on was coming in.

Michael Malone would stake out the house tonight, making sure Kyle didn't slip out or invite someone in.

He forced down the emotion that played through him at the thought because he could fully pay attention to her now.

"So what are you planning on doing with me?" She put a hand on her hip and gave him her sauciest smile. That was a smile he intended to keep on her face.

"First I'm going to show you that your legs aren't important." He marched right up to her and hauled her into a fireman's hold over his shoulder.

She yelped at what was probably a shocking change of perspective. "I only said that to get you in the right headspace. I know you don't care."

"Oh, I care. I care a lot." He slapped her ass with his free hand, a playful swat that would serve as a warm-up. "And you're a brat."

"You're going to make me beg, aren't you?" She was breathless.

"I'm going to make you squirm and beg, and maybe I'll even

make you cry a little, but you'll like it or you'll tell me if it doesn't work for you. I'm not going to make this some training session, but we are learning each other's limits and what works for us as a couple. We talk during sex. We don't pretend like we make this spectacular without putting the work in."

She needed to understand that the heart of what he wanted wasn't merely spankings and blow jobs, though he did want that and intended to get to both this evening. At the base of his needs was communication. He needed to talk to her, to connect with her.

"Yes. I want all of that," she replied and did some of the squirming he'd promised she would do.

He slapped her ass again and she gasped. The first one had been playful. This one was all business, and a tight sound came from her throat.

A shudder went through her body as he turned into his bedroom. It was the one room that had nice stuff in it that wasn't connected to the Internet. He had a big comfy bed and a dresser that was half empty, two nightstands, and all the room they would need to be comfortable.

Was he already thinking about moving her in? He shoved the thought aside because being with her like this meant being in the moment.

He lowered her to the bed and stared at her. She looked perfect just the way she was, with her pink-tipped nipples and a flush on her skin. He gripped her ankles and flipped her over. The scars she worried about were on her back where they'd worked on her spine. Where it had broken and she'd been forced to put herself back together again.

He let his fingers trace the scars.

"What are you doing?" Noelle started to roll over.

He needed to show her what he wanted. He spread her legs and moved in between them, pinning her to the bed and leaning over to breathe his command into her ear. "I am looking at you, touching you, learning you, and you're going to let me. You have your safe words. Unless you want to use them, you'll be still and let me have my way with you."

He nipped the nape of her neck and she shuddered again, her

breath hitching and that sweet ass of hers wriggling against him.

Yeah, she liked a bite of pain. That was good for him because he liked to take a nibble every now and then.

He stood again, satisfied she would obey him now. It was time to show her how well he intended to take care of her—and how kinky he could get. He didn't want her thinking about her legs. He knew she'd brought it up to force him to react, but he also knew they'd been an issue tonight. She would think about them, think about whether they moved like other subs' moved, like other women.

He was going to make sure they didn't move at all.

His kit was sitting right outside the closet, so it was easy to pull out the rope he kept in there.

"The anticipation part is hard. I don't know what you're going to do," she said.

That was the fun part for him. "You'll learn to trust me. Part of what we're going to do is see what works for you and what doesn't."

"You work for me. It works so well when you kiss me."

"Good, then we know that works. Now let's see how you feel about bondage." He wasn't falling for her ploy. She was trying to get immediately to the good stuff, and he wanted to play. She needed to learn that he was the boss when it came to this.

"Bondage?" She started to try to turn again.

He caught her ankles and laid a quick three slaps to her ass, the skin getting a sweet shade of pink. "Yes, bondage, and you're going to learn all about long spankings if you don't stay still."

She laid her head down, and he could see the way she bit her bottom lip and how her hands fisted in the comforter. Patience wasn't her strong suit. But he would teach her that the waiting led to something incredible.

"Now I'm going to stand you up and we'll get this part out of the way. Tell me something, Noelle. Have you ever been tied up before?" He flipped her over and helped her stand. "Ankles together."

"You're tying my legs?"

He dropped a kiss on her nose and smoothed her hair back. "Yes, unless it's going to bother you."

She shook her head. "No. I'd like to try."

"Good. I'm going to use a basic pattern This is called Hishi," he explained and then dropped to his knees which put him in an excellent position to wrap the length around her hips. And be close to that part of her he would spend so much time on tonight. After she'd learned some patience. "The rope is jute, and you should get used to the feel. I'm going to use a diamond pattern."

He wrapped the length around her twice before tying it over and around and letting the remaining length brush her pussy.

A sigh came from her and he worked the rope in a tie right above her ankles. While he worked, he touched her. He stroked her calves and thighs and her ass as he formed the diamond pattern that would hold her tight for him.

Noelle stayed still, her eyes on him as he finished the last tie. "So you have me helpless. What now?"

"Have you figured out why I like this?"

She shook her head. "No. I'm not sure I like it. I do feel vulnerable."

"I want you to bend over and put your hands on the edge of the bed. I won't let you fall, and if you experience any discomfort in your back, I'll have you out in seconds." He had a knife handy for that exact situation. "But I want you to try it because I think this can eventually make you feel secure and might help you focus on the part of your body I want you to concentrate on."

"You've tied up my entire lower half, so I'm sure I'll be thinking about it," she complained.

"It's good we're getting this all out in private because if you're this salty on the dungeon floor, I'll have to do more than spank you." She'd been right to push him because he was settled now. He could handle this. He could take care of her and he could figure out what was going on with Kyle. He could definitely take care of her tonight. "Hands on the bed."

She leaned over awkwardly. He stood back, ready to catch her if she needed it, but wanting her to explore this, too.

"This is weird, Hutch. I feel both contained and exposed at the same time."

That was because with her legs all tied up, this position not only put her backside on fabulous display, it also exposed her pussy. He let his fingers brush over her labia. "Yes, this is ripe and ready for play.

Do you have any idea how tight you would be if I fucked you like this? I would have to force my way in, and you would feel every inch."

He let his fingers play, rubbing and caressing and giving her a hint of what was to come. She was already wet, her arousal coating his fingers.

"Tell me what you've played around with before. We had to go over hard and soft limits quickly this evening. I want to know what toys you feel comfortable with."

"Well, I'm starting to like rope but never tried it before. All of my relationships have been vanilla, like stale vanilla," she admitted. "The best sex I'd had up until a couple of nights ago was with a vibrator."

"So you masturbate?"

"Yep." Every word came out shaky as she responded to the finger slowly fucking inside her. "The sad thing is my stepmom helped me buy my first vibrator because I was worried it wouldn't work. My clitoris that is. It was after my accident."

He pressed between her thighs and found that pearl of hers. "Are you talking about this, sweetheart?"

Her breath caught. "Yes. Oh, yes. That's exactly the spot."

She wasn't getting off that easily. He moved his finger back. "It works quite well, and I'm glad you had your stepmom to help you. I had my hand, and then I spent time in juvie hoping I didn't learn anything at all about sex. I didn't, by the way. My time in juvie was actually okay. It sucked, but less than being on the street. The Army was also a dry spell for me, but things picked up when I worked for the Agency. Did you experiment in college?"

"With flavorless sex, yes," she replied. "Come on, Hutch. I was close."

"Do you know what else changes when you're in this position?"

"What?" The question came out on a sigh. A bratty sigh.

"What I slap when I spank you." He drew his hand back and laid a gentle smack right on her pussy.

A low moan came from Noelle's throat as he spanked her again and again. He went light in the beginning, raising the impact until he hit ten.

"How are you feeling now?"

She sniffled. "I don't know whether to cry or beg."

"Then you're exactly where I want you to be." He spanked her again. "Tell me how this makes you feel."

"It makes me feel like my body is a live wire," she replied. "It makes me feel like I kind of hate you, but I don't want you to stop either."

He let his hands move over her curves until he found her breasts. His dick pressed against the seam of her ass. He was so fucking hard, but he had a point to make. He cupped her breasts, loving the contrast of her silky-smooth skin and those pointed, pouty nipples. He rolled them between his thumb and forefinger. "I don't want to stop. I want to do such dirty things to you, baby. And you're going to let me."

"Yes. Yes, I am."

That was what he wanted to hear. He pinched down lightly on her nipples, and her ass rubbed against his dick. "I'm going to help you get to your knees. You're going to ease down to the floor and then you're going to suck my cock."

"Oh, god. Hutch, I haven't had much experience with that," she said, her body moving against his. "The time I tried it didn't go great."

"Did he tell you what he wanted?"

Her chest swelled, pressing her breasts into his hands. "No. He just shoved it at me, and apparently I have a small mouth."

It was tempting to drop his pants and shove his cock in, but he wanted to feel her mouth on him. "I'm going to tell you what I want from you. I'm going to let you play and explore and run your tongue all over me. I loved tasting you the other night. I can't stop thinking of how sweet you are. I want you to taste me. Will you do that for me?"

"Yes. I want that."

"But you have to tell me if you're uncomfortable." He was already thinking about buying some pillows and bolsters. If he did, she would be comfy when he twisted and turned her so he could fuck her hard.

"I'm uncomfortable right now," she shot back. "And you're not doing anything about it."

Oh, she was such a brat. He straightened up and placed a hand on the small of her back before peppering her backside with smacks that made her moan and call out his name.

He touched her pussy again, sliding his finger inside and then out again and again until she was on the edge and he withdrew.

Noelle cursed under her breath, her sweet Southern accent incongruous with the dirty words coming out of her mouth. He intended to make sure this was the only time his baby ever cursed him. But this was *his* time.

He helped her stand, turning her so he could bring her close. Her arms wound around him as he kissed her before gently easing her down to her knees.

"You're still not undressed. That's the only thing that bothers me," Noelle said, sitting back and seeming comfortable.

He pulled his shirt over his head and tossed it aside. He could give her what she wanted. "I'm sorry. I was far too busy looking at you. You're prettier than me."

Her lips curled. She reached up and undid the buckle of his belt. "I feel pretty like this. I liked wearing fet wear tonight and I like the rope."

He was glad because he intended to have her in one of the two a whole lot of the time. And he was deeply grateful that she'd moved past that idiot's words tonight. She was listening to the people who mattered. He toed out of his sneakers and his socks joined them. "I like to tie you up."

She eased the fly of his jeans open, and he felt his cock jump, eager to play. He'd concentrated on her the first night they'd made love. His whole focus had been on worshiping her, but they needed this connection, too. It was okay for him to take this because Noelle needed to give to him, too.

She also needed to explore, and it looked like she was starting with his dick. She wrapped her hand around his cock, and he felt every muscle in his body tighten. Her hand was soft and warm as she stroked him. The way her eyes took him in was even hotter than the feel of her hand. There wasn't hesitation in her gaze. There was hunger.

He was ready for her to eat him up.

* * * *

Noelle had never spent so much time on sex, and she reveled in it. This was what had been missing. Perhaps not merely the time spent or the care. It wouldn't have worked with another man. She was attuned to this one, to the way he cared for her, worshipped her body with his.

It was time to show him she adored him, too. And that she could play some wicked games.

She ran her hands from his chest to his abdomen. He was gorgeous, all muscled and tan, like he spent time in the sun working out, perfecting a body that was stunning to begin with. She drew her hands to where she'd uncovered his cock, tracing the line of neatly trimmed hair. She eased his jeans and boxers down so they were around his hips and she had full access to his cock.

Like the rest of Hutch, his dick was a thing of beauty.

She brushed her fingers over his hard flesh, moving from the base to the bulb, memorizing the soft feeling of the skin versus the strength it encased. She let the tip of her finger trace the ridge where the cockhead began, teasing the sensitive cap.

"I want to feel your tongue on me, Noelle," Hutch commanded.

She leaned over and licked the head of his cock, taking in the drop of arousal that had beaded there. Salty and masculine, she liked the way he tasted, too.

She definitely liked the tremble that went through his body and how his hand found her hair.

"That feels so fucking good. You're going to pay me back aren't you, brat?"

She liked being his brat. She was always the good girl, but here alone with Hutch she could explore another side of herself. She wasn't going to thank that ass Jeffrey, but she was happy things had worked out the way they had because she couldn't imagine exploring without Hutch. "I think I might like to play."

He hissed as she sucked the head of his cock behind her lips. All of her previous worry was shoved to the side because he would tell her what he liked. He wouldn't prevaricate. She could try whatever she liked, and he would guide her to what gave him the greatest pleasure.

Trusting him gave her a freedom she'd never known before. So did having her legs tied. She wasn't worried about being awkward or how they looked. He'd been careful as he'd tied her, making certain every inch of her skin got his loving attention before binding her legs together and making her helpless against him.

It was odd because she'd been helpless before. She would have thought being tied up would make her feel panicked, but a warmth had come over her, and then a pounding excitement that Hutch could do whatever he wanted with her. He could play with her and fuck her and spank her.

Wow, she liked being spanked. There was an ache in her cheeks that she could still feel. Every slap he'd given her had gone straight to her pussy, and she was wetter than she could have imagined.

She glanced up and Hutch was staring down at her, his eyes filled with dark desire. He was watching her, watching her tongue as it licked across his cock, watching as she took him into her mouth and laved him with affection.

She stroked him and cupped his tight balls and enjoyed the power she wielded over this man. It wasn't anything she would ever abuse. She trusted him, but the idea that he trusted her was important, too. Hutch had been through so much, but he was open and honest with her. He was willing to be vulnerable.

They could be great together.

She worked the underside of his cock, running over and over it with the tip of her tongue.

"I thought you said you weren't good at this," Hutch said, a growl to his tone.

She'd been awkward at this, but she was all tied up and had recently had her pussy spanked by the hottest Dom in the world. There was no room for awkward in her life today. And she also thought Hutch was far kinkier than her previous experiments. To test that theory, she gave him the barest scrape of her teeth over his cock.

His hand tightened on her hair. "That's right, baby. Fuck, that felt good."

She sucked him in and dragged her mouth over another inch

before pulling back. She liked the way his balls had tightened, ready to go off.

"Take more." He was getting demanding.

She did as he asked, drawing him in deeper and hollowing out her cheeks to suck at him hard. She found a rhythm, moving her body in time with his as he took a bit of control and started to thrust in and pull out. The hand in her hair led her, showing her exactly what he wanted. She whirled her tongue around, fighting because he was so big in her mouth.

He tugged on her hair, pulling her off. "As much as I want to come, I would rather do it inside you. I want to feel how tight the rope makes that pussy of yours."

He kicked off his jeans and stood naked in front of her. He reached down and simply lifted her up like she weighed nothing at all. She expected him to transfer her to the bed, but he gripped her ass and brought her breasts to his lips, sucking one in and making her squirm. He nipped at her, sending a thrill down her spine. She sank her fingers into his hair and held him to her while he moved from breast to breast.

"This isn't casual for me," Hutch said as he moved her to the bed. He laid her back and stared down at her bound legs. "I know you think we're only together for as long as the case…"

She shook her head. "No. I was stubborn about the class, but I won't be stubborn about this. I don't want an end date, Hutch. I want to date you, sleep with you, be with you for however long it works for us."

He took her ankles in his hands, sending warmth all through her. "I think this might work for me forever. You should be ready for that. And I am so ready for this."

He flipped her over and she was suddenly face first on the soft comforter. He tugged on her hips and her feet were on the floor again, her breasts flat against the bed. "You solid?"

He was asking if she was going to fall. She took a minute to make sure she had her balance. He was treating her like his favorite fuck toy but still thinking about her comfort. It was all she could ask of a lover. "I'm good. I'm better than good."

She heard the sound of a condom wrapper being torn open and wished she could watch him roll it over his cock, watch him stroking himself, but she suspected there would be many chances to come.

He wanted her in his life, and not for a couple of weeks. He wanted to try a real relationship with her, and there wasn't anything she wanted more than for them to have that chance.

And then she wasn't thinking about anything but that big cock teasing at her pussy. She could feel him there, his hands on her hips. She could feel him everywhere—in the way the rope rubbed against her skin and how her nipples ached slightly from his teeth, in the ache in her ass from his hand spanking her, and in the taste of him still on her tongue. He surrounded her, and it was the most intimate experience of her life.

"You're so pretty like this, all tied up and ready to take my cock. Did I tell you how good your mouth felt?" Hutch's hands roamed over her curves as he started to press against her.

She had to catch her breath at the sensation because he felt enormous. He'd felt big before, but this position he'd put her in made her so much tighter.

He gripped her hips as he started to impale her on his cock.

She gasped at the first long thrust. He held himself against her.

"You okay?" He was a chatty top.

"No." She was going to be completely honest with him. "I'm dying because you won't fuck me."

She felt his hand run down her spine. "I love it when you talk dirty in that Southern accent. It gets me hot. I'm going to fuck you, baby. I'm going to fuck you until you can't take it anymore and you scream out my name and wake Kyle up."

She bit her bottom lip because she wasn't going to do that. She could keep quiet.

He dragged his cock out and then immediately thrust back in, and he hit some magical place that made her shake. He was the only one who'd ever stroked her in exactly the right way. Until the other night she hadn't known that place existed. She'd managed to give herself orgasms, but they'd all been about stimulating her clitoris. Hutch managed to press a button inside her pussy that made her see stars.

"I can make you do it," Hutch promised. "I can take that ladylike exterior of yours and strip it away to reveal my sexy sub. That's what you are right now. You can be the smartest person in the room during the day, but at night in our bed you're my sub. Your job is to offer me your body and take my cock any way I want you to."

She loved it when he talked nasty, too. Like her, he had a daytime persona. He was the nice guy, the guy who always had some candy for the kids, who was always willing to help. But here with her he was the dirty Dom.

This was a place that was only for them.

His right hand moved around her waist to settle against her clit, and the minute he rubbed her, she couldn't hold back another second. The pleasure hit her like a wave and she cried out, not caring that someone might hear her. She was everything Hutch had said she was.

His.

She felt him stiffen behind her and he went wild, pumping into her until he finally fell to the bed beside her.

He had the sweetest smile on his face as he helped her up to join him. He kissed her and smoothed back her hair. "You'll be careful at work."

He was compromising. She could do the same. "I will. I promise. I won't take any chances."

"Because we're together now and we have to take care of each other," he said. "We have to honor what's important to each other. You are the most important thing to me."

He was going to make her cry but he kissed her again, and she let him take over. She let everything float away and trusted in her Dom.

Chapter Thirteen

"Do you ever listen to anything I say? Anything?" Kyle stood in the living room, a mug of coffee in one hand as he pointed to the clothes on the floor.

Hutch bit back a grin and scooped up Noelle's clothes. He had to stop tossing her underwear around every time she slept with him or she would get the wrong idea. "My living room in my house is a perfectly safe place."

"It's not safe for me." Kyle shook his head and moved to the windows that overlooked his front yard and driveway. He stood there staring out. "And tell your girl she's not very quiet. I need earplugs." He turned slightly, one side of his mouth curving up in a half smile. "Congrats, though. I take it you two are now solidly together? Or are you playing it by ear?"

"Together. I'm not playing at all." He tossed Noelle's laundry in the basket with his own. Being here at his place had some drawbacks, but having a full washer and dryer he didn't have to go two floors down to find was not one of them.

And having access to his kit hadn't been one of them either. Tonight he would introduce her to the crop, and maybe some handcuffs. She seemed to like being bound.

"Excellent, because having spent time with her, I think she would be good for you," Kyle said quietly. "I think she's a good woman."

"You think?"

Kyle shrugged. "You can never be a hundred percent sure. People can trick you."

He knew that better than most. "Yes, but only some people. A woman like Noelle would never trick me."

"I hope so." Kyle sighed and then moved to the kitchen. "So why do you not have dishes? You have coffee mugs and a bunch of barware, but you seem to run on paper plates."

"He had a crazy ex. She tossed them at his head when she found him playing video games with the guy she was cheating on him with." Noelle walked out of the hallway looking sunny in a yellow dress and white flats.

"That's a good explanation," Kyle said with a laugh. "You have a creative mind."

"She does, but not about this. I really did have every plate and bowl I owned tossed at my head because I wasn't sad enough," he admitted.

"I still don't think she was your worst." Noelle grabbed a mug. "He was friends with benefits with a woman CIA operative who threw knives at him after she realized he only considered her a friend."

"Kelly with the knives. Good times." He'd been grateful she'd only been trying to make him pee his pants.

"You told the new girlfriend about the old ones? Isn't that something you shouldn't do for a couple of years?" Kyle asked, pouring Noelle some coffee.

They'd been up most of the night. When he hadn't been on top of her, they'd lain in bed and talked. They'd talked about sex and their previous relationships and how sad his had been. He probably should have glossed over a couple of those, but he'd been honest with her. She'd told him how hard it had been to date in college, how hard it still could be because being in a relationship with her meant adapting to moving slower, to planning out every date to accommodate her needs.

His heart had clenched because she'd been trying to warn him.

She didn't understand that making things comfortable and easy for her would be one of his favorite things in life. He liked planning. It was a thing no one understood about him. He enjoyed the notion that he could be important to someone he cared about. Hell, once he'd given up a year of his life, walked willingly back into hell because a man he thought of as a brother had asked him to. He wasn't about to be scared off at the prospect of not being able to take Noelle on a particularly rugged hike.

He got into her space because it had been a whole ten minutes since he'd kissed her last. "We move on our own time." He brushed his lips over hers. "You want some breakfast? I've got frozen waffles and maybe some eggs."

She sighed, a happy sound, and wrapped an arm around him, hugging him close. "Tempting, but I think I'll grab something on my way in. Pete texted me and he's got the experiment ready for me. I'm hoping to run it a couple of times today."

He didn't want her to work at all. Well, he didn't want her working at Genedyne until they figured out what was going on. The thought of her going into that building alone scared the shit out of him. Kyle would be somewhere close, but he wouldn't be standing over Noelle making sure no one could get to her. "I'll be there at five."

She stepped back. "Hutch, I might need to work late."

"I'll be there at five, and you can work right here in this house."

She stared at him as though trying to figure out how far to push him. She finally grimaced. "Fine, but I have to have this report done by Monday."

"I would rather you worked on Saturday than late at night." He would bet a lot of people worked Saturdays at a place like Genedyne. She wouldn't even be alone in her lab, which he knew was part of the attraction of working at night, but he couldn't let her do it now.

She frowned but still went up on her toes to kiss him. "Fine. But I better get to the office. Are you coming with us? Your car is still dead, right?"

Yeah, he hadn't even thought about the fact that he'd fucked up his battery. But he had a plan in place. "Theo and Erin live a couple of doors down, and whichever one isn't on kid patrol can give me a ride."

They switched off carpool duties for their son and daughter, and whoever had the day off had an hour alone in the house. He still had forty minutes until he needed to head into the office.

But maybe he should go with Noelle. He could take a train from Genedyne to the McKay-Taggart building.

"Let's head out if we're stopping somewhere to pick up breakfast." Kyle put his mug in the sink. "I'm getting to sit in on some fun meetings today, and I'm supposed to cover a dinner date tonight. I might end up at Jessica's, so you should pick Noelle up. I'll leave the car and take an Uber back here because I don't want Jessica's driver to know we've switched locations."

"I'll come in with you." He should take a shower. Big Tag had a famously sensitive nose, and he could smell sex on a dude from five miles away. And he did not stint on the sarcasm.

"I'll be fine. Kyle is an excellent driver, and he's learned how to make small talk." Noelle took a long swig of coffee before her mug joined Kyle's.

"I have to talk about stupid shit or she starts in on her relationships. All of them," Kyle admitted. "I know a lot about her feelings. So we talk about dogs and TV shows I pretend I watch so I don't have to know more about her feelings."

Kyle was an asshole. "Fine. Take care of her. Text me when she's safe in the lab."

God, he hoped she would be safe in the lab.

Noelle kissed him again and then walked off, her cane in her right hand. Stretchy sex seemed to have done wonders for her.

It sure had done wonders for him. Noelle made her way out to the garage, and Kyle glanced back as he walked after her.

"Dude, take a shower. You smell like sex." Kyle shook his head and the door closed.

He was surrounded by assholes. He found his phone and texted Theo, who promised to pick him up in half an hour and made fun of him for his nonfunctional car. Hutch was making his way to the bathroom when the phone trilled.

Michael. Hutch slid his thumb across the screen. "Hey, Mike. You heading out?"

Michael had been assigned to watch the house overnight.

"I thought I might follow them to work. Just in case. What's going on? I don't buy the story about testing Kyle," Michael said over the line.

Big Tag was slipping. "It's probably coming from the bodyguard unit. You know Fisher is always trying new things out."

"And when I ask Fisher about it, what do you think he'll say?" Michael asked.

Hutch sighed. "Please don't."

"All right. This is one of those things I shouldn't ask about so I won't. But I don't feel right tailing one of our own," Michael admitted. "He left the house last night."

Hutch stopped. "He turned my security system off?"

"He must have because I watched him go for a jog. That was all he did. He ran around the block for almost an hour, made a phone call and talked for about twenty minutes, and then slipped back in the house."

Hutch fisted his hand, anger and fear curling in his gut. "I'm going to check the logs on the system. If he left us vulnerable, I'll kill him myself."

What the fuck had he been thinking? And who did he call at that time of night? It might be time to take a hard look at Kyle's phone and computer and his presence on the web. He hadn't because he rather thought Tag was being paranoid, but now he had to consider the fact that Kyle was putting Noelle in danger.

"You're worried about him?" Michael asked. "You don't have to tell me anything. I'm only trying to figure out how to handle this detail. I'm supposed to hand the reins over to Boomer this afternoon."

Boomer wasn't good at blending in, and sometimes he got distracted by food trucks. Or ice cream trucks. But he would be useful if Hutch decided to snipe Kyle. "I think you should bring in Jamal. He knows how to not be seen, and he won't talk."

For a six-and-a-half-foot heavily muscled Black dude, Jamal moved like a ghost, could oddly blend in when he needed to, and was absolutely one of the most solid guys McKay-Taggart had hired in the last couple of years.

"I'll talk to him, and I'll talk to Wade as well. We can watch Kyle for a few days, rotating shifts. Damn, I like him. I really like his brother. If he's doing something he shouldn't, Grace is going to be devastated," Michael said with a long sigh.

"Hopefully he's just a dude who likes to jog. He didn't meet anyone?"

"I couldn't follow him closely at that time of night," Michael admitted. "Don't you have a tracker on his phone? Give me access."

He did. Hutch opened his laptop and did not like what he saw. "He must have a second cell because according to my report, he didn't leave his room all night. Damn it. I do not want to tell Sean Taggart his stepson is doing shady shit."

"Have we considered he's an Agency plant? He was Navy. It would have been easy enough to recruit him, and they would look at him because of his ties to Big Tag."

Well, it hadn't taken Michael long to get there. It didn't surprise Hutch since Michael used to be on the same CIA team he'd been on. They knew all the hallmarks of an undercover operative. "I hope that's all it is. I hope he's reporting back to the Agency and that's the extent of it. But we need to know."

"All right. I'll follow them and then Jamal can take over this afternoon. I'll see you at the office?"

"Yeah, I'm coming in with Theo." Hutch pulled up his security system. His shower was going to be a quick one. "We can talk more there. I've got a tracker on Noelle's car, but Kyle knows about it."

"I'll let Jamal know. See you in a couple of hours." Michael hung up the phone.

Hutch set down beside his laptop and stared at the report on the screen. According to that report the system had been engaged all night with no disruptions. Either Kyle had found a way out without setting off the alarm or he had some skills he hadn't mentioned when he hired on.

Had he hacked the system and changed the report? He hadn't told Kyle the password to disarm it. He'd taken care of that himself. The system had been locked down tight when he'd gotten up this morning.

He would have to look into the reports but he could do that from the office. He could access his home server from there. A shower was necessary, and he needed to talk to Tag. Things felt like they were getting dangerous, and he didn't want Noelle in the way.

He shut his laptop and started for the bathroom when he heard the doorbell ring. He considered ignoring it but caught a glimpse of who was standing on his porch through the half-open drapes.

He caught sight of a blue uniform. Police.

What had happened? He rushed to the door, a million bad thoughts going through his head.

"Officer?" Had something happened to Noelle? Had there been an accident? He wasn't being reasonable, but he couldn't in that moment.

So much of his life had been a tragedy. He couldn't handle it if something happened to her. She was the one thing he needed. He knew it in that moment. He was in love with Noelle LaVigne, and it wasn't going to go away. This feeling couldn't be placated by sleeping with her a thousand times. She was in his heart, and she would be there forever.

"Greg Hutchins?" The officer stood in front of him, his partner close. His squad car was parked on the street.

"Yes, what's happened?" *Please let her be okay.* He could handle anything if she was all right.

"Greg Hutchins, you're under arrest. You have the right to remain silent," the big officer said.

Yeah, he hadn't expected that at all.

* * * *

"Where exactly are you taking me? I want to talk to my lawyer." Hutch was still in shock twenty minutes later as he was ushered through the hallways of the Jack Evans Police Headquarters. It wasn't where he'd expected them to go. There was a district office far closer to his house, but they'd blown right past it and come to the main building downtown. If this was about what had happened with that asswipe Jeffrey, they should have gone to the nearest district to book him.

"Where you need to go," the smaller of the two officers said.

And now that he thought about it, something was wrong with his arrest. He'd thought he was getting hauled in because he'd beaten the crap out of an overly privileged douchebag, but now he suspected something else was going on. "What exactly am I under arrest for?"

No one had mentioned that. They'd simply thrown handcuffs on him and hauled him out to the car. It was lucky for him his door locked automatically or his house and all its contents would have been vulnerable.

Was that what was going on here? Was he being drawn away so someone could attempt to get a look at his system?

"I think they're calling it impeding a federal investigation," a familiar voice said as they rounded the corner. "They got me as I was dropping off the oldest kids at the middle school. Tash and Kenzie got real upset, but Kala taped the whole thing on her phone and laughed her ass off. Do not have kids."

Ian stood outside a door marked *Conference Room*, his hands cuffed. Unlike Hutch, someone had been nice to Tag and his hands were in front rather than behind his back.

Still, someone was probably going to die. Big Tag had deep ties to DPD. The chief was a member of Sanctum.

The conference room door came open and another familiar face walked out. Chris Taylor was dressed in a suit this morning, his badge around his neck. He didn't look like he'd slept much, but then he wouldn't have if he'd actually worked a full shift at his "second" job. He glanced down at the cuffs and sighed. "Get those cuffs off them. Who the hell told you to bring in Ian Taggart in handcuffs?"

The officer standing near Ian immediately went to work. "It was not my idea, Detective. I realized who I was supposed to arrest and damn near crapped my pants. Luckily, the big guy was in a pretty good mood."

"My arresting officer showed up with coffee and lemon donuts," Ian said as the cuffs came off his wrists. "What did you get?"

"Potentially syphilis, since I don't think anyone's cleaned the back of that squad car in forty years." Hutch winced as his arms were free to move again. It was so unfair. He hadn't even gotten a cup of coffee this morning.

"Donuts?" Taylor asked.

The officer shrugged. "Everyone knows the big guy likes them, and I am hoping he understands I was merely following orders. The fed told us we had to arrest them and put them in handcuffs. She wanted to put the fear of God in them. I tried to tell her about Big Tag, but she did not get it. Hence the lemon donuts, and you should know I let him call his wife. Write me up if you want to but this whole assignment stinks."

"What does my guy have to do with McKay-Taggart?" The officer who'd arrested Hutch put his cuffs back on his belt.

"He's my cybersecurity expert," Big Tag explained. "He's the guy who your cybercrimes head calls when he needs help. Hutch, are you going to feel like helping the next time the lieutenant calls?"

It sucked that almost no one was scared of him. Tag got donuts and phone calls, and Hutch got a stain on his jeans that might never go away. "Definitely not, and I will mention why. I'm also feeling a little hack coming on. Maybe it's a cough from whatever I picked up in that car, or maybe it's the kind of thing that gets an officer's name on a no-fly list."

The officer held his hands up. "Man, I was following orders and I will clean the car." He looked to the other officer. "Donuts? You're an asshole, Jones."

"I'm a motherfucking genius, since I know not to piss off the dudes who work with brass," Jones replied. "You were trying to show off for the feds."

The officers walked away, still bickering.

"Please don't hack him, Mr. Hutchins. I'm sorry it went down this way, but you stepped in the middle of something big, and I can't have you busting up a six-month multiagency investigation," Taylor explained. "Come on in. We'll do what we should have done the minute you walked into the building with Noelle LaVigne."

Finally they would get a debrief.

It struck him forcibly that this meeting was him and Ian, and only him and Ian. He walked into the conference room and sat down at the table, leaning over to whisper Ian's way. "Why didn't they bring in Kyle?"

Ian's jaw tightened. "Because I suspect they're investigating him, too."

Taylor sat down across from them. "I am truly sorry she decided to bring you in this way. You need to understand that DPD isn't the lead in this investigation."

A whole lot of things fell into place. "Cara is the fed, right? She's got impeccable credentials. We even looked up her socials and they go back at least ten years."

"The FBI knows how to put together a cover." Cara moved from the back of the room. She wasn't in the boho clothes she normally wore. She was in a power suit, her blonde hair in a neat bun. "And we know when all our hard work is about to get blown out of the water. Mr. Taggart, I'm Caressa Thompson. I'm with the Dallas office in the criminal investigative division, and I've been investigating Jessica Layne and Genedyne for over a year. How did you become involved with Noelle LaVigne? I have to assume Mr. Hutchins is working and not playing her for some reason."

Tag looked his way. "She got through your cover? Did MaeBe fuck up?"

"Oh, Chris recognized him," Cara explained. "The cover was actually quite good. If Chris hadn't seen you before I would absolutely believe you're just a guy Noelle brought from home."

Chris nodded. "You gave a talk last year at a conference I went to. It was about how local police departments can use new facial recognition tech."

Hutch frowned Tag's way. "See, I told you I shouldn't do that conference."

Tag's eyes rolled. "You wanted to sit at home and drink beer. Next time I'll remember to send you in with a disguise. I'll let my girls dress you up. With a haircut and some glitter no one will recognize you."

"So I would like an answer to my question." Cara seemed unfazed by Tag's sarcasm. "How did you get involved with Noelle LaVigne?"

"I'd like to have not been dragged out of my house," Hutch replied. "We can't always get what we want."

"Mr. Hutchins, I need to remind you that I don't have to let you go at the end of this meeting," Cara said with an impatient sigh. "You truly are impeding an investigation."

"By protecting my client? I'm involved in this investigation because Noelle is a client of McKay-Taggart, and I think you had something to do with that." He wasn't a fool. "First of all, I need to remind you that I'm not some kid from a small town who's going to buy your line of bullshit. You're pissed because you're the one who turned on my client's monitoring system when I turned it off. You've been watching and listening to Ms. LaVigne, and you better hope that you have a warrant authorizing it because I intend to challenge it."

Cara's face flushed slightly, proving she wasn't as cold as she wanted him to think. "Ms. LaVigne is part of an important investigation."

"She better be because I suspect you're the one who got on her system and downloaded confidential files." His initial confusion was rapidly becoming anger. "You stripped her of her privacy, and you're potentially endangering her life's work. You know damn well she's not involved in whatever you're investigating Jessica Layne for. You're using an innocent young woman and placing her in danger without even giving her a warning about it. I find your investigation dangerous and cynical, and if you push me, I'll talk about it publicly."

"Hutch," Tag began.

Hutch shook his head. "No. She wants to arrest me? I'll show her how I can really impede an investigation. You think I haven't done it before?"

"I am well aware of your arrest record, Mr. Hutchins," Cara shot back.

"Then you're aware that he was a kid who did the right thing and got his ass thrown in juvie for it." Tag leaned forward, his eyes narrowing in that way that let Hutch know he was ready for a fight. "He went to juvie because the DA's office refused to do their job."

"I don't know any of this," Chris complained. "Juvenile records are supposed to be sealed. What don't I know and how will it affect this investigation? We can't have a criminal close to such an important player."

Cara softened slightly and looked Hutch's way. "He's not a criminal. He was a kid who broke the law to try to do the right thing. A girl at his high school...she went to a college party and got drunk and some football players took advantage."

"The word you're looking for is rape." He wouldn't sugarcoat it, and he'd been fucking happy to set his ass in jail. "They taped the whole thing, and then their parents worked with the DA to cover it up.

I was in a smaller town then, and no one wanted to lose the conference championship. So I hacked the system and I sent that tape to a couple of reporters."

"Hutch did more time than the football players," Ian explained.

"Yeah, but they didn't play again, and their names are still out there." He would circulate the story every few years. Every time one of those fuckers thought it was gone. "I was sixteen and I barely knew that girl. What do you think I'll do for a woman I care about?"

"Your prior arrest doesn't concern me or my bosses. But I do have something that does concern me." Cara's spine straightened and she leaned toward Ian. "Do you know that your...what do you call them...your operative is sleeping with the client?"

Ian chuckled. "Yeah, if I fired them all for that I wouldn't have any employees. It's kind of a perk of hiring my firm. McKay-Taggart. Serving your security needs and getting you off. It's our new slogan."

Hutch couldn't help himself. If there was one thing he couldn't stand it was hypocrisy. "Does your boss know you're sleeping with the locals? Or was that scene in the lobby for show?"

Ian was the one sitting up straighter now. The boss loved some gossip. "The detective's doing the fed?"

"Oh, yeah," Hutch said under his breath. "Blew their cover wide open last night."

Cara looked like she was ready to breathe fire.

Chris put a hand on her arm. "Don't. You know he's right and that's why you're angry." He looked Hutch's way. "Special Agent Thompson and I used to be engaged. We broke it off two years ago when she joined the FBI. Working on this assignment together brought back certain feelings, and we allowed them to cloud our judgment last night. If we'd had our heads in the game, this wouldn't have happened. We would have known to keep you in the lobby until that light went off. It takes about a half an hour to cycle on that system, right? The light was still on when you got up to the apartment. That's why you packed her up and left."

"Yes. I assume you're the ones who turned it on, and you did last night because you knew we would be late." He remembered Cara specifically asking about that night. "She thinks you're her friend, you know."

Cara seemed to soften slightly. "I am. At least I hope I am. She's involved in something criminal, and she doesn't know it. Or I could be wrong and she's a big part of it. It's precisely why I can't tell her I'm with the FBI. We're at a delicate time, and I've got to figure out how to handle this."

"What exactly are you investigating? The death of Madison Wallace?" He wanted to know what concerned the feds most.

"I was investigating Layne and her company before Madison Wallace was killed," Cara explained. "She's not the first mysterious death around Jessica Layne."

"You're talking about her business partner?" Ian asked.

Cara nodded. "And last year a business rival of hers died in a mysterious car accident. They were fighting over rights to patent a process concerning a new leap forward in eye tracking tech. Genedyne's case was considered the weaker of the two. There have been rumors for years that what Layne really does is bet on tech. She decides something is going to be big, and by either corporate espionage or clever trickery, she forces a legal fight for the patent. In this case, she was going up against a much smaller firm, and when the lead developer died, the firm's investment cash dried up."

"Hence, they were unable to fight the legal battle," Chris continued, "and Genedyne won the patent. The investors quickly found their way to Jessica Layne. There's a pattern of what I would consider fraudulent use of the legal system to better her company."

"I haven't heard anything about new eye tracking tech." Hutch kept up with everything that was new in the industry. He oftentimes collaborated with Adam Miles on how to perfect facial recognition methods. Eye tracking was in its infancy, and like many new high-tech things, had its start in video games. But the uses were wide and varying.

"That's because she hasn't used the patent yet," Cara explained. "She's sitting on it, using it to gain capital, but we've seen no attempts to actually bring it to market. It's one of the reasons I need to look at her financials. There are other reasons. I believe she might be working with some other tech firms to steal ideas, patents, even actual money from smaller firms. If I can prove that they're working together, I can charge them with a number of crimes. I can also force a wider investigation into what I think is collusion amongst a group of tech firms."

"I don't see how you could possibly think Noelle is involved in that," Hutch replied.

"I don't know that she is. I know she seems perfectly innocent, but there were files on her system that make me worry." Cara sat back. "And that's all I can tell you right now. I have decisions to make. If you were who you said you were, it would be simple since I would let things play out. But you aren't, and I have the added complication of your partner."

Oh, now they were getting somewhere. "What's your problem with Kyle?"

Cara looked back to Ian. "It's not something I'm willing to discuss with the man he considers his uncle."

"I know everything you know, probably more." All of the sarcasm had left Ian's tone. "I'm concerned about Kyle and his previous attachments, both professional and personal, and I'm definitely worried about the ones he refuses to talk about. So why don't we cut to the chase. You need to explain what you want from us or let us go. I'll let you in on a secret. The officer who helpfully allowed me to use my phone doesn't realize what a paranoid bastard I am. I have protocols in place. I didn't call my Charlie. I called my lawyer, and he should be here…"

There was a knock on the door that proved Big Tag had impeccable timing. Chris went to open it. He stared a hole through Cara when he looked back. "Mitchell Bradford is here, and my chief is, too. The lawyer said something about the DA being on speed dial."

Ah, Maia Brighton, the gift that kept giving, even if it sometimes bit a man on the ass. Literally. She was the duly elected Dallas district attorney and a long time…associate of Tag's. He wouldn't call them friends, but Maia was part of the community and would close ranks if she had to.

Tag grinned. "You gotta love a good lawyer. Mitch will have called my Charlie, and she'll be down here soon. You want to let me give her a ring to tell her to pick up some breakfast for Hutch on the way? We can still make this friendly. It's been a while since I was in handcuffs, and honestly, it's good to keep the kiddos guessing about whether their dad is a good guy or a bad guy. Keeps 'em on their toes. So you can have Charlie come in as a helpful partner or as a raging bitch whose man has been done wrong. I know which way I'd go. Also, I suspect you're going to need Hutch to cooperate or you'll both be off this case, and he honestly does think better when he's not hungry."

Cara stood and walked to the back of the conference room, Chris following behind her. They started in on a whispered discussion.

Big Tag sat back. "It's not a bad day. I'm going to get donuts and a breakfast sandwich. Charlie lets me off the cholesterol leash anytime I get arrested. I should do it more often. I haven't had a burger in a while. Hey, you know if we keep them talking, we could get lunch out of this."

Hutch frowned his way. "Noelle is in trouble. I don't know that I want Kyle around her. He snuck through my security system last night, and Michael says he called someone early in the morning. From a burner phone."

Ian groaned and let his head fall back. "Damn it. What has Michael figured out?"

"Pretty much everything we suspect," Hutch admitted. "He thinks he worked for the Agency and he might be reporting back to them. You know you shut Drake down hard after that last mission."

It hadn't been a mission so much as survival. Some of the team had been forced to put down a rogue CIA operative named Levi Green, and it had caused a wide rift between Tag and a man named Drake, who served as a sort of liaison between McKay-Taggart and the Agency. Drake seemed to be a good man, but he was a company man first and foremost, and that might mean using Big Tag's nephew to spy on him. It wouldn't be the first time the CIA had planted an operative in the office.

"Well, I should have suspected that, but Michael will keep his mouth shut," Ian replied. "We need to make a big decision, Hutch. I think they're about to ask you to work for them."

"I work for you, and I'm not going to do anything that might put Noelle in danger. I won't cross that line. Not even for you."

A ghost of a smile hit Ian's face. "Then Charlie did good. But Hutch, if they have even a sliver of evidence against Noelle, they'll have leverage. We can blow their investigation up and then Noelle likely loses her job and perhaps her reputation, depending on how bitter the feds want to be. Her boss won't help her. She'll probably end up getting sued, and she doesn't have the money to fight Layne in court. Or you can step in and do the job they were setting her up to do."

His gut clenched as the truth hit him. They'd always been ready to use Noelle. They'd simply been looking for the leverage to force her to do it. "They want someone to hack Genedyne's systems."

"Of course they do," Ian replied. "So this is your call. You want to blow it up, let's do it. You want to try to give Noelle as much cover as possible by making a deal with the feds, we can do that, too. It's up to you."

"What about Kyle?"

"Kyle is my problem," Ian replied. "And I have to figure out how much time I have to solve it before I'm the one who has to blow up my brother's whole world."

Noelle wanted to work late tonight. Kyle would be working late, too, because Jessica Layne had a date. If he did his job properly, he could have Noelle out of this in a matter of a couple of hours. "I want it in writing that if I do this, they won't prosecute Noelle for anything they find."

He knew she wasn't guilty, but a good prosecutor could twist things to suit the investigation. He wanted Noelle out of this.

Cara stepped back to the table. "All right. I'm ready to lay everything on the line."

Chris held her chair out, a seemingly habitual move. Hutch didn't miss the way the detective glanced down at her as he moved to his own seat. "I've convinced her you're trustworthy. Please don't make me a liar."

The door came open and Mitch Bradford strode in, a fierce frown on his face as he pointed at the detective and special agent. "I'm going to have both of your freaking badges. You arrested my client falsely and in front of his teenaged daughters' school? I'm going to sue the fuck out of this department and the two of you personally."

"Mitch, don't have a heart attack." Tag had his cell in his hand. "We're making a deal to keep Noelle safe. You hungry?"

Mitch set his briefcase on the table. "Noelle? My sister-in-law's stepdaughter? What the hell is Noelle into?"

"Nothing, but our friends here dragged her into some fairly wretched business," Hutch complained. "So I'm going to get her out. And tell Charlotte I need something sweet."

He *did* think better when he wasn't hungry.

Tag leaned over and whispered. "Dude, you should have taken a shower. You smell like sex."

He groaned and sat back as Mitch started to do his thing and prayed Noelle would forgive him for what he was about to do.

Chapter Fourteen

Noelle stared at the computer in front of her and sighed. She was close. So damn close to being done with this assignment that it seemed stupid to stop work and go back to Hutch's place where she would sit around and think about work.

Well, after he'd blown her mind because he would definitely do that. She was already considering how hot she could get him in the car ride home. Traffic didn't have to be boring, and one of their assignments was to push each other's limits.

But then she would worry about this damn report all weekend. He said he would let her come up to work tomorrow, but she could finish tonight, have that report on Jessica's desk, and then take the whole weekend off.

"Dr. LaVigne?"

She glanced up and a woman with dark hair stood at the front of her desk. She had a cart in front of her filled with envelopes of all sizes. She was probably in her late twenties and the pitch-black color of her hair was obviously not her natural color. The woman had fair skin that would have gone well with a blonde tone, but the stark makeup she had on marked her as a goth girl. She reminded Noelle the slightest bit of MaeBe, but without the other woman's infectious smile. "Yes?"

"I'm from the mailroom," the woman said. "I was stopping by to see if you have anything you need to send out."

"We have a mailroom?" She thought almost everyone used email and texts these days.

The woman smiled. "Oh, yes. Though it's almost exclusively used by the business floors. Snail mail is still a thing. I was told not to bother coming to the labs, but I had a couple of minutes before we close up and saw you in here. You had some tech journals."

She started to hand them over to Noelle when they slipped out of her hands and to the floor.

"I'm sorry," the woman said.

They'd landed far closer to Noelle. She leaned over to pick them up, one hand on her cane.

"I can be such a klutz." The woman maneuvered the cart so it wasn't between them. She held a hand out to help Noelle up.

"I'm good." She stood back up, her copy of the latest chemistry journal in her hand. "Thanks for this. I needed some light reading for the weekend. I usually get this delivered at home."

The dark-haired woman shrugged. "I think I heard something about the company ordering journals for the bigger labs. I think she meant for you to share them with your techs. It's some kind of continuing education thing. I don't know. I'm mailroom. The only magazine I read is *People*. I leave the other stuff to the smarter citizens of the world. Anyway, let me know if you need anything. I should get back downstairs before they think I'm talking too much."

Noelle nodded her way. "Thanks."

The woman pushed her cart into the outer lab as Pete walked in. He turned, looking at the woman.

"Who was that?" Pete asked.

She hadn't asked the woman's name. That had been a bit rude. "No idea. She said she was from the mailroom and dropped off a couple of magazines. Have you heard anything about a continuing education program?"

A brow rose over Pete's eyes. "Beyond the fact that Jessica firmly believes everyone should pay for their own education?"

Noelle set the journal down. "Yeah, I thought it was weird, too. Did you know we had a mailroom?"

Pete waved that off. "Oh, yeah. The upper floors still rely on snail mail. I sneak in my Christmas cards to avoid paying for stamps. Don't tell anyone. But they must have done some hiring lately because the last time I was down there it was all dudes."

"It's good they're diversifying." But the mailroom didn't matter. Hutch would be here any minute and she was going to try to convince him to stay with her for an hour or two while she finished up. "Are you heading out?"

"I'm running up to the gym. I was going to see if you wanted to join me. After what happened last time, I don't want you to go alone."

"Oh, my boyfriend's picking me up any minute." Hutch would flip if he caught her going to the gym again. She'd been ordered to stay out of the locker room until further notice. Hutch had been escorting her to the small gym in her building when she wanted to work out.

What would it be like when Hutch wasn't staying with her? Would he still spend time with her at night, or would they get back to being obsessed with work?

"Good. Then I'll leave you to it. Did the experiment finish up?" Pete settled his gym bag over his shoulder.

"It's uploading data right now." She glanced back at her screen. "It's going to take another hour or so. I'll probably be up here tomorrow."

Pete winced. "Sorry, Noelle. I've got a family party tomorrow. It's my brother's birthday, and we're all meeting for brunch. I can maybe make it after two or so. Or I can stay tonight."

"Don't worry about it." She was done with the physical experiments. "I'm doing nothing but running data and extrapolating at this point. I've got to have the report on the latest data to Jessica by Monday."

Pete looked thoughtful for a moment. "Huh. I must have heard wrong."

"What?"

"I heard that Jessica already met with investors about our project," Pete admitted. "I thought you were being extra careful since she's already presented the data."

There were some crazy rumors flying around. "No. She can't

present what she doesn't have. We'll probably need to go to a couple of meetings next week to get her ready and be prepared in case we need to explain things to the investors. I've never done this, but I know Madison went with Jessica when they got that ridiculous amount of cash for her project."

She remembered that Madison had dressed up for the occasion. She'd been in the locker room that afternoon, changing into her designer sheath. Noelle had watched as she'd reached up into her locker, feeling for something she'd hidden at the top. When she'd brought down a small magnetic box, she'd shown off the big diamond earrings hidden inside.

"There's this spot at the very top of all the lockers I can hide this. These earrings are worth more than your whole lab. I'm certainly not going to keep them in my purse," Madison had said as she'd fastened them on. *"Do I look like a million bucks? Because I need these suckers to give me about ten. Million, that is."*

Would Jessica want her to dress as flashy as Madison had? Madison wore sky-high heels and slinky dresses even when she was working in the lab. Noelle got the feeling her dressiest sneakers wouldn't make the cut for an important investor meeting. Did she have any shoes that would work? Or a dress? Maybe she wouldn't spend all her time working this weekend. She might need to go shopping.

"Yeah, I'm sure you're right." Pete started for the door. "Give me a call if you need anything. Definitely give me a call if you need to run the experiment again. That damn machine is being held together with tape at this point. I'll be happy when we can get a new one."

So would she. An influx of cash would help her enormously. A whole lot of the cash for her lab had gone to Madison last quarter. Now she was the one with the successful experiment, and she was ready to reap the rewards by buying a bunch of new equipment. It would be like Christmas. "I think this data is the last I need, but thanks. Have a good workout."

He strode out as Kyle was walking in. Kyle looked a bit pale and kept glancing back at the door.

"Are you okay?" She didn't see Hutch with him.

Kyle seemed to shake something off. "Yeah, I'm good. Just saw someone who reminded me of an ex. Like the worst ex ever. How are you doing?" Kyle stepped into the lab. He'd put his suitcoat on, a sure sign he was about to follow Jessica to someplace fancy. "Hutch texted me he's running late, but he should be downstairs in a couple of minutes. I thought I'd walk you down."

She frowned his way. "Is there any way I could convince him to let me stay a couple of hours?"

Kyle crossed his arms over his chest. "I don't think so. Not after what happened yesterday. He doesn't want you in here alone, and I have to go out tonight."

That brought up a good point. Kyle should know what Jessica was doing this evening. "I thought this was a date, but Pete mentioned a meeting with investors."

"She mentioned a date to me a couple of days ago, but from what I can tell this is a business dinner," Kyle explained. "She changed the restaurant from a French bistro to a steak house, and I overheard her assistant confirming a table for four. Why do you ask?"

"Pete thought she was pitching my research to investors." It didn't make any sense unless she was buttering them up for the real meeting next week. "But she doesn't have my supporting evidence, so it can't be that. I know you're not supposed to listen in."

"I'm literally being paid to spy on the woman," Kyle pointed out. "If you want me to figure out what she's pitching tonight, I will let you know. You ready to head down? I've got to meet Jessica at the limo in a couple of minutes."

She sighed because he didn't look like a man who was going to be persuaded. "I'll get my keycard."

She glanced down and it wasn't sitting on her desk. Where had she put it?

"Hey, baby. I brought us some dinner because I thought about it and you are going to feel better if you finish this thing."

All thoughts of anything else fled as she looked up and Hutch walked into the room, carrying a bag emblazoned with the Top logo. Her stomach growled, reminding her she'd only eaten about half the sandwich she'd bought at the deli downstairs. A few days before she'd thought the turkey on wheat had been a serviceable lunch, but then Hutch had started making her lunches. He put honey mustard and tomatoes on it, and she loved them. The one from downstairs was now bland.

She would miss him if they drifted apart at the end of this.

"Did you bring me something?" Kyle started to poke around in the bag Hutch had set on her desk. "I don't think I'm eating at this thing. What's the special tonight? Mom told me Sean was working on short ribs and they're delicious."

Hutch slapped at his hand. "No, I did not get you anything because we're not in a relationship, and as you have pointed out many times, you are an adult man capable of making your own lunch."

Kyle stared down at the bag with sad puppy eyes. "Only because I didn't know you're actually pretty good in the kitchen. I thought it was one of those things where a dude thinks he's good, but he pretty much sucks. Your breakfasts are solid. I missed it this morning. We need to get groceries again."

Because they'd abandoned the ones at her place the night before. None of that mattered because Hutch was here and he was letting her stay and finish up. She moved into his arms and wrapped herself around him. He hugged her tight and she realized what she'd been missing all day. Him.

He kissed her cheek and nuzzled her ear. "Hey, I missed you. It was a long day."

But he was still here and still willing to wait with her. "You, too. Thank you for dinner and thank you for letting me stay."

"Okay, I lost my appetite. You got this, brother?" Kyle was already at the door.

Hutch's lips curled up in a sexy grin as he stared down at her. "Oh, I got this. I got all of this."

His hands moved down to cup her ass. Kyle made a gagging sound and then he was gone.

"Alone at last." Hutch kissed her. "That is what I wanted all day."

"Well, since you are letting me finish this up tonight, I might not have to work this weekend," she whispered against his lips. "And then we can get a whole lot of alone time in."

His hands moved up her back. "I would love that."

He was such a handsome man with his blue eyes and golden

brown hair, a sharp jawline that had a hint of scruff covering it. She loved the way his muscles felt under her hands. She wasn't in his league. All of her insecurities flooded back in and she decided to simply ask. Wasn't that what she was supposed to do? "Hutch, what happens when this case is over?"

A quizzical expression hit his face, but he didn't let her go. "I suspect you won't be afraid anymore."

"I meant with us."

"What do you want to have happen? Because I know what I want, but I have been accused of moving way too fast. You, my darling, are a skittish chick."

She felt a smile cross her face because that was not the reply of a guy who was planning on ghosting her once this was done. "I am not." She went on her toes and kissed him before pulling away. She was starving, and whatever was in that bag smelled like heaven. "Skittish? What a silly word. I am reasonable and responsible, and one of us has to be."

"I am over-the-top romantic and reckless," he replied, moving in behind her. "One of us has to be. I got you the special tonight. It's half a roast chicken with lemon rosemary potatoes and asparagus. If you don't like it, you can have my burger."

The smell of the chicken hit her, and her stomach growled again. "Not on your life, although that is a lot of food."

Hutch shrugged. "I figured I'd try yours, too."

She couldn't stop smiling. He made her happy. Happier than she could remember being before. She had her work and she had a guy she could trust. What more could she ask for? "I suppose I could share. How did you get up here, anyway?"

"Kyle left my name as an approved guest. I also think that after what happened in the locker room, the security guys are happy to have someone up here with you." He kissed the nape of her neck and took a step back. "There's a piece of chocolate cake and a slice of whatever pie they made today. I definitely thought we could share those."

Because her man had a sweet tooth. "I think we can make that happen. Are you sure you're okay babysitting me? You can eat and then head home and pick me up."

He stared at her.

"Or you can be bored right here." He was right. The last time she'd been totally alone she'd gotten choked out. The truth of the matter was it could get creepy here at night.

"Thank you," he replied. "And I won't be bored. I've got my laptop. I can catch up on work, too. I've got some code I need to write for the website. And Big Tag wants me to hack the new Japanese toilets Adam bought for his company. They're super high tech, complete with wash cycles and a blow-dryer for your junk."

"You're going to hack a toilet?" He could also be a prankster. She would have to remember that.

"Yep. I'm going to turn the water pressure way up and the temp way down and see if we can hear Adam howl from our floor." He was sitting at her desk, a big smile on his face. "It's also an excellent way to figure out who actually uses them. They all say they don't. Jesse Murdoch said it was a waste of money, but I bet he ends up using the soothing wash cycle. Well, at least once."

Damn, she was in love with him. She couldn't even fool herself anymore. She was in love with Hutch. "You are a moron."

That smile didn't dim a watt. "But I'm your moron. Come here."

She moved into his arms. Dinner might have to wait.

He started kissing her when the door came open again and Kyle walked through, pulling at his tie.

"She is not a nice boss. And that is all I am saying," Kyle grumbled and then proceeded to contradict himself by saying more. "She replaced me with Austin. Austin is a putz."

"What did you do?" Hutch's face had completely lost its humor. And his horniness.

They started to argue.

It looked like dinner was back on, and she was definitely going to have to share.

* * * *

"Are you sure it's okay he's in there with her?" Kyle stood in front of the window that connected the lab's main room to one of what she'd called the experiment rooms. There was a big MRI machine along with a bunch of technical equipment. Noelle was running a test to see how much of the helium she could catch and recycle off the machine.

Something had gone wrong and she'd called Pete, who'd happened to still be in the building. The engineer was in there with her.

"He works with her every day," Hutch pointed out. "I don't see why it's a problem."

Hutch stared down at the screen in front of him and wished like hell he didn't have to do what he was going to do. What he wanted to do was scoop Noelle up and get her the hell out of here because every instinct in his body was telling him something was wrong.

Why had Kyle suddenly gotten himself taken off the security detail he'd been talking about all week? It was pretty coincidental that he would get bumped on the very night Hutch had to get his job done.

Was Kyle here to make sure he didn't do his job?

Kyle moved in behind him, his voice going low. "Are you going in tonight? I thought you wanted to wait until tomorrow night when I could watch your back."

That was what they'd discussed, which was precisely why it was so odd that Kyle was suddenly free tonight. "I'm doing some recon. I haven't spent much time in the building. I need to get a feel for what I'm going to have to do to get in."

"Did Ian get intel on Cara? Have you talked to Noelle about it?"

He turned to glare Kyle's way. "Dude, someone could be listening."

Kyle shrugged that worry off. "Nah, I check for bugs every day, and I've got a disruptor on me right now. It'll blast static if anyone's listening."

That was interesting. A disruptor was brand-new tech. It was so new most people didn't know about it. It wasn't on the market to the public yet, and Hutch hadn't been able to get his hands on one. The small device emitted a high-frequency tone that would render most listening devices useless. "That's impressive tech. You didn't get it from the office."

Not that Big Tag hadn't tried to find a way to buy a couple.

Kyle's jaw tightened, the expression on his face going stubborn before it fell. "I got it from a friend. Okay? Look, there's a lot about my time in the Navy I can't talk about."

"Because it's classified."

"Yeah."

"And the friend you got the disruptor from is probably classified, too." The friend was either some kind of intelligence agent or something far worse. The friend could be a corporate spy who looked to Kyle for help.

Kyle sighed. "The friend I got it from is dead. I don't talk about her because…I don't talk about her. But she's been on my mind lately. That must be why I thought I saw her earlier. It was a woman who looked a little like her, though not really. It was more the way she moved."

Was he talking about Julia Ennis? "A girlfriend?"

Kyle chuckled, a humorless sound. "She's the reason I don't believe in love. She's the one I misread. Look, I didn't talk to Big Tag about the disruptor because I figured he would ask me to give it to him. I need it."

What other tech did he have? "Is that how you got through my security system last night?"

The slightest flush stained his cheeks. "How did you… Did it show up on the logs? Because I thought it wouldn't."

"It wouldn't have if I hadn't written specific protocols. It's not a normal security system." Not a total lie, but he wasn't about to tell Kyle that he'd gotten caught through good old-fashioned human eyesight. That would lead to questions of why the hell Michael Malone was watching him. No, he'd found using words like *protocols* threw off the people who weren't hard-core hackers.

"I'm sorry. I shouldn't have done it." Kyle sank into the chair beside him. "I need you to know that I have been in that apartment every night since we started the job. I swear I have. Last night, I just…I couldn't sleep, and you don't have a treadmill. Sometimes it's the only way I get myself tired enough to fall asleep. Last night I actually managed to doze off, but I woke up at two in the morning and I couldn't stay in bed."

"You couldn't stay in the house," Hutch accused.

Kyle shook his head. "No, I couldn't. I'm sorry. I had a shitty

276

dream and I had to burn it off."

That didn't explain the phone call he'd made or why he had two phones to begin with. He wasn't sure he could ask that question without giving up the fact that Michael had been following him. "You want to talk about it?"

"No."

"Okay." He couldn't force the guy to trust him.

Kyle pushed off the chair. "I knew this wouldn't work."

"The job? No, it probably won't work if you can't stay in a house with a client you're guarding."

"Well, I figured you would take care of her. It's not like she was alone."

It was time for some hard truth. He knew Tag wanted to keep Kyle around until he figured out what was happening, but Hutch wasn't going to let that secondary mission put Noelle in danger. "You're the one who is supposed to be watching our backs. Had I gotten the heads-up that you needed a break, I would have paid more attention to security."

Secondary mission? Now he had a third—getting the feds everything they wanted so they would leave Noelle alone. That was the deal he'd made this afternoon. He would find a way to get the financial records to prove Genedyne was a fraud and they would leave Noelle alone. Of course, he couldn't simply tell Noelle what he was doing. He'd had to sign an agreement that all of this would be confidential.

Or his pact to keep Noelle safe would dissolve, and she could be forced to risk her career and possibly her life to keep her research safe. The feds knew exactly how to bust a man's balls.

Kyle nodded and seemed to think something over. "That's fair. Have you talked to Big Tag?"

He didn't want to lie to the man, but he also wasn't sure Kyle wouldn't simply walk away. "I don't want to."

"It won't happen again." Kyle groaned and his head dropped back, an obviously frustrated move. "Or maybe it will. Fuck, I should never have come home."

"Why did you?"

Kyle's head came back up, and there was an unmistakable

weariness in his gaze. "I don't know. I guess I hoped it would make things better. I left because things didn't make sense anymore. I came back because I hoped being home would feel safe. I was in an accident. I'd gone into grad school."

Hutch nodded. "I remember hearing something about it."

"It might be why I feel such an affinity for Noelle. I know I said you should be suspicious of any human being who seems as nice as Noelle, but I honestly like her. I know something of what she went through. You can't exactly understand it."

"I can't? I assure you I've been through some shit."

Kyle shook his head. "You've been through all the shit, Hutch. Like you should be a walking pile of human garbage given what you've been through. Tell me something. Was there ever a time you didn't know the world was dangerous?"

His heart clenched because there was only one answer to that question. "No. I always knew."

"Well, I remember the moment the world changed for me. I had lost my dad, but I had my mom and my brother and I got through it. It was the accident that changed things."

Hutch remembered a bit of the story. "Your friend died, right?"

"Oh, yes, but friend isn't the right word. He was my brother. We met in first grade and he was always there for me. Don't get me wrong. My brother and I were close, but he's older than me and he was always more serious. I was closest to Kenny growing up. And then because some asshole ran a light, he wasn't there anymore. I'd dealt with death, but not in a visceral way. My dad's death seemed almost peaceful. I know it wasn't that way for my mom. She was careful in what she let us see. He was in an accident, too. He had surgery, but they knew he wouldn't pull through. He lingered for a week. I remember my dad telling me everything would be okay and that he would always love me. That wasn't how Kenny died."

"I thought he died on impact."

"Yeah, well, that was the story I told my mom," Kyle admitted. "He didn't. We'd been out to dinner with some friends. It got late, but everything was normal. Kenny had a meeting the next day, so he decided not to drink."

"That doesn't make it your fault."

"Oh, I don't know about that. It was my car. I drove us out there. Neither one of us was planning on getting toasted that night, but I was talking to a woman I met and we went through a bottle and a half of wine. When the time came, Kenny took my keys and he was sitting in the driver's seat. He took the full brunt of a car going forty-five miles an hour plowing into him. I was asleep and ended up with nothing more than a couple of scratches." Kyle's eyes seemed to be on something far away. "He was mad that he was dying. So fucking angry. He was mad at me."

"He was in pain and confused." Hutch wanted to give him some comfort.

"I don't know about that. Anyway, that second brush with death was unlike the first. I watched it, watched the blood pour as I tried to stop it, watched the fear as he realized there was no way out, watched the light die. I couldn't go on with my life the way I had before, so my stepdad and a friend of his convinced me to try the Navy. I didn't go into the Army because I didn't want to have to live up to the Taggart name. That's sad, right? It's not even my name, but I feel it."

Now he needed to play things carefully. "You didn't want to walk in those big-ass footsteps. I get that. So what did you do when the CIA called?"

Kyle huffed. "Of course everyone knows."

"It was a decent bet," Hutch said with a shrug. "You went into Special Forces training. The Agency watches those recruits, and the minute your name was placed in close proximity to a Taggart..."

"Yeah, my team worked with a Mr. Brown shortly after I got the assignment. I was recruited from there. Tag knows?" Kyle asked.

"He suspects, but you have to know he checked up on you."

"Well, I rather thought my handler would have covered it up better." Kyle sighed. "I'll talk to him about it. I'm not particularly proud of the work I did there. It's why I got out. I came home and it still doesn't make sense. It might be time for me to try something else."

Hutch knew exactly what he should try. "Have you tried talking about it? With Kai?"

Kyle's hands fisted at his sides. "Talking about it won't work."

"Have you tried it?"

"No. And I'm not going to."

Well, that was about as far as he could push the guy. Someone had to be open to therapy for it to work, and Kyle was kind of right about him being different. By the time he'd been plucked from juvie and offered a different life, he'd been ready to try anything. Kai Ferguson had been his therapist for years, and while he probably didn't need it anymore, he liked to go. It was good to have someone to purge to. In a lot of ways those sessions with Kai were a way to process what happened around him. He'd learned not to react emotionally but rather to allow his emotions to process and then act in a way that best represented who he wanted to be.

Did he want to lie to Noelle?

Did he even have a fucking choice?

Would it be wrong to ask for a session in the middle of an op?

"Have I lost you?" Kyle sounded irritated.

Hutch glanced back at his laptop. He had some programs running, trying to figure out the layout of Genedyne's system. It was complex, but definitely not undoable. "You said you didn't want to talk. So I thought we weren't talking."

A brow rose over Kyle's eyes. "Aren't you going to try to convince me?"

"Nope. That's your damage, and until you're ready to face it, no amount of me trying to convince you will work." He might need to get into the server room. He'd hoped he could do it all from here, but it would be infinitely easier with physical contact. How long would it take him? The server room was on the floor below the business level. MaeBe was on standby. He could bust through the keycard processor easy peasy, but it might set off a security alert.

"You think I don't face it?"

Now was the time when he would normally take a fucked-up dude out for a beer and gently coax him into telling the whole sad story. Dudes could be skittish, too. But Kyle wasn't the normal life-fucked-me-over story. Kyle might be dangerous, and he couldn't make him more suspicious than he already was. Telling him Tag knew he'd worked with the Agency was a calculated risk, but a fairly easy one to make.

Telling Kyle his uncle thought he might still be working for them would be a mistake, and Hutch didn't make mistakes like that.

"I think you risked our client at two this morning because you didn't want to face whatever you dreamed about," Hutch explained.

Kyle stopped. "You might have a point. Maybe coming here was a huge mistake."

"Where else would you go? I can assure you you'll have to sleep there, too."

"You're kind of an asshole."

"Well, somehow I don't think me coaxing you is going to work," Hutch pointed out. "You've made it perfectly clear that we aren't friends."

"How did I do that?"

"Friends don't bust through other friend's security systems when their friend's girlfriend is in danger. I mean, I got the point from all the crap you've said over the last couple of days, but that really drove it home."

Kyle's jaw dropped. "Crap I've said? I was joking."

He was missing the point. And rewriting history. "You literally said we weren't friends. Several times."

"Fine. We're friends." Kyle sat back down. "I'm not sure what to do or if I should even stay here. I can't talk to my brother about this. He wouldn't understand. David's a freaking college professor. He's never had to do the things I've done. The worst he's faced is pressure over publishing. He talks about that a lot. It's the pinnacle of bad shit in his world. How can I tell him I've killed people?"

Ah, now they were getting somewhere. It was hard for Hutch to believe that this was an act. He didn't think Kyle was that great an actor. It was odd, but he wouldn't peg Kyle as a brilliant operative. Kyle would be able to kill when he needed to, would probably be great at following a subject and analyzing a situation. But pretending would be hard for him. At least that was Hutch's take on the man.

Unfortunately, Hutch was good at it. And his time was running out. The guards who worked the building were about to take their dinner break, and for thirty minutes or so only the lobby-level guard would be actively watching the cameras. It wasn't supposed to be that way. The guards were scheduled to take separate dinner breaks, but the man and his woman counterpart seemed to be flirty according to

MaeBe, who'd cut into the feeds days ago and watched the guards like a soap opera playing out for her amusement.

Hutch closed his laptop. "I think he probably knows since you were on a team. You were in the military and you saw combat. It wouldn't shock him. He's probably worried about you, too, but you have to be willing to open up to someone. I've worked for the Agency. I've worked dangerous undercover ops. I've come back from more edges than you could imagine. If you honestly think whatever you have to say is going to shock someone like me, then you're wrong. So when you're ready to talk, I'll buy you a beer and you can tell me your shocking story and be disappointed when I explain the truth I've found out about the world."

For a moment he thought Kyle wasn't going to take the bait, but he finally looked Hutch's way. "What's that?"

"That when we feel our most alone," Hutch began, "when we think we're lost and in the woods and no one can ever find us, it's only because we aren't looking at all the other people who are in that dark place with us. It's a lie that you're alone. It's a lie you tell yourself because not being alone means there's no reason to turn away from the past. Not being alone means facing it all. It means letting it break you utterly because you can't heal until you break. And if you're not alone then it's okay to break because someone will be there to help you mend."

Kyle huffed. "Yeah. Sure. There's someone else out there who's been through what I have."

And that was all he could do. He couldn't force Kyle to trust him. He rather thought Kyle didn't want to trust anyone. "Like I said, when you're ready, find me or someone like me. Now I need you to make sure Noelle doesn't get murdered while I take a leak. I'm pretty sure I remember where the bathroom is."

"I think I can handle that." Kyle sat back. "Be careful."

"I'm going to the bathroom, man. Tonight all I'm doing is getting a feel for what it's going to take to get what we need. There's zero chance Noelle is done tonight. We'll get a shot tomorrow." He could always say he'd underestimated how fast she would work, but he was a bit worried that she would want to be back here tomorrow. Something had gone hinky with the MRI machine she'd been testing her theories on. She looked awfully cute with a wrench in her hand and goggles covering her eyes.

"All right. I'll keep an eye on her," Kyle promised. "I want to get out of here as soon as possible. I don't like the fact that Jessica booted me tonight. She hadn't mentioned anything about it up until I walked down to the limo. Then she dismissed me. I can assure you that she wasn't thinking about dismissing me this morning."

Hutch huffed. "Maybe she realized you're a douchebag."

"I'm serious, Hutch. Something changed this afternoon, and it affected the way she views me. I have to think she's up to something."

Perhaps Kyle was right. She'd changed her plans. She'd been going on a date and now she was having some kind of dinner meeting. "Do you know who she invited to that dinner?"

"I might have seen a list of names," Kyle admitted. "Jessica's assistant had it sitting on her desk. I didn't think much of it at the time. I remember them."

"Did you send the names to MaeBe?"

"I'll do it now. Sorry. Like I said, I've got a lot on my mind. I'm going to focus."

"You do that." Hutch walked out, but not before he grabbed the small pack he'd left on the edge of the desk. It contained his phone and a couple of attachments that weren't readily available in a tech store. When he was certain Kyle couldn't see him, he placed the comm device in his ear. It was linked to another set and didn't record, so it worked even in the presence of Kyle's anti-bug technology. "You there, MaeBe?"

"You know I am." MaeBe's voice came over the line. "What on earth were you talking to Kyle about? I couldn't hear anything, but that looked serious as hell. Is he like into Noelle? Is that what you're fighting about?"

He moved down the hallway, keeping his voice low. "No. He's not into Noelle, but I also think he shouldn't be into anyone right now. His situation is complicated, and you should be careful around him."

"Am I that obvious? Take the stairs to your right. The stairwells only require keycards on the ground floor," MaeBe advised. "Also, you're totally alone. There are a couple of people working late on the second floor, and some dudes hooking up hard on ten. They would not notice you even if you walked in. They're totally into each other."

It was good to have eyes on the building. MaeBe was at the McKay-Taggart building on a server that had been secured by Hutch and overseen by the goddess of the Internet, Chelsea Weston. She was safe. He, not so much. It had been a long time since he'd felt this kind of jangly anxiety that came with a boots-on-the-ground mission. Adrenaline made him chatty. "And you're not obvious, but I know you pretty well. I've seen how you look at him, and you're interested. I'm telling you to be careful, and that's all I can say."

"Huh, there's one other person in the building. How did I miss her?"

"I don't know. Perhaps it was the two hot dudes hooking up," Hutch quipped.

"It's weird. She's on the fourth floor, walking toward the elevators. I think she's heading home." MaeBe's voice had gone totally professional. "Hey, speaking of the devil, I got a text from Kyle. It's a list of names. What am I supposed to do with this? He is not very communicative."

It was good to know Kyle was succinct. "Those are the names of the people who are taking a meeting with Jessica even as we speak. She changed all of her plans to meet with those people. I haven't seen the names yet."

"Well, there seems to be an international flair to her guests. Dimitri Sidirov. Igor Krupin. Saeed Nasir."

Hutch stopped. "MaeBe, I need you to run those names now. Text Kyle and ask him for the name of the restaurant and figure out a way to break into the feeds around it. I want to know who they are, and I want recognition to confirm it."

"What are you thinking?"

His mind was racing, making connections. "I think the fact that she dismissed Kyle says something. She thinks Kyle lives with Noelle, and she's meeting with Russians and someone who could potentially be from the UAE. I want you to see if you can connect those names with natural gas companies."

He could hear her typing as he moved down the hallway.

"Wow, that was fast," MaeBe said over the line. "Okay, uhm, Mr. Sidirov represents a Russian energy company."

"They all do. I need dossiers on every one of them." Hutch took the stairs two at a time.

"Will do," MaeBe said. "It looks like Nasir is also with an energy company. Is this about natural gas?"

"No. It's about helium." Noelle's research was promising. He hustled up the next flight. He had to get the data he needed and then get Noelle out of here.

With her research. Every single file, every experiment. He could take it all and then erase it from Genedyne's servers. Then he would get a good lawyer because hell would be coming for her, but if he was right, it might be the only way to save Noelle's work.

"But Noelle's research isn't about finding helium," MaeBe said and then a gasp came over the line. "Oh, shit. Her research is about conserving helium. If she's right, the price goes down, and anyone who uses helium on their machines invests in her recycling techniques. You think Layne's selling Noelle's research to the people who will bury it."

"Think about it. What's really come out of Genedyne?" It was a question Cara had posed during the debrief today. "There's been a whole lot of press, but what's made it to market?"

"These kinds of innovations can take time," MaeBe offered.

"I don't think Jessica Layne has any plans to spend time and money to bring anything to fruition. Why would she when she can sell the process to someone who will or someone who will bury the whole thing? And she's got the right to do it because she owns it." This was why she hired young, hungry geniuses. She took their talent, made money off of it, and then buried them in legal fees. She was taking the best and brightest minds of a generation, wringing them dry, and tossing them out.

Anger thrummed through him, and he was happy he was about to take this whole house of cards down. If he could find what he needed in time.

"I'm approaching the server room."

"I can see that," MaeBe replied. "You should get in fast because the woman on the elevator pushed the number of your floor. She's going up, not down like I expected."

"Do we know who she is?"

"She hasn't looked up from her phone, so I haven't run her through facial recognition," MaeBe admitted.

He didn't like the sound of that. One thing went right though. The door to the server room came open, proving that days of learning this system had paid off. He slipped inside and immediately found what he needed. He pulled out a small drive and started to run through the company's financial records, copying everything he could and taking a virtual picture of what the server looked like in that moment. He would try to get in and out quietly, but there was always the possibility someone would figure out he'd been inside and try to flush the system. He needed proof of what was on this system at the moment.

"Hutch, I need you to be quiet." MaeBe's voice was barely a whisper, as though she was worried someone might hear her from across the city.

A chill went through him. "What's happening?"

"Our friend is approaching the door, and she has a keycard in her hand," MaeBe explained. "She's going in. Fuck. The system just registered Noelle's card. She's using Noelle's keycard."

The door started to come open, and Hutch realized he was in trouble.

Chapter Fifteen

Hutch glanced down and realized he was seconds away from finishing his download. He moved behind one of the large servers.

Someone had either stolen or duped Noelle's keycard. Someone was setting Noelle up on the same night Jessica was meeting with men who would love to hide her research.

Whoever was coming through that door was actively working to steal Noelle's ideas, to take a future she'd worked hard for. Anger started to war with fear, though his training had taken over and a calm started to descend.

"She's moving in. She can't see you at this point." MaeBe's voice had gone calm. "She's pulling out a drive. Yours is finished, Hutch. It's done and all you need to do is get the fuck out of there as soon as you can. She's coming your way. Your best bet is to move around the opposite direction. She's coming the same way you came in. I think she's going for the same system."

Was it possible Cara had sent in her own person? The special agent seemed like a woman who might get impatient and try to do the job with her own people. If whoever the intruder was worked for the FBI, they probably wouldn't kill him. Of course they also probably wouldn't have used Noelle's keycard.

He couldn't risk it. Whoever was coming around the corner likely hadn't been trying to throw a suspicious coworker off the scent. If she was a pro, she would have a gun, and therefore the only advantage he had was the fact that she didn't know he was in here.

He wasn't carrying because Kyle would have asked why he'd grabbed a gun to go to the bathroom.

He hoped he had everything he needed because he was not going to get another chance at this.

He moved as quietly as he could, the hum of the machines around him giving him some cover. He caught sight of someone coming around the corner as he pocketed his drive and eased out of sight.

How quiet had the door been? He'd had to use a bit of force to push through, so it was probably on a self-closing hinge. Could he get out without her hearing or would the very act alert her?

"I'm in. Yes, I'm going to get it done, and I used the girl's keycard," a quiet voice said.

Hutch stopped, the idea of learning more information suddenly more important than getting out.

"I know. I can do things right sometimes. I only get tripped up over one thing." She was quiet for a moment. "Don't think I've forgotten for a second. I won't let personal feelings fuck up this job. I'm going quiet now. I expect payment upon delivery."

"Oh, I'm going to track this bitch," MaeBe promised in his ear. "I've got a good bead on her. I think if you stay where you are, we'll be okay. I'm watching her. She's not pulling financial data down. She's in another file. Fuck, she's pulling research. Noelle's research. She's downloading everything they have on the helium project."

He wanted to tell MaeBe to screenshot what she could, to capture the espionage in progress. They had to figure out who this was. If she erased the files…

Noelle was in the building. If she erased the files, Noelle would know immediately. Noelle would contact someone.

"I've got what we need. Tell our Russian friends I'll let them look at the real data and they can decide if Layne's insane offer is worth it. Hold on."

"Hutch, she's moving your way. I think she heard something." MaeBe's calm declaration sent a pulse of adrenaline through him.

"And she's got a Glock 9. She'll be coming from your left. Quick but quiet."

The ground beneath him was carpeted, and that would help enormously. He moved across the aisle toward the other side of the room, the one he'd come from. This was a game of cat and mouse, and he was worried he was about to be the mouse.

"Is someone here?" a feminine voice asked. "Sorry, I didn't know I wasn't alone. I'm new."

Sure she was. It was a good try, but he wasn't going to buy it. No one would if they'd heard her talking. She was trying to figure out where he was. Any sound at all would help.

Hutch moved, flattening out against the side of the machine at the end of the aisle.

"She's behind you, but she's stopped halfway down the aisle. I'll let you know if you need to move. For now, stay completely still. She obviously doesn't have backup watching," MaeBe pointed out.

If she did have her own MaeBe, the lady with the gun would know exactly where he was. She didn't seem to.

"I'm fine," the woman said, her voice quieter now. "Just out of practice and a bit paranoid. I'm on my way out, and I've already put the plan in motion. I'll meet Sidirov at the time and place we agreed to. No. No one will be able to tell I was ever here. Including Jessica Layne. She'll have to delete this chick's lifework herself if our client decides to make a deal. I'm going to create some chaos on my way out. I have plans in place. Despite my previous issues, I'm still a pro. And yes, I intend to tie up loose ends soon."

He stayed perfectly still, barely breathing.

"You're clear, but you should know that she introduced a program to the system," MaeBe began. "I'm not sure what it is but…fuck. She took out the CCTV, and I would bet anything it's going to erase the last ten minutes. That's going to set off an alarm. You need to get back to the lab. Now. I can't see anything, Hutch. She was walking to the elevator, but I don't know if she got on or not."

She could be standing right outside, waiting for him. And he had no weapon to defend himself with.

How long before they would notice he'd been gone too long and

Noelle might come looking for him? Kyle would either forbid it or come with her. Either way, she would know something was wrong.

He had to tell Noelle, but he couldn't do it here. She had to know what was happening with her research. And he had to protect her. There was one thing he could do to help her before they needed to get somewhere safe and stay there until he could work through this problem.

As quickly as he could, he found the files where Noelle's lab work was stored and copied it to his drive. He took a quick look around.

Madison Wallace's research was there, too. At least the files were. Every single one of them empty.

Had Jessica Layne sold Madison's research, too? Who had she met with before Madison's "accident"? He had a million questions, but his first responsibility was to protect Noelle at all costs.

"I'm coming out. If anything happens to me, call Kyle and have him get Noelle out of the building. Then call Big Tag. I want Noelle under twenty-four seven guard," he said. "And you tell him that I don't care what deal we made. She should know what's going on."

"You're going to tell her about the feds?"

MaeBe had been debriefed and was one of the only other people beside senior staff who knew about the deal they'd made.

"As soon as we're out of this building and I can be assured no one is listening, yes." He took a deep breath, slid the drive into his pocket, and opened the door.

Kyle was walking down the hall and stopped when he caught sight of Hutch. His gaze went from slightly concerned to steely in a heartbeat.

"What the fuck are you doing? Noelle is worried about you."

"You're supposed to be with her." He didn't like the fact that Kyle had left Noelle alone.

"It was this or bring her with me, and then she would know that you're a liar and you're hiding something from her." Kyle stopped in front of him. "And me. What is going on and why am I out of the loop?"

He didn't have time to deal with Kyle. "I saw an opportunity and I took it."

"Is MaeBe in your ear? Because if she is, then you didn't see an opportunity," Kyle insisted. "You planned this. You planned it when you let Noelle stay late. You planned it because you thought I wouldn't be here."

Well, no one had ever said Kyle was a dummy. "We will talk about this later. We need to get Noelle out of here now. Get the car and meet us at the front of the building."

He had to get out of this building with the information on that drive.

Kyle stared at him for a second before he nodded. "Fine. But we're going to have a long talk, and we might need to bring Ian in because if he approved this, I have a problem with him, too."

Hutch didn't look back as he jogged down the hallway, praying Kyle did his job. "Have the cameras come back on yet?"

"No," MaeBe said. "I'm blind. You should know I already sent Tag a text updating him. I thought you would be all right with that."

"Of course, but he's at Sanctum." It was a play night, and Tag tried not to miss Friday nights. "I want to know the minute those cameras come back up, and I want you to check CCTV anywhere around the building. I want to identify that woman."

He made it to the lab and Noelle was starting to pack up her laptop. He grabbed his own and shoved it into his satchel.

"Hey, I was worried you got lost." Noelle's eyes were wide, concern for him plain there.

He was crazy about this woman, and he prayed she could forgive him. He'd thought he could honor the deal with the feds, but now he knew he should have walked out of that meeting and laid it all out to her. He couldn't talk to her now because Pete was standing behind her.

"I told her it was likely that the janitors hadn't gotten to the men's room yet and you couldn't make yourself go in." Pete shuddered slightly. "Some of our techs, I swear they need to see the doctor. She doesn't understand because women's rooms are never nasty."

He needed a reason to leave and fast. "Hey, sweetie, I sent Kyle down to get the car. I got a call from home and something's happened to my mom."

She paled because she knew damn well his mother wasn't alive. She knew a whole lot about his family. She nodded. "Is she okay?"

"I don't know. I need to get home and call my dad. We might have to head down to Louisiana if it's serious."

Her grip tightened around her cane as she obviously realized something had gone wrong and she might not be coming back to the office soon. "Of course. Let's go."

"Hutch, I've got cameras again," MaeBe said in his ear. "Be careful what you say until you get in the car."

Well, of course they would come up now. Fuck.

"Go," Pete said. "I'll take care of closing everything up. Please let me know if I can make things easier on you."

She nodded and walked out of the lab with him.

The minute the door closed, she looked up at Hutch. "What's going on?"

"Like I said, I'm not sure. Dad was upset. He said something about an accident, but the doctor called him back in the middle of our conversation. I'm waiting for him to get in touch again."

Noelle stopped, and for a moment he worried she might argue with him. Then she started for the elevators. "I hope everyone is okay and not in danger."

Smart girl. "Me, too. Kyle is getting the car and we'll go back home and take it from there. Hopefully we'll have more information soon."

They made it to the elevator, the tension palpable between them. He reached out and took her free hand in his.

She was silent but entwined their fingers and turned his way. "I hope everything is okay."

He smoothed back her hair and stared down at her. "I'm going to make sure it is. Trust me, baby. I'm going to take care of things no matter what. I'm going to put you first."

She took a long breath and then tilted her head up. "Okay."

He kissed her, needing to be close to her. It had been a rough hour, and he wanted nothing more than to get her somewhere safe, wrap his arms around her and tell her everything.

He could also tell her he'd gotten all of her research because if he was right, it would be gone soon, and if she fought Genedyne, she might find herself in the same position as Madison Wallace.

He wasn't going to let that happen.

The doors opened and he stepped out. She let go of his hand and started around the corner.

"Hutch, something's happening. I need you to go out the back of the building. I can get you out," MaeBe said, her voice urgent in his ear.

He stopped, letting Noelle go slightly ahead of him. She rounded the corner. "What is it?"

"It's the cops. They're here and they have Kyle," MaeBe said. "Damn it. Why is Noelle walking out there? They've seen her, Hutch. The guard is taking her into custody."

Oh, that wasn't going to happen. "Call Tag."

He started toward Noelle. They wouldn't be able to see him until he fully entered the lobby.

"Hutch, stop. Think for a second," MaeBe pleaded. "They'll arrest you, too. They'll take the drive. We don't know who will get their hands on it. We don't know if you can get it back."

His feet felt planted to the marble floor. From his vantage, he could see the lobby guard gently leading Noelle out the front doors where blue and red lights made the whole place look eerie.

Kyle was on the ground, his hands cuffed behind his back and a burly officer standing over him.

"I need you to run to the back stairwell," MaeBe said. "I'm shutting the cams down and I've got Michael ready to pick you up. He's on his way. You're going to leave out the freight entrance and immediately take a right. Keep your head down and I'll get you to Michael and he'll take you to Sanctum."

Hutch hesitated.

"If she talks about you, they'll find you," MaeBe pointed out. "You can't help her right now. All you can do is save her research and get the feds the data they need. They can get her out. We don't even know if they're arresting her. This could be about Kyle."

He didn't think so. The mystery woman had said she'd put her plan in motion, and this felt like a plan.

He couldn't let Noelle's research fall into the trap.

With a pain in his heart, he turned and made his way to the back of the building. "All right. Get me out of here."

Walking away was the hardest thing he'd ever done.

* * * *

Noelle's hands were still shaking two hours later. She'd been arrested, put through the booking process, and then shown to this cold, quiet room. On the wall across from her hung the classic mirror through which someone would watch her.

But she'd been left in here alone for what felt like forever.

The moment when she'd realized something had gone terribly wrong played through her head. She'd walked out and seen the red and blue lights, realized it was Kyle on the ground, and then the kindly security guard had explained that they were here for her.

She'd glanced behind her and Hutch had been gone.

He'd left her. Left her alone to be arrested, to know her career was in ruins because she was being accused of stealing something from the company. She still didn't understand that part.

She definitely didn't understand where Hutch had gone and why he'd left her alone.

The door came open and a man entered. He wore a button-down shirt and slacks. His badge was in a lanyard around his neck. He was tall and older than the men who'd arrested her. There were threads of gray in his short, well-kept hair. He pulled out the chair across from her and settled in, a notepad in front of him.

"Noelle LaVigne, I am Detective Grady. Do you want to explain to me why you broke into the Genedyne server rooms this evening?"

"I would like to make a phone call." Her first thought was to call Hutch. She wanted to see him, to have him tell her everything was going to be okay.

But he'd left her. He'd left her and Kyle behind. She was starting to wonder if Hutch wasn't the reason she was here in the first place. He'd been gone so long, and then he'd wanted to hustle them out of the building.

He'd told Kyle he was going to the bathroom. What if he hadn't been? What if he'd been doing something else?

Trust me, baby. I'm going to take care of things no matter what.

I'm going to put you first.

So much for putting her first.

"You can have your phone call, but I need you to answer a few questions first. Is there any way this is a mix-up? I'm surprised a nice young woman like yourself is involved in something criminal."

"What exactly am I being accused of?" It would be nice to know why she was sitting here. She was a sheriff's daughter. She knew she should ask for a lawyer, but the whole day seemed surreal. This was some kind of nightmare, and she would wake up soon.

"You and your boyfriend broke into a part of the Genedyne building that was off limits to you. They've had several problems there in the last couple of weeks with people breaking in."

"I don't have to break in. I work there. And tonight I never left my lab," she replied. "I was in my lab from after lunch to a few minutes before you arrested me."

"That is not what the security logs say." He opened a folder that was sitting in front of him. "According to this, you used your security card to open the door to the server room at exactly nine forty-two this evening."

She looked down at the security logs and sure enough, her keycard registered as accessing the server room. There was one big problem with that. "That's impossible. I don't have clearance to get into that room."

"Yes, that's what we've been told, too. The logs clearly show that your card was used to enter the room. From what we can tell your security clearance was changed an hour before."

"I wouldn't know how to do that. I certainly don't have access to change security levels for an employee even if I did." She hadn't been able to find her card earlier. She'd thought she'd misplaced it. Hutch had distracted her from looking for it.

It had gone missing a few minutes after Hutch had brought her dinner and kissed her and changed all his previously important security protocols about her staying at work.

She was starting to get a bad feeling. Why wasn't Hutch up here trying to get her out? She hadn't seen Kyle since they'd put him in a separate squad car and raced off.

She was alone. Completely alone.

"I was in my lab. Someone else must have used my card. And Kyle isn't my boyfriend. He works for Genedyne, too. He's in security. He was in the lab at the time, too. As well as my engineer." She had witnesses. "His name is Pete Moore. You can talk to him and he'll tell you that Kyle and I were both in the lab."

Except for when Kyle went to look for Hutch.

"I will certainly do that," the detective said.

She wanted to say that he should check the security cameras that were all over the building, but then he might see that it had been Hutch who had crept into the server room. What had he done?

Why was she hesitating?

"I would pull the security camera footage, but somehow all the cameras mysteriously went out in the ten minutes before and after your card was used. Did you do that or was that…" He glanced down at the file again. "Kyle Hutchins?"

So they hadn't figured out that Kyle Hutchins was Kyle Hawthorne. Should she point that out? She was confused about how to handle this. Hutch had explained to her that the security guard at her building was Dallas police, and they weren't sure if he was investigating Jessica Layne or working for her. She didn't know if she should lay everything on the table or if that move would get her in even worse trouble. Before they'd taken her in Kyle had told her to stay quiet. He'd promised her someone would come for them. She folded her hands together to try to keep them from shaking. "It wasn't either of us. I wouldn't begin to know how to hack a system, and neither would Kyle. He works security. He's got access to the whole building. Why would we use my keycard if we were…what? Trying to screw with the computers? Why would we do that?"

"Because there are companies out there who would pay a lot of money to get the research on that system. You're not allowed to take home large parts of your research, are you? No one is. So all that research, all that cutting-edge knowledge, is in that room."

A chill went through her. "I wouldn't do that."

The detective pointed to his file. "But I have evidence that says you did. And it's not only companies that would be interested, is it? Other countries would love to get their hands on some of that data. According to your boss, there's a vast array of cutting-edge research, the kind of tech that could give a country an advantage."

He wasn't merely accusing her of stealing. He might be accusing her of spying, of treason.

How had Hutch done this to her? He hadn't told her he was going to take a look around the server. He'd taken her card and put her in a horrible position and then left her to take the punishment.

Her career was over. She would lose everything and she wasn't sure why. Why had he done it?

Why couldn't she point the finger his way? She should do it because everything was on the line for her and he'd left her out in the cold. She had no idea what he was doing.

Had someone taken him? Was she looking at this the wrong way? Maybe he was completely innocent and someone had taken him. Maybe she was sitting here feeling sorry for herself and he was being hurt.

Helpless. She felt so helpless.

"I can't do anything for you unless you talk to me." The detective's voice had softened. The good cop was in the building. "Noelle, I'm sure he talked you into this. He's a good-looking guy. Did he convince you he cared about you?"

Yes. Hutch had. Despite her better judgment, she'd fallen for his every line. He'd figured out exactly how to play her. He'd walked the fine line between making her feel cared for and appreciating her independence.

He was good, but then hadn't he told her flat out how good he was at undercover? Seducing her had likely been way easier than dealing with the evil doctor.

"Noelle? Are you all right?" The detective was frowning her way, making her wonder how long she'd been zoned out. "You have to know that Kyle Hutchins is in a room next door and he's talking. He's telling us everything."

"He's making a deal?" A numbness had settled over her, and she welcomed it. She wasn't going to cry now because she couldn't feel the pain.

The detective nodded. "That's exactly what he's doing."

"But I could make a deal first." She knew how this went. Even if she hadn't been a sheriff's daughter, she'd watched enough *Law and*

Order to play this scene out in her sleep.

"All you have to do is tell me the truth."

"Because that's what Kyle is doing." She didn't even know what the truth was. How hard had she been played? Had they set her up to take the fall? She couldn't help but remember how Kyle had told her Hutch would never be anything but honest with her.

"He's watching out for himself even as we speak," the detective affirmed. "You're a young woman with a future ahead of her. Don't you want to protect that?"

She had no future at all after this. Her project would be given to someone else, and they would erase her name entirely. If she was lucky she might be a footnote in a journal somewhere, but no one would hire her.

Jessica Layne would ruin her. Even if she managed to get out of jail time, she would spend everything she'd saved on fighting her former boss in a court of law.

Her dad was going to be so upset. He'd sacrificed to help her get here. He and Lila had worked hard to put her through college and grad school, and it had all been a waste.

"I would like to make a phone call." She didn't know who she would call. She should call her dad, but god, how was she going to tell him it had all gone wrong? Maybe she could call Cara. Cara was a reporter. She might know people who could help.

The detective huffed. "I can't help you if you won't help yourself."

There was one thing she could do to shut this down. "I want a lawyer. I have the right to an attorney, and you will provide me with one."

There was a knock on the door and then it came open and a familiar woman walked in, though she looked way different than she had the last time she'd seen her. Mistress Lea strode in wearing a dark business suit, her hair sleek. She carried a brilliant pink bag, and sky-high heels clicked along the floor.

She frowned down at the detective. "I'm Lea Stone, Ms. LaVigne's attorney. I would like to know why you're questioning my client without representation present because my client is an incredibly smart woman who knows not to talk to the police without proper representation. So I think you're the one who's fucking up right now."

Detective Grady sighed, a long-suffering sound. "She's all yours."

"In my defense, I didn't realize I was your client, Miss…Miss Stone." She'd been about to call the woman *Mistress*. Even out of fet wear Lea Stone kind of scared her. She filled the small room with her presence.

Lea's dark eyes pinned her. "Yes, you are, and we're getting out of here now. I believe the detective will find this has all been a mistake. You can apologize now, Detective. It might go a long ways to calming my client down after her false arrest."

"False arrest?" The detective stood. "Are you fucking with me? Have you read this file?"

"Take it up with the DA." A shit-eating grin crossed Lea's face. "My partner and I have been talking to Ms. Brighton all evening, and her office has come to the conclusion that this was all one big mistake."

"Maia Brighton?" The detective took a step back as though he'd realized the danger he was in.

"The bitch herself. She's on her way in," Lea explained. "She will be after she talks to your chief."

Another knock and an older man was poking his head in. "Grady, cut her loose. We've got problems, and I need you in my office in ten to talk to the DA."

Grady went pale. "Of course, Lieutenant. I'll be right there."

He strode out without a backward glance.

"What just happened?" Noelle's head was reeling.

"Big Tag happened." Lea turned. "Come along. We're leaving before they decide if they're going to fight or not. Right now, they're dealing with shock and awe."

"Shock and awe?"

"The district attorney. She's been informed about the case and she's taking exception to having DPD do Jessica Layne's dirty work. I honestly don't know what's going on. I was having a nice night at Sanctum disciplining a gorgeous, naughty boy, and then Mitch and I were on our way here. He's getting Kyle, who managed to be so obnoxious they actually threw him in a cell," Lea explained. "Let's go. I want you processed out as soon as possible."

Noelle was on her feet. "I want to know what's happening. Where is Hutch?"

"He was at Sanctum the last time I saw him. He was with Big Tag and a couple of civies I didn't recognize." Lea's foot tapped on the floor. "Do you want to stay here?"

There was an easy answer to that. "No. I want to go home."

"Then it's sad that I have strict instructions to take you back to Sanctum," Lea announced.

Noelle shook her head. "I'm going home. I want out of all of this."

And by *home* she meant she was packing up her bags and heading back to Papillon.

Lea's eyes rolled. "I knew you were going to be a pain in my ass the minute I saw you." She sighed. "All right. I'll try to avoid stuffing you into my car in front of a police station by giving you the talk. I don't know exactly what went down. I suspect there are layers upon layers to this thing, but our problem right now is you're upset with your boyfriend."

"He's not my boyfriend."

"Oh, is he not? Because I recently changed my whole training program rules for him. He's your boyfriend and he pissed you off by not getting his ass arrested with you. He's waiting for you at Sanctum. Face him like the grown-ass adult woman you are and make him either explain his actions or pay for them. Do not sneak off in order to avoid confrontation because confrontation will find you one way or another. Do you want to be the sad sub who gets hauled into interrogation rooms, or the badass bitch who makes cops so scared they're willing to do almost anything to keep you happy? It's your choice." Lea turned and started out. "And know that I *will* stuff your ass in the car. You're going to Sanctum. Spend the car ride deciding how you want to deal with your man."

Noelle forced herself to follow the Domme.

Maybe it was time she faced Hutch. But he wasn't her man. He wasn't going to be anything to her but a regret.

Chapter Sixteen

"She's not answering her phone. She has her phone back, right? Lea said she was processing out half an hour ago. The police would give it back to her." Hutch paced the conference room floor.

Sanctum's conference room was there for the numerous times play nights had gotten interrupted by some case they were all on. More than once in his time with McKay-Taggart he'd gone from spanking a sub to sitting in this conference room hacking into the CCTV feeds of a European country because an op had gone south.

This one had gone so far south it might be rounding north again, and it was the most important case of his career because he'd fallen madly in love with his client.

"She's not answering her phone because she's probably still in shock." Big Tag had changed out of his leathers, though it seemed his night had sucked before Hutch's issues had arisen. Charlotte had gone home to deal with some kind of teen girl problem, and that had left Tag growly. "Have we figured out why our mystery lady left the cameras on while she stole the data and then turned them off as she left? Why not simply turn them off when she's ready to access the data?"

"Because that would tip off security." Hutch was guessing here, but Kyle had mentioned that security monitored the cameras from their phones from time to time. They could be alerted if the systems went out. It would be a calculated risk on the operative's part. She balanced the risk of someone watching one particular camera among hundreds at precisely the right time versus the absolute certainty of the alarm going off. "She shut it down when she was okay with the chaos the alarm would create. She'd already gotten away, and she could erase whatever she liked."

Tag's hands had fisted. "MaeBe, I want a name."

MaeBe looked up from her computer. She'd made it to the club before he had and apparently taken the brunt of Big Tag's bad mood. "I can't get a name if I can't see a face."

"What does that mean?" Tag stalked over to her, looking over her shoulder. "I thought you said she walked out of the building. Did she find a way to take out every CCTV camera in downtown Dallas?"

"No, CCTV is working. I can show you that she walked from the Genedyne building three blocks to a hotel where I lose her. And yes, I've made note of the hotel and I'm investigating, but I would bet she's not a guest. This woman planned her op carefully, and that means she planned how she would get away. I would bet she met someone there and they left via the underground parking garage. It's what I would do if I wanted to go unseen."

"Show him. He doesn't understand how she could keep her face down for that long." Hutch moved in behind Tag. He'd been down here while Tag had dealt with Cara and Chris. He'd been trying to track the woman who'd fucked up his life because this had been one long setup.

MaeBe's fingers raced across the keys, bringing up the moment the woman walked out of the Genedyne building.

"What is she wearing?" Tag asked, pointing to the odd glasses on the woman's face.

"She's wearing state-of-the-art, fuck-the-facial-recognition-software gear," MaeBe stated flatly. "The LED lights confuse the AI. She can smile right at the camera and I get nothing. It's even bending the light around her face slightly so I can't print it out and get anything useful. She presents as female. She's roughly five foot seven, and that's all I can tell you. The jacket she's wearing is shapeless. She knew exactly what she was doing, and that was getting away with stealing Noelle's research."

"How is she able to see anything with those lights on?" Tag leaned in, looking at the screen.

"Like MaeBe said, that's state of the art. There was a professor in Japan years ago who played around with using LED light to fool an AI. This looks like someone's taken his work to the next level," Hutch explained. "And maybe using meta materials to bend light around her face. Again, not something that's on the market."

"So she's our Collective friend," Tag surmised.

"Or something like it." Hutch was sure they weren't calling themselves The Collective these days, but it was the same shit. It was corporations at war with each other and willing to burn down the world for fun and profits.

The fact that they couldn't ID the woman who'd stolen Noelle's research made anger roll in his gut.

But that was nothing compared to the anxiety of not being with her, of knowing she was going through something horrible and not being able to do anything about it. After Michael had picked him up, he'd worked as fast as he could. He'd immediately called in Tag, who'd gotten Mitch and Lea on the case. He hoped the booking process had taken a while and they'd managed to get her out of there before she'd been taken to a cell.

The door came open and Chris Taylor walked in, Cara moving behind him. "You had to sic the DA on them? Do you know the kind of hell I'm going to catch once this story gets around? No one outside of major crimes knows what I'm working on right now, but they'll find out eventually, and I'm going to catch hell for sending in the dragon."

"I have questions about involving her, too. Maia Brighton's got quite a reputation," Cara complained.

"A reputation for being a man-eating, ruthless she-demon?" Hutch had known her for years. He'd avoided falling even temporarily into her web, unlike many of his friends.

"Hey, don't misrepresent a long-time… Well, she's not really a friend." Tag took his place at the head of the table. "And she is a true pansexual. She'll take it from anyone she finds vaguely attractive.

Maia is many things. The one thing no one can accuse her of is being corrupt. There's zero threat of her working with Layne. In fact, she'll happily help you take her down. But for tonight she's the only thing keeping my people out of jail. I don't know what is going on with this third party. Hutch is going to give us an update on what he thinks is going on as soon as our friends get here." Tag looked down at his phone. "And they're coming in now. Lea's got Noelle. Mitch had more trouble getting Kyle out because they'd tossed him in a cell. He's running a couple of minutes behind."

She was here. Thank god. "I'm going to meet her."

"Does she know about me?" Cara asked.

"No. I took the deal seriously." It had been a mistake on his part. "But she has to know everything now."

"Agreed." Cara took a seat next to Chris. "We need to protect her. It's obvious she's not involved in this."

If only they'd figured that out days ago. He pushed through the conference room door and out into the hallway. The first floor of Sanctum was fairly normal looking. It was where the offices and locker rooms were. He could hear the sound of industrial music pulsing from above.

He wished he was up there with Noelle, wished they were a Dom and a sub, enjoying a night for themselves.

Instead he had to tell her that everything she'd worked for was at risk.

The good news was he'd saved her research. All of it. He'd risked his neck and put her first. She was going to understand, and he was going to figure out how to fix this for her.

He strode to the lobby, though there wasn't much to the lobby of Sanctum. There was a security desk that was manned by one of the Doms on play nights. The rest of the time a state-of-the-art security system protected the building.

He watched as Lea strode up and the guard allowed her in, followed by Noelle. She leaned on her cane as though the day had taken a toll on her body.

His whole soul softened as she walked in, and he rushed to her. "Noelle."

He wrapped his arms around her, needing to assure himself that she was safe. He breathed her in and brushed his lips against her hair. It took him a moment to realize she wasn't hugging him back.

"Good luck with that one, Hutch," Lea said. "She's already fired me, so I don't think you'll be around for long."

She'd done what? He stepped back. "Baby, you can't fire Lea. She's the best defense attorney in Dallas. We managed to get the charges dropped tonight, but I have a feeling Jessica Layne will come back fighting. Lea, you're not fired."

Lea started for the locker room. "And this fucks up my training class because she also quit that. I planned for a certain amount of couples, and now I don't have that number. This is why I shouldn't deal with tourists," she muttered.

"You don't get to make that decision," Noelle said quietly after Lea was gone. "I'm here because your friend there wouldn't let me be anywhere else, so I'm going to let you know that if you ever come near me again, I'll get a restraining order."

Okay, she didn't have the whole story. She'd been through a lot, and he could understand why she pinned it on him. "Noelle, we need to talk."

She shook her head. "No, we don't. The whole drive over here I thought about what I would say to you, and I realized I don't need to say anything at all. I don't need to listen to you justify your actions. Maybe that's not true. I do need to let you know that you won't break me."

His heart ached at those words. "I would never do that. Never. I'm sorry I had to run, but you'll understand once I explain."

She stared at him, not a hint of affection in her eyes. "Did you or did you not break into the server room and download data?"

His heart seemed to clench because she didn't look like a woman who wanted to listen to explanations. "Yes, but I did it for you."

A humorless chuckle huffed from her. "For me? You broke into my employer's secure computer systems for me?"

He needed to tell her what he'd discovered and she would understand. "Yes, and come into the conference room and I'll explain everything. A lot has happened tonight. I'm sorry you had to go through that alone, but I had a good reason."

"How did you know? I walked from behind the elevators and the guard was waiting for me, but he didn't see you. How did you know to stop? Why didn't you follow me?"

He wasn't going to lie to her. "MaeBe had cut into the cameras and she saw them. I had her in my ear, but she didn't say anything until it was too late. You have to know I would have gotten you out if I could have."

"Oh, tonight has proven that I don't know anything at all. You're the mastermind. How long have you known you were going to do this?"

"In the beginning we talked about the fact that I might need to get on the systems." Hutch felt the need to defend himself. "It was the whole point of getting Kyle a job at Genedyne."

"I thought the point was protecting me," she shot back. "I didn't feel protected today, Hutch. I felt used."

"Used?" He understood her anger, but she needed to think for a second. "If I had gone in with you, it would have been much longer before we could have gotten you out."

"So MaeBe wouldn't have called someone in?"

He sighed. "Of course she would have, but getting myself arrested would have led to questions we don't want to answer, and it would have led to us losing all the data I pulled down. Including your research."

That seemed to stop her in her tracks. "You downloaded my research?"

At least now he had her attention. "Yes, I went in to gather intel for the feds."

"The feds?"

This was another tricky part. "I spent most of the day with the FBI special agent who is investigating Genedyne for fraud. The whole company, including you, baby. I made a deal with her to keep you out of any prosecution, but I had to get the financial records."

"Her? Who is *her*? I thought Chris Taylor was probably the one watching me," she began, and then it was easy to see that big brain of hers making the leap. Her head shook and there was a shine to her eyes. "Cara. Of course. She came along at the right time. I was lonely and happy to have a friend."

"I think she likes you. She made that deal to protect you without hesitation, Noelle." He could save this. He could show her that she wasn't alone even though she felt that way. He could make her understand that he'd done everything he'd done with her safety in mind. "Part of the deal was not giving up Cara's cover until the end of the op. I was following the rules of the deal but I shouldn't have. I should have told you what I was doing."

"That you were going to steal my keycard and ruin my career? Yeah, I would have liked to have known that was coming."

"I know it seems bad now, but I was trying to save your career," Hutch explained.

"Hutch, can you do this in the conference room?" Big Tag stood in the hallway. "I have to get home at some point in time tonight."

"Yes, we wouldn't want the ruining of my life to inconvenience you, Mr. Taggart," Noelle said, a bite to her tone. "How about I call a ride and then you can go home immediately?"

"Ian," Hutch began because he knew what it took to stir the beast in his boss, and that beast was close to the surface tonight.

"I would love for you to do that, Ms. LaVigne." Ian's voice had gone soft—a sure sign that he was about to go volcanic. "I started my day getting arrested in front of the middle school my daughters go to, and all because of a case I took for zero dollars."

"Well, you did a great job," Noelle replied. "Your guy cost me my job and my dignity. I'll be sure to put that in my online review."

He turned to his boss. "She's upset. She doesn't mean any of this."

"I know, and if I'd had a less shitty day, I would be more patient, but I'm sick of little girls who think they know what they're doing. I'm sick of children who tear up the people around them because they don't know how to handle their emotions," Tag bit out. "Ms. LaVigne, you should understand if you weren't Armie LaVigne's daughter, I'd toss your ass out on the street because if you can't do us the courtesy of listening to a debrief, then I don't care what happens to you. But you are, and I owe your father. So this is how the evening is going to go. You can sit and listen, or I can have a guard escort you upstairs to one of our safe rooms where you will wait until your father can come pick you up."

Noelle's jaw went tight, and a single tear fell on her cheek. "I'm sorry I was rude."

"Your whole world feels like it fell apart." Hutch moved to her side. Ian was being too hard on her. "It's okay."

She ignored him, choosing to look to Ian. "I would prefer it if you didn't call my father."

Tag shook his head. "You can call him or I will. I'm sorry. I can't be a businessman here. I'm a father, and I know how I would feel if my daughter had been arrested and no one bothered to tell me. You've got until tomorrow morning. I'll be contacting your dad at ten a.m."

"Ian, maybe we should talk..." Hutch began.

"All right." Noelle interrupted him. "It doesn't seem like I'm left with many choices. I will listen to this debrief of yours. Am I going to be able to talk to the people who had me arrested? Is Cara in there? Why didn't she question me?"

"Because she didn't have you arrested at all. That's what I've been trying to tell you." At least he would have a chance to explain. He would rather do it privately, but he could make her understand any way she would allow it.

"There's a third party at play." Tag seemed to relax slightly. "We should talk in the conference room. It looks like Mitch is back with Kyle."

There was the beep of the front door opening and Kyle walked in. Unlike Noelle, he truly looked worse for the wear. There was a cut on his lip, and his normally controlled hair was unruly. There was a blood stain on the shirt he wore.

Kyle looked Noelle over. "You do okay in there?"

Noelle sniffled, the first sign that she wasn't completely in control. "They told me you were throwing me under the bus."

Kyle snorted. "Like I would do that." He looked to Ian. "I got mouthy and pushy to buy us some time. Also, I hate those interview rooms. They're cold and I can't make friends. I think I joined the prison softball team."

Tag showed his first real smile. "I'm sure you'll be a hit. You going to take it out on him or me?"

Kyle smiled, but it was a kind of scary thing. "Oh, I'm taking it out on him."

Were they talking about him? Hutch started to ask but then Kyle reared back and popped him right on the nose. Pain flared, and Hutch felt a momentary nausea as he cradled his nose.

"That's for getting me arrested, you asshole. And for not trusting me. You lied to me," Kyle said. "The only reason I'm staying on this assignment is for Noelle. And we're not friends again."

Hutch saw the moment Noelle started to reach for him and then pulled back.

"Can we get through this? I'd like to get some rest." Noelle looked to Kyle like he was going to save her.

"I'll make sure you get home after this is over," Kyle promised. "I could use some rest myself."

She thought Kyle would escort her home and leave him out in the cold? Well, she was wrong. He watched as Kyle led her into the conference room, his mind turning ruthless.

"Don't kill him," Tag said, looking down at his nose. "It's not even broken."

It was good to know someone didn't underestimate him.

"Damn, what happened?" Mitchell Bradford walked in the door. "Fuck. That had to be Kyle. He's psychotic, you know. There's something wrong with him. From what I can tell he started at least two fights and then told me how fun his night had been."

"Yeah, the kid's got issues," Tag agreed.

"Is this still my op?" Hutch asked.

Tag frowned. "Man, she's pissed. I don't know that you want this op anymore."

"I want it." And he wanted her.

"All right. How do you want to play this?" Tag asked.

Mitch groaned. "I don't need to hear this, do I? Because if it involves holding a woman against her will, then I should go back to the dungeon. You know that place where illegal stuff doesn't happen?"

"You should definitely go." Because Hutch had no plans to let Noelle ditch him tonight.

Or ever.

* * * *

Noelle had to force herself to sit across from the woman who'd been her first real friend in Dallas. She figured if she could get through that last meeting with Hutch, she could handle one more liar.

"I need you to understand that I never thought you were truly involved in what I believe Jessica Layne is doing." Cara leaned forward. She sat beside Chris, and Noelle had to admit they made an attractive couple.

"Were you lying about knowing him from before?" Noelle asked the question, the words feeling numb in her mouth. That was a problem because she couldn't seem to make herself feel anything. She'd watched Kyle hit Hutch and emotion had swelled inside her, and then it had gone out like a flame snuffed.

Maybe she had lied and Hutch had broken her.

Cara stared at her like she didn't want to answer the question at all. "We were engaged two years ago. I left DPD to join the FBI, and we broke up shortly after that. This assignment was the first time we'd seen each other in a while."

"Noelle, we never meant to hurt you." Chris was out of the suit he wore for his cover job. He wore jeans and a T-shirt, his dark hair slicked back. "You unfortunately got caught in the middle of a long-term covert investigation. What happened tonight was not something we were aware of or we would have found a way to shut it down. No one on our team wanted you arrested."

"Yeah, well, your team needs to do better because we made you the first day we walked in the door." Kyle settled in beside her.

If that punch had been any indication, Kyle hadn't been in on Hutch's plans either. She'd wanted so much to go to Hutch. When he'd wrapped his arms around her, she'd wanted nothing more than to hug him and cry against his shoulder. The impulse had been right there to believe everything he said and let him handle it all.

She couldn't because letting him handle it had cost her everything.

Why had he downloaded her work?

"You didn't make anyone." MaeBe looked up from her laptop. "I did. I remembered you from a conference about a year ago."

Cara turned his way. "And you didn't remember the young woman with purple hair and a nose ring?"

Chris shrugged. "She looks like every techie in our department, to tell you the truth. Or CSI. I won't even go into the women who work in the morgue."

MaeBe frowned. "I take exception to your attack on my individuality." She focused her gaze on Noelle. "Are you all right?"

"Why would you care?" This wasn't her. She wasn't cold and unfeeling. MaeBe had been doing her job, but it felt personal.

MaeBe's eyes widened, and Noelle realized she wasn't wearing her normal makeup. She wasn't wearing any at all, and her eyes were slightly puffy. Had she cried it off? "I absolutely care. I've been worried about you and Kyle."

"Then perhaps you should have given me a heads-up that I was about to get arrested," Kyle replied, his voice cold as ice. "Instead, you calmly saved your boy and let Noelle and I give him cover."

"That's not what happened. When that woman broke in and she used Noelle's keycard, I thought my heart was going to stop. I haven't been calm since the moment I realized the whole thing had gone to hell." MaeBe's face had flushed.

The door came open and Big Tag and Hutch walked through.

"What woman?" Noelle had stuck on that part of MaeBe's story. "I thought Hutch had taken my keycard."

Hutch's nose was slightly swollen, but it oddly didn't make him any less attractive. "I don't need your keycard, Noelle. I wouldn't have done that because that would have left a footprint in the logs. Which is exactly what the woman who did use your card wanted."

"What woman?" Was there something more here? It wouldn't change the fact that he'd lied to her and taken away her options, but she wanted to know what was happening.

"I didn't see a woman," Kyle admitted. "I only saw Hutch slinking out of the server room when he told me he was going to the bathroom."

"And from what I understand, you snuck through his security system last night when you were supposed to be on duty." Big Tag sent Kyle a glare that could have frozen fire. "I am going to assume you have an explanation and that you want me to believe you."

Kyle's jaw tightened, but he sat back as though letting the matter rest for now.

Why would Kyle have slipped out of the house?

Hutch took a deep breath and sank down into his chair. "Noelle, I was arrested this morning, and in this case it *was* Cara and Chris."

"We thought it was odd that a McKay-Taggart employee moved in with a person of interest," Cara explained. "But he's cybersecurity, so we both bet that he was hired to figure out who had accessed your computer. That was me, of course. I did that. When Hutch showed up at your apartment, I made the decision at the time to not approach. Your father has ties to McKay-Taggart. I assumed they were with you out of an abundance of caution because of the break-in on the floor below you."

"We realized you were going to fuck up everything when you caught us together the night before and then took off. You were careful about not saying anything that would give away what you were truly doing. We couldn't risk you actually taking Noelle out of the city," Chris admitted. "We needed Noelle in the Genedyne building."

"Because they were going to ask you to do what I did this evening," Hutch pointed out. "They were going to offer you a deal. Your cooperation in exchange for a promise of no prosecution."

"What would I have been prosecuted for? What is Jessica doing? And was the break-in below about me?" She had a million questions, and she wanted the answers to all of them. Because she worried if she didn't have them, she might allow herself to believe anything Hutch told her. He was close, and she wanted the comfort of his hand in hers, but she couldn't be that woman. He'd ruined her life and hadn't even brought her into the discussion of it. He was supposed to protect her, not make decisions for her.

"I'll take the easy one," Chris offered. "I don't make decisions on who to prosecute or not. I was the one who broke in the floor below. I did it because it was the only way to access your apartment's hub without anyone knowing."

"You hacked her smart system from the direct line," Hutch explained. "It's why it didn't show up in the logs. Did the resident come home while you were doing it?"

Chris nodded. "Yeah, this has been a clusterfuck of an assignment the whole time. The resident brought a date home, and I had to make it look good. I quickly hid her laptop and trashed the place a little and told her I'd gotten a call that someone had entered the apartment. She bought it."

"So you were watching me through my smart system?" The idea that people had been watching her made her sick. How could she ever not feel eyes on her again?

"Yes," Cara replied bluntly. "But only the last few weeks, and only to ensure you weren't actively working with Layne."

There was so much she didn't understand. "Why me? I'm not close to Layne."

"Because my person on the inside might have said that if anyone was working with her, it was you. Look, I didn't realize how angry she was at first. I had to check out her claims. She was honest about a lot of things, just not you," Cara said.

"Are you talking about Madison?" It was the only thing that made sense.

Cara put a hand on the folder she'd brought in. "Yes. Madison contacted the FBI when she started to suspect what was going on at Genedyne. It was six months ago. We spent a long time with Madison trying to get us the information we needed to prove what's happening at Genedyne. Madison inferred that you might be in on it in the beginning. I came to realize she said that because she was angry with you for stealing one of her techs."

Noelle took a deep breath because this was a lot to process. "Was she talking about Pete?"

"Yes," Cara replied. "She admitted it later on. She was jealous of you because everyone wanted to work for you. She knew what the rumors about her were. But the reason I've stuck close to you is that before Madison died, she sent out a single text, and it was your name. I think that was all she was able to do. Her phone was destroyed in the fire, so if she put any information in but wasn't able to send it out, we'll never know."

"My name? Why would she do that?" She'd known Madison hated her, but the extent hit her squarely. Madison had tried to implicate her in... "What am I being accused of?"

"Nothing," Hutch said quickly. "They know you had nothing to do with this."

"Then why would you be worried I could be prosecuted?" His story didn't make sense to her.

"It's a leverage tool," Chris admitted. "One the feds use a lot. Even if they know you don't have a level of culpability that would make prosecution reasonable, they will use the threat to gain your cooperation."

Noelle turned to Cara. "Is that what you were going to do?"

"If I had to." Cara sent Chris a frown. "It's not like the cops don't use it, too."

"I cut a deal with them." Hutch broke into the conversation. "That's what I was doing this morning. I was ensuring that they don't have any leverage over you."

"But you didn't even ask me if I wanted you to do that," Noelle shot back.

Hutch's eyes narrowed. "Of course you did."

"Hutch, what did you trade for my safety? Shouldn't I have had a say in that?" She understood that he might have thought he was doing what was best for her, but he'd made a life-changing choice without giving her any input.

Hutch stared back at her, not giving an inch. "I traded the information they need to prove that Genedyne is involved in fraud."

"Apparently he also caught a third party." Big Tag was studying her. "Hutch wasn't the one who used your keycard, and he definitely wasn't the one who called the police. The woman who was in the server room with Hutch downloaded your research."

"Why would she do that?" She was starting to feel queasy.

"I don't know," Tag continued. "Why would Jessica Layne meet with representatives from three of the biggest natural gas companies in the world this evening?"

That information stopped Noelle in her tracks. "Why would natural gas companies want to invest in my technology? Helium is often found when they drill for natural gas. Helium is something they sell, and it would be in their best interest to keep the prices high. Maybe she was meeting with them for another reason."

"Then why would she have gotten rid of me?" Kyle asked that question. "She made a last-minute decision to take that meeting, and when she did, she ensured I wasn't there, even standing outside the restaurant because she knew I would talk to you about it. Damn it. She's selling your research to keep it from being used. That's the fraud."

"That explains why Madison's research files were empty." Hutch placed a thumb drive on the table. "These are some financial records that hopefully prove another one of Jessica Layne's scams. She's finding investors for Genedyne by sending them fraudulent research. She's taking everyone's reports and making the numbers look better than they really are."

"I haven't given her my numbers," Noelle replied.

Cara slid that folder across the table. "Then why did she print out this report earlier today? This is what she did to Madison. This is what she did to her original partner, too. Madison was working on a cancer project. Shortly before she died, Jessica Layne met with some of the biggest pharmaceutical companies in the world."

God, could this be true? "Madison told me her research was going to change the world. But she was working on a biochemical solution to pollution."

"And sometimes the greatest breakthroughs are made by accident," Cara pointed out. "What Madison discovered was that the bacteria she manipulated to basically eat pollution, ate tumors as well. She hadn't even started real experiments on it yet, but she had high hopes that it could potentially lead to a breakthrough."

"But that could be worth a lot of money. Why would Jessica squash that research?" Her brain was racing with the implications.

"Because Genedyne is a house of cards," Chris explained. "She's running it like a multi-level marketing scheme. She pays investors and her legal team by bringing in new investors and selling promising research to people who would like that research to never reach the marketplace. From what Hutch has given us, we believe that she sold Madison's research to that pharmaceutical consortium for fifty million dollars."

"She's selling my research and getting rid of me. She killed Madison." That truth felt like a kick in the gut.

"Good." Tag sat up straighter. "We're all on the same page now. In light of this new information, can we all agree Noelle is potentially in physical danger?"

"Why have her arrested?" MaeBe spoke up. "What was our spy doing there? She said she was meeting with Sidirov, so I would bet she's not working for Jessica Layne."

"No, she's working as a corporate spy, trying to get the real research. If they have the pure data, they can prove Layne's lying about how far along the research is and knock the price down in exchange for not talking about it," Hutch surmised. "Someone in the corporate world caught on to her shakedown. They had you arrested to create chaos and to discredit you in case they decide not to pay at all."

"They're driving down the price of my work." She thought she'd been stunned before.

"Genedyne is literally built on nothing. It's a work of fiction fueled by fear of Jessica Layne," Cara pronounced. "And I'm going to take her down. Hutch gave us an excellent start, and he believes no one is going to even question that he has the financial data because Layne will be so concerned with the data breach on research."

His eyes were intense as he stared at her. "That was not my intention."

But he would use it. She understood that. There was no reason to put his investigation at risk when the damage was already done.

Jessica Layne had taken everything from her. Including Hutch, since she now knew what he truly thought of her. He might care about her, but he'd lied to her.

It seemed like everyone had. There was only one way to handle it. She had to fight, had to throw all of her personal feelings to the side and survive this the best way she could.

She turned to Cara. "I'm going to help you. What do you want me to do?"

Chapter Seventeen

Two hours later Noelle sat on a spanking bench contemplating the turns her life had taken.

When she'd woken up this morning, she'd had a promising career, a relationship with a man she was falling in love with, and a nice apartment that she could feel comfortable in.

Now her career was in shambles, her boyfriend had lied to her, and she was a prisoner in a dungeon. She wasn't technically in the dungeon, but Sanctum had one. The second floor was a big old dungeon complete with a hamster wheel that was being used by her bodyguard, who needed to literally run away from his demons.

She was confused and on edge, and she wasn't sure what to do with it. She was never going to be able to sleep.

Was this how Madison had felt before someone had set her lab on fire with her in it?

Why had Madison texted her name to Cara?

Why had Hutch done what he'd done?

The questions pounded at her brain, making her hands shake with the need to… She wasn't even sure what she needed to do, and that was part of the problem.

Tomorrow she'd promised to call her father, and then she would probably have to go back to Louisiana because they couldn't keep a

24/7 guard on her for long. She would go home and be that poor pitiful girl she'd been. She loved Papillon, but gossip was a big part of life there, and she would be a story. A cautionary tale about what happened when a young woman tried to fly too high.

Sanctum was her home for now. Given what had happened to Madison, they hadn't been willing to risk even letting her go back to Hutch's place. She was stuck in what they called a "safe room."

It was late and Sanctum had finally closed down, though Hutch and Big Tag were still talking, and MaeBe had promised to run by Noelle's place to grab some clothes for her. Kyle had been the one to settle her into this room. She wondered how many other "safe" houses had spanking benches in them.

Tomorrow Chris and Cara would figure out if they had enough data to charge Jessica Layne. They would decide if she would try to get more. There had been a lot of talk about how she would get back into the building. Hutch had shot every single scenario full of holes until the special agent had thrown up her hands and told Ian Taggart she would talk to him tomorrow.

Where the hell would she be in a week's time? Back in Papillon, hoping someone would let her teach high school chemistry? Would she be fighting off a lawsuit that would take everything she had? Jessica Layne wasn't known for backing down. Even if she was in the middle of an indictment, she would still come after Noelle.

Her life was utterly changed, and she had no idea how to stop it.

There was no stopping it. This would change her life as surely as the car accident had. She'd never seen it coming, and it would affect her forever.

There was a knock on her door, and there was no question who was on the other side. "Go away, Hutch."

She didn't need to hear about how heroic he'd been. She didn't need to hear about how he'd risked everything to ensure she wasn't prosecuted for a crime she hadn't even come close to committing. Did he think she didn't know anything about the law? She'd grown up in a law enforcement family.

The door opened even though she was sure she'd locked it. This man didn't need keys to get through a door. He'd proven that tonight. Of course she was also in a space he felt comfortable in.

He walked into the room carrying his laptop bag and another she recognized from her place. It looked like MaeBe had found one of Noelle's tote bags and filled it with a change of clothes. She didn't care about any of it.

"Noelle, we need to talk. You are not taking part in this investigation."

She got to her feet, reaching for her cane because she had to go toe to toe with this man. "You don't get to make that choice for me. You've made enough choices for me."

His gorgeous face looked confused for a moment. "Is that why you're upset with me? You think I made a choice for you? Baby, what other choice was there to make?"

"I don't know because I wasn't allowed to make one."

"What should I have done?" The question came out quiet, his sincerity hard to deny.

But her anger had a place, too. "You should have told me what was happening. Not only am I the woman you were sleeping with, I was your client. And don't tell me you couldn't have found a time."

"I was going to explain everything to you this evening." Every word he said was soft, as though he knew she was a powder keg and he didn't want to be the one who made her explode.

The trouble was she kind of wanted to explode in a spectacular fashion. It might be better to destroy everything good left. She could do it herself before anyone else had the chance.

"After you ruined my career."

He paled slightly. "I didn't have any intention of ruining your career. Did you forget the part where your boss was selling your research to the bad guys? Did you think they're going to hire you to finish it and take away a part of their business?"

Yes, this was what she wanted. She wanted to snarl his way and have him claw at her, too. That would feel good and then she wouldn't have to miss him when he was gone. If they burned down everything they had, he would be nothing more than a regret. "Do not call me naïve."

"If the shoe…" He stopped and took a long breath. "I'll insert that shoe right in my mouth. Noelle, I did not come up here to argue with you. I came here to give you what I didn't give Cara and Chris."

He held out a thumb drive. "I switched your research data to a new drive and erased it off the one I gave to them. Only you and I and MaeBe and Tag know that I downloaded your research data. It should be almost everything that was on the Genedyne system. You updated the file twenty minutes before I downloaded it, so I think it's almost everything."

She stared at that drive knowing there was a woman out there delivering the same information to a group of businessmen who would store it away and never look at it again. Whose only use for all her hard work was to trash it so it didn't dent their profits. Those people only cared about their bottom line and not about the fact that her work would make it easier and cheaper to advance humanity.

"What do you want me to do with that?" All of her numbness was starting to melt, giving way to a bubbling rage that threatened to overwhelm her. Rage and fear and sorrow. It was all being held back by that wall of ice that had started to crack the minute he'd walked into the room.

Because Hutch is safe. Because even though he did something dumb, he did it for the right reasons.

No. No. Fucking no. She wasn't giving in. She wanted one good thing to come out of this, but how could it be him?

He didn't put you in this position. He tried to get you out. Put yourself in his place.

He was still holding the drive. "I expect you to take it and do something with it."

He was the naïve one now. "And what's that? Because at the end of the day it's not mine. It belongs to Genedyne, and she has the right to use it however she wants. She has the right to sell it. God, how stupid was I? I even read the contract and I still signed it."

"Because you were young and hungry and she offered you everything you needed to get started," Hutch insisted. "I'm going to get a copy of your contract, and Mitch will find a loophole. There's always a loophole. Lea will ensure that no criminal charges even come close to touching you. You have people who will look out for you. Jessica Layne knew what she was doing, and she took advantage of you. You are not the stupid one."

Oh, but she had been. So stupid. Her stepmom had even pointed out how the contract heavily favored the company, but had she listened to her? No. She'd known better. She'd known that this was how the business worked.

His hand was up, offering her all she couldn't take. It was hers. Her work. Her soul. And she'd stupidly sold it all because she'd thought she was smarter than anyone else.

Without thought, she slapped that dumb drive out of his hand. It hit the wall, pinged onto the floor, and she started moving toward it with every intention of smashing it into pieces. She needed to, needed to destroy something the way she'd been destroyed.

Hutch's arm went around her waist, hauling her back against him. "Don't you dare."

She tried to push his arm away. "Why? It doesn't mean anything. Not a damn thing."

"It means everything because if her company is a fraud then they can't enforce your contract. And honestly, even if they tried to, I'll find a way to get this back for you," he whispered. "I won't let this happen. I won't let them take it."

She wanted to believe him, wanted to throw all of this on him. She could take the drive and work on what she could while she didn't have access to a lab and let Hutch and his superhero team get her out of this nightmare. But she didn't think he could fix this. "You can't, and if you think I'll let you do anything for me again, you're wrong."

He went stiff behind her and then relaxed. "It's okay. Take it out on me. You're angry. I can handle it. I know what this feels like. You need to get it out or it will poison everything in your life."

Rage threatened to bubble up, and it suddenly was too much. The day had been horrible. She'd been left with nothing. Nothing.

And she couldn't scream. She couldn't cry. She couldn't breathe. It was right there. Her rage needed an outlet. Her fear needed to come out or it would drown her.

Her sorrow... It was hers and they'd taken that from her, too. "Please."

Hutch turned her in his arms and there were tears in his eyes as he looked down at her. "What do you need?"

"I can't..." She could barely breathe. Her hands were shaking, and she wasn't sure what was happening. The world felt utterly out of control.

Hutch's jaw tightened. "I can. I can make this right and I will. I need you to understand that I will change the whole fucking world for you. I won't stop. Not even if you can't forgive me."

His hand came up and tangled in her hair, giving her a bite of pain that sliced through her, forcing her to focus.

He was offering her his dominance, offering to take control, to pull out everything that was making her cold and unfeeling.

She shouldn't let him. She should hold on to her anger, but in that moment, she wasn't alone. She was back in that car, her whole future ripped out from under her, surrounded by wreckage, but a hand was there to help pull her out. She didn't have to drag herself out. All she had to do was take this man's hand.

All she had to do was be brave.

"I can't tell you I'm going to stay with you." She couldn't make that decision. Or maybe she couldn't say it because she also couldn't imagine leaving him. The thought left a hole inside her.

"Then I'll have to convince you because I love you, Noelle. You might not be ready to hear that yet, but it's there. I love you and it won't stop because you can't love me back. I will always be here for you."

She wasn't ready to hear that yet, but she needed him tonight. She needed what only he could give her.

"I don't want you to be tender. I need…I need you to make me cry, make me scream."

"Because it won't come out any other way," Hutch said, his eyes taking her in. "I will help you. Always. I know exactly where you are, and I know how to bring you home."

His hand twisted in her hair again, biting through the fog that had enveloped her.

She didn't know where home was anymore. Maybe Hutch had been right in the beginning. Maybe the city was too much for her. Maybe she belonged back in Papillon where it was safe.

Except it wasn't. Nowhere was safe. Nothing was promised. No tomorrow was promised. No happiness. No joy was certain.

"I don't think I can trust you again," she said, wanting to push him.

"Hush. You think I don't know where you are? I do. And I spit every bit of bile I had when I came back. No one knows this but two weeks after I came home from saving Theo, I was ready to leave again. I didn't know where I was going. I only knew I didn't trust anyone anymore. I couldn't sit there and watch everyone go on with their lives. So I quit and Big Tag...he threw me in his car and brought me here and he pushed me until we beat the shit out of each other. I needed that release. I couldn't find it any other way, and then we sat down with Kai and we were bleeding and I couldn't see out of one eye and I told them everything that happened to me. Things I'd sworn I wouldn't tell anyone, and I cried. I'm not ashamed that I cried. Feeling emotions is what we're meant to do, and I'm so glad Tag didn't let me go. I'm grateful he didn't leave me in that dark place alone, and he knew how to get me where I needed to go. I wouldn't ever leave you alone."

She didn't want to think about what kind of a man Hutch was. Good. Loyal. True.

Had it all been a lie? If it had been, why would he be here now? What did he gain?

Hutch pulled his shirt over his head and tossed it to the side.

He picked her up, her cane clanging to the floor. "The good news is you selected the Rumpus Room. That's what we call this room. There are several privacy rooms we also use as bedrooms if we need to, and you picked the one with the spanking bench."

She'd walked into the first door she'd come to, but it was obvious Hutch thought it was destiny.

Where would she be if she hadn't met him? Things would have played out the way they had, and she would have been alone. She wouldn't have had someone to hold her the way Hutch was.

Was he the only real thing in this world she found herself in?

Hutch strode over to the spanking bench and set her on her feet in front of it. He gripped the neckline of the dress she wore and she gasped as he ripped it open, exposing her in an instant. She didn't complain about the loss of the clothing. She liked the sound of the fabric tearing, enjoyed the savage look in his eyes. She shrugged out of the remnants of her dress, letting them slip to the ground. Her body was starting to heat up, nipples already stiff and wanting.

This was what she needed. She didn't need to cry. She didn't need to shout out her pain. She needed his hands on her. She needed to forget everything for the next hour, and then she would decide what to do later.

Hutch moved into her space, his mouth a flat line as he gripped the nape of her neck with one hand. The other hand found the back of her bra and twisted it off with the ease of a man who'd been taking bras off women for years.

She let that thought go because he seemed to want her. It didn't matter what he'd done before. He seemed to need *her*.

God knew she needed him.

He tossed her bra away and his hand found her breast. "You're strong enough to handle what happened today and what will happen in the future."

She shook her head. "I don't want to talk."

He tweaked her nipple, a hard twist that made her knees go weak. "We don't have to talk about you and me, but we will talk about this. We will talk about the fact that you are not stupid."

Or she could say her safe word and make him go away. She could curl up into a ball and be the fragile thing she'd always worried she was deep inside.

He tightened his fingers, pushing her to the point of pain.

"I'm not stupid," she said on a breathless whisper.

He eased back. "Good. You are young and so fucking smart, and you made a mistake. Lay down on the bench. Your breasts go on either side, your ass will be in the air."

"Should I…" she began because she was still in her underwear.

"You know what, brat? If you're going to question me, then stand right there and don't move. You want extra punishment? I can do that. You're in my house now. I know exactly how to deal with you."

She was stripped down and should feel more vulnerable than ever, and yet something had calmed inside her. It was the fact that she knew she didn't have to think about anything but her body for the next few hours. She would get rest. Hutch would spank her and she would cry, and then she would sleep and figure it all out in the morning.

Yes, that was why her hands weren't shaking anymore. She was going to get sex and she would feel better.

Hutch was back, standing in front of her and holding something in his hands. He held up small clamps and her breath hitched. They were tweezer clamps meant for her nipples.

"You seem to require a big bite of pain tonight. Do you remember your safe word?" His voice had gone deeper than before, his eyes losing their softness. Hutch had found his top space, and she realized that perhaps he needed this as much as she did.

If she worked on the assumption that Hutch cared about her— maybe even loved her—then today had been hard on him, too.

"Yes." She didn't want to think about him as anything but the man giving her what she needed. It wasn't good or kind of her, but she wanted to be selfish for once.

"Then we should begin. Hands behind your back. Present your breasts to me."

She reached her hands around and threaded them together. The hold made her breasts thrust out, nipples puckering. Hutch palmed a breast and then took the nipple between his thumb and forefinger.

"Have you played around with clamps before?" Hutch asked, his whole focus on her.

No one in the world could ever make her feel like she was the center of the universe the way this man could. When he focused on her, she knew she was all he was thinking about.

Had he truly been thinking about her today? Had his only thought been to protect her?

"No. I've only ever played with a vibrator, and then only with myself."

He slid the clamp over her nipple and gently tightened the small screw. "Then it's good I picked a beginner clamp. I would love to see you in clamps with weights, ones that bite into your nipples and turn them a ruby red. But these will do for now."

The clamp bit gently into her and made her deeply aware of her breasts. She took a deep breath as he worked on the other breast. A silky heat flashed over her skin, making the world seem softer than it had been moments before.

She could survive this. She could make it through the night without breaking down. If she didn't break, then she might wake up harder and stronger than she'd been before.

She might be strong enough to walk away from him.

Because you were stupid, and you don't deserve him. Because you'll drag him down the way you do everything. You can only keep it up for so long.

She gasped as she felt tears pulse. Was she punishing herself? She hadn't had thoughts like that since after the accident. Or maybe it had been before. She'd always wondered if she was the reason her parents hadn't worked. It was a child's question, and she knew the answer, but that insecurity had found another place to go.

"Give in, Noelle." Hutch's voice had gone soft again. "Give in and let me hold you."

She couldn't do that. He'd lied to her.

Had he? He'd told her he needed to be in that building, needed to get on the computers and see if he could find out what was happening.

He'd left her alone.

He'd saved her research because if he'd been taken into custody, they could have lost it.

She was the reason she couldn't use it again. She'd done that. Not Hutch. She'd signed that contract when she'd known deep down it could hurt her. She'd signed it because she wanted so badly to start her career, wanted to jump over all those hoops instead of going through them.

"Fuck you, Hutch."

She couldn't. She couldn't do this with him. Except she was asking him to not leave her alone. It wasn't fair or right or even rational, but she wasn't ready to give in. This was the only way she could process what had happened today.

Her world had fallen apart and she kept trying to blame someone else, but it was her fucking fault.

If Hutch hadn't been there, things would have still gone down the way they had. She'd put herself on this path.

How did she tell everyone how far she'd fallen?

"Stop it." Hutch barked the words her way and then she was being led to the spanking bench. "Place yourself on that bench because it is obvious to me that nothing else is going to do. Be careful with the clamps. If they fall off, I'll know to make them tighter next time."

He held a hand out to help ease her down. Noelle felt the cool leather of the padded bench. It was built to support her chest but let her breasts dangle from either side, and she could feel the clamps dragging on her nipples, gravity playing its part to make the sensation sizzle. The middle bench cradled the length of her torso, ending at her pelvis and leaving her ass and pussy fully open to Hutch. Leaving her vulnerable.

Her hands found the cushioned arms of the bench, and her knees and legs were comfortable, too. It wasn't a hard position to be in, and she wondered if they should find something that would hurt more.

Then she wasn't worried about getting enough pain.

Hutch smacked her ass, and not a warm-up slap. He slapped her cheeks in a way that made her grit her teeth and bite back a moan.

"Is that what you want?" Hutch asked the question in a tortured growl. "Do you need me to punish you physically to go with all those mental gymnastics you're going through right now?"

How could he see through her? His questions made her feel far more vulnerable than being nearly naked and laid out for him.

She let her hands tighten around the bench she held onto as Hutch smacked her again. Somehow the spanking reminded her that she wasn't weak. She was strong. Her body would hold.

Was she still punishing herself for that, too? For the accident she'd had no control over?

Her body was strong. Even when it ached and needed support. It was strong enough to do what she needed it to do, and she'd learned that sometimes what she needed wasn't what others did.

Other people made mistakes. Did that mean they didn't deserve forgiveness?

Didn't she deserve it?

He slapped her ass until she could feel tears dripping from her eyes and the ice starting to really crack. The physical sensations of pain and arousal was starting to break through her reserve.

"You can be angry with me. You can hate me, Noelle, but this was not your fault."

"I can't..." She started to speak but it was hard to breathe between the emotion welling inside her and her body pulsing with feeling. She was starting to lose control.

"You can. You can put it all on me. I lied to you. She lied to you. She promised you the world and never meant a word of it," Hutch said gravely. "I promised I would take care of you and I didn't."

But he had. He was trying so hard even now.

He was giving himself up to save her from the pain of knowing she'd made this mistake.

Her body ached, but nothing like her soul did. "I can't…"

"You can," he insisted. "You can do anything, Noelle. Anything. This will not break you. I won't break you."

But he did. He broke her in the best way. Noelle let that wall finally come down, the one that kept her safe from all this emotion, the one that kept her away from him. Her wall came down because he was safety and love and risk, and that was okay. He was the one she could risk all the heartache on, the one she could share her pain with, the one who would never leave her alone.

He hadn't truly left her alone today. When he'd let her be arrested, he'd still been choosing her. The truth hit her squarely. He'd chosen her future over momentary discomfort. He'd believed she was strong enough to handle herself, and he'd made the call he'd been trained to make.

"I can't hate you." She finally got the words she needed to say out. "I can never hate you. I love you."

The wall came totally down and she sobbed. The events of the day—of the last several years—poured out of her. She'd made a terrible mistake, but she wasn't alone. She had a family who would forgive her, who wouldn't even think twice. They would open their arms and welcome her.

Hutch picked her up and carried her to the bed, and when she looked into his gorgeous eyes, they were shining with tears because he wouldn't hold back from her. He was strong enough to break, too. He'd put himself back together again and again.

"I love you, too," he said. "God, I love you so much."

She held on to him as the storm flowed through her. She'd tried to hold it back, but now she realized how much she needed this. How much had she held back because she'd had to prove to everyone that she was strong? She might not have cried like this since that first time her stepmom had pushed her until she'd believed she might walk again.

She could rebuild her wall and hide behind all the reasons she couldn't trust this feeling—they hadn't known each other long enough, their relationship was forged under pressure—or she could let her heart take over and accept that this man was everything she'd longed for.

She cried, letting the pain go. She'd been stupid, but she'd had the best of intentions. He should have told her what he was going to do, but he'd had the best of intentions.

She could let go of the pain, but she didn't have to let go of him.

"Baby, I have to get these off you." He smoothed back her hair and kissed her forehead.

She'd almost forgotten about the clamps. She sniffled and wiped at her eyes. She probably looked terrible, but Hutch was staring at her like she was the most beautiful thing in the world.

Any tragedy was survivable if the right person was holding her hand.

"They don't hurt."

He winced. "Probably because you're numbed out, and you're about to not be."

He eased the first clamp off and the blood flooded back into her nipple, making her bite back a scream. Hutch was immediately on top of her, his lips and tongue on the abused flesh, soothing it.

The pain had been momentary, but arousal started to flood through her. Between the ache in her ass and the sensation of having her nipples tortured and then loved, all she could think about was having his hands on her.

She could make it through the night if his hands stroked her.

She could make it through life if his hand held hers.

He dealt with the other nipple and then started to kiss his way down her body.

He'd given her a safe place to cry, and now he seemed determined to lavish her body with the affection she needed to connect to him. He ripped the thin material of her underwear and exposed her pussy. She didn't need a command to spread her thighs wide and offer herself up to him.

He took her up on the invitation, covering her pussy with his mouth and immediately spearing her with his tongue. He licked and sucked and fucked her pussy with ruthless precision, every touch pushing her toward the edge.

Her whole body tightened as the orgasm swept over her, making her shake with pleasure and something more—emotion poured through her. Love and affection and relief.

She wasn't sure what would happen next, but she would face it with him.

"Hutch, please," she whispered as he continued to lave her pussy. "I need you inside me."

He kissed her again and then moved up her body, covering her.

She placed her hands on his shoulders and knew this was forever.

* * * *

Hutch stared down at her for a moment, knowing what he wanted but still unsure. She'd had such a rough night and they hadn't talked yet. Still, what had begun as a desperate play to break her out of the spiral she'd been in had turned into the best night of his life. "I know I said I wouldn't take anything for myself, but you said it. You said you love me, and I won't let you take it back."

Her eyes were still red from crying, but there was the sweetest smile on her face. "I love you. I was wrong to deny it and I'm sorry I took it…"

He didn't need an apology. He knew damn well sometimes the pain was so great a person lashed out at the one they shouldn't. It was human nature, and she hadn't exactly tortured him for long. She'd been dealt a horrible blow, and he'd made it worse for her. "I'm here when you need me. For anything."

"Then kiss me and tire me out so I can sleep, and we'll face everything in the morning. Together."

There was a light in her eyes he'd worried had died. He was going to make this right for her. But first he was going to give her what she needed. What he needed.

He kissed her, well aware that her arousal was still on his lips and coating his tongue. He gave it all back to her because she should know that she was the sweetest thing he'd ever tasted. She should know that he would crave her for the rest of his life.

He kissed her until his cock couldn't last a second longer. Then he worked his jeans and boxers off. He didn't have a problem finding a condom. Not at Sanctum.

Someday in the future he wouldn't wear one at all. Someday he and the glorious woman underneath him would have nothing between them and they would make babies. They would start a family—the kind he hadn't had. Their babies would be smart and beautiful.

Just like their mom.

Everything he'd been through, it had been worth it to be here with her. "I love you."

He kissed her again as he brought them together. He sank his cock deep, surrounded by her heat. She wrapped her legs around him, winding her arms around his neck and enveloping his whole body.

This was what he needed every day for the rest of his life. He needed to surround himself with her.

"You feel so good," he whispered against her lips as he thrust in and dragged out.

Her nails bit into his back as she gasped and said his name.

Then he let himself go, let himself pound inside her, giving her everything he had until the wave crashed through him. He was suffused with pleasure and then warmth and peace as he sank down beside her, staying close for a moment.

He let his head find her breast and he listened to her heartbeat. "I was so worried."

Her hand smoothed his hair back. "I'm still worried. We have a lot to face tomorrow."

They did. "Cara will let us know if they have enough to move on Jessica in the morning. Have I told you how gorgeous and smart my girlfriend is? How I wake up every day and I'm happy to be with her?"

She groaned, but her hand kept stroking his hair. "You're impossible to stay mad at. But seriously, Hutch. I'm sorry. I was mad at myself. I've worked hard and it's all gone to hell, and I took it out on you."

"I should have told you what I was doing. You would have

known why I didn't join you." He whispered the words against her breast. "You were perfect. You gave them nothing, and I wouldn't have blamed you if you'd turned me in."

"I didn't even truly consider it," she admitted. "Even when I was confused and angry, I couldn't give you up. I'm surprised Kyle punched you, though. He was the one who yelled at me that you would come for us. He told me not to talk because our friend would get us out."

"He did?" He'd been surprised that Kyle had stayed on the job. And yet, if watching McKay-Taggart was Kyle's secret job, he would do anything to stay on. "Baby, I need you to be careful around Kyle."

He wasn't holding anything back. Not ever again.

"Why? Because he was mouthy with the cops? He was, you know. Totally mouthy. I kind of thought he was doing it so the attention was on him and not me," she said quietly. "I think he was trying to look out for me."

It would have been better for Kyle to lay low, but he hadn't. Still. "I'm supposed to watch Kyle and let our boss know if I think he's working for someone. For the CIA, or maybe someone worse."

She turned to her side, and he wished he hadn't brought it up. He wasn't ready to leave the bubble they'd found. But she needed to know.

"You think he's a spy?"

"I think he's suspicious, and I want you to be careful. You need to understand that even if I leave you alone with Kyle, someone else is watching. If anything happens, you'll still be protected." He kissed her forehead and with reluctance rolled out of bed to deal with the condom. Luckily the Rumpus Room came complete with a bathroom and a decadent shower where he could clean her up before he got her dirty all over again. "The good news is you won't be going back to Genedyne any time soon. You can come up to work with me."

He would watch over her.

He moved into the bathroom, getting rid of the condom and washing his hands.

Noelle was on her side when he returned, her head resting in her hand and a thoughtful look on her face. "I have to call my dad in the morning."

She was so much calmer. She'd needed to know he would never let her go, that no mistake either of them made had to mean the end if they clung to each other.

"It's going to be all right."

Her nose wrinkled. "You've never had an overprotective Cajun sheriff worried about you."

"I'll talk to him." He moved back into the room. "Unless you want to go home. I can take some time off."

It might be for the best.

"Let's see what Cara has to say in the morning." She reached her hand out toward him. "It might be nice to go home for a bit if you come with me. I'd like you to meet my parents."

And have an overly protective Cajun sheriff size him up? For her, he would do anything. "I'm going to have to have a long talk with your dad. I really did serve some time."

"He'll give you a medal for what you served time for." She squeezed his hand. "My dad will love you because you take such good care of me. But I do have some decisions to make. The truth is even if Cara arrests Jessica tomorrow, Genedyne still owns my research, and it's going to be hard to get it back."

He had some thoughts about that, but he didn't want to get her hopes up. "I'm going to let Mitch work on that. We have some work to do, too. I want to know who that woman was and why she had your keycard."

Noelle let go of his hand and sighed as she lay back. "It was the mail room chick. I didn't even think about her until now. The police told me someone used it, and I didn't know there had been anyone but you."

He sat down beside her, trying to focus on her face, but it was hard because there were her pretty nipples and they were a deep pink from the clamp and...damn it. Mail room chick. "Had you met her before?"

She shook her head. "No. We don't get snail mail. We do everything on computers. But she had a couple of journals she said the company had ordered for our lab. She dropped them. That was when she took my keycard."

"Did you get a good look at her?" They could get a sketch artist in and he could then use computer modeling to refine it. She thought she could avoid facial recognition software, but there were ways to work around her tech.

Noelle bit her bottom lip. "I don't know. I can probably give you a basic description. So the mail room woman was working for the gas company. It's crazy how many people don't want my work out in the world."

He'd been thinking about it all night and whether or not Kyle had anything to do with the incident. Kyle hadn't helped the woman who'd downloaded Noelle's research. If he had, he would have told her they were in the building and that Hutch was on the move. She would have either avoided the server room until he was out or killed him there.

"We're going to figure this out," he promised her. "And honestly, now that you don't have to go back to that building, Jessica probably isn't a physical threat. She'll have you where she wants you, on the outside. She might even think she's gotten away with it. She doesn't have to kill you. She can try to let the court system silence you."

Not that he would let up on her protection. Another reason to go to Louisiana with her. He bet he and Armie LaVigne could bond over how to protect Noelle.

Noelle sat up suddenly, her eyes going wide. "Madison texted Cara my name."

Oh, she'd put something together. He watched her as it was obvious her brain was working overtime. "Yes. Cara thinks she was interrupted. Likely it was when they took her and created the accident in her lab."

"She was in the building when she sent it out."

"Yes, according to the location service on her phone."

"Could she have been in the locker room?" Noelle asked.

There was no way of knowing exactly where she was. "I suppose so."

"Someone was going through lockers the day I got attacked. Madison's locker. My locker. What if they were looking for something Madison left me? The woman hated me, but I might be the only person she would trust to go up against Jessica Layne. She always teased me for being all upright and honorable. And our lockers were close. What if she was running and she knew she only had a moment to hide something?"

"But they've searched the lockers. You've used yours. You would have found something."

She shook her head. "But I didn't look up. I might not even be tall enough to feel for it. Madison kept a magnetic box in her locker. Our lockers were done by a designer, and they have an almost cathedral shape to them. Up at the top, Madison found a metal fastener she could put the magnet on. It's how she kept her expensive jewelry safe, but I never heard of anyone else using it like that."

"How big was it? Big enough for a thumb drive?" He wasn't interested in jewelry, but he would be in any type of data Madison might have pulled down when she'd figured out she was in danger. "How would she have gotten in your locker?"

"She was smart. She could have figured it out. Hell, she might have watched me and memorized the combo so she could play a prank or something. She did that a lot. Hutch, I think that's where it is. If she left me something, it's in that locker."

Hutch felt his jaw tighten because that meant what had happened that day wasn't a coincidence, and it hadn't been someone trying to hurt Noelle. They'd been looking for something. "They know she left you information."

"But they didn't find it," she insisted. "They looked in the locker, but I bet they didn't find it. Madison painted the magnetic box almost the same color as the locker. If you don't feel for it, you won't know it's there."

She was getting excited, but fear was what he felt.

Whatever was on that drive, Jessica Layne had been willing to kill for.

"I think I'm going to call Tag." He was going to move her. "There's clothes for you in that bag I brought in. Get dressed. I think we might make that trip to Louisiana tonight."

He would have someone bring him a car and take off. If Layne even had a whiff that there was an investigation, she would want all the loose ends tied up.

Noelle was a loose end.

"Why? Hutch, we need to get to that locker," Noelle said.

He grabbed her cane and handed it to her. "Someone will. I promise. But it won't be you."

He dragged his boxers and jeans on and reached for his cell just as it lit up and started to hum. Michael. He swiped to accept it because Michael had the night shift watching Kyle. Had he slipped out again? "What's going on?"

"We have company. I need…"

The line went dead.

And then the lights went out and Hutch realized the night had taken a deadly turn.

Chapter Eighteen

It was so dark. Without windows to let in any light, the room that moments before had felt warm and safe now sent a chill through Noelle.

"What's happening? Did we have a power failure?" She couldn't see Hutch at all. At least she'd managed to get her cane in her hand.

A light came on, splitting the utter darkness. Hutch held his cell in his hand and illuminated part of the room for her. "Cell service is out, and Michael said we had company. I need you to get dressed as quickly as possible, baby. I'm going to start my laptop and pull up our security feed."

"I thought we were safe here." She opened the bag MaeBe had dropped off for her and thanked the universe for underwear since hers had been ripped off. She quickly got into the jeans and T-shirt while Hutch hauled his laptop out with the hand that wasn't holding the flashlight.

"Even if someone cut our power, the security system has a backup," Hutch explained. "And if they think they can break in, they should think again. The windows are bulletproof, and the locks would take a long time to cut through. I can access the security cameras and listen in through the comm. It looks like the backup is already online."

"Who's Michael?" She picked up Hutch's shirt and handed it to him.

The laptop had turned on and glowed, making his face a bit ghost-like against the darkness of the rest of the room. "He's the man who's watching the man who's supposed to watch us."

Ah, the one they had trailing Kyle because they were worried he was a spy. She still hadn't completely processed that bit of information, but she couldn't see it. Still, she was grateful they had someone on the outside. "So he called and said we have trouble and then the power went out. We're in the middle of downtown Dallas. Who does he think is going to show up?"

Hutch handed her the cell that was working as a flashlight. "Where you live, Dallas is pretty vibrant. There are always people around. This is a warehouse district. No one lives here. Well, Kai and Kori live next door, but they're in California right now, so we're alone at this time of night. But if there's trouble, Michael will already have called someone in. He'll call Tag and Alex first, but Theo is closest. Still, even the cops are probably ten minutes out at this time of night. More if they're working an accident or something."

"How can he call if cell service is down?" She sat on the bed beside him, watching as he worked. She wasn't worried. Power went out a lot, and how would anyone know where they were?

"We don't know how far the outage goes. Maybe it's all on our end. Michael will figure it out." Hutch was always an optimist. And then his eyes went wide. "Oh, shit."

She looked at the screen where Hutch was staring and saw an eerie site.

Jessica Layne was standing out in the parking lot in front of Sanctum, five big men around her all in black tactical gear. They were all holding guns, and they hadn't come alone. They'd brought someone familiar with them.

"Is that MaeBe?" The question came out on a gasp because it was obvious MaeBe hadn't wanted to be with them. She was on her knees, a gun to the back of her head and blood on her face. It looked like she'd been worked over, one of her eyes almost swollen closed. She had a gag in her mouth and her hands were in zip ties that were so tight, Noelle could see blood on her wrists.

"Yes. They probably tagged her when she went by your apartment. Then they followed her, caught her when she tried to go home, and waited until the middle of the night when no one would be here." Hutch stood. "MaeBe isn't a field operative. She's never faced anything like this."

There was a brief knock and then the door came open. Kyle stood there, wearing sweats and a T-shirt. He also had a gun in his hand. "I want you both in the bathroom. I don't know what's going on, but until I do, you two are going to lockdown. You barricade this door and then lock yourself in the bathroom. Hutch, you carrying?"

Hutch frowned. "No, I'm not. I'm in Sanctum. I'm supposed to be safe."

Kyle didn't know what was happening outside. Noelle's heart was pounding as she heard a trill. Was that a cell? "I thought we didn't have service."

Hutch stood as Kyle pulled his cell out of his pocket. "Are you on Wi-Fi?"

Kyle nodded. "Yeah. I always move to Wi-Fi when I come in here. Service isn't great inside the club. I think Tag likes it that way. Shit. We don't have cell service because Jessica Layne's blocking it. Is she outside?"

Hutch nodded. "Yes. I'm going to assume she's taken over our Wi-Fi. She's got some great hackers on her staff, and after tonight we can assume she's got some we don't even know about. We can't call out, but she can call Kyle because she has his number and his phone is on Wi-Fi. Don't answer it. She can't be sure we're in here."

Noelle cried out when she saw Jessica nod to one of the men in all black who moved behind MaeBe.

He hauled her up by her hair and landed a wicked punch to MaeBe's midsection, tossing her to the concrete when he was done.

How much pain had MaeBe already taken? She wasn't a hardened operative. She was a goth girl who was good with computers and liked playing board games with her friends.

"I'm serious," Kyle said. "Lock yourself in the bathroom."

He hadn't seen what was happening outside. He had no idea they had MaeBe and she was in immediate danger.

The cell trilled again. Hutch had a hand on her arm. He would do anything to save her. Even give up another young woman. He was desperate and he would buy time, but Noelle couldn't buy it with MaeBe's life.

Kyle cared about MaeBe. How would he feel if she died in that parking lot and he could have answered that phone?

They needed to buy some time. Despite the fact that Jessica Layne had dampened cell phone reception, surely they'd triggered an alarm or the Michael person would find the edge of the cell bubble and make a call.

"They have MaeBe," she said, turning the laptop around. "I think they know we're here."

Kyle moved in, watching the laptop with no expression in his eyes, and then he swiped his finger across his phone's screen. "Hello?"

Hutch cursed under his breath and grabbed his boots, shoving them on his feet.

"Hello, Kyle. If that is your real name," a feminine voice said. "I should have known you were too good to be true. I thought I only had to worry about you talking to Noelle about my plans. But after tonight, I wonder if you don't have another agenda entirely. I think you'll find I have your bitch. I will trade her for another bitch, but if I don't see you down here soon with Noelle LaVigne, I'm going to kill this one."

"I don't have Noelle," Kyle replied, his tone bland. "But I have information that can help you."

"Then come out here," Jessica replied. "Now, or the girl dies."

The line went dead.

"You can't go out there. She'll figure out you're lying." Hutch was on his feet again. "I'm going for the security office. I'm going to reset everything and call the cops. You've got to know she's going to move as quickly as she can. She has to. We need to slow her down."

"And then MaeBe dies and Jessica tosses her body and she still gets away," Kyle said between clenched teeth. "I'll tell her I know where Noelle is. I'll negotiate to take her there. You call in anyone you can get. Take the gun. They won't let me keep it anyway. If they take me and MaeBe…"

Hutch stood in front of him, his shoulders slumping. "Then we'll find you."

"Tell Jessica you know what Madison left for me. That's what she's looking for. It's in my locker. I don't know exactly what it is, but I think it's data of some kind. Take them to the Genedyne building and it's in my locker in a magnetic security case at the top." Noelle didn't want to leave him with nothing. Her heart was pounding at the thought of Kyle going out there with no protection at all.

"Noelle, are you sure?" Hutch asked.

She nodded. "I'm not giving up MaeBe's life to make mine easier. We can get Jessica some other way." She looked to Kyle. "I figured out where it is a couple of minutes ago. Or where I'm pretty sure it is. I could go with you. I trust Hutch to save me."

"Fuck, no," Hutch began.

Kyle put a hand on her shoulder. "I promise we'll get her. Thank you, Noelle. But I'm going alone." He moved to the door. "Hutch, if anything happens to me, tell my mother I love her. And tell them all I'm sorry."

"Don't do this," Hutch said. "I can figure this out."

Kyle shook his head. "There are some things not even the smartest people can stop. I'm afraid this is one of them. If I die, save MaeBe. Please. Tell her... Fuck, don't tell her anything."

Kyle disappeared from view.

"I'm going to take the light. Turn on yours," Hutch ordered. "The control room is on the first floor. I'm going to get the lights back on. There's a monitor down there, so I should be able to see what's happening. You keep this one and don't come out of hiding until you see it's safe. I love you, Noelle."

And then he was gone, taking the light with him. He was gone in the shadows and she was alone.

The light from the laptop helped her find her cell and get her flashlight app on. She stared at the monitor for a few tense moments. Her hands were shaking as she watched the door open, Kyle appearing with his hands up.

Before he could even start to talk, one of Jessica's men rushed him.

One shot and Kyle went down. He hit his knees and then slumped to the pavement as the man who'd shot him moved around his body and caught the door before it closed.

Jessica walked by Kyle, making sure her designer shoes didn't touch the blood that was starting to pool. Even for a murder the woman wore five-inch heels and expensive clothing.

Noelle couldn't hear MaeBe's cries, but she could see the way the woman started to crawl toward Kyle, her bound hands coming out to reach for him.

For Kyle. Kyle had been shot in the chest and he was down. Was he dead? Oh god, he looked like he was dead. Hutch was out there and Jessica was in the building. She'd gotten in the building.

The laptop screen shook because her hands were trembling. Why? The question pierced through Noelle. Why had she shot Kyle? He'd told her he had what she wanted. Why had she shot Kyle without even giving him a chance to explain?

Because the information wasn't what Jessica wanted. She wanted Noelle.

Tears blurred the shadowy world around her as she watched Jessica walk past the cameras. She snapped her fingers and one of her guards fisted his hand in MaeBe's hair and started to drag her away from Kyle, her feet kicking as she fought.

Jessica was in the building and Hutch was out there. Hutch didn't know she'd breached the building because he was likely still trying to get to the ground floor. He might walk right into her trap, and Jessica wouldn't hesitate to kill him, too.

She bit back a sob at the thought of Hutch's body on the ground.

Then she saw it, saw Kyle's chest move.

He was alive. She might be able to save him.

"Noelle?"

Noelle stopped at the sound. Jessica was using the megaphone app she loved to use whenever she wanted to get someone's attention. It was an app she claimed she'd developed herself, and it turned a cell phone into a microphone that could blast her voice through the tiny speaker she carried in that designer bag of hers.

"Noelle, I've got your friend and I'm going to kill her. I already took care of that wannabe spy of yours. So you can show yourself or I'll have my guys blow this whore's purple head off. No one's coming, by the way. I've taken over all the systems. There's no alarm going out."

She hated Jessica, hated her and everything she stood for.

And Noelle was going to give her what she wanted because she had no other option.

She clutched her cane and forced herself to move because she couldn't let her friends die.

* * * *

Hutch followed Kyle down the stairs, lighting the path for them both. "I think this is a mistake. You need to know that Michael was watching the club tonight. He knows we're in trouble."

Kyle didn't stop moving. "Michael was outside? I didn't know we had... Shit. Michael's here to watch me. I'm not spying on my uncle. I can't talk about what I did for the Agency, but it's over. Mostly."

"It's about to all be over if you aren't careful." Hutch needed time. "Michael isn't going to leave us here. I doubt Jessica has any idea we had someone watching the club. MaeBe didn't know, so they couldn't have gotten it from her."

Couldn't have beaten it out of her. Couldn't have terrorized her until she couldn't take it anymore.

There was a humming sound, and a set of lights came on, the secondary lights that were powered by a small generator in case of outage. Sanctum could be dangerous in the dark, and Dallas often experienced storms that could cut power. The secondary lights were low but enough to allow him to pocket his cell.

"I can't leave her out there alone," Kyle said. "I'll buy us some time. If Jessica thinks the police are on their way, she'll kill MaeBe and run. I'm certain she's got a way out of the country, and she's probably got plenty of money in offshore accounts. She won't hesitate to dump MaeBe. I have to stop that."

He wasn't sure Kyle could stop anything. "Let me try to get in touch with Michael."

"There's no time."

"She won't kill MaeBe until she's absolutely sure she's got that information. I don't know what Madison left her, but I would bet it's at least her research. We know Jessica sold that research, and there would be a whole lot of angry pharma people if it still got out. I think Jessica believes Noelle knows more than she does."

"I'm not going to give up Noelle. I'm not giving up anyone." Kyle jogged down the rest of the stairs and started for the door. "Hurry and get where you need to be. I don't want to risk them seeing you or they'll try to get inside. I'm going to try to get her to take me to Genedyne. Contact Tag and get there as soon as possible."

Hutch didn't want to let Kyle go out there alone, but he knew what he would do if Noelle was the one being held. He would move heaven and earth to get to her. "I'll get everything back online and we'll come after you. I won't leave you alone."

Kyle glanced back, a sad smile on his face. "I kind of wish we could have had that beer now."

"We will. And I'll help you. I'll help you get through all of it. No matter what it is," Hutch promised.

"I almost believe you," Kyle said quietly. "Go. Save your girl. I'll try to save…well, the one who could have been mine if I hadn't fucked everything up. Bye, Hutch."

Hutch ran the rest of the way to the security office, his boots thudding along the floor. He had to get Sanctum functioning again. If he did it quickly, they might have a chance to save Kyle and MaeBe.

The backup security was working, as the keypad that locked the security room was lit. Hutch punched in his code and slammed into the office.

Adrenaline pumped hard through his body as he set the gun on the security desk and brought up the cameras. They were all outdoor cameras, pointed to the front entrance, the back courtyard where the basketball court was, the parking lot, and the rooftop terrace. Tag would never allow his member's privacy to be compromised, so there were no cameras inside the club. But he could make sure they didn't have anyone coming up from behind. He didn't think Jessica would have had time to map out more than the front entrance, though he supposed she could have hurt MaeBe enough to get her to talk.

MaeBe. Guilt sat in his gut as he raced through the code to bring the power back online. He'd asked MaeBe to get Noelle some clothes. He'd sent her alone because he hadn't thought anything of it. He'd only been thinking about Noelle.

If MaeBe died, it was on him.

The power should have been on. Everything he was seeing said the system hadn't been breached.

Fuck. She'd physically cut it. Or had the power company cut it. Well, she loved to make deals with other corporations. She would be using a cell jammer, and he would have to physically take that out, too. She hadn't been able to hack his system. She'd tried but his walls had held.

She couldn't get into the building unless...

Fuck. She wanted Kyle to come out because him coming out was her only way in. MaeBe couldn't get them inside. She wasn't on the board of Sanctum or an employee. Hutch had a keycard because he provided the club's IT needs. Kyle didn't work here, so they would have to get around him.

The breath knocked out of him as he looked to the screen and he saw Kyle take a bullet to the chest and fall forward.

The man who'd shot him moved quickly to catch the door before it closed. They hadn't even given Kyle a chance to speak, much less offer them a bargain.

Because he wasn't offering Jessica what she wanted.

Noelle.

She was coming for Noelle and Kyle was down.

Kyle might be dead.

He prayed Noelle would stay in the bathroom, that she'd done exactly as he'd asked and she'd left the laptop in the room so she couldn't see what had happened to Kyle, couldn't see how MaeBe tried to get to him, didn't know they were dragging her away like she was meaningless.

Rage lit inside him because they were treating his people like they meant nothing. Like they were fucking prey.

He was going to show them what it felt like to be prey.

He knew this club like the back of his hand. He opened the desk drawer where he happened to know the dungeon monitor kept a set of knives. He rolled the kit out. The gun might be too loud, and it would give away his position. There were five men and Layne, who was also carrying a small pistol.

He wouldn't hesitate. She'd walked into his house and threatened his people. She was a snake, and he was going to take her out.

He grabbed two small, sharp-as-fuck knives and the gun he would use if he needed it. He shoved one of the knives into the holster he had sewn into all of his boots. There was a shoulder holster for the gun wrapped around the chair. It was slightly too big, but it would work.

"Noelle, I've got your friend and I'm going to kill her. I already took care of that wannabe spy of yours. So you can show yourself or I'll have my guys blow this whore's purple head off. No one's coming, by the way. I've taken over all the systems. There's no alarm going out."

Jessica Layne seemed to have her own PA system. A narcissist to the bitter end, she was.

Would Noelle have heard that? The rooms upstairs were pretty well insulated. Not enough that he couldn't hear GN'R playing every time Charlotte and Big Tag decided to have a private session.

"I mean it, Noelle," Jessica was saying. "I already took out pretty Kyle. I'm tired of this one crying. If you come out now and give me what Madison sent you, we can talk. Madison wouldn't play the game. She wasn't smart. You can be smarter. You know there's a lot of money to be made."

Hutch glanced at the screens and saw someone jumping the ten-foot fence that closed in the basketball court. Michael moved with the ease of a man who'd worked for one of the world's premiere security teams for almost a decade. He hit the court in a crouch and then started moving for the door. Michael had been given a keycard earlier in the evening and used it to slide inside.

So he wouldn't be alone. Michael would be coming in, and he knew what to do. And if Michael was making his way in, that meant he'd put out a call.

Hutch moved to the door. He couldn't see where anyone was inside the building, but he knew the club's blind spots. Knife in hand, he started to make his way down the hall and toward the lobby. He peeked around. The lights were sporadic, placed only as backups so a person inside could make their way. They sent long shadows. He flattened against the wall and risked a look into the lobby.

One man stood at the base of the stairs, guarding it for the rest who'd gone into the dungeon. He pulled a radio from his utility belt. "We're clear here. No sign of the girl."

There was the sound of static, and then a deep voice came over the radio. "Keep a look out. We don't know if the other male is here. We're giving this thing five minutes and then we'll torch the place. According to our friend no one's here, but she lied about Kyle, so I suspect this is where they stashed LaVigne."

Hutch moved quickly and quietly before the man could turn. He hadn't been in the field in a long time, but his body remembered this dance. He eased behind his prey, securing the man with his free hand, and before he could even start to struggle, Hutch found the man's jugular and sank his knife in. It took real force to slit a throat, but adrenaline gave Hutch the strength he needed. He lowered the man to the floor.

His hands were bloody. He'd hoped to never see his hands covered in a man's blood again, but this was necessary. The stairs were steep, and he couldn't see the landing from this vantage. He was contemplating taking the back stairs that led from the men's locker room to the west side of the dungeon when something moved out of the corner of his eye.

He turned and Kyle was shuffling his body to the door. He was covered in blood and held a hand to his chest, but the tough motherfucker was on his feet.

"Noelle, she's running out of time," Layne said over her loudspeaker.

Hutch opened the door as quietly as he could and helped Kyle in.

"MaeBe's still alive?" Kyle whispered the question.

"Yes," he whispered back. "And Michael's on his way. I'm stashing you here. Try not to die."

He helped him to the security desk. It was the only cover he could easily get Kyle to.

"I'm here." A familiar voice floated down from above.

Noelle. Damn it.

"You should spank her more," Kyle said. "Way more."

Oh, he would. He would slap that girl's ass silly if they got out of this. "Stay alive, brother. You hear me?"

347

Kyle nodded and sagged down to the floor. "You, too."

"She's coming down from the third floor." The dead man's radio was talking again. "Everyone come back to the rally point. We'll move out as soon as the queen is ready."

Oh, Jessica Layne was not a freaking queen. She was a user, a parasite. She'd spent her whole adult life stepping on the people around her, dragging them down because it was the only way she could succeed. She hurt people because it was easier to take from them than to do for herself.

He wasn't going to let Noelle be her latest victim.

He pulled the second knife out of his boot and handed it to Kyle. He couldn't leave the man without a way to defend himself.

"Please let MaeBe go. I'll come with you," Noelle offered.

He was going to spank the hell out of her. Hutch couldn't take the safe route. He was going to have to go right up the stairs and try to sneak around the edge of the dungeon. Michael would almost surely be coming from the opposite side. If they could trap Layne in the middle, they could take her down.

"What the hell kind of name is MaeBe?" Layne wasn't using the app now. Her voice was softer, but he could easily hear her. "And this seems like an odd place to hide, but then you have hidden depths, Noelle. I honestly bought your 'I'm a sweet country girl' act. Who could have guessed that you would play such hardball? Too bad you're playing against the best."

Hutch clung to the shadows now as he moved up the stairs.

"I'm not playing at all," Noelle replied.

"I disagree. You downloaded your research last night," Jessica accused. "Did you make a deal with Sidirov and the others? Because they won't pay more than ten million now. I could have gotten twenty out of them if you hadn't fucked everything up."

"I didn't do anything. You've got another enemy." Noelle's voice sounded closer now.

"When you're as good as I am, you make a few," Jessica admitted. "But don't even try to lie to me. Austin had an alarm on the system, and he's the one who caught you."

"Is he the one who nearly killed me in the locker room?" Noelle asked.

Jessica huffed. "Honey, if he'd wanted to kill you, he would have. We were being thorough. We hadn't thought to check the lockers. You interrupted him. Then Pete almost caught him. I'm probably going to kill that little fucker, too."

"You can't think you're going to get away with this. There's a federal investigation." Noelle's voice trembled.

Hutch made it to the top step. He was safe in the shadows. There was less light in the dungeon than there had been downstairs. He moved toward the lounge where one day he would sit with Noelle on his lap, talking to his friends and relaxing.

Because there was no way this was the end.

Noelle was moving down the stairs from the third floor, carefully using her cane and holding the railing. Two guards were at the bottom, and a third stood behind Layne. That left one unaccounted for, but he had to take the chance.

MaeBe was on the floor, close to the guard near Layne. She was so still he worried she was already dead.

"Isn't there always?" Jessica mused. "I'm a powerful woman. Someone always wants to take me down, but they can't. They try and try, but I'm better than they are. I'm smarter. I understand the world."

"You lie and cheat and steal. You make nothing." Noelle sounded stronger now.

"I make the world," Layne snarled back. "You think your ideas mean something? Without me you're nothing. You're all sad, pathetic creatures who have no idea how the world works. You see, Noelle, in this life you're either a queen or a peasant. There's no in between. The feds can try, but I assure you I'll come out stronger than ever, and then I'll make those feds pay. The key is to not give up. If someone hurts you, never let up. I'll sue them all, and when they run out of money, I'll keep talking. I control the narrative. The press sees what I want them to see, and then one day the little investigator will take some pills because they won't be able to handle what I throw at them. So you're going to give me what I want and pray I don't decide to go after your family."

He moved around one of the pillars. He was still fifty feet away, and Noelle had no cover. Then he saw something moving across the dungeon. A shadow, shifting past the equipment.

Michael was here.

"I could find a way to sue that father of yours," Layne continued. "Law enforcement is easy. One little scandal and they're done. Or that clinic your stepmom runs. I can bankrupt them in a heartbeat. You know what? That's a much better threat. Bentley, you can kill the girl. We'll leave her here."

Noelle cried out and the guard next to MaeBe turned, but MaeBe twisted her body, kicking her foot up and catching the fucker in his dick. A shot rang out and Michael moved in, firing once and catching the man who'd been about to kill MaeBe.

The two guards near Noelle started to fire Michael's way. Noelle proved she wasn't some shrinking violet. She brought her cane up and knocked the guard to her right in the head.

Hutch stepped out and fired, hitting the guard to Noelle's right, but not before he got a shot off. Hutch felt fire light through his left side, but he couldn't give in to that pain. He pushed forward, firing the second guard's way. "Take cover, Noelle."

Noelle moved straight for MaeBe, huddling over the other woman.

They were going to have a long talk about the meaning of the word *cover*.

Layne started running for the stairs, panicking and proving she let other people do her dirty work.

Hutch took out the other guard. Four down, and Layne could run but she couldn't hide because he heard the sweet sound of sirens.

Where was number five?

Then he felt his left side explode with pain again and realized that number five had been coming up behind him. He'd been somewhere in the lounge.

Hutch stumbled but made it to Noelle in time to put his body over hers.

A big figure in all black pointed a gun his way. "Guess if I'm going to jail, I should do some crime."

Hutch heard Noelle crying but he tensed, praying Michael would at least be able to save the women.

A knife thudded into the man's eye. Even through his pain, Hutch recognized that had been a hell of a throw. The sight was both beautiful and utterly horrific. It caused the man to drop his gun, and then his torso was peppered with shots.

Hutch managed to turn, and Kyle was standing at the top of the stairs. He started to limp over, and Hutch saw his chest was wrapped in…was that duct tape?

"Where did Layne go?" Michael was the only one who wasn't dying. He looked all whole and shit. Hadn't even gotten blood on his clothes.

Noelle was moving under him.

"Her well-dressed corpse is at the bottom of the stairs," Kyle managed through obvious pain. "She shouldn't have run in those heels. Broke her neck. MaeBe?"

Hutch groaned as Noelle got out from under him and he hit the floor.

"Kyle?" MaeBe was crying. "I thought you were dead."

From his place on the floor, he saw MaeBe struggle to her feet.

Noelle's sweet face hovered over his. "Hutch? You've been shot."

Yep, she was a smart one. "Multiple times. Tag's going to yell at me because blood is hard on these floors."

Tears fell from her eyes. "Don't joke. Please. I love you so much. Please stay with me."

He reached up with his good hand. "I'm going to be okay, baby. Ask Kyle where he put the duct tape."

He heard the sound of the officers rushing in as Noelle cried and the world went dark.

Chapter Nineteen

The woman formerly known as Julia Ennis stood to the right of the nurses' station. She had a clipboard in her hand and a professional-looking nametag. When the nurse had asked why she was walking the floor, she'd explained that she was with oversight and doing the first of her reports to the hospital board. This particular system was so large the nurse had simply shrugged and went about her business.

Of course if the nurse had called, she would have discovered that there really was an oversight committee and the name she was using was on it.

The hospital system was owned by a larger healthcare system, and that system was owned by a multinational conglomerate, and so on and so on, until no one could truly understand how much of the world was run by a few incredibly powerful men.

Men who were going to be deeply upset that she'd been outplayed by a naïve chemist and a dumbass, do-gooder hacker.

She couldn't explain to them that she thought it had been the presence of Kyle Hawthorne that had done her in. Like he always did.

After all, he'd been the one to kill her.

The door came open and two kids strode out. Carys and Luke Taggart. Carys was fifteen with auburn hair, and Luke was eleven and already had an inch on his sister. Neither looked like Kyle, but they

352

might be a fun way to twist a knife in his heart since she knew how much he cared for his half siblings.

They walked by, chattering like the sheep they were about something Aidan had done and how someone named Kala was going to end up in military school if she didn't stop making trouble.

She barely heard them since that door was taking a while to close and she could see him.

Kyle. The love of her life. The man she intended to pay back for the hell he'd put her through.

She didn't know if she would kill him yet. He really was too beautiful to die, but love was supposed to be forever. It wasn't supposed to wilt simply because one of the lovers found out the other understood the world and her place in it. He'd folded quickly when he'd discovered her side job and brought the CIA down on her head.

She'd barely survived him. He'd cost her everything, even her face since she'd needed surgery to hide the fact that she wasn't as dead as they thought she was.

Yet here she was—just a girl standing in front of a boy's hospital room asking him to love her.

Her cell phone buzzed and she sighed because the door was closed again, and it would be a while before she got another glimpse of him. She stepped away and answered the call. She didn't need to look at the number. There was only one person who ever called. Kyle had cost her all her other relationships. Not that there had been many. A few women and men she referred to as friends. Her mom had been useful from time to time.

Now there was only the man on the other end of this call, the one who sent her out to do the bidding of her bosses.

"Hello?"

"I'd like to know why I'm hearing rumors about Drew Lawless buying Genedyne."

Fuck. She felt her jaw tighten. She'd wondered why the tech billionaire had visited the day before. He'd shown up with his wife and kids and disappeared into the hospital room Kyle was sharing with Greg Hutchins. Lawless wasn't in her group. The truth of the matter was Lawless wasn't big enough to be welcomed into the Consortium, even if he hadn't been an uptight Boy Scout no one trusted. But he was big enough to do some damage. "I suspect Taggart called him in. Or Hutchins. He's done some work for Lawless's company over the years, and he's still friends with Lawless's brother-in-law. I suspect he's trying to save Noelle LaVigne's work."

"But we wanted to quash LaVigne's work. It isn't in our best interests to have the price of helium go down at this time," the deep voice said.

"Then we'll have to find another way because I seriously doubt Lawless can be convinced to change his mind." Her own brain was working, putting together the hows and whys. "I've heard he's putting a lot of money into quantum computing. Having access to cheap helium will help enormously until he can figure out how to make the systems work at a more reasonable temperature."

The fact that quantum machines still only functioned at near absolute zero was a drawback Lawless would love to solve, and apparently he meant to do it by buying himself a tech think tank and all of the research ever done under Jessica Layne's name.

"I don't like it and neither does the board. LaVigne found Madison Wallace's research and released it to the public. Do you understand what that means?"

It meant that somewhere down the line a whole bunch of people might not die from cancer or need ridiculously expensive treatments. Still, he was overreacting. "So our medical groups should get right on that." She sighed. "I know this has been a clusterfuck of a week, but at least Layne won't be a problem anymore. I'll ensure we have a few of our people embedded at the new Genedyne so we can keep an eye on anything coming down the pipeline and perhaps discredit the research we need to."

"See that you do. I'll call you in a few days with a new assignment."

The line went dead, and she slid the phone back into her pocket.

The Taggart kids were coming back, sodas in hand after what must have been a visit to the vending machines. They'd picked up a friend.

Mae Beatrice Vaughn. Such a silly name for a whore. She actually looked way better with all those bruises. It was unfortunate that Layne and her men had failed to do any long-term damage to the idiot her Kyle made puppy eyes at.

The purple-haired moron wasn't worthy of Kyle, but in some ways Julia understood. What they'd had had been so passionate, so overwhelming, that he needed a bleating sheep in his life after their relationship.

She watched as MaeBe walked along with Kyle's half siblings. The door came open, and there was no way to miss the light in Kyle's eyes when he caught sight of the trio.

Her heart clenched and she hated the fact that the look on his face wasn't for her.

He was her one weakness. She should slip into his room and end it, but she couldn't.

Perhaps it would be more fun to burn his world down around him.

Starting with his family. He loved his brother David. It might be fun to play with him. Yes, that would be a good start, but in the end she would take them all down.

* * * *

"Grace, he's fine. He took a bullet to the lung, covered it with duct tape, and still managed to take out the bad guys," Sean Taggart was saying.

"Uh, I took two bullets, and Kyle wouldn't share the duct tape, so you might ask him to share that sandwich." Hutch looked to the sad cup of gelatin the nurse had brought him as a snack and prayed the celebrated chef would take pity on him.

"Eat your Jell-O, dude." Kyle gave him a shit-eating grin. Getting shot and going through surgery had done odd things for his mood. The normally taciturn guy had been positively cheery since they'd wheeled them into this room for a couple of days recovery.

Grace sent her son a frown and brought a second bag over to Hutch's bed. "Of course we brought you some lunch. And a slice of chocolate cake."

His stomach rumbled.

"Should you be eating that?" Kyle asked. "I got a lung shot, but you got hit twice in the abdomen."

"It missed my stomach." He'd been lucky. A couple of days here and he could recover at his place, where Noelle and her stepmom had already been working to make the house more comfortable. They'd been shopping in between Noelle taking meetings with Drew Lawless.

That had been his idea. Even with Jessica Layne dead, there were legal difficulties involving all the research that had been done at Genedyne and who owned it. Drew Lawless had been happy to pick it all up for a multimillion dollar song, and Noelle was going to take the lead when it came to the research portion of the new company.

"You both deserve good food," Grace said with a smile as she put the bag on his tray. "After what you two went through, you should both take a nice long rest. I'm happy to hear that Noelle's parents are staying with you for a while."

"Lila's going to stay for a week. She wants to make sure I recover all right." Noelle's stepmom was a force of nature who'd had everyone in the hospital hopping. "Her dad is taking her brothers back to Louisiana tomorrow. They're afraid I might be too fragile to be around the boys. They like to destroy things."

Her brothers were awesome and sweet. Armie LaVigne was on the scary side, but once Noelle had explained how he'd taken that second bullet for her, he'd warmed considerably.

"They seem like lovely people," Grace said. "And your Noelle is so smart."

She was smart and kind and so gorgeous it hurt to look at her. He already missed her.

"Hey, did they figure out who the other agent was?" Sean Taggart had been filled in on the entire op.

"MaeBe and Noelle both gave us descriptions and we had a police artist sketch the suspect, but she's a ghost," Kyle admitted. "I don't think we have to worry about her again. She did her job and she'll move on to the next one."

"Now that we found the material Madison Wallace hid in Noelle's locker, there's no reason for anyone to come after Noelle for anything but to curry favor with the new boss." It had felt good to be able to make that happen for her. Genedyne would be what it was supposed to be. It would be a place where scientists tried to change the world.

"I can't believe you just put it out there," Grace said with a shake of her head. "That was an amazingly generous thing to do. The company could have kept it."

"Noelle wanted to do it, and she convinced Lawless." His future wife had a huge heart. "Madison's research is promising, but it's in its infancy. Now there will be a race to see who can make it work first. And that means we might cure cancer. There are things no one should put a price tag on."

Grace looked down at him. "Do you know how proud your mother would be of you?"

His mom. She'd been caught in such a bad place, and sometimes he only remembered her crying and wanting to hide. But there had been times when she'd snuck in late at night and crawled into bed with him and held him when he'd been sick. When she'd told him she loved him.

"I hope so." He often wondered what would have happened if his mother had lived. She would have loved Noelle.

"I know so," Grace promised.

And then the door opened and Carys and Luke were back with the drinks they'd gone to get, and MaeBe walked in with a smile, though her face was still healing. Grace had a huge hug for MaeBe, and Kyle seemed to have lost interest in his food because all his attention was focused on her.

It wasn't a minute before Noelle walked in and brought all of the sunshine in the world with her.

"Hey," she said, moving to his bedside. "Lila and I bought dishes and all new sheets for the bed. Yours are terrible. I hope you don't mind."

He reached for her hand. "I supplied our house. You make it livable."

It hadn't been a home without her. She leaned over and kissed him and then they were all talking. MaeBe was describing how she was definitely taking more self-defense classes. Grace was talking about David's research, and Sean was going on about the new specials at Top.

Hutch sat back and enjoyed the family he had.

Hours later, while Noelle napped in the chair beside him, Hutch relished the quiet.

"Hey, man," Kyle said softly. "We're friends again, right?"

He would be friends with any dude who could duct tape his own body and make it up the stairs in time to knife a guy who was trying to kill him. "Yeah."

Kyle sighed. "I think you know more about me than you're saying. I think Michael followed me for a couple of days."

This was one subject they hadn't broached. "If he did, it's only because Big Tag was worried."

"I was calling a man named Drake." Kyle let the admission sit for a moment. "That night I snuck out of your house, I called Drake. He was my handler when I did work for the Agency."

"I know him."

"I don't work for him anymore," Kyle said. "But he was there on the worst day of my life. I don't think I make it through without Drake. There's a day that I'm trying to piece together, and he's helping me. It's got nothing to do with McKay-Taggart, and the woman at the center of it is dead."

"Julia?"

Kyle groaned. "Damn, Tag's good. Yeah. She's gone. She was working for some bad people and tried to drag me into it. Just know that it's over and I'm not working for anyone but Tag."

"Okay." He believed Kyle. He understood what it meant to have a dark past. He hoped Kyle could find the light.

"I'm going to take you up on that beer someday," Kyle said quietly.

"Whenever you're ready," Hutch promised.

It was what family did. They were there when a man was ready to change.

Noelle's hand reached out to find his.

He squeezed it and let himself rest.

Epilogue

Papillon, LA
Six months later

Michael Malone looked out over the patio of the bed and breakfast where Hutch's wedding reception was taking place. He felt that familiar sense of joy with a twinge of regret that he got every time he'd gone to a wedding in the last five or six years.

A lot of his friends had gotten married. His twin had married years ago. JT and Nina had two kids Michael adored. Everyone was settling. Even his ex-fiancée. He'd gotten that invite in the mail and wondered why he'd made the freaking decision to stay friends with her.

Because she was a good woman who deserved all the happiness in the world. She simply hadn't been right for him, and he hadn't been the man for her.

He was starting to think there wasn't a woman in the world for him.

"Hey, did you try the punch?" Big Tag moved in beside him. He'd ditched his jacket and tie and seemed more relaxed for it. "There's a lot of rum in this sucker."

"Yeah, it's an interesting place. And Hutch's new inlaws seem cool." They were all out on the dance floor, swaying to the music and enjoying the evening. Hutch was in the middle of it all, his new wife in his arms.

"Oh, this whole place is insane," Tag said with a smile. "I like it."

Tag always had loved some well-intentioned chaos. "Did you like the gator? They act like run-ins with large reptiles are no big deal."

Tag shrugged a big shoulder. "Hutch says his name is Otis and he's kind of the town's mascot. I thought he smelled like ass, and he made me happy my girls are content with Bud, who can be easily groomed."

Maybe he should get a dog and forget the whole wife and kids' thing. He and Fido could live happily until Fido died and he had to start over again.

He was getting maudlin in his old age.

"You okay?" Taggart asked him the question like he was worried.

When the boss got worried, he tended to do things. Like set a man up. Michael smiled what he hoped was his brightest smile. "Of course. I'm at a wedding. There were some pretty cute bridesmaids."

Tag's eyes rolled. "Yeah, you're really into the mid-twenties set. All of Noelle's friends are babies."

He hadn't noticed. He didn't notice much of anything these days. He worked a lot. He sat through family events he didn't truly feel a part of. He was drifting and completely unsure how to get back on track. "It's probably better that way. Hutch can be surprisingly mean when it comes to revenge. Or pranks. Adam is still talking about the colonic his smart toilet gave him."

That got Tag laughing. "Ah, good times, man. Good times."

He took a sip of his punch and then put a hand on Michael's shoulder.

Michael knew that shoulder pat. It was Tag's I-need-a-favor shoulder pat. "What is it?"

"Am I that easy to read now? Well, it's probably true. I've got a job for you when we get back to Dallas."

That wasn't anything new. "I figured you would. You keep us pretty busy."

"It's a job of a sensitive nature," Tag allowed.

"Okay. What's it involve? The Agency? Are we still looking for the woman who set Noelle up?" He'd like to find her. "Is it about Kyle?"

"I'm not worried about Kyle anymore," Tag admitted. "He's a good kid. He's got some shit to work through, but who doesn't? No. It's more about the client than anything else. The job itself is pretty straightforward. I've got a client who's worried about his business. He thinks he might have a corporate spy in his midst, and he needs someone to get close to the woman to find out what's going on."

Close to meant he might have to romance someone. The thought made him sigh. "Tag, I don't know that I'm the right agent."

"It's Vanessa Hale."

He turned to Tag. "The film star? She's in Dallas?"

Tag nodded. "She's left the industry entirely. She was raised here. Her mom died recently, and she moved home. She's living in the house her mom left her."

Vanessa Hale had made a splash a decade ago when she'd first shown up on-screen. She'd been declared a rising star, but somewhere along the way she'd gotten off track. He didn't follow the Hollywood gossip, but even he had heard about the starlet's scandals and her marriage that had everyone labeling her a gold digger.

"Isn't she married to a billionaire?" She'd married some old man and become a trophy wife and sparked a million tabloid stories.

"Oh, he died last year and her husband's son took her to court, and she got left with nothing. She was given a pittance, and that was sucked up by legal fees," Tag explained. "She came home with very little."

He had to admit, he was intrigued. And Vanessa Hale was a beautiful woman. At least she had been. "Are you saying she's being accused of spying on someone?"

"She took a job a couple of months back, and now there are some problems with the firm," Tag explained.

"Why me?" The truth hit him. "Damn it. You think she'll get close to me because of who I am."

His father and brother ran Malone Oil. Michael worked but had a trust fund that would always ensure a certain type of woman found him attractive. He was bait.

"I don't think that will hurt. My client thinks you might be able to draw her in," Tag said. "She's described her perfect man, and you fit the bill physically. Dani's gotten close to her. That's another worry."

Suspicion flared hard. Tag had buried the lead on this one. "Dani? Danielle Lodge-Taylor? Ian, is the client Julian Lodge?"

"Yes, and Vanessa Hale, as a new employee in Julian's financial firm, gets club access. I need you to go into The Club and find out what's going on with her."

It would be a tightrope he would have to walk. Julian Lodge had been Big Tag's first investor and now a friend. He wasn't merely a client. Julian was part of Ian's family.

And Vanessa was intriguing. "Is she a sub?"

"Yes, which is why you will be her Dom mentor at The Club. I know this is a big ask."

Michael didn't hesitate. "I'll do it."

"No shoptalk." Charlotte Taggart wore a blue dress that clung to her every curve. She reached out a hand to her husband as bouncy vibrant zydeco began to play.

Ian let her start to lead him toward the dance floor. "We'll talk more later. Apparently I dance now."

He always danced with his wife. Ian gave Charlotte his everything because they were a pair.

He wasn't going to be a part of a pair, but it might be fun to get close to a woman like Vanessa Hale. Shameless. Likely with a soul as hard as a rock. He could play some fun games with her and not worry about breaking her heart.

Since she probably didn't have one.

It might be fun to be her Dom. She would be under his control, at his mercy.

And he would have none.

Michael, Vanessa, and the whole McKay-Taggart crew will return in *The Dom Identity*.

Author's Note

I'm often asked by generous readers how they can help get the word out about a book they enjoyed. There are so many ways to help an author you like. Leave a review. If your e-reader allows you to lend a book to a friend, please share it. Go to Goodreads and connect with others. Recommend the books you love because stories are meant to be shared. Thank you so much for reading this book and for supporting all the authors you love!

The Dom Identity

Masters and Mercenaries: Reloaded, Book 2
By Lexi Blake
Coming September 14, 2021

A man with everything

Michael Malone seems to have it all. A wealthy, loving family. A job that fulfills him. Friends he can count on. But something is missing. He's spent years watching his brother and close friends get married and start families, but it hasn't happened for him. When an assignment comes up to investigate fallen Hollywood star Vanessa Hale, he jumps at the chance. She's gorgeous and potentially deadly. Playing the spy game with her might be just the thing to take his mind off his troubles.

A woman with nothing left to lose

Vanessa Hale had big dreams that ended in scandal. She returned home with nothing but heartache and the desire to find her sister's killer. The trail points to someone at Lodge Corp, so taking a job with Julian Lodge's mysterious company is her best option for finding the truth. While she hunts for a killer during the day, she hopes to find some solace at night in The Club. Meeting the gorgeous, sexy and seemingly kind Michael Malone, their chemistry sparks in a way she's never felt before, and Vanessa thinks maybe her luck has finally changed.

A love that might save them both

When Michael's true motives are revealed, she will have to find a way to forgive his betrayal. The killer has made Vanessa their next target. Working together and stopping this monster is the only chance for them to have the real love they both deserve.

Treasured
Masters and Mercenaries, Book 21.5
By Lexi Blake

David Hawthorne has a great life. His job as a professor at a prestigious Dallas college is everything he hoped for. Now that his brother is back from the Navy, life seems to be settling down. All he needs to do is finish the book he's working on and his tenure will be assured. When he gets invited to interview a reclusive expert, he knows he's gotten lucky. But being the stepson of Sean Taggart comes with its drawbacks, including an overprotective mom who sends a security detail to keep him safe. He doesn't need a bodyguard, but when Tessa Santiago shows up on his doorstep, the idea of her giving him close cover doesn't seem so bad.

Tessa has always excelled at most anything she tried, except romance. The whole relationship thing just didn't work out for her. She's not looking for love, and she's certainly not looking for it with an academic who happens to be connected to her boss's family. The last thing she wants is to escort an overly pampered pretentious man-child around South America to ensure he doesn't get into trouble. Still, there's something about David that calls to her. In addition to watching his back, she will have to avoid falling into the trap of soulful eyes and a deep voice that gets her heart racing.

But when the seemingly simple mission turns into a treacherous race for a hidden artifact, David and Tess know this assignment could cost them far more than their jobs. If they can overcome the odds, the lost treasure might not be their most valuable reward.

About Lexi Blake

New York Times bestselling author Lexi Blake lives in North Texas with her husband and three kids. Since starting her publishing journey in 2010, she's sold over three million copies of her books. She began writing at a young age, concentrating on plays and journalism. It wasn't until she started writing romance that she found success. She likes to find humor in the strangest places and believes in happy endings.

Connect with Lexi online:

Facebook: Lexi Blake
Twitter: authorlexiblake
Website: www.LexiBlake.net
Instagram: www.instagram.com